Strahd Van Zarovich, vampire lord, lay on the coffin's satin lining, his dark eyes closed, his gaunt features pale and waxy. His hands were folded across his chest, and he appeared perfectly composed. The master of Castle Ravenloft looked, as he was, quite dead.

"Thank the Morninglord it's still daytime," the cleric murmured. Jander nodded, moving Strahd's hands so that Sasha could place the sharpened stake over the vampire's heart. The cleric positioned the weapon, said a quick prayer, and raised the hammer.

We've got you now, you bastard, Jander thought with a sudden burst of self-satisfied hatred.

Ravenloft is a netherworld of evil, a place of darkness that can be reached from any world—escape is a different matter entirely. The unlucky who stumble into the Dark Domain find themselves trapped in lands filled with vampires, werebeasts, zombies, and worse.

Each novel in the series is a complete story in itself, revealing the chilling tales of the beleaguered heroes and powerful evil lords who populate the Dark Domain.

Novels

Vampire of the Mists
Christie Golden

Knight of the Black Rose
James Lowder
Available in December 1991

BOOKS

Vampire of the Mists

Christie Golden

TSR Inc.

VAMPIRE OF THE MISTS

First Printing: September 1991
Printed in the United States of America
Library of Congress Catalog Card Number: 90-71506

9 8 7 6 5 4 3 2 1

ISBN: 1-56076-155-5

TSR, Inc.
P.O. Box 756
Lake Geneva, WI 53147
U.S.A.

TSR, Ltd.
120 Church End, Cherry Hinton
Cambridge CB1 3LB
United Kingdom

This book is lovingly (and gratefully)
dedicated to my parents,
James R. Golden and Elizabeth C. Golden,
who might not believe in elves or vampires,
but who always believed in me.

Thanks also must go to Veleda and Robert,
for always reading everything
and usually liking most of it.

And, finally, thanks to TSR
for letting a first-timer
cast her own dark shadows on Ravenloft,
and to my editor, Jim Lowder,
for his patience, guidance, and support.

He that can smile at death, as we know him; who can flourish in the midst of diseases that kill off whole peoples. Oh, if such a one was to come from God, and not the Devil, what a force for good might he not be in this world of ours.

—Bram Stoker, *Dracula*

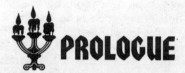 **PROLOGUE**

The last rays of the dying sun filtered through the stained glass windows of the castle's chapel and cast pools of fading color upon the stone floor. The only other light came from a small brazier that glowed on the altar. The Most High Priest of Barovia continued with his task until his old eyes could no longer see clearly. Finally, annoyed at the necessary interruption, he placed the amulet aside and lit enough candles so that he could continue.

The warm glow from the tapers illuminated the altar, but left most of the chapel shadowed. No longer a place for holy symbols and rites, the low wooden altar had been transformed into a workman's bench and was cluttered with tools for delicate metal work: small hammers, tongs, a smooth-faced jeweler's anvil, wax lumps for molds. The white-haired priest lit the last candle and hurried back to the amulet. It was a demanding master; its plaintive call for completion hammered at his brain.

The Most High Priest had been crafting the amulet for many weeks now, working with a feverish intensity that had not let him rest as he neared the task's completion. Yet he was not tired. Energy seemed to course through his veins even as it guided his clumsy, unschooled hands. The amulet was making itself. His gnarled fingers were but the tools.

Part of him felt guilty. He was neglecting his duties as priest and comforter to a frightened people. The intensity of the goblin attacks was increasing, but the Most High Priest sent his assistant to administer rites for the growing number of dead. The voice of the amulet reassured him that he had been assigned a greater task. He was forging more than a piece of jewelry, it told him. The amulet was to be a weapon the likes of which this sorry world had never seen. The enemy it was being crafted to fight was far worse than the goblins—an enemy who had yet to darken Barovia.

The Most High Priest paused, his hands trembling from the strain, and rubbed his bloodshot eyes before resuming the task. Following the instructions in his head, he had blended two old things to create this new one. The crystal was the gift of the earth. The platinum in which he had set the quartz was likewise ancient, although his fingers marked the precious metal with runes of love rather than violence. The pendant was shaped like a sunburst, and when the stone was placed in the center, it was as full of light and beauty as a miniature sun.

Carefully, the old priest carved the last rune. He blinked the sweat out of his eyes and examined his handiwork. There was one more thing he had to do. He draped the platinum pendant about his neck, tucking it into his robes so that it would not be seen. He patted his pouch to reassure himself that the letter he had written several days before was still there, and smiled slightly. The uncanny energy yet filled him, and he hurried from the altar and down the long torchlit halls of the castle with the speed and sureness of one many years younger.

One of the lord's servants heard him burst through the double doors of the chapel. Struggling to match the old man's pace, the servant inquired, "What now, Your Blessedness?"

"A horse," the Most High Priest snapped, not even bothering to glance at the man. Silently the younger man sprinted ahead to do the priest's bidding. Before the master of the castle had left for war, he had told the servants that His Blessedness was to be obeyed in all things. Swift though the servant was, the priest paced nervously outside the castle's beautifully carved doors for several minutes before a stable boy brought him his steed. The Most High Priest practically leaped into the saddle before he yanked his mount's head sharply around and clattered out of the courtyard. He was going to the Circle to complete the divine errand.

The night grew misty as the priest and the horse galloped down the Old Svalich road. Flying chunks of mud spattered man and beast, but the traveler was oblivious. He urged the animal on to greater speed at the prompting of the amulet. Impatiently he abandoned the road and took to the Svalich Woods. He did not know a shortcut, but the amulet did. At last, he reached his destination—a circle of large stones just outside the limits of the village of Barovia.

He tried to dismount, retrieve the amulet, and run to the center of the circle all at the same time, but all he accomplished was entangling his feet in his flowing robes and falling heavily to the earth. This old body can't give much more, he thought grimly as he rose. He sank down in the heart of the stone circle next to a large, flat rock, and laid the amulet down reverently.

The final blessing, he thought, and all is done. . . .

The young novice found the priest in the same spot late the next morning. The face of the Most High Priest was peaceful and curiously unlined in death. Gray lips curved in a faint, sweet smile. One hand held the sunburst pendant, the other, a note. The young man, his eyes full of tears, had to blink several times before he could read the last words the priest had written.

Here is the gods' gift to a troubled land. Use it well and with reverence, but pass the secret only from priest to priest. The family of the ravens shall descend, and this is to be the holy symbol of their kind. Its power is kin to that of the sun: light and warmth. It is a last hope to hold back the Shadow that shall fall upon this sad realm.

ONE

The *Queen's Pride* out of Evermeet rocked serenely in the inky water of Waterdeep Harbor. A playful night breeze stirred the catamaran's ropes, which slapped noisily against the boat in the relative quiet of the late hour. The wind increased, causing the standard to snap energetically, its heraldic image of a gold tree against a dark blue, star-filled sky billowing. In the distance, buoys chimed friendly warnings. The smell of fish and brine hung heavily in the cool, damp air.

From the safety of an alleyway, a lone figure gazed longingly at the catamaran. Selune's light turned the gold elf's skin and hair to a pearly white and his worn blue tunic to a gray similar to his cloak and breeches. Faded silver trim on the tunic still caught the milky radiance of the moon.

Jander Sunstar was tall for his race, nearly five foot nine, and slender. His features were clean and sharp, softened now with remembered pain. Elven ears tapered into graceful points, almost but not quite lost in the flowing gold of his hair. The boots that made no sound on the water-swollen boards of the dock were of supple gray leather and reached to mid-thigh. A dagger, simple and sheathed, adorned his left hip.

Jander's silver eyes were filled with sorrow. How many decades had it been since he had seen a ship from his homeland? Glorious Evermeet, land of beauty and harmony. He would never see it again. Thin, long fingers closed tightly about the cape, pulling it closer to hide him from prying eyes.

The elf could bear no more. He turned away and moved quietly from the dock and into the heart of the city that men called Waterdeep. This place, too, had been his home for a time, before the wanderlust had called him to his doom.

Jander seldom ventured into the city any more. It was becoming too crowded for his liking. He lived in a small cave beyond the city limits, where there were still trees and silence to be found. There Jander indulged his innate, elven love of beauty and nature by planting and tending a small garden of night-blooming flowers. Tonight, though, a great need drove the elf to steal into the Dock Ward. He moved in absolute silence with a deadly purpose, his gray leather boots making no sound along the cobblestones. Jander ignored the taverns, shops and warehouses. He was heading for the worst place in the city, where the most tortured souls on Toril wept away their meaningless lives amid squalor and pain. The elf turned a corner, his sharp features gaunt with hunger, his gray cape fluttering behind him.

Money could buy cures for just about anything in Waterdeep. There was a cleric for your wounds, a mage for your good fortune. Sometimes, however, the gods would not listen to the prayers of their priests, and sometimes spells went wrong. Horribly wrong.

Once, the unfortunates whose mental illnesses could not be helped by magic were locked away in cellars or cast out on the streets. Some particularly vicious people even arranged for their inconvenient mad relations to "disappear." Today, though, in the civilized year of 1072, there was a place for the incurably insane.

As he approached the large stone-and-wood building, Jander winced. Even outside, his sensitive ears were pained by the cacophony exploding within. Madhouses were places of more horror than haunted cas-

tles, he mused; here truly could be found the wailings of
the damned. He did not enjoy coming here to feed, and
did so only every few years, when the great thirst would
not be slaked with animal's blood. Steeling himself for
what awaited him within, Jander stepped up to the
door.

There were two main cells in the asylum, one for
males and one for females. Other, smaller cells housed
inmates who were too violent for the main cells and
those few pathetic souls whose former sex had been so
distorted that it could not be distinguished. As a rule,
Jander never entered the individual cells. He might be a
vampire, but he could take only so much pain and ugli-
ness.

He was nothing but tendrils of mist at first, creeping
through the cracks in the wooden door of the women's
cell. The mist took on color—blue and silver and gold—
then a being that some might have mistaken for an angel stood where the formless fog had been.

Torches in sconces too high for the inmates to reach
provided ample illumination. Too many of the lunatics
were afraid of the dark for the place not to be lit so.
Straw and moldering pallets covered the floor. There
were chamber pots, but few of the inmates used them.
Every few weeks, the city-appointed keepers would remove the inmates and douse the area with bucketfuls of
water, a process that did little to sanitize the filthy
place.

With the grace of a cat, Jander threaded his way
through the scattered madwomen, turning his blond
head this way and that, his silver eyes raking the scene.
Some of the lunatics scattered at his approach, to hud-
dle whimpering in corners. Others ignored him. Some
even fawned on him. From these he gently disengaged
himself.

It had been nearly half a century since he had been
here, and he recognized none of the inmates. Some
were fairly normal-looking, old women whose minds
had faded and then quietly disappeared altogether.

Some were misshapen monstrosities, victims of spells gone awry or perhaps even deliberate malice, who howled their anguish as they huddled in corners. The saddest were the ones who were almost sane, who could have functioned outside with a little aid but whose relatives couldn't be bothered to help them.

The growing population of Waterdeep had led to an increase in the number and variety of inmates. Most of them were human, although here and there Jander recognized the squat forms of dwarves or halflings. There were, thank the gods, no elves. Over in one corner of the damp, chilly place, one woman methodically tore at a bleeding stump of an arm with a hand that was covered with scales. Her legs were also reptilian and ended in the clawed toes of a lizardman. The expressionless face was completely human. Another lay almost at the vampire's feet, shielding her head with her arms. As Jander stepped over her, she shifted. The vampire flinched. The face she turned up to him was completely featureless save for the red slash of a mouth.

"They're coming, you know," a voice bellowed in his ear. "All those eyes on their stalks, waving at you, and the mouths, the mouths . . ." The madwoman became completely incoherent and began to suck on her fingers. Jander closed his eyes. He hated this pace. He would take sustenance quickly and leave.

This method of feeding did little actual harm to the inmates. Jander could materialize within the cell, partake of enough fluid to last until the next time his hunger demanded human blood, and disappear. Seldom did he even drain enough of the precious fluid to leave a victim weak the next morning. The keepers had no reason to check the throats of the patients. Consequently the small, insignificant marks were never noticed.

One woman lay huddled on a dirty straw pallet toward the back of the stone enclosure, separate from the rest. At first glance, she didn't look much different from the regular inmates of the asylum. Her long dark hair was tangled, and her pale limbs were dirty. She wore the ugly brown shift that was the standard garb in the hell-hole. Hardly more than a scrap of material, it offered little protection against the damp chill of the place and none at all against the fumbling of the demented inhabitants. Perhaps feeling his gaze, she looked up.

She was quite shockingly beautiful, and a soft cry of pain and wonder escaped Jander's lips. Though her hair was matted and filthy, it must have been a captivating shade of auburn once. Her eyes were large and shiny with tears. Even as he watched, they filled and drops coursed through the dirt on her pale face. Her lips were pink, perfect roses in a porcelain face, and they trembled slightly. The vampire had not seen such beauty in far too long; he certainly never expected to see it here. Captivated, he went to her and knelt beside her. She kept her luminous brown gaze even with his.

"I greet you," he said, his voice sweet and full of music. The girl did not respond, only continued looking at him with huge, soft eyes. "My name is Jander," he said, keeping his voice gentle. "What's yours? Where are you from?" Her lips moved then. Jander tensed, hoping, yet no sound issued forth. Disappointment filling him, he got to his feet. She still gazed up at him trustingly. Gods, so beautiful . . . Who could have sent her to this horrible place?

"I wish I could take you out of here," he told her sadly, "but I couldn't look after you during the day." He turned away from her. She gasped and reached out for him, her eyes filling with tears again.

"Sir!" she sobbed, holding her arms up to him. Jander didn't know what to do. Fully five centuries had passed since anything beautiful had deigned to touch him, and here was this tragically radiant girl reaching out for him. He hesitated, then sat down beside her and tentatively folded her into his arms.

"Shh, shh," he soothed, as if she were a child. He held her while she cried herself to sleep, then he laid her back down on her pallet. The vampire rose, careful not to disturb her, and tended to his hunger elsewhere in the room.

His heart was lighter than it had been for several long and empty years. Jander had found something beautiful in a hellish place, something that wasn't afraid of him. It had to be nurtured. He knew he would be back tomorrow night.

And so he was, bringing with him real food—meat from a traveler's fire, and bread and fruit pilfered from a careless shop owner. Vampires made excellent thieves, Jander had discovered, although few of them needed to pursue such a profession.

"Well again," he greeted her. She stared up at him, then her lips curved in a cautious, fleeting smile. His heart turned over, and he smiled broadly in return. The elf sat down beside the woman and handed her the food. She stared at it, confused.

"It's food," Jander explained. "You eat it." He mimed putting the bread in his mouth. The girl still didn't understand. Jander would have eaten a bite himself, just to show her, but he could no longer digest anything but blood.

A scuffling at his back gave him an idea. An old woman was staring hungrily at the bread. "Watch," he told the girl, and tore off a chunk of bread. The old woman grabbed at the offered food and chewed hungrily. The dark-haired girl smiled and nodded in comprehension. She rose with purpose and began handing out the food he had brought to the other inmates, glancing back at him with a happy smile.

Jander had to laugh, even though he was annoyed. The girl needed food; she was positively emaciated. She shouldn't be doling out what he had brought her—

He bolted upright. The lovely madwoman moved among her fellow inmates with a deliberate sense of purpose, sharing her food with practiced grace. As though she had taken care of people before, Jander thought. He was by her side in an instant, turning her to face him. "Dear gods," he whispered, "you weren't born this way, were you?"

She smiled serenely at him and continued with her task. He was shaken, filled with a sudden delirious hope. If she had been sane before, might she become sane again? Might he be able to bring her back from the brink of madness?

One thing was certain. He had to try.

Prior to meeting his "flower," Jander had merely existed, going from night to night, taking nourishment from animal blood. He tended his night garden, finding comfort in working with the soil and watching things grow. Since he had become a vampire, he had lived as an outcast from all the things he had most loved when he was alive.

But his undead state mattered not to this mysterious young woman in the asylum. She always seemed pleased to see him, even if she spoke in little more than fragments of words he did not recognize. Over the coming weeks, Jander finally succeeded in making her eat what he brought, and she began to gain weight.

One night, toward the beginning of fall, they sat together. Suddenly she tensed, drawing away from his embrace, a worried frown on her lips. "What is it?" Jander asked.

The girl seemed not to hear him. Abruptly she got to her feet, her attention still directed inward. Growing concerned, Jander reached up to tug gently on her dress.

The girl screamed, sparking accompanying shrieks from the other inmates that built to a hellish crescendo. She began to wring her hands, every muscle in her thin body taut with what appeared to be sheer terror. Frantically the madwoman glanced about, as if seeking an escape. She moaned low, the cry of a trapped animal, and hurled herself against the wall, clawing at the rough stone with her fingers, then pounding the unyielding surface desperately.

"No!" Jander cried. Swiftly he was by her side, pulling her away from her single-minded task. His strong golden hands closed tightly about her wrists. She struggled against him for a few moments, wailing piteously, then went limp against his chest. Bloody handprints dotted the stone wall, and a warm dampness trickled down onto his long fingers. She had cut her hands quite badly, and her palms and lower arms were sticky with blood.

Jander licked his lips, his hunger whetted, his silver gaze held by the torchlight flickering on the redness. Then he dragged his eyes back to the girl's. What he saw in their depths moved him.

Something flickered, like a candle flame. It was so brief, he hardly believed he saw it, but there it was. A flash of sanity, clear and bright as the sun on water, came and went.

"Oh, my little one," Jander said brokenly, "what happened to you?"

That was the first time he had seen her mysterious frenzy, but it was not the last. The contrast between the woman's wretched state and the serenity she displayed most of the time pained the elf. She would be fine for several days, perhaps even weeks or months. Then, without warning, her inner calm would shatter and she would again try to claw her way through the solid stone, desperately attempting to flee from some pursuing horror that existed only in her mad mind.

Jander did what he could to protect her from her self-inflicted pain, pinning her arms behind her back or to her sides, occasionally holding her in a grip so tight no movement was possible. She would eventually quiet down and become the tranquil flower she had been previously. After one such outburst, Jander held her as the tension ebbed from her body. He allowed himself to rest his head on her hair, content that she was now no longer struggling. She pulled back a little and looked up at him, and her lips moved soundlessly. Jander tensed. She placed a hand to her heart and babbled a strange combination of sounds. He shook his head, not understanding. Again, a meaningless gibber and then, quite clearly she said, "Anna."

Jander was dumfounded. "Is that your name? Anna?"

She nodded, her eyes alert.

"I'm Jander," he said and was surprised at how keenly he wanted to hear his name on those sweet pink lips. Anna had again retreated into herself, however, and the dull glaze dimmed those wonderful eyes. There would be no more speech from her tonight. The vampire was not distressed. There were many nights to come in which he would, he was confident, win Anna's trust and, he hoped, restore her sanity.

Winter was hard on the inhabitants of the madhouse. Jander stole some blankets and tried to keep Anna as warm as he could. He wished he could simply leave the warm woolens with her, but the guards would notice and grow suspicious as to their origins. It wasn't until spring that he won his next victory.

Jander had materialized in the cell just after twilight had bled to black. His garden was in full bloom, and he had collected a small bouquet for Anna. Perhaps they would win from her that radiant smile he had glimpsed a few times before. It was only after the mist congealed into his slender form that she recognized him, smiling a welcome that lit up her face and made her look sane again. She reached up to him, like a child to a beloved parent who has been too long away.

He placed the fragrant gift in her white arms. "For you, my dear," he said, his silky voice filled with gentleness.

Anna buried her face in the flowers, then raised her large, soft eyes to his. "Sir!" she cried happily, tossing the flowers to the stone floor and hugging him tightly.

Joyously he returned her embrace. As he held her affectionately, he gradually became aware that his feelings for her had changed. Until this moment, he had thought of her as a wounded young forest animal, in need of gentleness and care. He had attended to her so, denying the truth that now rushed to be revealed. Whether he wished it so or not, Jander was deeply in love.

As if she somehow sensed the change in the elf, Anna clasped him closer still, one small hand gently playing with the soft gold hair at the back of his neck. Emotions that had hitherto been as dead as his body suddenly flared to new life. Passion mixed sharply with the thirst of a vampire; the scent of her blood was overwhelming. Jander yielded to all his emotions and, with a groan, kissed Anna's throat, his fangs emerging quickly and purposefully. Yet he was gentle as his sharp teeth pierced the white flesh of her neck; his was the embrace of a lover, not a predator. And if she gasped a little with the first quick pangs, she did not pull away.

*   *   *   *   *

Jander was about to materialize in the asylum when the voices reached his ears. He flattened himself against the door, a blue and gray shadow, and listened intently to the voices within.

"Such a pretty thing," came one, gentle and warm.

"Aye, indeed," the second agreed. Jander recognized the voice of one of the guards. "Been that way for over a hunnert years. Me grandfather use t'work here, and she ain't changed since then."

"Really? Oh, poor child. Look! I think she understands me!"

"Ah, she's just foolin' ye. She don't understand nothing. Ain't for a hundred years."

"Yes, so you said before." The voice was significantly cooler than before. Jander grinned to himself. Any champion of Anna's was a friend of his. He shifted his position and placed one pointed ear to the stone.

What the guard said disturbed him. Had she really been trapped here, unchanging, for over a century? Mentally he ticked off the seasons. Time was nothing to a vampire, but he was shocked when he determined that he had been visiting Anna for over a decade.

The kind voice continued. "Lathander is the god of hope, and hope comes fresh every day with the dawn.

Don't forget that, my son. What caused this woman's suffering?"

"We think it's a spell, sir. Don't nobody stay that way that long without it being caused by some kind o' magic."

Jander tensed, his hands reflexively balling into fists. Magic! That would explain a great deal. He fought to quell the anger that welled up inside him at the mention of the arcane arts.

The elven vampire hated magic. Once, it had been part of his very nature. Even now, he still had a bit of elven magic at his control; his skill with the soil was only a minor example. Over the years, however, magic had failed to aid him in truly important matters. Now he did not trust it even in good hands, and to hear that Anna had probably been the focus of some evil spell enraged him. He deliberately forced himself to be calm and listen.

"Has anyone tried to remove the spell?"

"Nope. She's got no family, no one to pay for it."

Jander chewed his lower lip nervously. If the cleric of Lathander tried to free Anna from the magic that had kept her alive all these years, he might very well kill her. Apparently the priest had the same thought. "I would try, but I'm afraid to. It could be dangerous."

The guard laughed, a harsh, nasal sound. "What kind of a life has she got now? Dead might be better."

Jander's eyes narrowed in anger. "Perhaps," came the voice of the priest, definitely icy now, "if you took better care of your wards, this place might not be the sewer it is. I shall speak to your superior."

The vampire heard the sound of the cell door opening and melted back into the shadows. He watched as the priest of Lathander strode out, inhaling the fresh air gratefully. The human was young, only in his mid-thirties or so, and bore himself with a quiet grace. He wore his brown hair long, and his robes, though beautifully colored in shades of gold and pink, were simple. From his bearing and what he had said in the asylum, the priest ranked high in Jander's eyes. Besides, the elf had always favored the teachings of Lathander "Morninglord," the gold-skinned god of dawn and beginnings—at least, he had favored them up until the great darkness had fallen upon him, barring the dawn from his sight forever.

Once the guard had resumed his position outside the women's ward, Jander transformed into a mist and crept inside. He went to Anna at once, gathering her in his arms and holding her tightly. "Magic. Magic has done this to you. Oh, Anna." Suddenly overwhelmed by his empathy for her plight, he placed his hands on either side of her face and kissed her deeply—and started back in surprised pain, one golden hand reaching to touch his smarting, bitten lip.

Anna, caught up in her frenzy, screamed and pounded the walls. As always, Jander was beside her, calming her. When the moment had passed and she looked at him, her eyes were full of remorse. Jander embraced her tentatively, relieved, gently bridging the rift that he had unconsciously caused.

He did not ever try to kiss her again. Somehow, that token of affection triggered something in her mad mind. "Who did this to you, my love?" he whispered, holding her tenderly, not expecting a response.

She said, quite clearly, "Barovia." Nothing more would she reveal.

Barovia. The word sat oddly on the vampire's tongue as he repeated it. Was it a person's name, or that of a place, a word in her strange language for an action or idea? He had no way of knowing. All he knew was that something or someone connected with the word "Barovia" was responsible for Anna's present condition.

He would find out who.

 **TWO**

Days and nights ran their course in Waterdeep. Another year passed, and another, but time meant nothing to the undead creature and the ensorceled madwoman. A little progress was made, but not much. Jander, however, had the patience of the dead and took comfort in each tiny victory.

It was in midwinter, nearly three decades after the elf had first met Anna, that time began to run out.

He appeared in the cell as soon as night had embraced the land, carrying food and blankets. Anna lay huddled in a corner and did not greet him with her customary warm smile. "Anna?" She did not move at the sound of his voice. Suddenly frightened, Jander rushed to her and stroked her hair gently with his hand. "Anna, my dear, what is it?"

Carefully he turned her over, and his heart sank. "Oh, gods," he breathed. Anna's face, usually pale from lack of exposure to the sun, was flushed. He felt her forehead, noting with alarm its burning heat and dryness. Her breathing was rapid and shallow, and her eyes were unnaturally bright.

Jander felt the icy hand of panic close about his insides. It had been so long since he had struggled against an illness he had almost forgotten what to do. A fever. How did one tend a fever? The vampire began to tremble. Angrily he forced himself to remain calm. The vampire wrapped his beloved in a blanket and held her through the night as she shivered and moaned. The fever did not break.

For the next four days he tended her thus, forcing water down her throat and talking to her until his own throat was dry. The weight she had gained through his care melted off her, but still her fever did not break. Jander reached a decision.

All his love would not be enough to cure her. He had to find someone who had medical skills. Clearly the keepers of this place didn't even care enough to try to heal one ill lunatic. Jander hoped he knew someone who would.

He strode down the deserted streets of Waterdeep, not bothering to keep to the shadows this time. He passed through the seamy dock area and entered the more refined Castle Ward. The human population was increasing, and the city had grown considerably since Jander last was in this area of the city. Some of the new buildings confused him momentarily, but at last he found what he was looking for.

The Spires of the Morning was still an attractive building. Brand new when Jander had been here a hundred or so years ago, it was a little weatherbeaten by time, but not much. The building was made of stone, but the door was wooden, painstakingly carved with a representation of Lathander Morninglord. The god was depicted as a beautiful young man dressed in flowing robes with the sun rising behind him. Jander hesitated, then knocked urgently.

No one answered. Impatiently he pounded on the ornate wooden door again. Above him, someone opened the shutters and peered down at him. Jander couldn't see the speaker, but his voice was full of sleepy amusement.

"No need to break the door down, my friend. It is open to all who would enter. Come in!"

There was no way that Jander could enter a holy

house, even if he had been invited. "I cannot," Jander called up. "My message is too urgent. There is sickness in the asylum. Will you come?"

The priest did not hesitate. "Of course. Give me just a—" Jander had already gone, running swiftly back to the madhouse. The priest arrived within a half-hour with a variety of herbs and holy symbols. Jander recognized him as the young priest he had overheard talking with the guard thirty years earlier. He was in his early sixties now, but still handsome. His hair was white, but as long and thick as the elf remembered, and though his face was lined, it was filled with concern and kindness.

Jander let him inside. "Over there," he told the pink-robed cleric. "In the corner. She's got a fever."

The white-haired priest knelt beside the girl and began to examine her gently. The lines about his brown eyes deepened. "How long has she been like this?"

"Four days, now."

"Why wasn't I called in earlier?"

"I don't know."

The cleric shot him a fierce look. "You're one of the guards, you ought to have—"

"No, I'm not, I'm just . . . a friend. Can you help her?"

The priest seemed about to say something more, but the look on Jander's worried features stopped him. "I'll try, my son."

The hours ticked by with agonizing slowness. The priest prayed and chanted, administered herbs, bathed the unconscious girl with holy water, all to no avail. At last, looking tired and haggard, he shook his head and began to pack up his things. "I am truly sorry. She is in the hands of the gods now. I have done all I can."

Jander shook his head, uncomprehending. "No. You're a *priest*. You've got to be able to do something!"

"I'm not the Morninglord," the priest said. He smiled sadly. "Although you might be. Every time I see a sunrise elf, my breath catches in my throat. I wonder if your people might not be closer to the gods than we mortals, as you look so much like him."

"So I've been told," Jander snapped, "but if I were a god, do you think I'd let her die?"

The priest did not take offense, simply regarded the elf with pity. "This is an illness beyond my ability to cure. I think it may be magical. Perhaps it has something to do with her unaging state. If I try to do anything more for her, I could kill her."

Jander had never felt so helpless. He gazed at Anna, his eyes wide with pain. "Magic," he whispered. "Damn all magic."

"Come, my son," said the priest gently, laying a hand on Jander's shoulder and trying to steer him toward the door. "You're liable to take ill yourself. You feel cold already."

The golden vampire shrugged off the priest's hand. "No," he said. "I'm staying."

"But—"

Jander fixed the old man with his silver gaze.

"Well, perhaps you're right," the priest relented. "I'm sure she could use some comfort." He walked over to the wooden door of the cell and tugged it open.

"Lord—"

The cleric paused. "Yes, my son."

"Thank you."

The priest smiled sadly. "I'll pray for her. And for you," he added, then he was gone.

Alone with the madwomen, Jander sank down beside the woman he had taken care of for thirty summers. Anna's fever still hadn't broken, and, although she was now conscious, she obviously failed to recognize him. Jander laid his cheek on her hair and tightened his grave-cold hand on her shoulder.

He made the deadly decision without even thinking about it. It was the only option left to him. Anna was dying, but Jander could not bear to be parted from her. "Anna, my love," he said softly, "if there were any other way for us to be together . . ."

The elf's slender hand brushed her cheek, hot and dry

and red with her life's blood. Unable to hold back any longer, Jander kissed that cheek. Corpse-cold lips slid down her jaw to her throat, pressed against the beating vein. Had he thought any deity would have cared, he would have said a prayer for the success that night's endeavor. What he was attempting held danger as well as promise. There came the familiar, bittersweet ache in his mouth as his fangs emerged, ready to pierce soft white skin and take sustenance. Swiftly, before his courage could fail him, Jander bit deeply into Anna's throat, deeper than he had ever gone before. The skin resisted an instant, then popped and yielded a gush of hot fluid.

Anna gasped and struggled against the pain. The vampire's strength was more than mortal, and she could not escape his grasp. Gradually she quieted, then went limp.

Jander drank eagerly, the warm, coppery-tasting fluid flowing easily down his throat. The life force it carried began to seep through him, renewing his power and rekindling his senses. It had been a long time since he had permitted himself such a banquet; he had almost forgotten the elation and heat a true feeding engendered. He felt himself surrendering to the pleasure. Dimly he noticed the change as the flavor began to turn ashy and empty.

Abruptly he stopped. He had almost gone too far; he had almost drained her dry in his hunger. Quickly, still cradling her limp form in one powerful arm, he slashed a deep gash in his own throat with a clawlike nail. New blood—Anna's blood—pumped from the incision. Jander moved her like a doll, placing her mouth to his throat. "Drink, my love," he said hoarsely, "drink, and be one with me!"

There was no movement. Suddenly afraid, he shoved her face into the wound. "Anna, *drink*!" She tried feebly to push him away, and he cast a frantic glance down at her.

She smiled serenely, lucidly up at him through a ruddy mask of blood. Heartbeats away from her death, some fraction of sanity had returned, like a benediction, to the tortured girl. Her mind was obviously her own for the moment, and she had made a choice. She refused the eternal undeath he was foisting upon her. Her strength was ebbing, but she mustered enough energy to lift a small hand to touch his golden face, content, even happy with her decision.

"Sir," she whispered, a single tear sliding down her ashen cheek. Her magnificent eyes closed for the last time, then her head fell back limply across his trembling arm.

"Anna?" Jander knew she was dead, of course, but he kept repeating dazedly, "Anna? Anna?"

Sanity returned to him shortly before dawn.

His eyes were closed when he again became aware of his surroundings. The first thing he noticed was the silence. Not a single groan or whimper floated to his ears. No breath, no rustle, no sound at all. Next came the smell—a hot, coppery scent that was as familiar as his own name.

He was lying on the cold stone floor and attempted to rise. It was then that he discovered that he had been in his lupine form over the past few hours. Silver eyes still shut, Jander ran a pink tongue about his jaws, tasting the fluid that had given off the copper smell. What had he done? He did not want to know, but he had to face his deeds. Slowly the gold-furred wolf opened his silver eyes.

He had left not one of the miserable wretches alive. The sight of the slaughter greeted him like some obscene carnival tableau. The madwomen lay strewn about like a child's forgotten toys, some on their pallets, some on the floor, all with their throats gaping open like second mouths. Here and there were the mutilated corpses of the guards who had foolishly tried to stop the carnage. Red was the predominant color now instead of the flat gray of stone. It looked as though the same child who had tossed the corpses carelessly aside had hurled bucketfuls of crimson about.

A low moan escaped Jander. The vampire couldn't even remember attacking them. He had killed before, often. He had enjoyed killing before, occasionally. However, he had not known he was capable of such total butchery. The people who now lay in ghastly puddles of gore had not been his enemies. They had not even been food for his unnatural, cursed hunger. This was wanton murder, and the part of Jander that was still elven, the part that still loved light and music and beauty, was appalled.

The full horror of what he had done settled on Jander like dust on a gravestone. Those slain by a vampire were doomed to rise again as vampires themselves. He wasn't sure if these pitiful wretches would—he had merely ripped them apart, he thought with grim humor, not drained them of blood. Still, it was a thought that would chill any heart: one hundred insane vampires wandering the night landscape of the Sword Coast.

Jander turned his shocked gaze back to Anna. He changed then, his sleek, golden wolf limbs dissolving into mist and reforming gracefully into his elven manifestation. He gathered the dead girl's slight frame in his arms and held her tightly for a few moments. Tenderly he laid her corpse out on the straw, cleaning her bloody face as best he could.

Jander had tried to make Anna his mate, but she would not drink his blood. When she rose a few nights from now as an undead, she would be only a weak, servile vampire: his slave. That was all she would ever be, for all eternity, for slaves could never become true individuals while their maker existed. "Oh, Anna, I never wanted that for you," he said brokenly. "Death would have been better."

The elven vampire rose slowly, wearily, and glanced around at the dead bodies until he found what was left of a guard. He searched the bloody corpse until he found a ring of keys, then unlocked the heavy wooden door and went to the other main cell. He wondered if he was doing the right thing for a brief second, but pushed his hesitation aside. Jander inserted the large skeleton key into the lock, turned it twice, then pushed open the door. Most of the madmen within took no notice of him, but a few crept timidly to the door and peered out cautiously. With a cry, the elf ran about the large cell, waving his arms and herding the inmates toward freedom. When the last one had left, Jander went to the individual cells and unlocked them as well, swallowing his revulsion.

Now the asylum was empty, save for the dead. The vampire returned to the women's cell, and knelt beside Anna for the last time. He allowed himself one final kiss, a gift that she had been too frightened to grant him in life. Then Jander removed a torch from its sconce on the wall and tossed it into the straw that covered the cell's floor. It caught quickly, and for a few minutes the elf hesitated.

His existence was a wretched one. It was tempting to end it here, to burn to charred flesh along with Anna. The thought had occurred to the miserable vampire more than once over the last several centuries, but always Jander had decided against suicide. There were worse things than vampires, and Jander would become one should he die.

The smoke became black and thick before the elf hurried outside into the fresh, cold night air. He did not want to watch as Anna's body burned, but he knew it was the only way to send her tortured soul to a final rest.

Jander walked silently westward, pulling his cape tight about his slender frame. The bitterness of the midwinter night was not uncomfortable to him. The touch of a vampire was cold if he had not fed, but the undead never felt the chill themselves. As he strode down the empty streets toward the city limits, he could hear sounds of wakefulness behind him. He hoped that aid would not come before Anna's body had been completely destroyed.

The elven vampire left Waterdeep behind him, heading for the comfort of the forest. The grass beneath Jander's feet was coated with frost, but it made no sound under the tread of his gray boots. The large trees were bare, and their silent, massive shapes did not invite his touch. Nevertheless, the elf leaned his back against the trunk of one and lifted his eyes to the sky. The moon was half-full, fading before the lavender and pink tinge of the approaching morning. He had a good half-hour, though, before he needed to seek the dark shelter of his cave.

The predawn beauty felt more like a rebuff than a re-assurance to the stricken vampire. He was undead; he could hope for no acceptance anywhere. Even Anna had rejected the living death he offered. For thirty years she had been the one hope that had made his existence bearable. Now there was nothing, no one. Who would spare sympathy for the plight of a vampire?

"I did not choose this life!" Jander raged to the empty air. "I did nothing to earn it! Have I not suffered in this state? Is there no mercy for such as me?"

The night remained still. It did not answer him. He clenched his fists. "Anna!" he wailed, his voice shattering the night. He fell to his knees. "Anna . . ." He had killed the thing he loved best. It made no difference that that had not been his intent.

Perhaps, came a thought like a whisper, you freed her. The vampire grasped at this hope. He forced himself to remember her dreamy insanity, and the anger that had been directed at himself and his undead state began to focus elsewhere. She had been something beautiful that had brushed his life, had given him a reason for continuing his existence. Now, he had a new reason: revenge. Jander already felt certain that someone had done something terrible to Anna, something that had driven her over the edge of sanity.

That was a greater sin than his. Filled with new resolve, he raised his arms to the paling sky. "Hear me, gods! Hear me, powers of darkness and pain! If there is one who harmed her, I will find him. I will destroy him. Punish me if you will, for my hands are not clean. *But* deny me not my revenge!"

Not in five hundred years of undeath or in two hundred years as a living being had Jander spoken with such anguish. His hatred poisoned the words, and the good, clean earth of Toril shrank from the bitterness he spewed forth. But there were other powers, far more corrupt than anything that dwelt in Toril, and they drank Jander's tainted curse like nectar.

As it was a seaport, Waterdeep had its share of fogs. But years later, the inhabitants of the Dock Ward would speak in hushed tones about the malevolent mist that appeared suddenly on that particular dawn. It rolled in from the sea like a ghost ship. It was damp and chill, as was every fog, yet there was something uncanny about it. Those awake retreated into their homes or huddled in their boats until it passed them by. Those yet abed frowned in their sleep as dreams were transformed into nightmares. It came as if guided, rolling through the streets of the ward to the west. It passed over the dock area quickly, leaving behind a hazy morning. The noon sun burned away the last traces of the strange mist, and the sunset that evening was stunning.

Jander never saw that sunset on Toril, nor the clear night that followed. When the mist rolled in, it engulfed him completely. His mind was as clouded with hot thoughts of vengeance as the forest was with the weird mist, but the vampire retained enough presence of mind to realize that he didn't have much time to return to his cave.

He took the shape of a bat and flew toward the dank underground lair he called home. The mist would obscure normal vision. Bats, however, navigated by emitting high sounds that bounced off objects and returned to sensitive ears. Jander was surprised to find that the shrill shrieks he produced as he flapped his leathery wings never echoed back to him. Resolutely he flew on, grimly crushing any notion that he might become lost in this dense, gray fog.

After an alarmingly long time, an echo bounced

back. Jander fluttered to the ground, changing yet again into his elven form. The fog was lifting. It dissipated as quickly as it had come, revealing a landscape so completely transformed that Jander couldn't believe the evidence of his eyes.

For one thing, he had been fleeing the dawn. Judging from the position of the moon, it wasn't even midnight yet. The elf frowned. The moon was wrong, too. It had been only half-full when he left, he thought to himself. Now it was full. Even the stars bore no resemblance to the constellations he had come to know through centuries of observation. Everything was alien.

What was going on? For a moment, Jander wondered if he had spent too many nights among the insane. Perhaps he, too, had lost his reason. Whatever the explanation, as far as his senses could determine he was no longer in Waterdeep. Judging by the unfamiliar stars, he wasn't even in Toril anymore.

He shivered, though the air was balmy and full of the scents of spring. *Magic.*

The moon slipped in and out of cloud banks, alternately obscuring and revealing Jander's new surroundings. Instead of frost-crusted grass, the elf discovered he was standing on a road, well-kept enough but clearly not often traveled. The shapes of the tall trees that fringed the side of the path were large and seemed to hover over him. They were apple trees, in full bloom, and they scattered petals on the ground as the breeze stirred them. The road wound through a pass up ahead, then took a steep downward turn. Jander strode to the crest, and peered down into the valley.

Nestled in the valley was a huge ring of dense fog. From his vantage point, Jander could see that there was a village inside the circle, and north of the road a forbidding-looking castle perched like a vulture over the town.

A mournful howl rent the air, one quickly joined by a dozen others. A fell harmony was raised, and the source drew closer by the minute. The wolf pack did not worry

Jander. He was no lycanthrope, but he knew what it was to run four-footed over the hills with the scent of the quarry hot in his nostrils. He had yet to meet a beast that did not bow to his command.

The howls increased. Jander threw back his head, found the slight wind, and sniffed, catching a wild, musky scent. As the pack cleared a small hill the moonlight caught their bright eyes. They were enormous—great, shaggy shapes of shadow and darkness. Jander kept his keen silver gaze even with the pack leader's. Wolf and vampire regarded one another for a moment. The leader glanced back at his companions, then down at Jander again. He cocked his head and twitched his ears, considering.

The elf was a bit taken aback. Always before, the mental commands he had issued had been immediately obeyed. Jander narrowed his eyes and increased his concentration. *Leave*, he told them silently. He sensed their strength of will, their cunning, their threat, but they made no move to obey. *Leave!*

At last the mighty beasts slipped away and were engulfed by the night. "Fare you well, brothers," Jander said. He was alone again.

The moon was swallowed by a cloud. With a deadly swiftness, the night was subtly transformed. The whiteness of the apple blossoms looked like shrouds. The hard-packed dirt road twined away like a snake. Long though he might for the sun, Jander was a denizen of darkness, and knew he had nothing to fear from it. Still, he felt a shiver touch his spine like an icy finger.

Once, as an elf in whose veins warm blood circulated, he had known this dread of shadows. Even then, he did not fear the cloak of darkness itself, but rather what it hid from view. Now he was one of those terrifying, hidden things. Yet Jander was afraid of the night in this strange land. The very soil under his feet felt wrong. He had called the wolves "brothers," but that was out of habit, not a sense of kinship. Those wolves had no ties with him. Had he not had the strength of will to turn

them, he knew they would have leaped upon him and
torn him to pieces for the sheer pleasure of doing so.
Wolves in Faerun, with a few exceptions, were merely
beasts, travelers under the black skies in search of food
and nothing more. But those huge, shaggy beasts staring balefully down at him had been full of malice.

He again turned his attention to the only evidences of
civilization he could find, but they offered no reassur-
ance. The town that lay below him looked imprisoned
by that ring of unnatural fog. The brooding castle had
an aura about it that boded ill.

Jander sighed. He had no idea where he was or how
he had come to be there. The only ones who could tell
him anything dwelt in the village and in the castle. The
elf decided on the village, as he would be more likely to
pass unnoticed there. Suddenly he remembered his
clothing, drenched with the blood of the innocent victims in the asylum. He certainly couldn't show up in the
village with that on his garb.

Jander glanced down at his tunic to examine just how
bad the stains were, and he received another shock on
this night laden with surprises. His clothing was completely clean. Whoever or whatever had brought him
here had seen to it that he would be free to mingle with
the place's population.

The elf smiled grimly. He had the most curious feeling that he was under surveillance. Then I'll let whoever
is watching know that I will not be intimidated, he decided. Jander tugged the hood of his cape from his
head and shook his hair free. He had vowed to go on a
mission of revenge, and if he had to conduct it here, so
be it.

His mind filled with memories of Anna, he strode
surely down the road toward the fog-encircled village.

 **THREE**

It seemed to take an eternity for the house to fall quiet. Anastasia pulled the embroidered coverlets up to her chin, feigning sleep, and tried to still her hammering heart.

Moonlight managed to find its way into the spacious, well-furnished room through the cracks in the shutters, laying fingers of milky light across the features of Anastasia's slumbering sister. Ludmilla's impish face was serene in sleep, and her dark hair was spread across the white pillow. The child was only ten, and having her share Anastasia's room made it difficult for the seventeen-year-old to do what she had been doing for the last few weeks.

Anastasia shifted, the rustling of the fine sheets sounding deafeningly loud in the silent room, and continued to wait. When at last she could hear no stirring, neither from her parents' chamber nor the servants' quarters downstairs, the girl slipped out of bed, fully dressed in her simplest clothes: a linen blouse and plain skirt. She reached for a ribbon that lay on the table by her bed and tied her hair back, then tugged on a pair of boots.

Her palms were damp as she rummaged beneath the mattress for the length of rope she had hidden there. At one point, Ludmilla moaned in her sleep. Anastasia froze, but the girl did not awaken. The older girl closed her eyes in relief. Knotting one end securely around the heavy bedpost, Anastasia opened the shutters and window as quietly as she could and let the rope fall to the ground, paying out its length. She took a breath and said a quick prayer, then gathered all her courage and began to descend.

She had hoped Petya would be waiting for her, but to her disappointment his slender form did not materialize from the shadows. Anastasia cursed under her breath as she paced back and forth, her pale face drawn and nervous. Waiting so close to the house was dangerous. Her father might take it into his head to get some air, and he'd flay her alive if he caught her out here. She could just see him now, his bald pate gleaming with sweat, his heavy jowls trembling: "Remember who you are! You are the burgomaster's daughter, not a common prostitute!"

No, staying here would be courting disaster. Anastasia decided not to wait any longer. She scurried along the dark streets of the village, wrapping the black cloak around her to conceal her identity should she encounter anyone, though it was unlikely. Hardly anyone ventured outside at night anymore. The burgomaster's daughter made haste, knowing the moonlight made her vulnerable, but grateful that at least she could see where she was going. She left the road and followed the overgrown path, stumbling a little, to the ring of stones on the hill where she had met Petya before.

Everything loomed larger at night. Every tree was a scowling giant, every rock a misshapen threat. The old people of the town used to speak of a time when Barovia was almost as safe during the night as at midday. Goodwife Yelena, for instance, used to tell Anastasia that "The most dangerous thing about the night then was the dung pile you couldn't see in the dark."

Anastasia grinned through her apprehension as she reached the circle and sank down in the shadow of a stone. She recalled how her mother had scowled at

Yelena and bustled Anastasia away, but the goodwife had made Anastasia laugh. The girl's nostalgic smile began to fade. The good things of which Yelena had spoken had disappeared even before the old woman was born. Now the night sheltered things that Anastasia didn't even want to think about. Folk had been found literally ripped to pieces by wolf packs. Others spoke of corpses empty of blood. People even muttered against Count Strahd.

Count Strahd. The wind seemed to sigh the name, tossing it back and forth in the tops of the trees. A shower of apple blossom petals fluttered, ghostlike, to the earth. Anastasia shivered and drew her cloak about her more tightly. She leaned back against the large rock, somehow comforted by its solid presence. This spot was rumored to have been a sacred place once, but now it was just a ring of stones.

Anastasia tried to redirect her thoughts to her gypsy lover. Their illicit romance was dangerous—and exciting. The Vistani had an air of mystery about them that drew Anastasia to the young, swaggering Petya. His dark eyes were full of magic, and his touch knowing and skillful. He walked with a sense of freedom that Anastasia, cowed by her father and the whipped attitude of the entire village, drank like wine. She wondered if she wasn't more in love with the gypsy lifestyle than she was with Petya.

A wolf howled, shattering her pleasant thoughts. Her heart began to beat quickly. "Hurry, Petya," she whispered.

The wolves, it was said, were Strahd's creatures. Anastasia had met Barovia's lord only once, just a few nights ago, and once would certainly be enough. He had attended the annual spring celebration hosted by her father. Strahd was tall and lean, she remembered, with carefully combed black hair and deep-set dark eyes. He was immaculately dressed in a beautifully tailored black outfit, highlighted with bright touches of red like drops of blood. The count had smiled oddly when the burgomaster presented his eldest daughter, and he had regarded Anastasia with a look of appraisal that made her very uncomfortable. When he kissed her hand, she'd mustered all her control not to scream; the touch of his lips had been like ice.

Some said the count dabbled in magic. Others said that the ladies he fancied tended to disappear.

Anastasia gasped quietly at a sound in the night. Clutching the cloak closed with a hand that trembled, she tried to melt into the stone.

The sound came again—footsteps, slow and deliberate. They were coming right toward her. So much for the circle protecting her. Her father's warnings about corpses empty of blood returned unbidden to her mind.

A hand clamped down on her mouth.

Anastasia's heart leaped in horror, and she struggled against her attacker. She kicked and scratched, fear giving her added strength. Abruptly the moon cleared a cloud, and she realized it was only Petya, his grin even larger than normal. His swarthy face appeared white in the moonlight that drained the color from his bright, beaded vest and voluminous red pants.

"You—" Anastasia sobbed for breath as Petya crowed with laughter. She launched herself at him, her small fists pummeling his slender chest, and they fell together on the earth. Anastasia was still struggling, her face hot from embarrassment, when Petya pinned her underneath him.

She glared up at him, but her anger was rapidly fading. "You crazy Vistani devil!" she hissed, teasingly now. He waggled his dark eyebrows in a playful imitation of a villain in a mummer's play and bent to kiss her.

As Anastasia kissed him back, she realized distantly that the night was not nearly so cold anymore.

* * * * *

An hour later, Petya reluctantly bade goodnight to Anastasia, watching her as she climbed up the rope to her bedroom as nimbly as an over-laden pack horse. He sighed and shook his dark head.

It could not be said that he loved the burgomaster's daughter. He was certainly attracted to her and would miss her when his tribe moved on, but she fit into his world no better than he fit into hers. The burgomaster would never hear of his daughter wedding a gypsy, and the clannish Vistani would never permit Petya to bring a *giorgio* into the camp.

Ah, well. Such was life. He sniffed the fragrant air and shook off melancholy like a dog shakes off water. It was spring, and there were many things besides women to be enjoyed. Strong despite his small physique, Petya swung a heavy burlap sack onto his back. With a jaunty stride, he set off for the Wolf's Den. The inn would be filled with patrons waiting to be entertained by Petya's cleverness.

The Wolf's Den was not the cheeriest of places at the best of times. It was a whitewashed, three-story building, its eaves decorated with floral patterns. Its brightness outside, however, merely made for more contrast with the subdued interior. There were always too few lamps, so the taproom appeared to be couched in darkness. The fire that burned sulkily in the hearth did little to illuminate the room and even less to warm it. The inn profited little from the few who still dared venture out after nightfall and consequently seemed sadly underfrequented. The innkeeper himself was a surly sort, too lean and too tall in a town populated by thick-set, small people. He was pleasant enough with those he knew; newcomers he regarded with suspicion. Still, he would accept the money of strangers, provided he recognized the coin.

Had Petya been a little more experienced with the ways of the world, he would have sensed the subtle change that came over the inn's inhabitants when he sauntered in, whistling. If he had been even a few years older than his current seventeen, he would have stayed a polite amount of time and then returned to the safety of his own kind. Petya was young, however, and thoroughly convinced that he knew everything.

The Vistani cut an unusual figure, a bright-eyed, garishly clad fox capering among a pack of dark, brooding hounds. He clapped one man on the back, exchanged greetings with another, and tossed a coin in front of the scowling innkeeper. "A pint of your best, to celebrate the season, hey?"

Wordlessly the innkeeper plunked a mug down in front of Petya. "To your good health, gentlemen!" Flushed with his pleasure of the past hour, Petya took a long pull. His bright black eyes darted to the door where a figure seemed to be hesitating on the doorstep. "Enter, friend!" Petya bade the man, his exuberance embracing even a stranger on this, his night of conquest. "No man should be out of the company of his fellows when there's good drink to be had!"

"Indeed not, young sir," said the stranger, entering and sitting beside Petya.

The low chatter of the inn ceased as the patrons gazed, slack-jawed, at the golden-hued stranger. A few of them made the sign of protection against the evil eye and hurried outside. Others merely stared. Still others regarded the interloper with open hostility.

Inwardly Jander winced. His plan to unobtrusively gather information was obviously not going to work. The elf hadn't encountered this much hostility since he'd left Daggerdale. Fortunately the garrulous little gypsy boy at his side didn't suffer from the same reticence as the rest of the inn's customers.

"You have obviously traveled a long way," Petya said. "May I buy you a drink of *tuika*? It's a Barovian delicacy."

Barovia. Jander was hard put to conceal his elation. So this odd place was the land from which Anna had come. "No, thank you," he said politely. "I was wondering if the inn might have a room available."

"Then it'd be me you want to talk with, not this Vistani cur," the innkeeper growled, darting a decidedly angry look at the oblivious Petya. "Go earn your drinks,

Petya, or go back to your camp."

Petya leaned over and whispered in Jander's ear, "If you change your mind about the drink, the offer stands. I know what it's like to be an outsider in this town." With a mock bow to the innkeeper, Petya slipped off the stool and swaggered into a corner. He rummaged about in his sack and emerged beaming. In his dark hands, he held an astonishing variety of balls, clubs, and torches. He ignited his torches from those fastened to the wall, and they flared brightly. With a whoop, he began to deftly juggle the objects.

"The lad has talent," the elf remarked. "My name is Jander."

The innkeeper glowered at the stranger. "Sorry. Can't get you a room tonight."

"No vacancies?"

"Oh, there are plenty of vacancies, but we never take lodgers after nightfall."

"An inn that will not accept paying travelers?" Jander raised an eyebrow, and his lip curled with disdainful amusement.

"Come back tomorrow morning, and we'll discuss it then. We don't take lodgers after nightfall," he repeated.

Jander sized up the innkeeper. Beneath his rough speech and hostile demeanor the man emitted the iron tang of fear. Jander could smell it. He had been right about this land. This little village was being terrorized. He went to a shadowy corner of the room and pulled the hood of his cloak over his gleaming blond head. All his senses were alert as he listened unobtrusively to the subdued chatter around him. He heard various snatches of conversation: "Devil . . . stay inside . . . Strahd." That name cropped up in different conversations, and each time Jander heard it, he caught that whiff of fear. After listening in on various discussions, he concentrated on the one going on closest to him.

One man, rather young and with a thick black beard, took a gulp of ale. His companion, gray-haired with a two-day growth of stubble on his face, merely stared blankly at his own untouched mug. "I shouldn't have left," the older man said softly, his voice full of pain.

The younger man laid a hand on his arm. "When it's fever, it's best to be safe," he said gently. "You know that as well as I do, Da. No telling how catching it might be."

The man nodded, his eyes still haunted. "She was so young, so beautiful," he whispered brokenly. His sad brown eyes grew shiny. "My little Olya, my poor child."

The son's features reflected pain, sympathy, and an anger that seemed oddly out of place to Jander. "Has anyone told *him* yet?"

The bereaved father wiped his eyes with stubby fingers. "No. No one dares go to the castle with that kind of news."

"I'd wager he'll hear soon enough. The count has ways of finding out what he needs to know."

Abruptly the older man's expression altered, changing from one of grief to one filled with hatred. "I'm glad she's dead," he spat. "I'm glad she's dead so he can't get her and touch her with those cold hands of his—"

"Da!" the boy hissed, trying to quiet him. The older man began to sob harshly, and two other men from a nearby table helped the son walk the broken father to the door. The rest of the patrons watched silently.

Jander noticed that the gypsy boy Petya had ceased juggling. All his playfulness had vanished, and his dark eyes were alert and observant. The boy isn't quite the clown he pretends to be, Jander thought. Petya had stepped away from his burlap sack to watch the departing father and son, and as the vampire observed, one of the customers moved past the Vistani and dropped a small pouch into the bag. The mustached man, who had small, piggy eyes and a cruel mouth, ordered another ale and returned with it to his seat.

Jander was about to say something, then hesitated. Best not to draw more attention to himself. He would wait until the scene had played itself out. The customers took their seats, and the low murmur of conversation resumed.

Petya relit his torches and began to juggle them again. An instant later the cry of "Thief!" rang out. With speed greater than Jander would have credited them with, several men grabbed the astonished boy, yanking his arms behind his back and landing painful punches to his stomach. Petya's torches went flying, and other people scurried to put them out before the place caught fire.

The door slammed open. A big, beefy man with fat jowls and a thick, drooping mustache charged in. His clothing was much finer than the shirts and vests of the other patrons, and he had the air of one used to being obeyed. "Burgomaster Kartov!" exclaimed a greasy little man. "One of the Vistani has been caught picking Andrei's pocket!"

Andrei, the pig-eyed man with the cruel mouth, nodded vigorously. Kartov turned his angry glare upon the boy, who was clearly terrified. Nonetheless, Petya clenched his jaw and stared the larger man in the face.

"This man lies," he said coolly, his voice betraying nothing of the terror that filled Jander's nostrils. "I was only juggling for coins. I have been wrongly accused. Besides, if I had stolen the purse," he added with a sneer, "I would have done so without him noticing."

Kartov's hand came crashing down. Petya's head jerked to the side with the force of the blow, and blood trickled from his mouth.

A sharp cry pierced the air, and a girl launched herself at the burgomaster from the doorway. "Papa, no! Stop it!" Jander noted with clinical detachment that the girl's face, too, bore signs of a beating. Her father ignored her, shaking her off distractedly. All his white-hot anger was fixed on the Vistani.

"My people will take it ill if you harm me," Petya warned in a low voice. He was obviously not bluffing. Jander noticed that a few of the men looked uncomfortable. Apparently Vistani vengeance was nothing to be courted.

Clearly, though, Kartov was beyond reason. "*We* take

it ill when honest folk are robbed!" he roared back.

"Hang the bastard!" came a voice from the crowd. Jander could not locate who had uttered it first, but the chant was quickly taken up by the mob.

Kartov bent close to Petya. Only the gypsy and the vampire heard what the enraged parent hissed: "You'll wish you were in Castle Ravenloft by the time we're done with you. I know what you did to my daughter!"

Under his naturally dark skin tones, Petya went pale.

Ah, thought Jander with instant comprehension.

"Papa, no!" the girl screamed. "It's not his fault!"

Kartov spared her a furious glance. "Haven't you had enough?" he snarled. Jander watched with disgust. The elf despised bullies, and clearly the town was governed by a prime example. He wondered if this hot-tempered man was the mysterious "he" that the bereaved father had feared.

"I'll deal with you later, Anastasia," Kartov continued. "Right now, you're going to watch your lover die."

Anastasia began to sob. "No! Petya!" One of the men who had accompanied Kartov grabbed her and held her tightly.

Jander had to admire the youth's poise. "Kartov of Barovia," the gypsy began in a sing-song voice, "You shall rue this night's deeds. Boris Federovich Kartov, I curse y—" He choked as someone shoved a dirty rag into his mouth. Even though the curse hadn't been completed, some of the patrons were now hesitating to aid their burgomaster. Others, however, were grateful for the opportunity to translate their perpetual fear into action.

They yanked Petya's arms behind his back, tying the limbs tightly with the boy's own brightly colored scarf. Jeering and cursing him, they shoved the boy out the door. He stumbled over the threshold and hit the cobblestones hard, unable to break the fall with his bound hands. Raucous laughter burst from the crowd. Kartov pulled Petya to his feet by grabbing hold of the boy's silky black hair. Petya winced with pain.

The light from the open tavern door spilled out into the center square, its yellow brightness a sharp contrast to the subdued glow of the moon's light. Lights went on in all the houses along the open square. Shutters opened a crack and the inhabitants peered out curiously but cautiously.

The mob tumbled out into the night in a collective stream of enthusiasm, half-pushing, half-carrying the hapless Vistani. They were taking him toward the gallows at the end of the square. The pig-eyed lackey had run ahead and prepared the hangman's noose for its victim and waited, grinning viciously, as the crowd moved in his direction. Petya was dragged up the few steps onto the scaffold. He still struggled as the pig-eyed man draped the noose about his neck.

No one noticed when the elven stranger separated from the throng and vanished like a shadow into the night. However, they all heard the sound of the approaching wolf pack.

 **FOUR**

Their song soared before them as horns' music before hunters. The shrill melody rent the night, a gleeful sound that could freeze blood. Wolves had never before come straight for the village. Then again, much was afoot in Barovia that was best not examined too closely.

As uniform in their flight as they had been in their bloodthirst, the villagers scattered before the oncoming beasts. The crowd dispersed, shrieking in fear and stumbling toward what safety their small homes could afford. Still the sound closed in about them.

Anastasia took advantage of her captor's slackened grip to squirm free and scramble up the gallows steps. Ignoring her own terror, she forced her trembling fingers to undo Petya's bonds. Whoever had tied his hands had done it well. The scarf bit into his flesh, and she practically had to dig it out. She had almost loosened it enough for Petya to work free when her father's hand clamped down on her arm. "Anastasia, come! Hurry!"

At that moment a gigantic furry shape emerged from the shadows and leaped onto the wooden platform, hurling itself at Kartov. Its jaws remained closed, but the weight of its body sent both burgomaster and wolf tumbling from the platform to sprawl on the unyielding stone. As quickly as it sprang, the beast leaped off Kartov, nipping at his feet, almost herding him down

Burgomaster's Way toward his house. Kartov needed no further urging. He may have loved his daughter, but he loved himself more.

The eight wolves raced across the square, their howls clashing with the screams of their intended victims. They chased after fleeing villagers, scrabbled angrily at bolted doors, capered with bestial abandon at shuttered windows. One of them seized a wooden window sill in its mammoth jaws. The beam splintered with a loud crack and the wolf whimpered in stupid surprise at the pain.

Not a single one of the great beasts attacked Petya or Anastasia.

Anastasia continued to work at the scarf, and Petya struggled free. He grabbed her hand, and they clattered down the steps. A great gray she-wolf noticed the movement and swung her shaggy head toward them, growling. Petya lunged for a knotty branch one of the men from the tavern had dropped, then shoved Anastasia behind him. Gritting his teeth, Petya raised the stick. The wolf advanced on them slowly, her legs stiff and the hackles on her massive shoulders raised. Her eyes blazed with an amber glow.

"There's no need for that, Petya!" came a reproving voice. Petya gasped. Jander stepped in front of him, smiling slightly. "The pack is at my command." He turned to the beast. *Calm down, sister, calm down . . .* Clearly unhappy with her lot, the gray female sat down. She still growled, though, and her ears were flat against her head.

Jander looked about, making eye contact with the rest of the pack and issuing silent commands that were obeyed, albeit reluctantly. *Thank you, brothers. You may go now.* As one, the wolves sprang to their feet and sped into the shadows, shaking their heads to get the human stink out of delicate nostrils. Within a few seconds, all trace of them had vanished.

Petya and Anastasia gaped at Jander. Then Anastasia started to cry weakly, the strain of the evening finally catching up with her. The gypsy boy put a protective arm about her, but his black eyes never left Jander's. "What *are* you?" he demanded in a voice that betrayed nothing of the fear that Jander could smell.

Jander raised his eyebrows, feigning offense. "I am but a traveler from another land. I have saved your life here tonight, Petya. What more must a stranger do to win your trust? You told me that you knew what it was like to be an outsider here. Have you forgotten?"

Petya flushed. "I have never seen anyone like you before. You will forgive me if I still mistrust. Yet," he conceded, "we are in your debt. How can we repay you?"

"By getting out of here before the rest of the villagers get suspicious. Anastasia," the vampire said gently, "you'd best bid farewell to Petya. He won't be visiting the village again, not with the kind of greeting he is sure to receive."

Anastasia, who had mastered her tears, threw her lover an anguished look. "Our savior," Petya said, with a still-suspicious glance at Jander, "has the right of it, my darling. This is goodbye. My people, I think, will be on the move even sooner than we had planned." He grinned ruefully. "My Papa will be whipping me before morning, I'm sure, for the coins such a retreat will cost us."

It was with real affection that Petya gathered the girl into his arms for a last embrace, holding her as she sobbed against his chest and planting a gentle kiss on her head. At last Anastasia drew away from him and dragged a hand across her wet face. She took a deep breath to steady herself.

"Good sir, I do not know your name to thank you properly." Her voice quivered slightly.

Jander glanced around the square, worried that the villagers might be crawling out of their holes. It appeared that his little trick had succeeded extremely well. All the windows and doors remained securely fastened. "I am Jander Sunstar."

"Then, Jander Sunstar, I pledge my friendship to you. I will never forget what you have done for us tonight."

The tears threatened to overwhelm her, and she bit her lower lip. Unwilling to break down again, she fled toward her father's home. Petya's black eyes followed her, unusually somber.

"Your true love?" Jander did not mean to sound so sarcastic, but the words came out that way.

Petya was oblivious to any needling, however, and merely shook his dark head. "Nay. But I am fond of the girl and would not see her harmed. She has spirit, and that is rare in her village." He turned to face Jander, planting his fists on his hips. For his small stature, Petya was very sure of himself. His face was bruised and bloody, but he ignored the pain.

"I owe you my life. We Vistani do not take such debts lightly. Jander Sunstar, whatever you may be, you have demonstrated friendship to me here tonight. I offer the same." He paused and licked his lips. "I invite you to come with me to our encampment, where we may treat you with the honor you deserve." He bowed deeply.

Jander smiled to himself. His plan to win the gypsy's trust had worked. "Petya of the Vistani, I should be honored to visit your encampment."

Petya was pleased with the gracious reply. "Then let us go," he smiled. "This way," he said as he took the road headed west. Jander followed.

The lights of the village faded behind the gypsy and the vampire, and the night closed about them. Most of the dwellings were located well inside the town limits, but as he walked along the dirt road Jander saw a few lone homesteads. A small flock of sheep stood out like specters against the dark green of the grass.

"Tell me about yourself, Jander Sunstar. I do not think you are from this place."

Jander glanced down at his companion. "What makes you say that?"

"All those who dwell here look like the villagers."

"Yet your people live here, and you're not quite the same as the Barovians," Jander pointed out.

"We are travelers."

"Well, then, so am I."

Petya smiled, flashing white teeth in the moonlight. "Perhaps that is so. What is the name of your race?"

"I'm an elf," Jander answered. The term brought an unexpectedly delighted response from the gypsy.

"I *am* happy to have met you! I have never before seen an elf. Although," he added with a trace of self-importance, "I have heard the stories." Jander had to smile to himself. He would have given much to hear exactly what kind of tales Petya had listened to. "Then the mists must have brought you."

Jander was surprised. He certainly remembered the thick fog that had enveloped him, but he hadn't thought it the reason he had come to Barovia. "Does this happen often?"

"No, but it is not unknown. We ourselves travel the mists. Our tribe has only been here a short time." He stopped and pointed. Ahead roiled the mysterious fog through which Jander had passed earlier when he entered the village. It was a thick gray barrier that shifted and pulsed as if it possessed its own kind of malevolent life. Jander had not enjoyed passing through it when he entered the village a few hours earlier, but it had not harmed him any.

Petya shoved a dark hand into one of the voluminous pockets of his red pants and pulled out two small vials of a purplish liquid. "It is well that I put these here and not in my sack, hey?" He tossed Jander one of the vials, uncorked his own with a small "pop" and drained the contents. Jander examined his, wondering what he should do. He couldn't drink it, that was certain.

"Come, come!" Petya chided. "This is a potion that will let you pass safely through the fog."

"Why, is it dangerous?"

Petya stared, then shrugged. "You came through the mists, so you would not know. That is killing fog. It is poisonous. This," he held up his now-empty vial, "makes you immune to its effects."

Jander hesitated, then pretended to drink the liquid,

spitting it out the minute they entered the fog and Petya couldn't see him. The fog hadn't harmed him because he didn't breathe. Poison couldn't affect one who was already dead. The fog welcomed them, folding damp arms about them, trailing tendrils about their faces and down their backs. Jander would have lost Petya within minutes but for his infravision. He concentrated on the redness of Petya's warmth ahead of him. After several minutes, the fog lessened, then faded altogether.

"That's . . . uncanny," the vampire said.

"There is much that is uncanny in Barovia," the gypsy replied somberly.

"Yes, tell me about Barovia. I—" Jander broke off in mid-sentence. The poisonous fog had shut them off completely from their surroundings, even to the point of eliminating outside noises. Now the elf heard the bubbling of water a short distance away and glanced ahead down the path. It led directly to a small wooden bridge that arched over a fast-flowing, dark river about fifty feet wide. On the other side, the path continued, twisting ahead into the forest. Jander's sure footsteps faltered and his mind raced. As a vampire, he would be unable to cross the running water. Petya still believed him a living being—elven, and therefore alien, but alive. The music of the flowing water taunted him.

"Is something wrong?"

They drew closer. "I . . . have a confession. When I was young, I nearly drowned in a river. Ever since then, I've been deathly afraid of them. Is there no other way to your camp?"

Petya looked skeptical. "The bridge is secure, I promise you. Look." The youth scampered halfway across the wooden bridge and back like a rabbit. "I will guide you safely across." A crafty smile touched his lips. "You have asked me to trust you, and I have walked alone in the Barovian night with a stranger! Now it is your turn to trust me."

The elf glanced down into the swirling water, taking care that Petya did not notice that he had no reflection.

The river churned beneath the bridge, heedless of the
vampire's dilemma. Even if he could take his wolf form,
it was still too wide for him to jump. No, he would be
unable to cross the water. He had tried once, a few hundred years ago, and had doubled over in agony. He had
to make the attempt here, if for no other reason than to
convince Petya that his false phobia was crippling.

The elf slowly reached and took Petya's proffered
hand. For extra support, he felt Petya's arm go around
his back. Together, gypsy and vampire took a tentative
step onto the bridge. Jander moaned in pain and quickly stepped back onto the land. He could not do it. Before he realized what had happened, he was on Petya's
back.

"Petya—"

"A debt is a debt, *giorgio!*" The slender youth was surprisingly strong. Quickly and with a sure stride he
walked across the bridge, carrying Jander easily. Jander glanced down as they crossed, seeing the silver
glint of moonlight reflected in the water.

Petya reached the far shore, and Jander slipped to
the ground. "You are kind," he said to the boy. Petya
shrugged off the compliment.

"It is a good thing you fell in with me," the Vistani said
as they continued. The forest pressed in thickly about
them, and Jander noticed that Petya's footsteps were
almost as silent as his own. "You would have terrified
the villagers long before now. I assume you are a magi-
cian?"

Inwardly Jander grimaced, but it was a convenient
way to pass off his control of the wolves. "You could say
that."

"I understand these things. The villagers, they are too
frightened. Your kind of magic is most often found
practiced by the *akara.*"

Jander did not recognize the word, and raised an in-
quiring eyebrow. "*Akara?*" he repeated.

"Nosferatu," Petya explained, "vampires. The undead
who feed upon the blood of the living." He made a quick

sign of protection over his heart. Though it was as alien to Jander as the word Petya had used, he instinctively flinched. Fortunately, Petya didn't notice.

"Ah, I see," Jander replied. "You're right. I am lucky indeed that we met. Tell me more about this world. Is Barovia the name of the town?"

"Yes, and the name of the land as well." They passed beneath some hunching apple trees, their beautiful blossoms sharply at odds with their twisted appearance. Petya paused a moment, then leaped upward and seized a branch bursting with blossoms. It cracked loudly in the still night and showered him with petals. He tugged, and the branch came free in his hand. The youth inhaled its scent deeply, smiling.

"For my sister," he explained. "Flowers turn their anger, hey?" His smile deepened to a grin as he gave Jander a sly wink. "Do you have a lady, Jander? They can be very fine company, but sometimes they talk too much."

Jander was growing impatient. The boy was amusing, yes, and it had been far too long since Jander had been amused. He had rescued Petya's neck from the noose for information, however, not entertainment. "I heard the name Strahd at the inn, and mention of a place called Castle Ravenloft."

Petya's mercurial features now registered a true seriousness, and Jander smelled fear. "Let us not speak of these things in the dark," he said quickly. "We can talk about that tomorrow."

"Tonight," Jander pressed.

Something in the elf's tone caused Petya to look at him closely. "Very well," said the boy slowly, "though it is best not to talk of such dark things at all. Count Strahd Von Zarovich is the lord of this land. His home is Castle Ravenloft. He was a powerful warrior once, but now it is said he cultivates magic."

Magic. Would he never be free of it? Jander fought the urge to spit contemptuously. It was a stroke of ill luck indeed that the lord of this fell place was a mage.

"Do you think that's true? About magic?"

"It must be. He has ruled here far longer than any mortal man should."

"How long is that?"

Petya shrugged. "I do not know. We are not Barovian. We do not follow its history that much."

Jander considered the strange surroundings for a moment. "The fog answers to him, doesn't it?"

"The fog around the village, yes. It is under his control. But the mists that brought you to this land bow to no one."

"Who is Olya?"

Petya glanced at him again, a flicker of suspicion in his eyes. "A girl who died, as you obviously heard. It cannot interest you." A sharp twittering caused Jander to look up. A small gray and white bird, disturbed from its sleep, regarded him with a bright eye before settling back to its rest. "Mark that bird well, Jander. It is a *vista chiri*. When you see one of them, you know that the Vistani are not too far. They follow us, our little friends. It is said that they are the spirits of our ancestors, here to keep an eye on us. Come, we leave the path here. I know a shortcut."

Petya veered into the forests. Jander followed. It was quite dark here, as the thick trees that arched overhead cut off most of the moonlight. Giant roots crisscrossed the shadowy forest floor. Petya, however, navigated the tricky footing with a sure step and an air of complete safety. "The villagers seem to be afraid of the night," Jander ventured, "yet you stride off like a hero, Petya. There are wolves in this realm. Are you not afraid?"

"You speak with the wolves, Jander, and no self-respecting bandit would attack a Vistani." He grinned over his shoulder. "All Vistani can cast the Evil Eye, hey? As for not-so-mortal danger, the powers of this place have no effect on me. It is why Strahd—" He broke off and muttered a curse under his breath. "You loosen my tongue, elf, and that is not necessarily a good thing. I have spoken enough, perhaps too much.

Come, tell me of your land."

"I was born in a land called Evermeet, a place where only my own kind dwelt. I can't begin to tell you how beautiful it was. I used to play the flute and sing, and there was dancing in the groves in the summer. It was like nothing I have ever seen since." Jander's voice hardened. "And believe me, Petya, I have seen much."

Petya threw him a searching glance. "I do believe you, elf," he said softly and sincerely. "You may find a balm to your soul this night."

Jander and his unlikely ally threaded their way through the brooding darkness of Barovia's forests as Jander talked about Evermeet. Petya kept respectfully silent and listened, alerted perhaps by the deep tinge of sorrow in the elf's musical voice. They kept the river on their right for the most part, though its tones decreased in volume occasionally as they wandered deeper into the forest at places. At last the river's sound was replaced by others—horses' whinnies, dogs' barks, and the hum of human conversation.

They emerged from the shadows of the hunching trees, and Jander could see the glow from the fire in the distance. His sharp elven vision, enhanced by his skills as a vampire, enabled him to make out several dozen caravans. The wagons were gaily decorated things covered in bright hues and imaginative carvings. Many horses and the goats and chickens that served as the gypsies' livestock crowded the edge of the camp, and shadowy shapes moved about the fire.

The elf took in this inviting scenario only secondarily. To the north of the encampment rose a huge spire. The sky was black, dotted with tiny, cold points of light, but the shape silhouetted against it was blacker. A forbidding castle crowned the precipice. Jander recognized it as the same structure that he had seen from the road when he had first appeared in Barovia. He had wondered about it then. Now, he knew its dark identity.

Petya followed his gaze. "Yes," he said quietly, "that is Castle Ravenloft. Count Strahd dwells there."

 **FIVE**

Maruschka did not like children.

When Lara asked her to mind the baby while she danced, Maruschka couldn't politely decline. Now the young Vistani woman sat on a rough wooden stool, holding the unhappy child and frowning like a thunderstorm while Lara danced gracefully with her husband. The flickering light from the fire only served to show Maruschka that the baby had spat up the beet soup she had wrestled down his throat. When the fretful infant tried to insert the end of Maruschka's thick black braid into its rosy mouth, the girl decided that friendship went only so far.

Black eyes flashing, she strode through the dancers to Lara and shoved the baby at her. "Take him," she snapped in the Vistani tongue. "He's not spitting up on me again tonight."

Lara and her husband laughed and cuddled their child as Maruschka stalked off. "Ah, the gods would make a mistake in giving that one a baby," Lara chuckled, gazing after her friend with pitying affection.

"Aye," her husband agreed, taking his child and planting a kiss on the soft cheek. "Better that she follow her grandmother's path." The baby cooed and promptly went to sleep in his father's loving arms.

Maruschka's quick anger took her as far as the ring of

firelight that closed off the gypsy encampment. She flipped back her thick braid of glossy black hair and gazed down the path, then up at the stars. Four hours had passed since her little brother Petya had departed, swaggering and boasting as always. Four hours was ample time for him to get into plenty of trouble.

Maruschka had a feeling that something had gone wrong. She always listened when her inner senses spoke to her, for they were usually right. Many in the encampment had partial Sight. Lara could tell fortunes in the cards, for instance, and Keva sometimes heard voices that accurately foretold the future. Maruschka, however, had the complete Sight, the only one of her generation to be so blessed—or cursed.

She could scry in any surface, be it a cup of water, a ball of crystal, or a mirror. The cards always spoke to her about the questioner's destiny, as did tea leaves. Maruschka could also read palms and faces, and sometimes had occasional blinding flashes of knowledge. Such power made her respected in the tribe, but sometimes the tall, slender twenty-year-old longed to be merely an ordinary Vistani. At present, all her Sight told her was that Petya had gotten himself into trouble.

"He'll be returning shortly, child. Fret ye not," came a dry voice at her elbow. Maruschka jumped, then smiled and nodded at Madame Eva. The elderly woman had a disconcerting habit of creeping up unnoticed. It was wise to not talk behind her back. Some said it was wise to not even *think* behind her back. Maruschka thought those folk had the right of it.

No one knew quite how old Madame Eva was, and she never told. Her back was still straight, although her body was fragile and her face was wrinkled like Barovian plums left in the sun too long. She kept her white hair long and loose, flowing down her back like moonlight. Eva's eyes were bright and quick, and her Sight was still accurate. Though most of her teeth were gone and she lived on porridge, she was the most powerful person in the tribe, and none dared cross her. Maruschka honed her divination skills under Eva's strict tutelage and knew that she would become Seer of the tribe when the old gypsy woman lost the Sight.

Some of Maruschka's worry faded. She knew that if Eva said Petya would come home safely, then the boy would come to no harm.

"Aye, Petya's got the luck of the gods, all right. Half the towns we've visited would put his head on a stick if they could," she told Eva. The crone laughed, a raspy sound. "But I can't help but worry," the younger woman added. "He courts trouble like he courts those girls. He takes such foolish risks."

"There are some that would say that of me, too, child," Eva reminded her. "I seem to recall a certain girl who was convinced that I'd never leave Castle Ravenloft alive."

Now it was Maruschka's turn to laugh. "Well, Strahd is the very devil, Gran."

"Be that as it may, he has been good to the Folk. Ye would do well to remember that, child, should yer loyalties be divided. That any of us rest easy in our beds in this land is due to Strahd's generosity."

Suddenly a wave of love for the proud old gypsy woman swept through Maruschka, and she gave her grandmother a hug. "Also due to my gran's cleverness!"

Eva smiled a toothless grin. "That too," she agreed. Abruptly the old woman frowned. "Petya comes," she said, "and another."

"Brought another of his young ladies," Maruschka snorted, glancing down the path. Sure enough, two figures were approaching the encampment, but Petya was not accompanied by some pretty young maid. The gypsy girl had never seen anyone like this stranger before.

Maruschka heard Eva inhale in surprise. "One of the People," she said softly. Maruschka didn't understand Eva's use of the term. Before she could ask her grandmother about it, Petya was running toward them at top speed; Maruschka gasped when she saw his bruised faced. The boy skidded to a halt when he recognized Eva.

"Greetings, Gran," he said politely, bowing deeply. Eva didn't even spare him a glance, but kept her sharp eyes on the slender stranger who waited a short distance away.

"Why does the elf not come with ye?" she demanded.

"Petya, what happened to you?" Maruschka exclaimed.

The boy ignored them both. "First, Gran, you remember you told me to keep an eye on Olya Ivanova? She died tonight from fever."

Now Eva did look at her grandson, her bright eyes narrowing. "Are ye certain?"

"Her father and brother were in the tavern. Old Ivan is nearly mad from grief." Eva looked suddenly weary. Petya noticed her sudden change in demeanor. "Did I do right to tell you?" he queried, worried.

Eva nodded. "Yes, child. Though it is hardly good news, it is something worth knowing. Now," she regained her former mien, "answer me about the *giorgio*."

"He says among his people, it is rude to approach without an invitation."

"I have never heard such a rule among the Tel'Quessir," Eva retorted. "In any case, he is a *giorgio* and not welcome."

"Please, Gran, he saved my life tonight!" Petya pleaded.

"Petya, what have you done?" Maruschka's thin black brows drew together.

Quickly and with some embarrassment, Petya told them of the night's occurrences. Eva raised an eyebrow when he described Jander's powers, and a small smile quirked a corner of her mouth. "Very well," she said unexpectedly. "He may approach."

Petya grinned despite his swollen face, and he returned to fetch his comrade. "You seem to know the *giorgio's* kind," Maruschka said to Eva.

"He is a gold elf, also called a sunrise elf, from a world called Toril. The elven nation is to be respected and honored. I wonder, though, why such a one is here. Nonetheless, Petya is right. He has saved one of our

children, and for that, he is welcome—for this night only." She gathered her brightly colored shawl about her
thin shoulders. "It is late. Goodnight, child."

"Gran, don't you wish to greet the stranger?"

Eva shook her white head. "Nay. I must get these old
bones to bed. Tell him of the cave near the falls," she
added.

Maruschka nodded, though she was utterly confused.
She turned her attention back to Petya's strange new
friend, who was walking up to her with the grace and
silence of a cat.

He was of average height and very slender. His features were well-formed and yet delicate, the strange silver eyes large and compelling. His coloring fascinated
Maruschka, who found herself staring. She couldn't
help it. This *giorgio* was quite the most beautiful thing
Maruschka had ever seen.

"Jander Sunstar, this is my sister Maruschka," Petya
said. Jander bowed politely.

"Lady, I am honored."

Maruschka blushed, an unusual thing for her. This ali-
en being focused entirely on her, making her feel as
though she were the center of the universe. She had not
had many dealings with *giorgios* and was accustomed to
the Vistani mixture of rough affection and subtle defer-
ence. The elf's grace was new, and she liked it.

Her musing was rudely interrupted by a shout from
the campfire, and before she knew it there was a large
crowd behind her. "Who's the *giorgio*?" her father asked
in the Vistani tongue.

"An elf, Papa. He saved Petya from a hanging this
night. Gran said we were to make him welcome." There
was some resentful murmuring, but Eva's word was always obeyed and the throng reluctantly parted to admit
Jander into their midst.

The vampire had wondered about the reception he
would receive. He found that the dark visages of the
gypsies were reserved, but not hostile in the way the
faces of the Barovians had been. Petya spoke to them

rapidly in their own tongue, and Jander watched the faces change to expressions of surprise and then pleasure. Hands were extended, and smiles of welcome replaced the speculative gazes. Jander smiled back, cautiously. Arms were linked through his, and he was propelled to a special place at the fire amid much lively chatter and laughter.

Jander found himself the center of attention as the children clustered about his feet. Completely without embarrassment, they reached to clutch his gray cloak, run small, sticky hands through the gold of his hair, and tug on pointed ears. Their onslaught was unheralded, and Jander instinctively drew back, pushing the boys and girls away.

Maruschka reprimanded the children, and they scattered. A few of the more intrepid among them paused and crept back, to sit a little farther away from the golden *giorgio*. "I did not mean to alarm them," Jander apologized. "I have not been around people much in the last few years, certainly not children."

Maruschka sat down beside him on the wooden bench and shrugged, her blouse slipping off one dark shoulder. "They are a nuisance to me, too," she confided with a small laugh. "Animals are better. At least they can be trained."

Jander heard a small cough and glanced up, meeting the gaze of a rather uncomfortable-looking older man. "Sir, I thank you for the life of my son," the man said stiffly, "although the gods know, sometimes I want to kill him myself." He bowed once, then strode to where Petya was regaling an audience with an account of his escape.

To Jander's chagrin, Petya's father seized the boy by the ear with one hand and unbuckled his wide leather belt with the other. Petya yelped, wriggled free, and sped toward the forest. His father was quicker, and soon the two began jabbering heatedly. Petya had apparently been right about the punishment he would receive.

"Is your father really going to beat him?"

Maruschka grinned conspiratorially. "Watch."

The father and son continued arguing, their movements becoming ever more animated. Suddenly the older man grabbed the youth and hugged him tightly. Petya returned his father's embrace. When they parted and Petya's father began to examine the boy's injuries, both pairs of eyes were glistening with tears.

"Beat our children?" smiled Maruschka. "Jander, children are the most precious things in the world to our people. Maybe not to me, hey?" she amended with a laugh. "There are so few of us, you see. Still, one of these days Petya will grow up." Maruschka sighed.

"Do not wish that day too soon," Jander said softly. He had seen altogether too many flowers blossom and wither in his seven centuries. The thought of impish Petya aged and worn saddened him.

Maruschka noticed the change and gazed at him searchingly for a moment. Gravely she said, "Would you like me to tell your fortune?"

Jander sobered even further. "I can tell my own," he replied harshly. "There are no surprises for me, and it would give me no pleasure for you to make up a false future."

Had not Jander been so obviously downcast, Maruschka would have taken great offense at the implied insult to her talents. "I am a true Seer," she stated with pride, "and perhaps I can give you the answers you seek." He turned to look at her, his silvery eyes searching. "Perhaps I can tell you why you are here, sunrise elf of Toril."

Silver eyes narrowed, going catlike. "How did you know?"

"My gran knew. Madame Eva is the Seer and leader of our people, and she has been to your land. It is she who is responsible for your welcome here. She also told me to tell you that there is a cave not far from here, though I don't know why you would need to know that."

Jander was confused. Could this Madame Eva know that he was a vampire? Why else would he need a cave? Perhaps merely for shelter, as any mortal might. Still, it was interesting that Eva knew of Toril. "May I meet your grandmother, Maruschka? If she has visited my land, we might enjoy talking."

"She has gone to bed. She is very old and tires easily." Her red lips curved in a mock pout. "Why would you wish to spend time with an old lady when you have my company? Come, Jander Sunstar. Let me tell your fortune. I usually charge dearly for such a service. For the life of my brother, it is my gift. You would not insult me by refusing?" She glanced up at him through dark lashes, her tone coy and teasing. Jander remembered the fine art of flirtation, and it wakened a sense of nostalgia. That, too, had been denied him for centuries, that harmless coquetry and pleasant sparring between the sexes. Gone, like so much of his past . . .

"Very well. I accept."

"Come to our caravan. My cards are there."

Jander had to smile. "Is it safe to take a stranger into your home alone?"

She laughed, tossing back her thick black braid of hair and showing white, even teeth. "Hey, *giorgio*, we Vistani can take care of ourselves!" She patted the wide black leather belt that encircled her narrow waist, and he saw a small and clearly functional dagger tucked therein. Still smiling, she beckoned him toward her family's caravans.

As befitted the family of Madame Eva, the *vardos* were ornate creations. The one Maruschka was taking him to was small but beautiful. It was difficult to distinguish colors in the dim glow of the fire, but Jander could make out a woodland scene of stags and hares carved on the side. A piebald pony was tethered to the back, drowsing contentedly.

As Jander and Maruschka approached, the animal started to wakefulness, its ears pricked forward attentively. Rosy nostrils widened as it caught Jander's undead scent, and the beast began to neigh frantically, tugging at its rein and rearing. Maruschka went to the pony and tried to calm it, but the animal was wild in its terror.

Jander concentrated. He sent a silent command to the panicked animal, ordering it to be quiet. *Hush . . . calm down, little friend. . . .* The piebald obeyed, although it still shivered, brown eyes wide and rolling. Maruschka frowned and glanced over at Jander as she patted the pony's neck. The vampire smiled in what he hoped was a reassuring manner.

"Petya told you of the wolves. No doubt your pony can smell them on me yet."

"Yes, that must be it," Maruschka agreed slowly.

They climbed the few wooden stairs that led to the door of the *vardo*. Maruschka pulled the door open and went inside to light some lamps. Jander lingered outside, unable to enter until she bade him. The gypsy Seer stuck her dark head out after a few seconds. "What are you waiting for? Come in!"

Jander did so, ducking his head because of the low entrance. The *vardo* wasn't particularly large, and the many objects Maruschka had crammed inside made it appear even smaller. Five large, colorfully embroidered pillows were strewn on the floor, forming a ring about a large crystal ball that rested on a fancifully carved metal stand. Wooden shelves hosted an assortment of stones, beads, bones, and other trappings of gypsy fortune tellers. Maruschka's bed, at the far end of the *vardo*, was a small, sturdy pallet, covered with wolf skins and a woven woolen blanket. Three lamps, hung from hooks in the curved ceiling, provided ample lighting.

"Sit down while I try to find my cards," Maruschka invited. As Jander did so, lowering himself onto the surprisingly comfortable cushions, a sudden cawing sound caused him to glance up, startled. Tucked away in a corner was a large cage that housed a huge black bird. It fixed the elf with watchful black eyes. Before it could caw again, Jander sent one of his silent commands, and it subsided into slumber.

"That is Pika. His name means 'mischief.' I let him out now and then, and he brings home the oddest things sometimes. Ah, here they are." Maruschka emerged from rummaging under her bed with a pack of over-sized cards. Jander turned his gaze back to her. "Petya made these for me for my birthday a few months ago," she said. "I think you will find them beautiful." She handed the pack to Jander. "Shuffle them."

"How many times?"

Maruschka shrugged. "Until they feel right in your hands."

Jander mentally rolled his eyes and began to shuffle the cards with his long, golden hands. This was a waste of time, but perhaps he could get the girl talking about Strahd. Instinctively he knew Maruschka knew much more about the land and its lord than happy-go-lucky Petya. He also suspected that it would be harder to pry answers from her. Maruschka seated herself on a pillow opposite the vampire, gently pushing the crystal ball to one side. Her black eyes were fastened on his face.

Suddenly, he knew what she meant. The cards "felt" right. It was as if they had sent him a message, *That's enough, put us down now.* It surprised him. He'd always thought of gypsies as tricksters and performers, with little or no real magical knowledge. The Vistani, however, were clearly different.

He placed the cards down on the table. "Spread them out," said Maruschka. Her voice was different now, deeper, more mature. Her face, too, seemed older. Jander did as he was told. "Now select six cards."

She took the ones he gave her and carefully set the others aside. She turned over the first card. It depicted a beautiful shooting star, a rainbow of colors, carried by a woman equally as lovely. Jander was surprised that the apparently frivolous Petya had such a delicate sense of beauty. "This card is your distant past." She smiled. "It is the best card in the deck, full of gentleness, hope, and promise. What a beautiful soul you were then, Jander Sunstar."

The elf could not meet her eyes. Maruschka turned over the second card, and her expression grew sad. Jander was confused. It seemed like a good card. It depicted a pair of lovers walking through a green wood, hands clasped, the man looking suspiciously like Petya. "That doesn't look so bad," he ventured.

Maruschka shook her head. "It isn't, usually. This is the Lovers' card. But you see, it's upside down. That means that there was a parting. This is the recent past— you loved, and you lost her."

Jander began to seriously consider the idea that this woman could indeed predict the future.

Maruschka flipped the third card. It showed a blind woman carrying a set of scales. "You seek Justice." She frowned and touched the card gently. Her eyes grew distant. "You seek revenge," she amended softly.

When she turned over the next card, Maruschka was a bit startled. A scythe-wielding skeleton grinned up at her. She glanced up at Jander and noticed to her shock that the elf had a slight, sarcastic smile on his lips. "That's you," she blurted out. "I mean, this is your present. The card really means change, not death."

Jander's smile stayed. "My dear, I think in this case, it means exactly what it looks like."

Something was not right with Jander, Maruschka thought. "Are you a warrior, then?"

"I was, yes. Once. A long time ago. In a way, I still am. Please, go on. You've caught my interest now."

Maruschka hated the smile on the elf's face. It was bitter, self-mocking, and yet dangerous. She liked Jander better when he had been wrapped in melancholy, his strange, silver eyes full of a deep sorrow. Maruschka became aware that there was a menacing edge to this polished *giorgio*. He was slight, though, and she was sure that she could handle him in a fight. Nonetheless, her right hand crept slowly toward the knife in her belt. Maruschka turned the next card over with her left hand, closing her eyes as she saw what it was.

The Death card alarmed most people, but this was the card that every fortune teller hated to see turn up in a reading. It was the Tower. Petya in his whimsy had fashioned the building to look like Castle Ravenloft. It was in the process of shattering violently, hurling people to their deaths. "This one is bad," she murmured. "Very bad . . ." Her hand closed around the hilt of the dagger.

"All the more reason for me to believe in the truth of your reading," Jander replied mildly. "And Maruschka," his voice was gentle, "take your hand off your dagger. I have no intention of harming you."

Startled, she looked up and met silver eyes that were full of a gentle sorrow once more. The Vistani Seer felt ashamed of herself. She opened her mouth to apologize, and he waved a slender hand. "What does this ill-boding Tower card have to say to me?"

"The Tower is chaos, destruction. That will be the situation in the future for you."

"Lovely."

Maruschka hurried on. She turned the final card and smiled in relief. It was the Sun, her personal favorite in the deck. A small child, about three years old, reached chubby arms up to a glowing orb that hung just beyond its grasp. "The Sun represents success and victory. It also has much to do with children. If you are to get your justice, it will be through the Sun and through children." She glanced from the card to Jander, confident that she had brought some measure of happiness with this last card. Instead, his face was sadder than ever, his features weary and resigned. "The Sun is a very good card," she repeated.

"For most people, perhaps. Not for me. I thank you for taking the time, Maruschka. It was . . . enlightening. I must go, now." He rose gracefully. "You mentioned a cave?"

Maruschka could not bear to see him leave like that, so devoid of hope. After all, she'd been the one to insist on a fortune telling, not he, and it was because of the dark nature of the reading that Jander seemed so downcast.

"Stay with us a little more and watch the dancing. It is very seldom that we permit *giorgios* to see it, and though your lifespan be long, perhaps you will never see it again."

Jander had to laugh at her choice of words. "Life-span" indeed. Still, it would not do for him to be discourteous. These people had a freedom that few others in Barovia appeared to have, and who knew but when he might have to use their knowledge and skills again. "As you will, my lady. It has been long since I watched something so graceful as dancing."

He permitted her to lead him out, past the still-spooked piebald pony, back towards the ring of the blazing firelight. Sharp sounds of violins filled the air, and he could hear the cheerful jangle of tambourines and the underlying, heart-beat sound of a bodhran. Lithe shapes were silhouetted against the blaze. Laughter and clapping, and even occasionally pure, sweet singing in a foreign tongue spiraled up with the smoke into the inky black sky that arched above it all.

Jander drank in the scene with hunger and envy. The elf wanted so much to be part of this. Jander liked Petya. He liked the idle prattle combined with sharp insight that the boy spouted, sprinkled with lewd, lusty, *living* commentary about females and good wine and the vagabond lifestyle of his kind. The vampire liked the beautiful Seer and the keening yet joyous strains of the music that stroked his ears at the campfire.

Sadly Jander realized that he fed upon the living, spirited nature of these people as though it were another kind of blood. He started when he felt Maruschka's feather-light hand on his arm and tried to smile. Her eyes went dark, seductive, and he realized she had unbraided her long, black hair. It tumbled down her dusky shoulders like an ebony wave, and with a teasing smile, she went to join the others by the fire. They parted to admit her, and she merged effortlessly with their dance.

When Jander permitted himself to really watch what was happening, he knew a sharp pain at the wildness and beauty of the gypsy dancing. The young women were clad simply, in light cotton blouses of either white or cream and full, brightly colored skirts. As they moved in time with the music, their skirts billowed about them, revealing long, shapely legs. Long hair flowed down their backs. Laughter rippled from them, as natural and unforced as the sound of a tumbling stream.

Jander's silver eyes closed in a mixture of pain and joy. He had seen nothing like this for nearly seven hundred years, not since he had last watched the dancing in his native, magic-soaked groves of Evermeet. Unwillingly, his mind went back to those days of impossible innocence, when there was nothing ugly in any particle of his limited, sweet universe, and vampirism was only a little-cited legend told to tease children.

Maruschka stepped in front of him, her dusky hand taking his golden one. She tugged gently, urging him to rise and follow her to the fire as her partner. For a moment Jander hesitated, then, as if drawn by the orange flames, he joined her in the dance.

Undead for five centuries, his body still remembered how to respond to music. The vampire and the gypsy Seer whirled together, black eyes locked to silver, golden frame pressed to dusky brown. Jander surrendered to the moment, and suddenly it wasn't Maruschka he was dancing with, it was Anna. *Anna*, sane and smiling up at him with love in her eyes—

He could bear no more. The beauty of the music, the intoxication of being among people again, and the memory of the dead girl he had loved overwhelmed the vampire. To his horror, he felt tears sting his eyes. With a mumbled apology, he strode from the fire to the protective shadows of the nearest *vardo*. Maruschka followed.

"Jander, what's wrong?"

"Nothing, just . . . just leave me for a few moments, please. I'll be fine." He kept his face turned away from her. She left, reluctantly. Alone once more, Jander wiped at the tears of blood that had filled his eyes. One had escaped to make a red path down his face. He hoped no one had noticed in the uncertain, ruddy glow of the firelight.

A damp cloth fell to the earth at his feet. "Wipe your face, vampire," came a brusque voice.

SIX

Jander looked up sharply. There was no break in the dancing. This elderly woman seemed to be the only one who had noticed his tears. Keeping his eyes on her, he did as he was told.

"You have the better of me, my lady. What are you going to do about it?"

The old woman shrugged weakly, but Jander sensed that she had a will of finely tempered steel. "For the moment, nothing. You are our guest, and we would not so disgrace the traditions of our ancestors. Besides, you were betrayed by your tears. That is rare enough in this land, and rarer still for an undead creature. For the sake of what you once were, Jander Sunstar, you may depart safely. You may sleep tomorrow in a cave not far from here, near the Tser Pool. We shall not disturb you. But," she added, her voice resonant and strong, "henceforth you are our enemy. There is no place for you among the living. Go now, quickly."

Jander bowed courteously. "I would ask a favor, Madame Eva, for so I assume you to be. Do not tell Petya or Maruschka of my nature."

Eva frowned, and the vampire saw something of Maruschka's fire in the old woman's eyes. "I must warn them. They are my grandchildren."

Jander looked back at the dancing. Maruschka had

rejoined the dancers and whirled gaily, on fire with the music. Petya was in the center of a group of young women, gesticulating wildly, a grin on his face.

"I have had ample opportunity to harm them had I wished to. They are safe from me."

Eva's small, black eyes searched his silver ones, calculating. Then her withered face lost some of its sternness, and she said softly, "I will tell them only if I feel it necessary. But leave, now." She hesitated, then said, "Sweet water and light laughter."

It was a traditional elven farewell, and Jander bowed deeply. Swiftly he vanished into the night. Eva watched him go, then turned her attention back to her grandchildren. Maruschka had paused at that instant to catch her breath and was watching the vampire leave, disappointment plain on her dark face. At that moment, Petya came scurrying up to his grandmother.

"Gran! You didn't send him away, did you?" His voice was full of hurt, and he gazed at her accusingly. Eva sighed.

"Go fetch your sister," she told him. He hesitated, glancing after Jander, then went to do her bidding. Eva sank down on the nearest bench. Too old, Eva, she thought with a rueful chuckle. You're getting too old for this sort of thing.

"You wanted to see us, Gran?" Eva looked up at her grandchildren. Both of them were handsome young things, a credit to the tribe and to her. She was doing the right thing. She patted the bench on either side of her, and they sat obediently.

For a moment she didn't speak. "This is not a happy land," she began. "We stay here because of the pact I made with the lord of Barovia, a pact that is good for our people." She paused, searching for the right words. Petya fidgeted, anxious to get back to the adoring young women, and Maruschka merely sat patiently. "That does not mean there is not danger for us here," Eva continued. "Sometimes it is hard to recognize. Sometimes, it is cloaked in beauty."

It was Maruschka who understood first, although she didn't want to. "Jander is dangerous?"

Eva laid a withered hand on her granddaughter's. "Aye, my dear. Very."

Maruschka frowned. "No," she snapped, "I cannot believe it. I did a reading for him. He is not evil."

"I did not say he wished to be. There are times when men are not given a choice between evil or good."

"Gran, he saved my *life!*" Now Petya was angry with her, too. Eva wished she did not have to tell them, but Petya adored the elf and Maruschka was enraptured by him.

"Yes, he did, but you are never, ever, to see him again. Or you," she added to her granddaughter, who glared up at her with sullen dark eyes. Eva unfolded the damp handkerchief. "He wiped his face with this."

Petya took the rag and stared at Eva accusingly. "You let him go away injured?"

"Nay, little grandson," Eva said gently. "Those were the tears that fell from his eyes."

Maruschka gasped, her eyes wide. "No," she breathed, "he isn't . . . he can't be . . ."

"*Akara,*" Petya finished. He stood up abruptly. "Excuse me, Gran, but I must go back to the village."

Eva frowned. "I will not hear of such a foolish thing, not after what happened there to you tonight."

Emotions warred on Petya's face. "But, Gran—"

"No, and that is my final word." She rose with disgust. Much as she loved Petya and Maruschka, she shared Maruschka's views about children and arguing with them sapped her patience. "I have told you what I needed to, now do as you are told." She strode off to her *vardo.*

"Maruschka, I need your help," Petya said when Eva was out of hearing distance.

"Oh, no. I'm not getting involved in—"

"My . . . friend in the village. She, too, trusts Jander. We both pledged friendship to him. She must know what he is!" Petya's face reflected his great anguish.

Maruschka had never seen him so serious, and was a little surprised.

"Oh, all right, but I'll deny everything if you're caught," she warned.

Her brother beamed. "Then may I take your horse?"

* * * * *

Anastasia lay on her stomach, heedless of the tears trickling down into the pillow. The red welts on her back burned with a steady, ceaseless pain. Her right arm had fallen asleep, but she dared not move it and further provoke the pain.

Ludmilla had slept through it all, and Anastasia envied her. Ah, gods, she wept, if only Father would allow Mother to apply some healing ointment.

A handful of pebbles clattered against her window. Anastasia bolted up, her face contorting with torment. She gritted her teeth and somehow, slowly, rose from the bed and hobbled to the window. Reaching her arm up to the shutters to open them nearly caused her to faint, but she blinked hard and held onto consciousness. Gasping, she slowly eased the shutters back.

Petya was there, an agitated shadow in the moonlight. He didn't speak, but made motions that she was to come join him. Anastasia wanted to, but she didn't think her tortured body would let her.

At that moment, a sharp yell of outrage shattered the quiet of the late hour. As Anastasia watched, horrified, her father's servants streamed from the house. Two of them seized Petya by the arms while others brandished swords.

"Anastasia, what—" came Ludmilla's sleepy voice from behind the girl. Anastasia didn't have time for her sister now. She was moving for the door and stumbling down the stairs as fast as her battered body would permit. By the time she had staggered through the main entry hall and heaved open the heavy door to the cobblestone courtyard, she was gasping with exhaustion.

The wind had risen and the temperature had dropped. Cold, moist air buffeted her body.

Petya was no longer on his feet. He would have sprawled limply on the cobblestones, but his body was being pulled taut by Kartov's servants, one on each arm. The burgomaster himself was wielding the riding crop he had used earlier on his daughter. He grunted with each blow, and sweat flew from him despite the sudden chill in the air. He had already struck the hapless Vistani several times, and Petya's back was becoming a red, pulpy mass. The rhythmic crack of whip on flesh was a sharp counterpoint to the low rumble of an approaching storm.

Anastasia's throat went absolutely dry, and the scene swam before her for an instant. Then she summoned all her energy. "*No!*" she screamed in a voice that seemed much too loud to have erupted from her.

Kartov paused and threw her a murderous glance, but Anastasia refused to be cowed. The pain retreated as a slow-boiling rage began to fill her chest. "*I said no,*" she repeated, in a voice as soft and deadly as a wolf's low growl. "Ivan," she snapped at her father's valet, "let him go."

Ivan hesitated, glancing from father to daughter. The gray-haired head servant had never disobeyed his master before, but there was something about Anastasia that unnerved him. She stood ramrod straight, her dark hair whipping about her pale face. "My lord?" Ivan queried. The burgomaster didn't even spare him a glance.

Anastasia walked boldly to her father, closing the distance between them with a slow, sure step. Kartov raised the crop, ready to strike her upturned, bruised face.

"Aawoooooo," Anastasia mockingly howled.

Kartov's face went white. The thunder rumbled again, louder this time. Anastasia continued, "Why don't you tell Ivan how you fled before the wolves this evening?" Filled with absolute confidence and a cold hatred, she reached out and calmly plucked the bloody crop from her father's grasp. Kartov made no move to stop her. "I didn't run," she said quietly. She turned to the gypsy boy. "And neither did he. Ivan," she repeated, giving the head servant a cool look, "you may let him go now."

Stunned and confused, Ivan did as he was told. The other servant followed suit, and they exited as quickly as they could without breaking into an outright run. The rest of the servants followed their lead. Petya fell to the cobblestones, unconscious, but Anastasia didn't go to him at once. She kept her icy gaze fastened on her father. Kartov couldn't meet her accusing eyes. He had been exposed as a coward tonight, and his daughter was never going to let him forget that. With a guttural curse, he stormed back into the house, slamming the door shut behind him.

Now Anastasia did turn to her injured lover, ignoring the pain of her own back to kneel beside him and cradle his head in her lap. She smoothed his silky, sweat-matted hair lovingly, and his eyelids fluttered open. "Anastasia," he rasped, "Jander—"

"Shh, shh, don't try to talk. I'm going to take you inside where we can treat your back properly. Do you think you can walk?"

"Listen to me!" Petya spoke with a desperate urgency. "The elf—tonight—we pledged friendship. Remember?" Confused, Anastasia nodded. "He's a vampire . . . we can't . . ." The effort was too much for him, and he collapsed in her arms, again unconscious.

Anastasia felt gooseflesh rise along her limbs, and not from the chill of the rain-pregnant air. The golden being that had rescued them was a dead creature that fed on blood? It didn't seem possible. Still, Petya would hardly have come back into the village if he hadn't felt it very important. She glanced down again at his back, and hatred for her father rose afresh in her heart. Jander Sunstar might very well be a vampire. Looking at her father's handiwork, however, the burgomaster's daughter felt she'd sooner cast her lot with the golden undead creature than her own blood kin.

A gigantic flash of lightning illuminated the courtyard. Its glare was so brilliant that Anastasia winced. The crack of thunder that followed immediately was nearly deafening, and Anastasia felt the ground tremble from it. Sheets of rain spewed from the cloud-filled sky, stinging her back as they struck in hard little droplets. The rain woke Petya, who coughed and moaned in pain. At last he was able, with her help, to get to his feet and stumble toward the door. Anastasia saw the slender shape of her mother silhouetted against the light from the house and smiled to herself.

Another flash of lightning, another sharp, deep roll of thunder. It was rumored that Strahd's magic extended to weather control. "The ring of fog around the village is his to command," the old goodwife Yelena had told Anastasia long ago. "It is there to keep us a little bit blinded. The wind and the rain is his anger, and the lightning his sword of vengeance."

Anastasia could barely see through the cold, heavy downpour and began to shiver violently as she slogged toward the house. If the storm was Strahd's anger, she mused with a flash of dark humor, he must have received some very bad news.

* * * * *

The land permitted Jander to dream.

Yet he did not enter a dreamscape in the same fashion as humans did; elves required very little sleep, and when they needed to rest or refresh themselves, they controlled the degree to which they relaxed. This first day in Barovia, however, as he waited for the onslaught of night, Jander dreamed.

He had easily located the cave of which Eva had spoken. It was deep and dark, a perfect resting place for one for whom sunlight was lethal. The elf trusted Madame Eva's word, but he planned to rest lightly, not sleep. Should it prove to be a trap, the Vistani would be surprised to find a wakeful vampire. He would be more than a match for them.

Now he sat deep in the earth, well away from the mouth of the cave. Jander drew his legs up to his chest and folded his arms across his knees. He leaned his head back against the rough stone and closed his silver eyes.

He was playing his favorite game: remembering the sunlight. Jander imagined the golden hue was spreading toward him from the mouth of the cave. The elf pictured the sunlight puddle in hollows and trickle across stones, and felt an ache in his chest. It was a game he had played too many thousands of days. He would dream of the sunlight and wonder if today was the day that would find him brave enough to step out into it. It was not the fear of death that held him back; it was the fear of what the sun would do to him.

On Toril, there existed a creature known as a crimson death. This hideous, gaseous monster, which gorged itself on blood, was linked to vampires in legends. Some claimed that the crimson death was the soul of a slain vampire, doomed to wander. The thought of becoming such a being kept Jander to the night and the shadows, away from the beloved sun.

His family had been named for the light. It was the most heartbreakingly beautiful thing Jander knew, this golden radiance that changed the color of everything it touched. As a living being, Jander had reveled in the day, loving its warm caress and its fiery brightness.

When he was growing up on Evermeet, Jander would herald the dawn with his flute. His friends used to tease him about it. "Do you think the dawn will not come unless you pipe it in, Jander?" they had joked. He was now, of course, forever condemned to only think about the light and remember its touch.

In his dream, the vampire glanced at the cave's entrance. A shadow blocked the sun's path. Jander drew back, ready to attack. The figure at the mouth of the cave stepped out enough so that he could see who it was.

It was Anna.

She was dressed, not in the horrid brown shift of the madhouse, but in a bodice and skirt that accentuated her beauty and her ripe yet maidenly figure. She seemed utterly, completely real, but Jander realized at once that she was only alive in his mind. Anna peered in, her eyes dilating in the gloom, and smiled at him. "Why don't you come join me?"

Because it was a dream, because he wanted to join her more than he'd wanted anything in seven hundred years, the dream-Jander rose and walked out into the bright Barovian morning.

"Much better, isn't it?"

Anna's small, soft fingers twined about his long ones as she smiled up at him. Dear gods, but she was so beautiful. Her sun-kissed face was a mercurial pool of expressions, her mouth ripe and ready to smile, her eyes the bright warm brown of a deer's. He had never seen her like this when she was alive. The insane girl with the pale skin and still features that he remembered was a mere shadow of this radiant being.

He was so wrapped up in her that a few minutes passed before he became aware of the miracle. He could no longer smell her blood. Somehow, in this delirious dream-state, he had ceased to be a vampire and was only Jander Sunstar, a gold elf, once again. He felt the sun's warmth on his hair, and, as he turned to her, she squinted and looked away.

"The sun on your hair is too bright!" she laughed, blinking. He laughed, too, a carefree, ringing laugh that could only issue from a living throat. He kissed her red mouth, wanting only this sweetness, thrilled to the core of his being that he had no desire for her blood. She responded as he had dreamed she would, with a joy that caught him by surprise.

"Anna," he whispered, running his long, thin fingers through her thick hair. "I never meant to hurt you, my love, I'm so sorry . . ."

She shook her head, smiling brightly, her eyes warm and lively. "Nay, Jander Sunstar, did you think I did not know? Through the madness that had claimed me, you still shone."

"Anna," he gripped her arms tightly, "Tell me who did it to you."

Her smile broadened. "You must discover who destroyed my mind. That is your test."

"Test? I don't understand . . ."

Abruptly she was gone, and Jander was alone in the cave again. He started, shaken out of his dream by a harsh whinny from outside. The cave was pitch black; a slightly less dark oval marked its entrance. Jander discovered he was trembling. He had experienced his share of dreams and nightmares, but this had possessed the qualities of both. It had pained him to see Anna again, even if it had only been in his own wistful imagination. Yet he hoped that they would meet again.

The horse outside neighed and pawed the ground. Another one whinnied. He could smell the beasts' warm, animal scent, mixed with the fragrances of oiled leather, metal, and the sweet hay the animals had eaten. Nostalgia gave way to curiosity. Why would horses be there?

Best to be safe, Jander thought to himself as he took another sniff. There was no scent of humans anywhere nearby. Cautiously the vampire emerged from the cave.

There was nothing unusual about the two horses, save their absolute blackness. Not a white blaze or sock marred the inky color of their coats, although their nostrils flared pinkly as they caught Jander's scent. They were clearly spellbound by powerful magic, for they did not even quail as the vampire approached and laid graceful hands upon their sleek ebony necks. He had loved horses, once, and they him. He deeply missed the animals.

With a final, reluctant pat, Jander dropped his hand from the horses' necks and turned his attention to the vehicle the black beasts drew. It was a large, spacious carriage, well-crafted and jaunty. The interior was fine red leather, and there was actually glass in the windows. Only someone quite wealthy would squander so much on a carriage, he noted. Jander walked slowly around the vehicle, examining the fine quality of the wood and the symmetry of the wheels.

There was a place in the front where the driver of the carriage would sit. Only there was no driver. The reins were neatly tied together and draped across the seat. Standing out against the lush black and red of the carriage was a crisp white envelope. Jander took it, instantly recognizing the fine quality of the paper. The red wax that sealed the envelope was imprinted with the likeness of a bird; it was too small for Jander to determine what type. He broke the seal and began to read.

> *Unto the Visitor in my Land,*
> *Jander Sunstar,*
> *Count Strahd Von Zarovich, Lord of Barovia,*
> *sends greetings.*
>
> *Good Sir, I pray you accept my humble*
> *Hospitality and dine with me tonight in Castle*
> *Ravenloft. I have many Questions for you, as I am*
> *certain you have many for me. I shall endeavor to*
> *assuage your natural Curiosity about the Land as*
> *best I might.*
>
> *The Carriage shall bear you to the Castle safely.*
> *I urge you to accept my Invitation, and I await your*
> *arrival with pleasurable anticipation.*
>
> *Count Strahd Von Zarovich*

Carefully Jander folded the note, thinking. He should have realized that the Vistani would give the master of the land such fascinating news that an elf had stumbled into Barovia. He could hardly blame them. What troubled him was his own reluctance to accept the invitation. Wasn't this what he wanted? Who better to answer questions than the ruler of this wretched place?

Jander unfolded the note and read it again, trying to uncover some hidden meaning. He'd be walking into the wolf's den with a bared throat, but the wolf might be in for a surprise himself. He had no option. Strahd would find him eventually, he was sure. "Well," Jander said to the horses, who swiveled their ears in his direction, "let's get you two back to your stable and me to the master."

As he approached the carriage door, it swung open for him. He hesitated, then climbed in. The instant he pulled the door shut behind him, the horses began to trot purposefully. Jander sat back in the incredibly comfortable cushions and resolved, whatever awaited him at the end of the journey, to enjoy the ride there.

The horses trotted along the trail, picking up their pace as they turned onto the road. The road again crossed over the river, this time providing Jander with a breathtaking view of a waterfall. They were so close, the windows were spattered with spray.

The by-now familiar ring of poisonous fog enveloped them, and Jander was forcefully reminded of the mist that had transported him from Waterdeep to Barovia. He found himself pressing his face up against the glass, hoping against hope that the strange mist had risen again and was taking him home. The fog lasted for about three hundred feet, then cleared as abruptly as it had risen. Jander looked through the small window back at the swirling gray mass, and shook his head.

The horses found a comfortable, swift pace and settled into it, moving at a steady speed northward. They were heading into the mountains now, and the horses slowed but continued moving steadily. The road veered toward the east and divided after a time.

Jander glanced at the road that forked off toward his left. Huge gates towered in the distance. They were massive things, apparently made of iron and flanked on either side by large stone statues. It seemed as though both statues were missing their heads. For the moment, the gates were open. When they were closed, however, they effectively blocked the only road leading into the village from the west.

The steady clip of the horse's hooves continued, and soon Jander could see Castle Ravenloft looming ahead. A cold finger of fear traced its way along his spine. It was an alien sensation to the vampire, who'd had nothing to fear from any being, alive or dead, for several centuries.

Here, however, could lie a key Anna's identity. Anna, beautiful and vulnerable, driven to insanity by someone's cruelty . . . *someone who called this world home.* Jander's hands balled into fists. Perhaps Castle Ravenloft's master would have some answers.

The horses took him up to the gates, then the carriage halted. Jander got out and gazed up at the castle. He could easily see why the horses had stopped. Between two guardhouses of ruined stonework lay the entrance to the castle—a precarious-looking wooden drawbridge that hung from chains that appeared old and rusted. There was a thousand-foot drop into the misty canyon below. From their eternal perch atop the stone walls, two gargoyles gazed down at him. They were hideous things, and the grins upon their stone faces did nothing to soften their appearances.

The elf gave the horses a last pat—for himself; it could hardly have been pleasurable to the frightened animals—and they galloped off, the carriage jolting crazily behind them.

Jander examined the drawbridge. It definitely looked unsafe. There were times, he mused as he changed into bat form and fluttered safely across the crevice, when being a vampire definitely had its advantages. Once across, he changed back into elven form and continued on.

He passed through a covered entryway, alert for any kind of attack. The entryway was damp and slimy and smelled of decay, but nothing happened. The portcullis at the entrance was raised; it looked as though it had been in that state for some time. The wood here, too, was starting to rot. The entryway opened into a large, dark courtyard, and Jander looked up at Castle Ravenloft.

It was indeed impressive. The closed main doors were huge, elaborately decorated with battle scenes so realistic they seemed to move. The carving was both delicate and bold, and so vibrant that it seemed out of place in the dark, neglected fortress. Two large torches fixed to either side of the doors flickered in the wind. The knockers were made of brass; had they been polished, no doubt they would have gleamed magnificently. Now they were only a dull, brownish gold. Shaped like ravens' heads, the knockers possessed eyes formed of glittering jewels. Jander hesitated, then seized one of the knockers and slammed it home three times.

The sound reverberated with a low boom and lingered in the air. For a few tense minutes, there was no answer, only the sound of the wind behind him. Jander fought to stay calm, but his nervousness increased by the second.

Then with a low, deep groan, the massive doors creaked open. They moved slowly, protesting every inch of ground they yielded. Warm light spilled out into the courtyard.

Jander lingered outside, the moonlight silvering his golden hair. "Count?" he called, his query sounding thin and frightened. He mentally rebuked himself. "Your Excellency, it is Jander Sunstar," he called again, willing himself to sound strong and determined. "I am here by your invitation, but I shall not enter unless I am bidden."

Silence greeted his statement, but, somehow, Jander knew that he had been heard. A deep, mellifluous sound emanated from the depths of the torchlit entry hall. It was the most beautiful and the most frightening voice Jander had ever heard, and it caressed his ears even as he recognized the danger it promised.

"Enter, Jander Sunstar. I am Count Strahd Von Zarovich, and I bid you welcome."

 **SEVEN**

For a moment, Jander was frozen by Strahd's voice. Angrily, he shook off his paralysis. He mentally took a deep breath, steeled himself for whatever might await him within, and crossed the threshold into Castle Ravenloft.

The floor of the hall was a smooth gray stone that seemed cut from the living rock of the mountain, worn in the center with the passage of generations of former inhabitants. The torches that lined the massive walls guttered in the damp air and threw an uncertain light over the suits of armor that stood rusty sentry beneath them. Jander did not yet see his host, and his eyes flickered about. "Count Von Zarovich?" he called.

"Come in, my friend," the beautiful, deadly voice answered him.

The elf had gone about twenty feet into the hall when a second set of doors in front of him swung open. He paused, then continued on. He caught a movement out of the corner of his eye and started, baring his abruptly lengthening fangs and hissing. An instant later, though, he realized with some embarrassment that it was only a trick of the light. Four statues of dragons stared balefully down at him, and their eyes, like the eyes of the door knockers, were made of jewels. The precious stones had merely reflected the torches' light.

Some of the tension left Jander's body as he continued onward. He passed through another set of doors that opened to his touch, and entered a large room. This was the main entry. To his left, a wide staircase twisted up into the darkness. Circling the rim of the domed ceiling were more of the stone gargoyles that had greeted him earlier. He glanced upward at the ceiling they were guarding, and for an instant his qualms faded in the face of the beauty he saw there.

The ceiling was covered with magnificent frescoes. Jander's eye wandered from hunting parties to battles, from jousts to knightings. Sadly the frescoes were well on their way to ruin. The master of Castle Ravenloft apparently cared little for maintaining his castle and the beauty it housed. The elf returned his attention to finding his host.

Straight ahead two bronze doors stood closed. Jander had taken a step toward them when the silky voice said, "I am pleased you have come. You are welcome in my home."

Jander turned to see his host descending the carpeted staircase, a candelabra in one strong hand.

Count Strahd Von Zarovich was quite tall, over six feet, and his body was lithe and clearly powerful. He was dressed in a formal fashion, with black pants and coat and white vest and shirt. A crimson bow on his neck stood out like a splash of blood, matching a large red jewel at his throat. His skin was extremely pale, practically bone-white. In sharp contrast, the count's eyes were dark and piercing. They missed nothing as they roamed over Jander with a hint of curiosity, coming at last to meet the elf's silver gaze evenly. Thick, carefully styled black hair did not quite disguise a slight point to the count's ears. Strahd's expression was pleasant, but the smile of welcome seemed double-edged.

Jander bowed as Strahd approached. "I thank you for your invitation, Count. It's an honor to be received by the lord of Barovia."

Strahd's smile widened, and this time it was tinged

with a definite malice. "I am pleased you feel that way, Jander Sunstar. Not many deem my castle so welcoming an environment."

"Ah, but perhaps they were not extended so gracious an invitation."

It was a daring comment, and something red flickered deep in the count's black eyes. Strahd smiled and nodded, acknowledging the barb. "Very true indeed. You are not one to hide behind false courtesies, I see. That is well. I did indeed ask you here for my own reasons—as I'm certain you came for yours. Nevertheless, my welcome is genuine, I do assure you."

They stood gazing at one another, for all the world like two strange wolves circling. Yet neither was ready to cower and admit defeat. "You may call me Strahd," the count said at last. "I do not know your rank, but you are clearly closer to an equal of mine than those odious peasants and my mindless servants. Please, follow me. We shall be more comfortable elsewhere, and besides," Strahd smiled coldly, "I have so few visitors that I like to display some of my home's magnificence." He turned and began to ascend the staircase. "I suppose you are wondering how I knew where to find you."

"Not at all. Clearly, you are in league with the Vistani."

"Yes, my little gypsy compatriots. An altogether better class of people than the villagers." They had reached a landing, and Jander looked around. Here were more of the elaborate frescoes he had admired earlier, these depicting an attack on the mountain upon which the castle was built. As before, however, they were in a sad state of disrepair. Jander could make out what remained of an inscription: T   OBL N KIN   LEE B   OR TH   OW R O   O Y S M   OF RA EN   . He followed Strahd as they began to ascend another flight of stairs. "Did you observe the fog as you approached?" the count queried.

"Yes, the ring of mist about the village is rather curious."

"It is a good thing you are past breathing, my friend. That fog is there by my command. It is poisonous. The gypsies, for their services, have been granted knowledge of a certain potion that enables them to move through the fog unharmed. They make a tidy fortune selling passage through the mist, and I keep my larders well stocked. A sound business transaction, is it not?"

They emerged at the end of an enormous hall. Moonlight pooled onto the stone floor from a window on their right. The hall loomed even bigger in its emptiness. A large throne rested at the far end from where they stood, and that was all. "In other times, this was the audience hall. It is not used often now, as you might expect." The two continued on, passing through elaborately carved doors into a small corridor. Two suits of armor stood lonely vigils in nearly obscured alcoves. Strahd stepped up to one of the alcoves, made a movement with his thin fingers that Jander did not quite catch, and the outline of a door appeared. Strahd pushed it gently, and it swung open.

Jander tensed. The rumors about Strahd were true. The lord of the land was a mage.

The elf swallowed his distaste and followed Strahd obediently as his host took him up yet another flight of stairs. By now, Jander was a bit confused. The place was a maze. "Do you dwell here alone, Strahd?"

"Oh, no. I have servants, of a sort, and the villagers supply me with whatever I may need or want. The inhabitants of the little town are quite docile, and, as I have mentioned, the gypsies and I have an agreement. It is well you chose not to harm them. I must commend you on your self-restraint."

"Why should I wish to harm them?"

Strahd stopped abruptly and swung around to face Jander. He began to smile conspiratorially, red lips pulling back from white teeth. Jander was shocked to see Strahd's incisors grow and sharpen. "The thirst calls commandingly, does it not, Jander Sunstar?"

The elf could only stare. No wonder Strahd had wanted to see him! No wonder the people were so afraid in this besieged town. Strahd continued gazing at Jander for a moment, pleased with his guest's stunned reaction. Apparently satisfied that he had put the impertinent elf in his place, the count turned with a sweep of his cape and continued upward.

The stairs ended, and Jander found himself in a large hall. A gaping hole in the ceiling let in the moon's pale light and illuminated a long row of statues. "My noble ancestors," Strahd said drily, "all of whom I have done my best to anger, ignore, or thwart. Some of them aren't quite . . . gone, you see." And Jander did see that some of the statues seemed to wear anguished expressions. Others, of course, were mere stone. The head of one had been removed, and Jander, curious, tried to make out the name on the base of the statue.

"Jander!" Strahd's tone was imperious, and the elf hastened to catch up with his host. Another brief corridor, then the count opened the door to a room that shared little of the general decay that seemed to plague much of Ravenloft.

"My study," said Strahd, with more warmth than Jander had yet heard from him. A large fire burned comfortably in the hearth, its ruddy glow infusing the room with heat and light. The walls were lined with hundreds of books, and Jander caught the scent of well-oiled leather. Strahd obviously valued his literature. Jander entered after the other vampire. No bare stone here; the floor was covered with a beautiful rug. The count took a seat in one of the large, scarlet velvet cushioned chairs and indicated that Jander take the other one.

"Please do sit. This is my favorite room. I have much time for reflection and contemplation." Jander sat down obediently, and for a moment they were quiet, enjoying the comfort of the room.

"I understand," Strahd said at last, "that you rescued one of the Vistani last evening." Jander nodded. "You are quite the do-gooder, aren't you?" Strahd's rich voice was tinged with contempt.

Jander bristled. "Is there elven blood in your line, Strahd?" he asked abruptly. "Your ears are pointed."

Strahd raised one hand as if to touch an ear, then he deliberately folded his hands together. "Actually, no," he admitted, "though I occasionally do spread that rumor." His eyes narrowed, and when he spoke again, it was with a deliberateness that was casual and yet unmistakable. "No one but my slaves and a few of the Vistani know of my nature. I should like it to remain so, and I would be greatly displeased if I learned that someone had revealed my secret. I have chosen to share my confidence with you because I feel we could learn from one another."

So, we come to the real purpose for the invitation, thought Jander. The whole terribly polite conversation and labyrinthine tour had been a thinly disguised bout of testing, and now the trial was to begin in earnest. Jander shifted and crossed his legs, making himself comfortable. He met Strahd's gaze evenly. "Secrets are dangerous things," he said. "They become good bargaining chips in the wrong hands."

"I hope," said Strahd slowly, and this time there was no mistaking the threat in his voice, "that yours are not the wrong hands."

Jander allowed himself a smile. "Suppose they were. Suppose I were to reveal your identity as an undead. We 'akara' are not a very sociable group. What would you do to me?"

Strahd dropped the pretense of courtesy altogether, and the hint of red deep in his eyes blazed. "I would destroy you."

"How could you do that? Make me your slave?" Jander sat up and leaned his elbows on his knees. "I am not here to oppose you. On the contrary, I agree that we have much knowledge to share, and I hope we can become allies. I am not some peasant fool or one of your docile minions. You may be the lord of the land—"

"I *am* the land!"

The deep voice was thunder now, and the red light in Strahd's eyes leaped angrily. Jander wondered if he had gone too far, if perhaps Strahd had some mysterious power that could destroy him.

"I am Barovia!" Strahd raged. "It has given me power, and I give it what it wants." His lip curled in a sneer. "I am the First Vampire. Unlike you and every other undead, *I* need no invitation to enter a dwelling. Here, every home is my home. All creatures are mine, to do with as I will."

He sank back in the chair and slitted his eyes. Jander heard a skittering of nails along the stone floor, and three large wolves trotted into the study. They curled up, panting happily, at Strahd's feet. "These," said the count proudly, "are my children. They obey my every whim."

One of the wolves rose, its pose tense and alert. Stiffly it strode to the stone hearth and lay back down, exposing its throat. It whimpered, and Jander scented fear. A second wolf got to its feet with equal stiffness. It stalked over to its prone companion and unexpectedly bit deeply into its comrade's jugular. Blood gushed forth, staining both beasts and the gray stone of the hearth. The first wolf kicked and flailed frantically, but the second wolf merely sank its teeth in deeper. The wolf spasmed and died. Its killer released its grip and licked its jaws. Head held low, the animal belly-crept to its master's feet. Idly Strahd ran a hand along its smooth head. The third wolf was curled into a tight ball, trembling.

Jander half rose in protest, but something in Strahd's gaze stopped him. The self-styled "First Vampire" was daring him to show weakness, to protest the wanton slaying of the beast. Slowly Jander sat back down, his eyes never leaving Strahd's. The animal-loving elf was indeed angry at the careless cruelty the other vampire had displayed, but there was a better way to show it.

He gazed at the two remaining wolves, then touched the murdering wolf's mind gently. *Rest.* The gray beast closed its eyes and obeyed, curling up and quickly going to sleep. He turned his thoughts, cool and reassuring, to the other wolf.

Come, my friend. Come to me. She whuffed slightly, her ears swiveling toward the front. With a sound that was half-growl, half-whimper, she bounded toward Jander. The animal made a ridiculous attempt to crawl into his lap, and he smiled a little as he gently pushed her down. She lay at his feet, gazing up at him adoringly, every muscle intent on satisfying whatever her new master's next whim might be. The elf patted her head. Jander raised his eyes from the wolf to the count and allowed himself a slight smile.

Strahd, he could tell, was angry, but there was also admiration on that cold face. "Impressive," the count purred, the word rumbling from his chest. "Most impressive indeed. Always the wolves have answered to me and no other call. It is clear that the land's master may learn from the land's visitor." He nodded slightly.

Something subtle had changed. Jander somehow knew that he had just been reclassified in Strahd's eyes. He hoped that was a good thing. "This, actually, was why I invited you here tonight," the count continued.

"So I assumed." Jander threw out the comment as a test. Strahd frowned slightly and his aquiline nostrils flared, but he didn't rise to the bait.

"Eva told me that your world is called Toril," Strahd continued. "I am greatly intrigued by other lands. I would enjoy hearing your story."

The crisis had passed, for the moment. Jander allowed his guard to relax slightly. "Before I answer your questions, I have a few of my own." Strahd waved a hand, indicating that Jander should proceed. "Was there a woman in this land named Anna?"

Strahd smiled a little. "That is a common name. You'll have to be more specific."

Now that he had begun, Jander found he was loathe to continue. Somehow it seemed vulgar to expose Anna's condition to a stranger, but he forced that feeling aside. It was the only way to find the answers he so desperately sought. "She was insane," he said quietly. "She was tall and tanned, with long, reddish brown hair. She was very beautiful. I believed her to be the victim of a spell. You see, I knew her for many years, and she never aged."

Strahd shook his head. "Regretfully I can think of no one who meets all those qualifications. That is not to say that there has not been such a one in the town, or perhaps even in Vallaki, a fishing village not far from here. Insanity is not unusual in this place. As for magic, I am the only one I know of who performs the arcane arts in Barovia. And Jander, my friend, I have never cast a spell on a woman named Anna. I give you my word." His voice was utterly sincere, and to Jander's surprise, the elf found himself believing him. "I know what it is to have lost a love—more than once I have sipped at that particular bitter cup." Strahd suddenly looked weary.

Jander's hopes faded quietly. Somehow, perhaps too quickly, he had assumed that Strahd would know about Anna, could tell him who had broken the beautiful young woman's will.

"Any further questions?" Strahd's tone of voice suggested that he hoped the answer would be negative, but Jander pressed on.

"How could I find out more about her?"

"You are welcome to peruse the books in my library," Strahd offered, gesturing expansively. "All other records are in the old church down in the village, however, and I doubt you'll be going there." The more familiar, masterful Strahd had returned, smiling at Jander slyly.

Jander had to smile himself, but his expression was tinged with sadness. "You're right. You mentioned a place called Vallaki. Where is that? What sort of people live there? What records have they—"

Strahd's raven brows drew together, and he gestured impatiently. "All these things I can certainly tell you, but must you solve your little mystery tonight?"

Strahd had a point, and Jander saw that the count was rapidly losing interest. "You're right. Curious as I am about this place, you must be equally as curious about me. My arrival here in Barovia is a mystery. One of the Vistani said the mists brought me."

"Ah, the mists, the mists," Strahd mused, his eyes gazing into the fire. "They come for many, it would seem. They came for me—they came for my entire realm, some years ago. That was when I became as you see me now." He smiled, revealing the long, white fangs that he had not bothered to retract. "A gift from the powers of this place—eternal life."

The elf supposed Strahd was right, after a fashion. Jander had never hungered for such an "eternal life" as humans did. Elvenkind lived several centuries. This was why, he assumed, he had never heard of many other elven undead. Their nature was not well suited to that kind of existence; elves tended to lack that driving, desperate desire for things not granted to them by the fates. When he became a vampire, Jander himself would have preferred to die by his own hand rather than exist as he now did, but the legend of the crimson death would not permit him so easy an escape.

Uncomfortable with the dark turn his thoughts had taken, Jander changed the subject. "You speak of Barovia as though it were a living being. The Vistani, too, spoke of the land's powers. What is Barovia, exactly? Why does it bring people in through the mists?"

Strahd did not answer at once. He rose and went to the fire, laying a hand on the ornate mantlepiece. "I will answer your questions later. After all," he smiled grimly, "do we not have all the time in the world?" After a pause, he added, "I would feed. Will you join me? It is becoming increasingly difficult to find wanderers in Barovia after nightfall. I keep a supply on hand at all times."

Jander winced inwardly. He envisioned a prison of barely alive beings, kept like livestock to feed this darkly elegant lord. Yet could he condemn such behavior, he who had fed for years on madmen? "Thank you, no. I prefer animal blood until I become more familiar with the territory."

Strahd laughed outright at that. It was a chilling sound, and Jander waited it out patiently. "Ah, Jander, if I may call you that, you cannot subsist on beast blood here."

"Perhaps you cannot, Your Excellency, but I shall. I'm sorry if that offends you."

"No, no, it only amuses me. The forest is your own, but I do not think your thirst shall be quenched by the beasts of the Svalich Woods. Somehow I don't believe you'll find them . . . suitable. Perhaps I shall see you when you return. Jander, I am the master here," Strahd said bluntly. "You are to be my guest, for as long as you like."

"And if I said to you, 'Thank you, Your Excellency, but I wish to leave tonight'?"

"Then I would say, 'You are free to go. But your questions will remain unanswered.'"

Jander laughed aloud at that, and even Strahd smiled with less than his usual iciness. "My curiosity, Count, is the best chain in the world. Thank you. I accept your offer of hospitality."

"What are your requirements for rest? There are crypts below us, and you would be welcome to—"

"Thank you, no. I need very little sleep and no coffin. With your permission, I would like to have the free run of the castle during daylight hours. As long as I am sheltered from the sun, I shall be unharmed."

Jander noted with a slight hint of smugness that he had caught Strahd completely off guard. Shock registered for an instant in those deep black eyes. Strahd recovered quickly, but Jander knew he had scored another point with the debonair master of Castle Ravenloft. "My home is yours, with one exception. That room, there—" he extended a long, thin finger and pointed to a wooden door across the room "—is not to be entered. What I keep there is my business. Should you try to disobey me, you will find the door magically locked. I ask you to respect my wishes."

Jander was curious, but he certainly had no right to pry. If the count wanted a secret room, he was welcome to his privacy. "Certainly."

"Then I bid you good night—and good hunting."

 **EIGHT**

Jander moved slowly through the forest, silent as a wolf along the deer trail he had found. His infravision and the leaf-filtered moonlight turned the forest into a moving tapestry of shadow and wisps of curling ground-fog, and all around him were the soft sounds and movements of life, the subtle scent of warm blood. A squirrel skittered along a tree limb above his head, leaping with daring grace into a neighboring tree. A gray fox, her coat brindled in shadow-shades, froze in a puddle of moonlight a yard down the trail, wide eyes locked on the terrifying, unexpected shape of the elven vampire. For a moment the two hunters stared at each other. Then the vixen melted back into the forest, ceding Jander her prey.

There, Jander thought, his infravision finding the soft heat of a big brown hare crouched among the roots and low hanging branches of a great yew tree. Softly, with the same exertion of will that had brought the wolves answering his call, Jander set calm upon the beast. *The fox is gone, and all is safe.*

Silence hung in the woods. Only the breeze traveled along the forest floor, moving gently in the litter of years, stirring the dried brown leaves, rattling the fallen needles of the pines. The hare barely twitched when the long, strong hands closed over its ears and hindquarters. The fangs that tore open its throat were sharper than the teeth of the fox.

Jander gulped eagerly, hunger overcoming the strange taste of the blood. He tossed the drained corpse at the spot where the vixen had disappeared and frowned as he wiped his mouth. There was a strange tang to the hare's blood, a kind of smoky sweetness.

Suddenly Jander's stomach roiled, and he felt dizzy. His knees buckled, and he dropped to all fours, vomiting up the blood he had just consumed until there was nothing left. He sat back, shaking. The rabbit had been ill, that was all, and he would simply have to feed again.

He called a deer this time, a healthy doe who fixed him with mournful brown eyes as he drained her of her life-blood. Again the taste was unpleasant, and again the blood would not stay in his stomach. Jander couldn't understand it. While he occasionally needed human blood, in Waterdeep he had existed for years at a time on the animal population. He had sensed something not quite right about this place from the moment he had arrived. Perhaps the mist had somehow altered him so that beast blood was no longer drinkable. It was the only reason he could think of, illogical though it seemed.

Strahd had known this and made a halfhearted attempt to warn Jander. The master of Ravenloft, while granting the elf victory with the wolves, probably enjoyed knowing that he would be vomiting helplessly after sampling the unpalatable blood. The score with Strahd was now even.

Much as he loathed the idea, here in Barovia Jander would have to find human blood if he were to survive. The golden vampire spent the next four hours in a fruitless quest for unwary humans. He changed into his wolf form and covered many miles, senses alert for the presence of prey. A few times he ran into some of Strahd's slaves: pale, sharp-featured vampiresses, who frowned and hissed at him before changing into bat form. Jander toyed with the idea of attacking the gypsy encampment, but dismissed the impulse at once. The Vistani were more canny than the villagers, and, although Jander fed delicately, the sharp-eyed gypsies would notice the small marks. Besides, Jander was Strahd's "guest" for the moment, and a violation of the pact would be sure to anger the count. No other humans could be scented in the woods, and a quick prowl through the village only proved that the Barovians were safely ensconced within their homes. Ravenous, tired, and frustrated, Jander exchanged his lupine form for that of a bat and flew toward the castle.

Unpleasant though the prospect was, the vampire would have to accept Strahd's invitation to dinner.

He landed on a walkway that stretched most of the way around the castle. Transforming from bat to mist to elf, Jander made his way to Strahd's study. He found he liked the place, although he had always been one for the open woods rather than enclosed spaces. The study, however, seemed just a little less lonely than the other parts of the castle, and at this moment Jander had no desire to be reminded of his loneliness. As he entered the room, he caught a sweet, teasing fragrance.

Human blood.

His hunger now knife-sharp, the vampire followed the scent through the double doors. Next to the study was a formal bed chamber, large and lavish. The single window was covered by thick red velvet drapes, open now to let in the liquid moonlight. It silvered the room, catching the dull glint of beautiful but tarnished candelabras and revealing finely crafted tables and other furniture. The bed itself had no doubt once been a dream of luxury, but now the rich linens had rotted and the canopies had been eaten away by moths.

Jander did not particularly notice the decor. He was staring sadly at the figure the moonlight had turned into a slender young ghost.

She was standing by the window, looking with longing out across the dark landscape. A tear trickled down her face, glinting in the moonlight like a pearl on alabaster. She seemed frightened, but resigned. Jander's approach was silent, and the young woman didn't sense his presence at once. He watched as she turned away from the window and sat on the bed. The maiden was an alluring combination of girl and woman. That she was an adult was evident by the swell of her hips and breasts. Her pale, round face, however, was practically still a child's, with large, terror-filled eyes fringed with long, sooty lashes. The ruddiness in her cheeks and the cherry hue of her sweet-looking mouth caused Jander to stir with bloodthirst.

"My lady," he began.

She gasped and drew back. Instinctively she tried to cover herself, then with an effort lowered the bed-clothes. She was clad only in a thin chemise. Taking a deep breath, she summoned her courage. "His Excellency Count Strahd Von Zarovich has sent me for your pleasure," she said in a young, sweet voice. "I am to tell you that I am untouched here—" she placed a finger to her throat "—and here—" she cupped her hands about the mound between her legs. Blood filled her cheeks, and she dropped her eyes, long black hair obscuring her features. "Such is my master's gift to his new friend." The sweet voice trembled.

Jander's hunger soured, but did not vanish altogether. He knew that many vampires sated a variety of appetites on their quiescent victims. Clearly Strahd enjoyed sporting with his prey, but Jander loathed the practice. Was it not enough to drain innocents of their lifeblood without violating their souls and bodies? He wanted desperately to be able to send this young woman home safely to her family, but his upper jaw was throbbing and his fangs were already lengthening in response to the sweet fragrance of blood. Hunger tore at him, and his conscience, as always, unraveled before that implacable need to feed upon the red life fluid.

He eased himself down on the bed and patted the spot beside him. "What is your name, little one?" He kept his voice soft.

"Natasha," she replied, her eyes still not meeting his.

"Come here, Natasha," he bade her gently. She crept toward him, and over the fragrance of blood he could smell the metallic scent of her fear. He brushed her dark hair away from her forehead gently, with great sorrow. She closed her eyes, shaking violently. "How did Strahd get you to come here?"

Natasha licked her lips. "He sent his carriage to the village," she replied. "He knew me and asked my father to send me. We must obey our lord in all things."

"Did you know why he wanted you to come?"

She shook her dark head. "No," she whispered, her eyes brimming with tears. All at once her control shattered. "*Yes!* Oh, gods, please, please don't hurt me! Let me go home! I'll do whatever you want, only don't make me like you, please, please. . . ."

"Poor child," he murmured. "Look at me, Natasha." His calm command penetrated her hysteria, and she met his hypnotic silver gaze. "You're not afraid of me any more, are you?"

"N-no," she said, beginning to lose herself in his gaze.

"Good. Do you trust me, Natasha? Do you trust me not to hurt you any more than I must?"

Her brown eyes locked with his, Natasha nodded slowly. Gently Jander placed his golden hands on her white face and tilted her head to one side. The jugular was now exposed, and it throbbed rhythmically in the silver light flooding the room. Quickly he bared his fangs and embedded them in the inviting flesh of her throat.

Once his body tasted the blood, it took over quickly. Jander fed deeply, forgetting how innocent the young woman was and knowing only the rush of heat and renewal of strength her blood was imparting. It took a great deal of control to stop feeding before he had drained her dry, but he did. The vampire licked the sticky fluid off his lips, placing the girl down on the pillows as he did so. Her breathing was shallow and she was dreadfully pale, but life was still hers.

He rose and went to the window. The moon, waning

but still mostly full, provided an eerie white backdrop for a sudden flurry of bats. Jander gazed out over the landscape of dark greens and purples, then closed the shutters, checking to make sure they were securely fastened.

He sat back down on the bed, thinking. Back in Waterdeep, a hare had been enough to get him by each evening. Now, he had almost killed a young woman with his hunger. Jander had spent centuries away from the very nature of his curse—to hunt and feed upon the blood of humans. He had, in his own way, denied that nature, pretending that if he fed upon animals, or only took what he needed from humans, he would somehow not be as evil as other vampires. He was unable to run from himself any more, and he was filled with self-loathing. Yet even that terrible emotion could not assuage his hunger.

That knowledge lay heavy in his heart, and he buried his face in his hands with a heavy, very mortal sigh. "Anna," he moaned softly, "Anna, I miss you so much."

"Do you really?"

The sun reigned in the sky, and Jander lay sprawled on the bed. He glanced up to see who had spoken and found Anna gazing down on him affectionately. She had planted her sun-browned hands on her hips, and her auburn hair, made red by the sun, tumbled down her back. Her eyes were full of warm laughter.

"Do you really miss me?" she asked again.

Jander, aware of this pseudo-dream state, still could not help but answer, "More than life, my dearest."

She came to him then, folded him in the warmth of her embrace, and he smelled the perfume of soap and sunlight upon her skin and nothing more. Anna went to the window and opened the shutters with a broad gesture; the glorious sunlight spilled in, washing over Jander like a river of light.

So real, he thought to himself, so sweetly real.

He noticed that somehow the neglected rooms were bright and cheerful, the furnishings polished and the decorations well-kept. Hand in hand, the two lovers descended the stairs, pausing to peer into rooms that spoke eloquently of loving care.

Outside, two milk-white steeds awaited them. As he drew near one of the horses, it nuzzled him affectionately. He discovered he had an apple in his hand. The elf fed it to the beast, who crunched it gratefully. Jander and Anna mounted and galloped off through the beautiful, late spring afternoon. Glancing over his shoulder, he saw Castle Ravenloft as a beautiful home, the seat of a great and noble family.

A few blissful hours later, they watered their thirsty mounts at Tser Pool. While the beasts drank, Jander and Anna lay together beneath a large tree, smelling the fresh earth and enjoying the leaf-filtered sun. A playful breeze stirred the leaves. Jander listened to the music of the water and the twittering birds, then spoke. "Why do you come to me like this?"

She was lying with her head on his chest and craned her neck to look at him. Her brown eyes searched his thoughtfully. "Do you wish me to stop?"

"No! Only, it isn't real."

"Who's to say what is real and what is an illusion? We are together. Isn't that enough? Besides—" her voice became teasing "—I don't want you to forget about me."

He brought her hand to his lips and kissed the tip of each finger. "Never."

"But you have. You know where to begin your search, but you have not done so. Jander, my love, avenge me." She had changed; her wondrous eyes had filled with tears. "For all that we lost because of my madness . . . *Avenge me!*"

Jander bolted out of the dream, utterly disoriented. He felt uncomfortably hot and slightly nauseous. He had fallen asleep in the bed chamber after he had fed upon Natasha. The shutters were closed tightly against the deadly sunlight, but enough light filtered in to cause him discomfort. Jander's senses were again heightened, and he closed his eyes in pain at being brought back to his dark reality.

After checking to see that Natasha was sleeping peacefully, the elf returned to the study to peruse Strahd's voluminous library. For a moment he was slightly daunted by the sheer number of books available. For years Jander had been cloistered in a cave with no company save that of the insane he fed upon. The elf felt a bit awkward in a place so crowded with history and literature. These volumes were beautiful things. Jander took a moment to admire the tooling of the leather covers. Some bore what the elf assumed to be the count's crest—a large black raven. Others had different symbols. A strikingly beautiful one which recurred now and then was a large sunburst.

"Well, might as well start at the beginning," he muttered to himself, and, picking a shelf, began to peruse the titles. *Coats of Arms of the Von Zarovich Line. Skin and Steel: A History of the Ba'al Verzi. Legends from the Circle. Tales of the Night. The Art of Kalimar Kandru. Barovia: Year 15 to the Present.*

Jander was delighted with the variety and pulled down a handful. Laden with books, he set a huge pile down beside one of the chairs and randomly picked a title. *Skin and Steel: A History of the Ba'al Verzi.* The cover featured a bloody skull. The elf frowned. He doubted he'd find a clue about Anna here. Then again, maybe he would. He opened it, inhaling the musty fragrance of the old book, and began to read.

In these civilized times, the long-dead author had written in his introduction, *it is difficult for us to imagine the kind of society that had assassins as open, thriving members of the community. In our country's turbulent eighth century, being an assassin, or Ba'al Verzi, was comparable with being a politician or a popular artist. One could name one's price and did, often receiving huge sums of money from individuals for protection.*

The Ba'al Verzi wore colorful, decorative clothing, with their symbol—the bleeding skull—prominently displayed. Their weapon was a blade of great beauty and frightening significance. The hilt was made of the skin

*from the Ba'al Verzi's first victim and was crafted by the
assassin himself. The first kill had to be someone the
Ba'al Verzi knew. This was demanded by tradition to dis-
courage all but the most hardened to know the secrets
and earn the protection of the Ba'al Verzi . . .*

Jander shuddered and almost threw the book to the
carpeted floor. He picked up another book, *Words of
Wisdom*, and dove into it eagerly to shake the image of
the Ba'al Verzi knife from his mind. His tactic worked,
for this was a collection of sacred poetry for some long-
forgotten god.

> *For the sun is mine, and moon,*
> *And all things of love and light;*
> *For the morn is mine, and noon,*
> *And all things of day and night.*
>
> *Harken to me, sons and daughters:*
> *Hear the wisdom in the waters.*
> *Listen to the river's laughter:*
> *Joy and peace shall flow thereafter.*

The rather simple poems gave the elf no clue as to
the fate of his beloved Anna. They did, however, calm
him and remind him that there was yet some beauty in
this dark land to which the treacherous mists had
brought him.

There were no windows in the enclosed study, so Jander had no idea how much time had passed. When he
returned to check on the girl, he was surprised to find
that it was well after sunset. Natasha slept like she was
already one of the undead. As he bent to examine her,
she moaned in her sleep and rolled over. Her throat was
bruised, but color was starting to return to her cheeks.

"They all look so inviting when they sleep," came a
smooth voice at his ear. "I trust she met your stand-
ards?" Strahd was at his elbow, smiling thinly.

"A little young for me, but then again, it is hard to
find an appropriate age when one is over seven hun-

dred," Jander quipped, startled and determined not to admit it. He had been alone so long, he had forgotten how silent vampires were.

Strahd frowned a little. "Seven hundred?" He clearly thought Jander was speaking in jest. "Ah—I see. You are counting your years as a living being."

"Well, yes," Jander admitted, "but that's only two centuries. I've been a vampire for five hundred years."

Strahd was silent. "I cannot even conceive of such a thing," he said at last. "I am barely past my first century. You make me feel like a child again. What a great deal I have to learn from you!"

Seeing the hunger for knowledge in Strahd's eyes, Jander was not so sure that being the wise old sage was a good thing in this place. Fortunately Strahd changed the subject. "Are you hungry, my friend?"

The bloodthirst called. "Yes," Jander replied.

That night they went hunting together; the first of countless nights they would spend thus. One of the gypsies had noticed a small party of intrepid—or foolish—travelers who had arrived too late to obtain a place at the inn. Jander remembered the sour-faced innkeeper and his refusal to admit patrons after dark. Of course none of the village's terrified, xenophobic inhabitants would accept the strangers, either. So the little band—three men, two women, and a child—had built a makeshift camp near the bridge across the River Ivlis.

Jander and Strahd had assumed their wolf forms for speed and practicality. Three real wolves and two slaves in wolf form joined them as they ran, speeding down through the Svalich Woods with one driving need foremost in their minds. The night was clear and cool, with just enough dampness to carry scents clearly. They located the little party from several yards away. The great black animal that was Strahd shimmered, faded to mist, then reformed. Following his host's lead, Jander transformed to elf form. They moved with the silence of the nightfall itself, creeping up on their unsuspecting prey. The wolves and Strahd's slaves circled around the little clearing to block off any retreat.

Jander and Strahd did not attack at once. They waited with patience until an owl had hooted twice and the moon had migrated a few degrees. Only then, in the damp, chill silence, did they descend.

The strangers were easy prey, easier than the two vampires had any right to expect. One big, hirsute man, allegedly on guard duty, was snoring against a tree, his unsheathed sword fallen from his limp hand. He was the first to go. Strahd materialized in front of him, gripped him by the tunic and promptly buried his fangs in his throat. The man's eyes flew open and his mouth gaped in a soundless cry, but Strahd drained him rapidly and soon the eyes fluttered shut.

While Strahd feasted, Jander took the other man. He could not have heard anything—Strahd and Jander were more silent than silence itself—but, warned perhaps by some inner instinct, he bolted upright, crying out a warning. Jander sent an unspoken command to one of the wolves who had accompanied the two vampires, and the beast sprang. It pinned the man, who was not small, easily beneath its bulk. Jander took over from there, moving with speed and silence to bury his white teeth in his victim's throat. A raven-haired slave hovered near, hissing, waiting to take the elf's leavings.

The vampire went not for the jugular, but for the carotid artery. This was no time for leisurely feeding— Jander's undead body demanded sustenance. As his teeth sank into the exposed neck, blood spurted out, pumped directly from the heart. The vampire gulped frantically as the warm, salty liquid shot down his throat. He wondered with a touch of macabre humor if vampires could drown in their victim's blood.

The third man screamed. Thin, tall, and pale with fear, he fumbled for his weapon as Strahd's hand clamped down on his wrist, snapping it easily. While two of the wolves bounded after the fleeing women, cornering them, Strahd again feasted on scarlet lifeblood. He dropped the unconscious man like a toy and turned his attention to the women. Two of his slaves were there before him, desperately hungry but yielding to their master. The vampiresses seized the women and held them ready for the count.

The mortal women were both in their thirties and slim, wearing men's simple clothing. One had long, fiery red hair and glared defiantly at Strahd while she squirmed in the vampiress's grip. The other was blond and wore her hair cropped short. The second vampiress held her tightly, but the woman's little boy, who was shrieking in terror, clung to his mother's waist. The sound was high and painful to sensitive vampire ears. Strahd advanced menacingly toward the boy.

"In the name of Torm the True, have mercy, he's just a baby . . ."

Jander had finished his grisly meal, and was wiping his mouth with the back of his gold-skinned hand when he heard the woman's plea. He glanced at her, startled. Torm the True—or the Foolish, or Brave—was a god of his home. Blood covered his clothing and face, and his gesture had accomplished little save to smear the liquid even further. He rose, a ghastly picture of crimson and gold, a fairy-tale hero who had suddenly, inexplicably, been cast in the role of the villain.

The little boy was still screaming. Strahd's black brows came together. Snarling he bared his fangs and reached a long, slim hand toward the boy. "Run, Martyn!" the woman screamed. With the last, desperate strength granted to a mother defending her child, she tore free of the vampiress's grip and lunged at Strahd.

A wolf leaped gracefully and tore her throat out before she had gone more than two steps. Blood drenched her tunic. The blond woman's body crumpled at her child's feet. "No!" cried the redhead, turning a gaze filled with horror and hatred to Strahd. He met her eyes evenly, exerting his powerful will.

"She deserved it, did she not?"

The redhead blinked. "No, she's just . . ."

"No," continued Strahd, his voice smooth and calm,

"she tried to thwart me. That is a grave error. Do you not agree?"

The redhead licked dry lips. "That is a grave error," she repeated dully, mesmerized by the vampire.

"That's better." Strahd turned his attention to the boy, who huddled shivering by his mother's body. The child had gone into shock. "He is too small for us to take with us. Besides, I am satisfied. Do you care for him, Jander?" he queried, indicating the child.

Jander's hunger was sated. The elf looked at the boy, and a sudden misery overwhelmed him. He did not want the child. He wanted to leave this place. He wanted to go home. He wanted Anna. "No," he said, softly. "Don't let them have him, either," he added, looking at the sultry, famished vampiresses. "The bearded man back by the tree is still alive. They can feed there."

The count said, "As you wish," and the vampiresses scurried to feed on the unconscious human. Strahd addressed the redhead, who was still staring at the corpse of her friend. He extended a hand. "Come, my dear," he said in his most affable tone. "You shall come to Castle Ravenloft."

"And the boy?" Jander prodded.

Strahd spared the child only a cursory glance. "Do what you will. I am not hungry." With the woman at his side, Strahd began the long walk back to Castle Ravenloft. Jander glanced at the three men. They were all still alive, though barely. The elf did not slay his victim because he had no wish to take a life, and Strahd had spared his prey because he preferred emptying the veins of women, thus providing himself with more slavish, female vampires.

The boy started to blink, looking around confusedly. His blue eyes met Jander's. Unable to bear the innocent's gaze, the elf turned on his heel and left the youth, throat unmarked.

Moments passed, then the boy spoke.

"Morninglord?" he whispered.

NINE

The next afternoon, when Jander awoke from a few fitful hours of slumber, he decided to explore the intricacies of Castle Ravenloft. He knew he should go back to the study and read more of the literature there, but his curiosity about the castle would be ignored no longer. One of the things that had led to the elf's forsaking the beauty and peace of his homeland was his insatiable inquisitiveness. Ravenloft was a marvel of architectural oddities, craftsmanship, history, and time-ravaged beauty, and Jander looked forward to investigating the place.

It was when he entered the audience hall that he had his first encounter with one of Strahd's "servants." Jander had gingerly seated himself in the ornate throne. He noted with a mixture of appreciation and disgust how beautifully the wood had been worked—and how neglected it had been over the decades. Suddenly he tensed. He had caught a faint sound of clattering behind him.

He leaped from the chair, ready to fight. Five skeletons stared sightlessly at him. Shreds of muscle tissue still clung to dried bones, and they all wore rotted fragments of a uniform. By their matching garb and the swords they carried, Jander guessed that they had originally been guards of Castle Ravenloft. They completely ignored him, pattered about the room in a parody of a patrol, then took up sentry positions in the guard post adjacent to the hall.

Jander watched them sadly. He had always felt sorry for skeletons. They were not in and of themselves evil creatures, and the elven part of him felt great pity for the souls forbidden to rest as they ought. Jander suspected that the count had kept these and any other "guardians" away from him during his first day or so in Ravenloft so that Strahd could give the skeletons instructions not to harm the castle's only willing guest. The elf wondered, with no small amount of unease, just how many other creatures dwelt within these dark, chilly walls.

He decided to find out.

Jander rose from the throne and continued wandering down the long hall. At the far end, the hall opened onto a long balcony. The backs of two more beautiful thrones were turned toward Jander. For a brief second, Jander wondered if a skeleton or something more horrible might be lurking in one of those thrones, waiting for him.

Angry at his nervousness, he dismissed the thought and approached the thrones. He stretched out a trembling, gold-skinned hand. Slowly he placed it on the back of the throne and closed his eyes in embarrassed relief. No one was sitting in the ornate chair. Judging by the layer of dust, no one had sat here for years. It was ridiculous even to have worried. What could any of Strahd's creatures have done to him?

The elf stepped forward, resting one hand on each of the thrones, and peered down from the balcony. His beauty-loving nature was disheartened by what he saw.

The room below was a sad sight. Once it had been the chapel of Castle Ravenloft, and, like apparently everything else here, had been beautiful and rich. Now, the stained glass windows were boarded up, although here and there shafts of multicolored light trickled in. The pews had been overturned, and it looked like long, sharp claws had raked grooves in the fine wood. Some of the benches were broken. Dust lay over everything like a blanket, and the altar had been defaced.

Even from this distance, Jander could tell there was nothing holy about the place anymore. That certainly was appropriate for a castle where a vampire was lord. With a rueful shake of his golden head, Jander continued his explorations.

He wandered back down to the main level, descending the wide staircase and entering the great entry hall. He took a left at the bottom of the stairs, passing through a long, dusty corridor. It was lined with statues. Jander read the inscriptions on a few of them as he passed. Some of the names he recognized from *Legends from the Circle*. Unlike the room full of figures on the floor above, these statues seemed to represent figures from literature or myth, rather than specific historical personages. Jander did not like the fact that the eyes of the statues seemed to follow him as he progressed down the hall.

The chapel was his goal. When he had been alive, he had always enjoyed visiting holy houses, provided they were run by honest priests who served a good and just god. Such places, in his mind, were almost as close to the grace of the gods as the outdoors. Almost, but not quite. He had not been inside a holy place since he had become undead, and he hoped that, since the chapel had been defiled, it might permit him entry.

He reached out a golden hand to push open the double doors when a soft rattling behind him made him pause. He turned to encounter another skeleton.

This one was clad, not in armor or a ragged uniform, but in tattered bits of fine clothing and jewelry. It was obviously a guard of the chapel, and Jander thought it must be what was left of the ancient priest of this place. He paused, but the skeleton made no further move to block his entrance.

Jander had glimpsed the ruination from the balcony above. Now, as he entered the erstwhile sanctuary, he saw the wreckage from a closer vantage. Mourning the lost beauty, he walked amidst the rubble, trailing his hands in the ages-old dust. The elf paused before the altar. Disrespectful hands had traced obscene images and runes of hatred in the thick layers of dust. Suddenly angry, Jander smeared the offenses with his hand, obliterating them.

He was a vampire. Truly holy places did not welcome him. Jander had discovered that. He was an outcast from all of the things he loved—nature, the sunlight, sacred spaces. He could accept that, even accept evil as part of his world. But the passing of five centuries still had not taught Jander to be unmoved by the destruction of beauty, and the elf began to wonder if there wasn't something he could do to restore the castle's former grace.

He sat down in one of the undamaged pews for a time, thinking. He was so lost in his reverie that he didn't notice the gradual fading of the light. "Lost in prayer, perhaps?" came the cool tones of the count's voice.

Jander glanced up. "Perhaps. How are you this evening?"

"Quite well, thank you. I am hungry, however. Do you care to come sample my acquisition of last night?"

Jander winced inwardly, but was careful not to let his expression show. Acquisition. That's all the woman was to Strahd. Not a human being . . . "No, I think I shall decline. I've an urge to explore the woods on my own tonight, if you don't mind."

"Not at all. By the way, there is more nourishment for your little maiden in the main hall. I have fresh food delivered every few days. It keeps the gossip down in the village and gives the townsfolk something to do besides drink. Besides, our charges must keep their strength up if they're to be any good at all to us, hmm?"

The count turned with a flourish and departed in unnatural silence. Jander quickly followed, eager to get some wholesome food into little Natasha's body. He had the meager consolation that it was as much for her own good as his.

He prepared her a plate of rare beef, vegetables, and fruit. When he entered her chamber, he found that the color had started to return to her cheeks. She watched him with listless eyes as he arranged her plate.

"Good evening, Natasha." She didn't answer. "I've brought something for you to eat. You must be hungry."

"No," she said softly. He paused in his cutting of the meat and caught her gaze.

"I think you'll find that you're very hungry indeed, and that this is exactly what you want." He didn't like to force her to eat, but she needed the nourishment. The thought came to him grimly, no, Jander, *you* need the nourishment.

He ignored the voice in his head and continued preparing her food. His "suggestion" worked. Natasha, sniffing appreciatively, tried to sit up. He helped her, placing a pillow behind her back. She was too weak to manage the utensils, so the elf fed her himself. Quickly, painfully, he thought of Anna. *Avenge me.* Tomorrow he would return to the study.

When Natasha finished, she looked at him curiously. "What's your name?"

"Jander," he replied, pleased that she had asked.

"You're different from the count."

Jander smiled a little as he gathered up the dirty dishes. "Yes, I suppose I am."

"You're not going to make me . . ." Her voice trailed off, frightened.

"A vampire? No. I can't let you leave here, though. You know too much and you could hurt me. Do you understand?"

The young woman nodded, but her face fell. She reached to touch the tiny holes in her throat, and her eyes flickered back to the elf's. Jander's face grew sad. "I must feed, even as you must," he said in a gentle voice, indicating the meal he had brought her. "You understand that, too?" She nodded slowly.

He loathed himself more than usual as he laid aside the dishes, took the girl in his arms, and took sustenance from her, contenting himself with the minimum of the red fluid that he needed. When he had finished, he eased her down on the bed again. Jander pulled the coverlet up and allowed himself to smooth her hair as she closed her eyes.

The elf opened the shutters and felt the cool night air on his face. He needed to get out of the castle, out into the woods, away from Natasha. Quickly the vampire became a gray mist, then a bat perched on the window sill for an instant before leaping into the air.

Jander flew for miles, gazing at the landscape beneath him. The elf enjoyed all his forms. While his elven body was the one he preferred, there was much to be said for the freedom of the gold wolf who ran through the verdant woods in silence and savagery and the airborne grace of a small brown bat. Beneath him the Ivlis twined its sparkling, serpentine way through the forest and fields. The ring of fog about the village was evident, swirling and pulsing. Jander could see the tiny orange spark that indicated the Vistani encampment. To the west, he knew, lay the small fishing village of Vallaki. He would have to travel there one night soon. Perhaps the populace was not quite so afraid of strangers there.

The bat dove and fluttered to the earth on a small hill between the forest and the river. Jander assumed his elven shape and lay down in the soft green grass. The dew did not bother him, and he felt comforted by the reassuring press of earth against his back, even if it was the earth of Barovia and not his homeland. Jander frowned. That was another thing. He had come here without any of his native soil, but had suffered no ill effects. His frown twisted into a bitter grin. Barovia, it seemed, was now his home.

He closed his eyes and offered his frenetic, racing thoughts to the tranquility of the glade. A golden hand reached out to touch the damp grass, stroking the blades gently, reverently. The wind sang in the trees, and he could hear the myriad songs of creatures serenading the night. They made a beautiful music. Once,

Jander too had made music, piping with joy and sorrow, laughter and love, his heart floating in the strains of the flute's piercing song. Would that he could ease his melancholy in that sweet sound again.

A thought popped into his head. He glanced up at the nearest tree. It swayed and sighed in the wind, its blossoms all but gone. An apple tree—a good choice. The elf hesitated, then drew his dagger and cut down a branch. Sitting on the river's bank, he worked all through that night, shaping a branch as he had a hundred times before. Though it had been literally ages since he had last fashioned a flute, his hands remembered the work. By the time Jander noticed that the dawn was on its way, much of his work had been completed. He frowned. When he transformed into a bat or wolf, his clothing changed with him. Would the flute change also if he tucked it into his belt?

Quickly, mindful of the morning's approach, he concentrated and assumed his bat form. The flute posed no problem. The bat that was Jander flew swiftly back toward the castle.

In the chapel, safely removed from the sun's rays, Jander spent most of the day engrossed in carving the flute. His eyelids drooped sometime during the middle of the day, and he lay down in one of the pews. He would only nap, he told himself as he pillowed his head on his arm and cradled the almost-finished flute. Just a few moments, just to rest his eyes . . .

"Why did you never play for me in the asylum?" came a voice sweet as sunlight. Jander's eyes flew open. Anna was sitting beside him in the polished wooden pew, looking at the beautifully carved flute with interest.

Jander blinked against the sunlight that streamed in through the stained glass windows. A rainbow of colors turned the chapel into an artist's palette of hues. The altar was ready for a service, its polished silver holy symbols winking in the violet and aqua light from the windows. The place was filled with peace and a quiet, restrained joy. Jander recalled a line from one of the poems: *Thy love is not one hue only, but a rainbow; for infinite are thy follower's joys.*

"It's beautiful, Jander," Anna said warmly, a delighted smile on her dear face. She held it out to him. "Play something for me, will you?"

He hadn't played for centuries; he had been unable to bring himself to try. Yet here, in the holy, radiant chapel, with Anna watching him eagerly, Jander found the courage to raise the flute to his lips. He took a breath, pursed his lips, and blew.

A discordant shriek issued forth, the sound of something in terrible, wracking pain. The flute twisted in his numb hands, turning into a foul black worm that writhed and hissed. Horrified, he dropped it, and it slid away from him. The entire room was now swathed in a malevolent darkness, much more evil than simple night. Things crouched in the shadows, and Jander, even with his infravision, could see only the red gleam of eyes. The elf groped for Anna, his hand closing on leathery flesh. A monstrous, contorted creature wearing Anna's clothing laughed at him, and the stench from its gaping, dripping jaws caused him to gag. *"Now you see the world as I did for over a century! How does it feel to be mad, Jander Sunstar?"*

With a cry, the vampire bolted upright. He was still alone in the ruined chapel. The day was winding down toward dusk. Nothing had changed. Trembling, Jander looked at the flute. He was determined to finish it despite the nightmare. "Anna," he whispered, "I didn't know what a torment it was to you . . . forgive me."

An hour later, he had finished the flute. It looked nothing like the ornate instrument in his nightmare, something for which Jander was quietly grateful. He still was afraid to raise it to his lips. Angry at his cowardice, he shoved the instrument in his belt and descended the stairs. He returned to the entry hall and wandered down into what he discovered was the main dining hall. A huge table, covered with dust, and dozens of chairs filled the room. Two sideboards, painstakingly tooled, flanked the table. It was the large object at the far end, covered with a sheet, that caught Jander's attention.

He had never seen anything like it, and he approached curiously. He removed the covering. The thing was made up of many hundreds of small pieces. A variety of pipes crowned its top, and many layers of ivory were laid next to one another like teeth. A bench was placed directly in front of it, and there was another row of objects below it.

"I see you have found my plaything," came Strahd's voice.

"What is it?" Jander asked, fascinated.

"It is a musical instrument," Strahd explained. Jander felt a hesitation in the other's manner and raised a curious eyebrow. "It is called an organ. The music it makes is very beautiful, very strong, and very . . . powerful. I used to be quite the virtuoso on it. That was a long time ago, however." He made as if to replace the covering, but Jander laid a hand on his arm.

"Could you play something for me?" he asked. "I loved music too, once. These halls are very silent. I should like to hear you play."

Strahd seemed torn. Jander could tell that part of him longed to caress the instrument once again, make it sing after all this time. Yet there was also apparently pain in the performing. Strahd hesitated so long that Jander felt certain he would refuse. To his surprise, the vampire said, "Very well. I would ask that you forgive any sour notes I might strike. It has been a long time."

As if he had not done so for centuries, Strahd seated himself at the massive organ, flipping the tails of his black outfit back with an automatic gesture. His long fingers twitched like spider legs as he placed them over the keys. Jander felt his own body tighten in response to the tension he could feel emanating from the other vampire.

With a blast of music like the sound from the gods' own horns, the organ sprang to majestic life. Sound rolled through the dining hall in sonorous waves, thrilling Jander to the core of his being. Haunting, demanding, beautiful, the music that flowed from Strahd's hands was all this and more. It was a magnificent thing, this organ music, and Jander was moved.

The piece Strahd performed was awe-inspiring in its magnitude, laden with sorrow and majesty. Jander listened, closing his eyes to aid his concentration, and allowed his body to respond as it would to the powerful pull of the music. The song ended, but Strahd was clearly loathe to relinquish the instrument, and his fingers wandered idly over the ivory keys.

Jander's own fingers wandered down to his belt and the wooden flute. The nightmare haunted him yet, daring him to play. Filled with a wondrous fear, he raised it to his lips.

He did not need to breathe to continue his undead existence. Speech required a deliberate intake of breath, but Jander had not filled his lungs as he now did for many a decade. Breathe in he did, and pursed his lips on the flute.

A sweet, pure sound issued forth, a bird's call to the rumbling waterfall of Strahd's organ. The count looked up, and something like delight mingled with surprise on his pale face. Together, the vampires created spontaneous music. The clear tones of the flute danced and skittered like light over the organ's deep chords. Sometimes the music was gentle, rippling, peaceful. Other times it swelled and burst like the waves crashing onto the shore, a vampiric music that reflected the inner pangs of its creators, the harmonies of the damned incarnated.

Simultaneously they finished their songs, and the silence pressed on their ears. They exchanged glances, and Jander could read his own pain in Strahd's dark eyes.

They could make music, but it was not the music mortals made. Mortals could never infuse their innocent instruments with the kind of wild pain and savage triumph that he and Strahd had just achieved in their duet. They had, for an instant, lost their pain in express-

ing it. The music had taken them away from their undead state, and they had exulted in the sensation.

In the uneasy quiet, Strahd lifted his hands from the
organ keys and folded them neatly in his lap. He looked
down at them, examining the long, sharp nails with a
casualness that belied the emotions Jander felt lay beneath the surface. Strahd had been moved, and by
something other than murder, power, rage, or grief. He
had been moved by beauty, and for a moment, he and
the elf had been kindred spirits.

The count raised his eyes to meet Jander's once
more, and there was merely the cool cunning in them
that the elf was beginning to know only too well. The
moment had passed, but it was not forgotten. Strahd
seemed to sense that he had somehow revealed some
vulnerable portion of his soul, so he deliberately
changed the subject.

"Enough of this," he said brusquely, yanking the covering over the instrument with what seemed to Jander
unnecessary vigor. "We have not talked as we promised
one another we would. Let us go to the study, where, I
see, you have been spending much of your time, and
you can tell me if my home is to your liking thus far."

"I have many books yet to read, Your Excellency, but
the ones I've seen so far have been . . . interesting. I notice that there are a few that are in a strange type of
shorthand," Jander commented as they climbed the
stairs.

"Ah, yes. Those are my personal records. I invented
the shorthand."

"It's very difficult to decipher. Could you teach it to
me?"

Strahd glanced at the elf. "Why?" The question was
sharp, cold.

"I'm still looking for a record of my lady," he said. "I
hoped that I would find something of use, but nothing's
turned up yet."

"Ah, I am sorry indeed. Of course I will teach you,"
Strahd offered. "Provided—" he paused and his tone

sharpened "—that you begin teaching *me*. I have learned much about vampirism on my own, with no guide whatsoever. Yet you can tell me more." They had arrived on the study, and Strahd sank down in one of the chairs, waving Jander into the other. "Now," ordered the count, "call the wolves."

Jander bristled at Strahd's tone, but forced his resentment down. He closed his eyes, and let his mind wander in search of a lupine brain. Gently he touched a wolf in the main entryway. *Come visit me, friend,* he told it. Jander sensed another one keeping guard in Natasha's room, and he likewise bade it come.

A few moments later, a gray wolf and a black one trotted into the study and sank down at the elf's feet. The count's thin lips twisted in a smile. "Now, I shall call them," he said. He placed the tips of his long fingers together and slitted his black eyes. The wolves inclined their heads in his direction, and one of them whined. They rose and went to him, one of them pawing at his chair.

Jander concentrated again. This time it was much harder to get through to the wolves' brains. He could feel Strahd's presence in their minds. He closed his eyes and focused his thoughts. The wolves grew agitated, their ears flat against their heads as they glanced from Strahd to Jander. Finally, cowed and obviously in pain, they crept trembling to Jander's feet.

Strahd's eyes flew open, and there was anger in their depths. "How did you do that?" he demanded.

Jander kept calm. "Control of animals and people is based on a vampire's will. All I did was—"

"Do you imply that *I* am weak-willed?"

"No, Your Excellency," Jander answered, a bit taken aback. "You are younger than I am and have had little practice. I was a slave for many years. I learned how to do what I do because it was the only way I could escape my master. Survival and freedom are good incentives, more so than a desire to play parlor tricks with animals."

Strahd held Jander's gaze for a moment, then nodded his dark head once, slowly. "I grant you that." He leaned back in the chair and placed his feet on the small, low table in front of him. Jander, a little confused, followed suit. The fire blazed in the hearth, and the two wolves dozed contentedly in its warmth. Jander could not help but be struck by the cozy normalcy of the scene, twisted only in that these two "drinking companions" drank blood instead of claret.

At length, Jander broke the silence. "Why can I no longer feed on animal blood here?" he queried. "For five hundred years, I have suffered no harm from it. Yet, here it makes me ill."

Strahd did not answer at once. "Things are different in Barovia."

"Well, that's rather obvious, but why? You claim to be 'the land,' Strahd. What's going on in this place?"

The count's jaw tightened. Jander had touched a nerve. He was resigned to that; there was no other way to get answers than to keep nudging the other vampire. "We are our own world, here in Barovia," said the count slowly. "Yet we are no world. It is my belief we are in an altogether unique plane of existence. I do not think you will find Barovia on any map. At least, not any more." He opened his dark eyes and looked at the other vampire. His expression was bitter. "Would you believe that I was once a noble, just warrior, Jander?"

This twist in conversation was not what Jander had expected. His confusion must have registered, for Strahd smiled thinly. "I see you have difficulty with the concept. Do not worry about insulting me, I have the same problem believing it myself. Things do change, do they not?

"If you can suspend your doubt, cast me in the following role. I was a warrior, and my causes were good. I united many countries; I defended many people. I fought fairly and well, and my army was without parallel. I grew up with a sword in my hand, and I came close to death so many times that I cannot even count them all.

"Then, all the fighting was done, and suddenly there was no place for me any more. I had become obsolete. I was used to leading warriors, not governing common folk, and even though I came from a long line of rulers, I had no wish to rule a country. My parents had died, and I was the eldest. The choice was not mine. So it was that I found myself the lord of Barovia."

Strahd rose and began to pace. His features, however, betrayed no inner turmoil. "At that time, Barovia was part of . . ." His beautiful voice trailed off, and confusion played about his eyes. He laughed a little. "Do you know, I cannot recall the name of my own homeland?" He paused, his eyes unfocused, trying to remember. Then he shrugged it off. "No matter. It is not important. No doubt, the land wishes me to forget."

Jander went cold inside despite the heat the flames emitted. The *land* wished Strahd to forget his country? Dear gods, was this place truly alive? The idea that he might forget Waterdeep and Evermeet filled him with fear. Painful though the memories might be, they sustained him. Another thought stabbed at him. Suppose the land wanted him to forget Anna? He made a silent vow to consciously remember her—and his quest for revenge on her behalf.

"Suffice to say that I was the law, and my laws were not kind." Strahd's liquid-silk voice startled Jander out of his reverie, and the elf refocused his thoughts. "I woke up one morning and discovered that my youth was gone," Strahd continued. "Vanished, and I had nothing to show for it."

"Surely," Jander offered, "your victories brought you comfort."

Strahd's upper lip curled contemptuously. "Comfort? The people hated me, and I could not care less about them. There was no solace. Only Death awaited me. Then . . . I had another chance at my youth."

A curious thing happened. Strahd's voice went soft. It became gentle, filled with a tenderness that Jander would never have expected from him. His eyes, too, lost their calculating stare and became almost human. His angular face with its high cheekbones relaxed in reverie. "I met *her.* Her name was Tatyana, and she came from the village. Another came between us, destroyed any chance that we might be happy together.

"I despaired. How could I fight against this youth, this bright young warrior who stole the only thing I ever loved?" Strahd's mask had slipped, and Jander knew that he was glimpsing the mortal man who had lived, a long time ago.

"I prayed for guidance, for revenge. And my prayers were answered. Death Himself appeared to me, and I made a bargain with Him—a pact, sealed with the blood of my rival, whom I slew on his wedding day to Tatyana.

"He had so enchanted Tatyana that she chose to follow him in death. The guards tried to kill me, but their arrows bounced harmlessly off this body. Death had not claimed me, but life had forsaken me.

"Thus was my pact with Death sealed, and my reward given. Somehow the land became no longer merely Barovia, but this strange, different realm into which you had the misfortune to stumble. So you see, Jander Sunstar, my friend, I understand your loss. I, too, am trapped here. I have not crossed the misty borders; always, my steps lead me back here, to this castle and its memories."

There was something unspoken in Strahd's tale that Jander could sense. He had lied somewhere in that story. Tainted as the tale was, the truth was much more horrible.

Once, when Jander had been alive, he had found a corpse that had been dead for a long time. The skin seemed taut and firm; yet when the elf prodded it tentatively with his sword, it burst open and began to writhe with maggots. This was the image his mind flashed to him when Strahd finished his story. Like the corpse, the tale appeared unpleasant but whole, still human on the outside. Jander knew that if he probed deeper, the dark reality of the tale would explode into the light like maggots from a corpse.

 **TEN**

"I'm sorry, Anna, but I found nothing."

In his dream, Jander leaned against the ornate mantel in the study. His arms were folded across his chest, and his gaze was on the carpeting. The elf didn't want to look at Anna. Somehow, he felt he had let her down, even though he had spent each afternoon for the last two weeks poring over every book he could read.

"It's all right, my love." Her voice was sad, though, and when Jander turned to look at her he found her sitting quietly in one of the red velvet chairs. "It's not your fault." She met his gaze and smiled sweetly, though her eyes were shiny with unshed tears.

His heart breaking, he went to her and laid his golden head in her lap. She ran her fingers through his bright hair. "I've read everything in here that I can. Strahd has even taught me how to read his own shorthand. There are no records, no documents—nothing that I can trace to you."

"But you are learning the history of my land."

Jander grimaced and pressed his face against the cool cotton of her blue skirt. That was true enough, although Barovia's was not a pleasant past.

"Perhaps there are answers to be found here in the castle," the sweet voice continued. "Perhaps very close at hand."

Jander lifted his head from her skirt and looked up. "Were you here in Castle Ravenloft?" She smiled mysteriously at him and did not answer. "Anna, *were you here?*"

He awoke in the study, his body stiff from sleeping in the chair. The elf stretched, wincing, then buried his head in his hands. His efforts consistently failed to yield fruit, and his dream-punctured sleep was hardly restful. Exhausted, he rose.

Out of the corner of his eye, he noticed the door to Strahd's private room. For a moment he wondered just what it was that the count guarded so jealously behind that locked and magically sealed door. Unfortunately Jander had promised his host not to pry. He rubbed his eyes, replaced the book he had been reading when he fell asleep back on the shelf, and left. If Anna wanted him to continue exploring the castle, he would do so.

After nightfall, the elf went to the room filled with statues. It was the dark of the moon, and the pale starlight that fell through the rows of high, arched windows did little to illuminate the still figures. Jander raised the torch he'd brought high to one side so that its light would not dazzle his eyes and wandered slowly from figure to figure.

The Von Zaroviches were an uncommonly handsome family, even allowing for the usual flattery of the artist. Strahd had warned Jander that not all of his ancestors were at peace, yet the elf felt uneasy as the distressed spirits bound to some of the stones seemed to shift and respond to his prowling inspection. Anger, frustration, rage, madness—the bound spirits seemed to hurl the pale echoes of their human emotions at his senses.

Overwhelming sorrow, betrayal, grief: here was another who did not rest comfortably in some glorious afterlife. This was the statue that had caught Jander's attention his first night in Ravenloft, the statue whose head lay at its feet. Jander knelt in the dust and gingerly lifted the stone head, turning the face to his own. Why was this one statue disfigured? The others were neglected, stretches of gray spider web spun between their limbs, shrouding their features, but this one alone was deliberately damaged. What rage had vented itself on the stone throat, Jander wondered. What guilt had set the head at the feet of the statue, refusing the final assault on its identity? Jander wiped the dust and cobwebs from the features, moved the torch to better study them. The features were handsome, masculine, but there was a sweetness about the expression that somehow reminded Jander of Anna, of the expression that had touched her face in those few, shatteringly brief moments of sanity.

"What spell bound you?" Jander asked the stone head, rising to his feet. He tried to set the head on the stump of the carved neck, still draped with a stone amulet. It teetered between his hands. Too much time had passed for it to sit in its proper place again. "I would release you if I could," Jander said softly, going to one knee to set the head down again, "and to the Nine Hells with Strahd."

The elf shifted the torch once more, peering at the inscription at the statue's base. Its worn and missing letters told him no more than it had that first night, when Strahd had so imperiously cut short his inspection. Jander straightened, brushing at the knees of his breeches, shivering a little. It seemed appropriate that his other destination this night was Castle Ravenloft's dungeon.

A heavy oaken door, bound with wide strips of tarnished brass, admitted him to the landing of a stone staircase. Stairways abounded in Castle Ravenloft, but this one was so worn that even Jander's sure feet slipped a little in the depressions worn in the gray stone.

The stair dropped away into darkness, and Jander was grateful for his torch as he passed under empty sconces, his free hand trailing down the damp wall. It seemed a long descent, ending at last in a space that was either a small room or a very large landing. The place made one feel trapped, with the steep darkness of the stairs behind and the silent threat of the doorways before and at either side.

Jander raised his torch a little, and the flickering light caught the leering features of gargoyles, grinning evilly from the walls. Startled, and angry because of it, Jander drew lips back from his lengthened fangs and snarled back at them.

He opened the door before him and entered a short hallway. Pushing through the crimson velvet that curtained off the end of the hall, the elf found himself on a balcony, as elegantly appointed as any in the castle. Two thrones were stationed at the end. What in the world was here for royalty to watch? He stepped closer.

Below him was a room like a small amphitheater. In the dim light, creatures that had once been men moved in a silent *danse macabre* among the torture instruments that had ended their mortal lives. A skeleton, the torchlight ruddy on its ivory skull and ribs, drew the lashes of a cat-o-nine-tails again and again through its fingers, as though pleased by the music of leather and metal skittering across bare bone. Nearby a zombie writhed in a parody of exhausted struggle, already-rotting flesh shredding against the iron manacles that bound it to the wall. Throughout the great chamber the dead played out the dramas of Strahd's humor, mocking their own deaths, dully tending the instruments that had tormented and destroyed them.

Swallowing his disgust, Jander leaped off the edge of the balcony. He landed lightly, lithe and golden grace among the shattered dead, and wrinkled his nose at the stench of them. With the smell of the dead came sound—faint moans and smothered shrieks, like the nightmare screaming of the souls of the enslaved, like the cries of the madwomen that had haunted his days and nights with Anna.

His face twisted, and he turned toward the sounds. A doorway stood on his left, a rectangular patch of deeper shadow in the chamber wall. He moved toward it, drawn by the sounds, which grew less faint as he grew closer.

The remembered din of the madhouse met him as he swung open the door and stepped into the dark hallway. Moans, sobbing, pitiful prayers assailed him from the corridor of cells before him. Figures moved in response to his sudden presence, some cowering into the shadows, others rushing forward, thrusting hands and arms through the bars in pleas for help or mercy—or oblivion. This was Strahd's larder. Jander stood for a moment, listening in pain. He had no right to release these people. In this castle, he was no more than Strahd's guest.

Jander was fiercely glad that Natasha had been given into his care, such as it was, and not shut away here in this dark place of horrors. Anxious to escape the sounds of suffering, the elf quickly ascended the curving flight of stairs, keeping his eyes straight ahead so that he didn't have to look on the wretches' faces.

Torches were positioned every few feet on the stair. There was a door ahead, but the room into which it opened was pitch black, too dark even for Jander's eyes to penetrate. He lifted one of the torches from its sconce and peered ahead. He had left the rooms of the dying. Now he emerged in the hall of the dead. Looming before him were the catacombs of the Von Zarovich line.

He stepped forward gingerly. A few dozen of Strahd's illustrious ancestors slept their last sleep here. At least, Jander hoped most of them were dust by now. He suspected that a few of those squat crypts housed inhabitants whose sleep was definitely uneasy.

Sounds too high for human hearing alerted him to the presence of thousands of bats. They covered the ceiling and walls, moving sluggishly, hiding their weak eyes from the unaccustomed brightness of Jander's torch. A few of them, particularly disturbed, dropped from their perches and fluttered about Jander crazily, emitting high squeaks. They resettled on the opposite wall, crowding aside their fellows. The floor and the tops of the crypts were coated with layers of bat excrement.

Mortals would know terror in this place, Jander mused. He only felt sad. The despair a choking gall in his throat, the elf returned the way he had come.

*   *   *   *   *

Evermeet! Evermeet! Home of the People,
Realm of sweet magic, land of the light;
Long have I tarried away from thy forests,
Long lie the shadows that darken to night.

Evermeet! Evermeet! East blow the breezes
That carry the fragrance of Evermeet's shore,
And soon the Realms will in truth be Forgotten
As thy lost, wayward child returns home once more.

Natasha's voice may have lacked the beauty of the elf woman's who had taught Jander this song, but the vampire didn't mind. It filled him with pleasure to hear someone sing the songs of his homeland here in this dark country. He had first played Natasha the melody on his flute. She had asked about the song, and he had obligingly taught it and others to her. They spent many hours, Jander on the flute and Natasha accompanying him with her sweet, sad, tired voice.

If Natasha was a prisoner within the gray walls of Ravenloft, she was very well-treated. Jander kept her strength up as much as he could. On days when her health permitted, she would accompany him about the castle, a quiet little ghost trailing behind him, her face white and strained but still able to smile occasionally.

Now she fell silent, looking at her hands. The elf had noticed how her voice had suddenly gotten thick on the line "lost, wayward child returns home once more." Concerned, Jander sat down beside her on the bed, placing a gentle, golden-skinned hand over her small white ones. "Are you ill, little one?" he asked gently. "Have I been draining you too much?"

She shook her head. Over the last two months, she

had grown to trust him, even, he hoped, to like him. "No, Jander, it's . . ." The girl gnawed her lower lip. "Jander, can't you let me go home? Please?"

Jander opened his mouth to reply when a cool voice from the doorway interrupted him.

"You are our guest here at Castle Ravenloft," Strahd purred, his voice low and dangerous. "It would be rude for us not to show you all the hospitality we can. Don't you agree, Jander?"

Quick anger stirred in the elf, but as always when he was with Strahd, he refused to give in to the emotion. "You are the host, Your Excellency, not I. Surely it is up to you to decide who receives your hospitality."

"Mmm, quite right. Jander, come to my study. We have not talked in a while." He left, cape swirling behind him, confident that Jander would follow. The elf gave the frightened Natasha what he hoped was a reassuring smile and hurried to catch the count.

As Jander stepped into the study, the four wolves who had been lounging by the fire rose stiffly. Their ears slowly flattened against their heads, and their dewlaps curled away from sharp yellow teeth. Somewhat surprised, Jander sent them a mental command. *It is only I, my friends. Calm yourselves!*

To his amazement, not one of the wolves backed down. Again he tried to touch their minds, only to find that there was some kind of block. He glanced over at Strahd. The count was sitting in his chair with his legs crossed and the tips of his fingers placed together. His gaunt face wore an extremely self-satisfied, predatory smile. If the emotion hadn't been so crass as to be distasteful to the elegant vampire, Strahd might have been accused of gloating.

"Very good, Strahd," Jander offered, a bit uneasily. "They're completely under your control. Now, if you'll call them off so I might join you?"

For a long moment neither Strahd nor his wolves moved. Then, as one, the four great beasts resumed their positions by the fire. They totally ignored Jander as he moved to his chair and sat down.

"I have been working on my willpower," Strahd said drily.

"You are an excellent student."

"Ah, but that is because you are a fine teacher. Yet," Strahd said in an almost regretful tone of voice, "I must take it upon myself to advise you, if I may?" He raised his raven brows, awaiting Jander's approval to proceed. The elven vampire nodded. "You ought to drain your little friend. That way, you would have a slave doing things for you instead of a patient upon whom you must wait."

Jander's silver eyes narrowed. "I have been meaning to talk to you about this, Strahd. You make far too many slaves."

To the elf's surprise, the count only laughed. "Is there such a thing as too many slaves?"

"Most definitely. As we vampires get older, we get stronger. We learn more. If you think there exists a single slave, vampire or not, who doesn't yearn to be free, you're greatly in error. What's more, you're in danger."

"Thank you, my friend, for your concern. I assure you, my slaves pose no threat to me. You underestimate my ability to, shall we say, keep the peace." He smiled the smile of a cat with a mouse.

Jander shrugged, refusing to play the game Strahd wanted. "As you will. I'm just giving you the benefit of my experience, take it or leave it. I have a question for you, however. You keep this room very well. Why do you allow the rest of your home to fall into such disrepair?"

"I treat what I value with care," the count replied simply. "I value my books. The rest does not mean that much to me. In life, Jander, I was a warrior. Fine weapons have always been my treasures, but over time I've learned that books, especially spellbooks, are to be coveted. Besides, what do the trappings of luxury have to offer me?"

"Beauty is its own reward," Jander replied. Strahd's lip curled in contempt, but he made no comment. "If you'll permit me," Jander continued cautiously, "I would like to restore some of Castle Ravenloft."

"You are not to bring anyone here," Strahd stated, his silky voice turning to ice. Red began to burn in the depths of his eyes. The wolves by the fire caught the change in the air and raised their heads quizzically.

"Of course not," Jander retorted, annoyed that Strahd would think such a thing. "I could do some work here myself. I would enjoy it very much."

"I fail to see the point."

Jander stroked his chin with his hand, searching for words. "I was not born to the darkness. Beauty, music, nature—these things are sources of great comfort to me. They help me to forget, as much as I *can* forget, what I am. Death doesn't end the hunger for those things, Strahd." He looked the count directly in the eye. "I've heard you perform music. I've seen how it touches you. We are vampires. Our existence isn't . . . it isn't *right*. That doesn't mean we can't lose ourselves for a moment in something that's beautiful.

"Appreciation of something just because it is a thing of beauty, because it's something right and natural and in harmony with its environment—that's a gift we can still possess." The elf's voice grew hard. "I don't intend to exile such little joys from my world. It's dark and lonely enough as it is."

Strahd looked at him keenly for a long while. Jander met that gaze without flinching. At last Strahd began to laugh. "What a puzzle you are to me, Jander Sunstar! You feed upon lifeblood, yet mourn the life you take. You are a being of shadow and night, yet you yearn to be surrounded by beauty. You are dead, but you cannot bear decay. What exactly are you? You can hardly be a vampire!"

"Be that as it may," said Jander, sadly but without a trace of self-pity, "that is precisely what I am."

Again, Strahd was silent. "Very well. Dabble with the castle as much as you like," he said, rising suddenly. "You will excuse me."

Jander remained in the study and read for a few hours, finishing a history of Barovia's ancient army. Apparently Strahd's boast about being a powerful warrior was based on fact. He had, thanks to his finely trained army, his skillful tactical maneuvering, and the devout prayers of the local priest, become the hero of great renown a century or so past.

On the ninth night of the attacks, our savior came charging through the Balinok Mountains. His name was Strahd Von Zarovich, and his army numbered thousands of brave men. Through that long night, Von Zarovich's army fought. It is said that the count was everywhere on the battlefield, and that he himself slew hundreds in the first hour.

The Most High Priest of Barovia, a young man named Kir, led the people in prayer. Precisely at midnight, he retreated to the castle chapel to meditate and plead for guidance. He was granted the use of the mysterious Holy Symbol of Ravenkind to wield against the goblin king. While the count fought and led his men to victory, the Holy Symbol was used in secret, as well. Afterward, Most High Priest Kir carefully hid the Holy Symbol in a secret place.

No one knows what the Holy Symbol looks like, or where it is hidden. To this day, no other priest has been able to find or use it. Unquestionably, however, its powerful magic aided our noble Count Strahd to his well-earned victory.

Jander raised a skeptical eyebrow. The whole thing sounded like Barovian propaganda. The people down in the village certainly didn't think of Strahd as their noble count and savior. The vampire carefully replaced the book on the shelf and returned to his room.

He was greeted by a sight that struck him to the bone.

Natasha lay sprawled on the bed. Her face was whiter than he had ever seen it, and an expression of fear was frozen on it. She was quite dead.

"If you bury her tonight," came a cold, smooth voice, "she shall rise in only a day or so. A fine little vampiress she will make, yes?"

Angrily Jander turned on the count. "Damn you for this!"

Strahd's thick eyebrows reached for his hairline. "I gave you the girl. She was growing older, losing her bloom. She'll stay just like this for as long as you like. Surely this was what you intended?"

Jander knew the action for what it was. Strahd was issuing a challenge, drawing a line and daring him to step across it. The count's supercilious quip, *What exactly are you? You can hardly be a vampire!* came racing back to haunt the elf. In a way Strahd was right. Jander glanced back at Natasha, remembering her sweet voice, her plea *please, don't make me like you.* This was what vampires did—feed upon the living and create others like themselves. Jander felt a wave of self-loathing.

He turned back to Strahd, with the little smile on his face that he knew maddened the count. "Of course it was, Strahd," he said pleasantly. "Now that you've made her into a vampire, she's your slave, not mine. You took her away from me. Don't I have the right to be angry with you for that?"

Strahd frowned. He could hardly argue with Jander's logic. "You are right. I apologize." Then he said, not hiding his fangs, "I shall find you another and make amends."

He bowed and left. Jander sank down onto the bed, sick. There was still time for him to mutilate Natasha's body so that she wouldn't rise as an undead, and then bury her. Damn him, the elf thought, Strahd always has the last word.

There was a garden in back of the chapel, gone to weeds from lack of care. A few small, sad flowers struggled valiantly against the choking roots of the other growth. Jander recognized overgrown rosebushes here and there. A little path of flagstones led through the garden to a balcony that overlooked a breathtaking drop into the rocky gorge a thousand feet below.

There, in the dying garden, Jander buried Natasha, using bits of broken board to scrape a hole in the hard earth. When he had finished his task, he sat down near the new grave. His gaze was caught by a beautiful, tiny flower near his left foot. It was purple and yellow, its blossom no bigger than his fingernail. A weed, no doubt, but lovely. The elf reached and plucked the flower, inhaling its sweet, light fragrance.

Suddenly he smiled. He could begin here, in the garden, to bring a little bit of beauty back into his world. All the place needed was a little bit of care and effort. Still holding the flower, Jander rose and cast a critical eye on the plants. Though straggly and neglected, all the rosebushes appeared to be alive. It wouldn't take much work at all to bring the garden back to life, maybe only a night or two.

Jander walked to the low stone wall that encircled the courtyard and peered down. A few hundred feet below a thick mist swirled, preventing the elf from seeing all the way to the bottom of the crevice. He could, however, see the fog-encircled village to the southeast of the castle.

He would go to the village tomorrow night and see if he could pry some information from the tight-lipped townsfolk. Or else to Vallaki, a little farther away. After all, he didn't know for certain that Anna had come from the village.

The sky was lightening in the east, the blackness fading to a dark gray. Melancholy settled over Jander like something tangible, and the brief joy the garden had afforded him slipped away. It was time for the elf to seek shelter away from the beloved sun.

A few miles away, the burgomaster's daughter also watched the dawn come in. She leaned against the window sill and gazed up at the menacing shadow of Castle Ravenloft. Anastasia sighed, and her eyes fell to the cobblestone courtyard beneath her. It had been three months since Petya had risked his life to warn her about the vampire; three months since Anastasia had stood up to her father and shamed him with his own fear. Life had become much better for all the women in the Kartov family since that night.

Still, Anastasia thought grimly as she stared unseeing into the bleak Barovian dawn, she didn't think anyone in her household would react well to the news that she was pregnant with a gypsy's child.

*   *   *   *   *

Jander's efforts to win the Barovians' trust failed miserably. Several times a week for many months he appeared at the Wolf's Den with a purse full of gold, but he was always regarded with suspicion. He chose the darkest corners and kept to himself, hoping that this tactic would garner more information than trying to directly engage one of the suspicious townspeople in conversation.

The vampire did indeed overhear much, but not what he wanted to hear. Vlad So-and-so's daughter had mysteriously disappeared. Mikhail Thus-and-such had heard a wolf howling and awakened to find the corpse of a half-human, half-animal creature on his doorstep. Irina on the other side of town had given birth to *something*, nobody was sure what; when they burned the tiny body it turned into a sticky goo and emitted a terrible stench. Irina went mad, they said, and they raised their glasses to her poor husband Igor. . . .

Jander listened and grew ill at the things they described. No wonder no one trusted him. He left a handful of coins on the table and rose, noting that the room fell silent and everyone had turned to look at him. The elf drew his gray cape tighter about his slender frame and hurried out the door.

"They said you came here now and then," came a female voice. "I was wondering if I'd be able to catch you."

Jander turned, raising a gold eyebrow when he saw a young woman standing by the door. A black cape did not quite disguise the full swell of her belly, and her upturned face was well illuminated by the light from the tavern door. Dead leaves swirled at her feet, scudding along with a dry, scraping sound. A polite distance away, two servants, a man and a woman, waited patiently. Quickly Jander reached and pulled the door closed so that the patrons of the inn wouldn't see them talking. "Anastasia, is it not?"

"Yes, it's me." She saw him looking at her servants. "Don't mind them. It's only my maid and my father's valet. I wanted to tell you about . . . well . . ." The burgomaster's daughter looked down at her curving stomach and smiled awkwardly. "It's Petya's. I'm keeping it. I haven't . . . He doesn't know."

Jander said nothing, only waited for her to continue. "Papa isn't quite the terror he used to be. Your wolves saw to that." She laughed, and the elf smiled as well. "I thought about giving the baby to the gypsies, but I know they wouldn't take it. Besides, it's something that will always remind me of Petya. Does that make sense? I'm babbling, I know, but . . ." She faltered and looked up at him, her dark-circled eyes very serious.

"You did a lot for me and Petya, more than you really know. This baby—" she rubbed her belly with one protective, loving hand "—is a kind of symbol of that for me. I'm going to tell it all about you, and you will have my child's friendship, as well as mine and Petya's." Her eyes searched his for a reaction.

Jander was moved. "My dear," he said, his voice soft and filled with a hint of surprised wonder, "you do me an honor in telling me this. I truly hope all goes well for you and your child."

Anastasia smiled up at him, relieved. "Here," she said on impulse, "it's kicking away like mad now. Would you like to feel it?"

The vampire almost declined, but the thought of touching such a new little life was more than he could bear. Cautiously he reached a hand to the girl's stomach. She took the hand and moved it about on her belly. "There!" Anastasia exclaimed triumphantly, looking to see the elf's reaction. Jander's eyes widened as he felt the tiny being moving. Quickly he pulled his hand away, balling it into a fist and holding it close to his heart.

"I must go, now," he said hurriedly, not meeting Anastasia's eyes. "Excuse me." Pulling his cape closed, he strode swiftly across the square and down the path that led toward Castle Ravenloft.

Anastasia watched him depart. The moon cleared a cloud, and its milky light flooded the square. She gasped a little, then shook her head, amazed at her temerity. Petya had told the truth about the elf—Jander cast no shadow. Instinctively she folded her hands about her unborn baby. "Little one," she said softly, "you may be the only child in Barovia who has been sworn a friend of a vampire."

Once Jander was out of sight, his body shimmered into mist and then into the shape of a gold-coated, silver-eyed wolf. He ran through the cool comfort of the Svalich Woods, concentrating on his movements and the play of taut muscles beneath shaggy fur. In the physical exertion, he tried to forget how much he longed to be a living being once again.

 **ELEVEN**

In the time following the unsettling encounter with Anastasia, the garden became Jander's comfort. On one particular night, almost ten years after his meeting with the pregnant woman, he worked at preparing the rose bushes for their winter's sleep by trimming them back. The other plants had already gone dormant, but he could feel their life beneath the sheltering soil. Come spring, the place would be filled with fragrant blossoms. Jander straightened and dusted off his dirty hands. He glanced at the sky. It was almost dawn.

The elf had been reading a book on furniture restoration and had left it in the study. When he went to retrieve it, Jander nearly collided with Strahd as the other vampire stepped out of the secret room.

"Jander! I thought you were in the village this evening," Strahd said, recovering his composure at once. He was carrying a large book in his left arm and holding a torch in his right. Quickly, tucking the book under his right arm, he pulled the door shut behind him with his left, blocking Jander's view into the room.

"I was. It's nearly dawn. You lost track of the time."

"So it seems. Well, I must to my coffin before the sun rises." He turned, placed the torch in its sconce, and began to murmur an incantation to seal the door magically.

"Are there books in that room?" Jander asked. "I'd

like to see if there are any records that might—"

Strahd stiffened and turned around slowly. "You are never," he said quietly, "*never* to ask me that again. Do you understand? This castle is mine, and what I choose to keep hidden from view is my own business. I have my reasons, and you are *never* to question them!" He clutched the book to his chest. "Leave me!"

In all their many sparring conversations, Jander had never before been the focus of the count's red-hot anger, and he was properly chastened. He nodded courteously and left for his quarters. Strahd spoke a harsh, guttural word, and the study door slammed shut behind the elf.

Jander went to his chamber, the room in which Natasha had died. He had since boarded up the window and sealed the cracks with pitch, so that he might sleep there comfortably during the day. He was tired and longed to lie down on the new down mattress he had asked Strahd to bring up from the village. Yet hunger nagged at his stomach. Reluctantly he left the comfortable room to descend into the prison that was Strahd's larder.

* * * * *

"Do you know who I am yet, Jander Sunstar?" came Anna's teasing voice. In his dream, Jander pretended to still be asleep, and when Anna bent over him he grabbed her and tumbled her onto the bed with him. She laughed, pushing him away halfheartedly, then hugged him tightly. The elf covered her sweet face with kisses.

"No, you little vixen, I *don't*," he replied to her question. "You don't seem to have existed here. There are no asylums, neither here nor in Vallaki. The Barovians keep their madmen to themselves or turn them loose to wander. Or else they die," he added, his eyes melancholy, "which, in this land, is the best thing for them."

"Perhaps," Anna said, one small hand stroking Jander's chest, "I wasn't in a madhouse."

He gaped at her, feeling very foolish. Of course. "Did you live in the village? Were you married? Anna, who was your family? What—"

"Jander, my friend, you distress yourself!" came a creamy cold voice that was definitely not Anna's. Jander opened his eyes to find that he had been clutching the down pillow to his chest. "Perhaps this room does not agree with you if you have such nightmares here," Strahd added, gazing at the elf.

The other vampire didn't even bother to reply, only sat up and rubbed his eyes with the heel of his hand. "Good evening, Strahd," he murmured.

The count pulled up a chair and seated himself with a flourish. "I have a gift for my friend."

A sullen slave entered, bearing a mahogany box, one foot by one and one-half, and about four inches deep. Strahd took the box and opened it. Jander's eyes widened.

Inside the velvet-lined case were the tools of a craftsman. Tiny bottles of colored powder were ready to be mixed. Three different sizes of styles, all silver-tipped, waited to be used for carving or engraving. There was an assortment of small hammers and chisels, as well. "These are merely to whet your appetite. Please let me know what else you may require in your work, and I shall provide it for you."

"They are a master's tools, Strahd," Jander said sincerely. "Thank you. I'll begin using them tonight."

"I have . . . something else planned for you this evening. If, of course, you care to join me."

* * * * *

"Behold the arrival of the Morninglord!"

Martyn Pelkar, better known to the impatient Barovians over the last ten years as Brother Martyn the Mad, stood on the wooden podium he himself had made and addressed anyone within earshot. Tall, lanky, with fair, curly hair and pale blue, rather fey eyes, the self-proclaimed priest of a god he called Lathander Morninglord stretched his arms up to the sky. He faced east as the sun crept slowly over the horizon.

"Every morning," muttered the baker, Vlad Rastolni-kov, as he busied himself with the morning's final batch of bread. The big man pounded the dough on the long table, venting his irritation on it. "Can't just shut his mouth, can he? No, he's got to come around here and bother everybody." The rest of his mumbling disappeared into his bushy black beard.

The bakery was a small building, the large oven in the back taking up most of the room. Only a few candles were lit toward the front, as the fire from the oven provided sufficient illumination for work in that area. There was a long table upon which Rastolnikov worked the bread, and a deep cabinet for the bowls and pans. When the loaves were ready, Rastolnikov's apprentice, Kolya, would hawk them in the market square.

Kolya, a plump boy who was overly fond of his master's wares, appeared at Rastolnikov's shoulder. "Are these ready for the oven yet, sir?" he asked.

Rastolnikov paused, white flour up to his elbows. Thick black brows drew together over equally black eyes. "What do you think I'm doing right now?" Kolya shrank back, cowed. "Ah, take a few minutes and get some air, Kolya. The heat has gone to your head."

"Thank you, master," Kolya replied, scurrying out into the square. He shivered in the morning and wished he had brought a cloak. The bakery had been sweltering, and now he felt the dewy chill.

"Be back in time for this last batch!" his master roared after him. Kolya headed down Market Street toward the old church. Behind him, Martyn still carried on with his dawn prayers, his gold and pink robes a startling contrast to the gray of the sky:

"We thank thee, O Morninglord, for this beautiful dawn and the glory of your new day. . . ."

"It's about time you got here."

Kolya gasped, then closed his eyes in relief when he saw that it was only Sasha Petrovich, the burgomaster's grandson, leaning against an abandoned building and grinning wickedly. He was wearing a simple cotton shirt and brown trousers, his cape draped over his shoulders. At the boy's feet was a large empty sack. "I was wondering if you'd ever get away from old Ratty."

"Sasha, you know I don't like it when you call my master that," Kolya protested halfheartedly. "Here," he offered the other boy half a fresh-baked loaf.

The boy reached out a brown hand and took the proffered bread eagerly, pausing to smell the yeasty scent appreciatively before taking a bite. "Ratty does make good bread," he admitted with his mouth full.

"We've got to hurry," Kolya prodded. "Martyn's already out in the square."

"I know, but he's as long-winded as my grandpapa. Especially when it's not raining. We've got plenty of time." They had reached the end of Market Street and stood gazing up at the church.

The building was old, its wood weathered. It had been falling apart until "Mad Martyn" had taken it for his god, Lathander. The young priest's labors had worked subtle changes: the door hung straight on its hinges, the windows were free of cobwebs and sparkled with new glass. The walkways were swept, and new roof tiles spotted the sharp, peaked roof with incongruous color, like the red caps of mushrooms dotting the brown litter of the forest floor. The evidence of fresh occupation was a little daunting, even to brash young Sasha. The old church was once again a holy place.

"I can't *believe* I let you talk me into stealing from a church," Kolya moaned.

"We're not stealing, we're just . . . borrowing." Sasha, shrugging off his momentary hesitation, tugged on the double entrance doors. They opened outward reluctantly, creaking. The two boys blinked, their eyes adjusting to the dimness within. There was a small center aisle, flanked by rows of pews on either side. Dust swam in the air. The altar at the end, however, was kept scrupulously neat. Sasha and Kolya saw a small pile of pink wooden disks in the center of the altar and a few simple but polished candlesticks with half-burned tapers. Next to the altar stood a large basin on a pedestal. A ray of sun crept in and caught the sparkle of water.

"Here we are," grinned Sasha triumphantly. He ran down the aisle, his booted feet making surprisingly little noise. "Well, come on, Kolya!" Reluctantly the other boy followed. Sasha handed him several small bottles. "You fill these up with the holy water, and I'll take the disks."

"Sasha, I know we're going to get in trouble for this," Kolya murmured as he dipped a bottle into the basin and bubbles formed on the water's glinting surface.

"Kolya, you're the one who's scared of the dark."

"Am not!"

"Are too. You're the one who said, 'Oh, Sasha, I'm *afraid* to go out there without anything to protect us!' Here we are, getting you some protection from the night creatures. So just shut up, all right? Aiee, what a coward! Cowardly Kolya, that's what I'm going to call you from now on." Disgusted, Sasha shoveled all the rosy disks into his sack. For good measure, he took the candleholders too. "I can get us some lamps and blankets. You're going to get the mirrors and the garlic, right?" Kolya didn't answer. "*Right?*"

Kolya wasn't listening. He was staring, horrified, out one of the holes in the stained glass window. "Sasha, he's coming!"

With the speed of a rabbit, the dark-haired youth seized his bag in one hand and his friend's collar in the other. Kolya stumbled and then found his footing, and together the two little thieves charged down the aisle. Sasha hit the heavy wooden doors running, and they swung outward, catching Brother Martyn full in the chest and tumbling the priest backward. Kolya and Sasha fell, too, but scrambled to their feet and took off as fast as they could.

The young priest lay gasping on the stairs until he got his breath back, then rose, wincing. He opened the doors and saw his altar at the far end completely bare. At first, Martyn was horrified. A smile, however, touched his mouth after a moment.

His god's actions were never clear to the slightly crazy priest. One thing Martyn knew, however: if those two boys wanted the holy objects badly enough to steal from a church, they were welcome to whatever protection the symbols could afford them. Martyn knew firsthand what lurked in the nightscape of Barovia.

A safe distance away, Sasha and Kolya collapsed at the foot of a massive oak tree. Sasha began to laugh hysterically, a merry whooping that made even the terrified Kolya grin and finally join in. "All right," Sasha said, wiping the tears from his face and resting a hand his laugh-weary stomach. "You've got to be getting back to Ratty. I'll meet you near the seamstress's shop at sundown. This is going to be so much fun!" Kolya wasn't so sure, but he nodded anyway.

The day wound down as usual. Kolya was late returning to the bakery and received a brief, floury spanking from his master. Sasha Petrovich had skipped his lessons, and his mother confronted him when he tried to sneak back into the mansion. She was sitting on the stair landing, waiting for him. Her face was worn and sad. She gazed down at him for a moment before speaking. "Why do you do this, Alexei Petrovich?"

Sasha shrugged. "I don't know."

"Don't you like learning things? Being smart?"

"Not in the summertime." He peered up at her with jet-black eyes. Anastasia had to laugh.

"Come sit beside me," she invited. Sasha obediently climbed the stairs to where she sat. Her arm went around him, and he leaned against her. "Sasha, I've told you about your father, and why it's so important to me that you behave well. It doesn't matter to us that you're half-gypsy, but there are some narrow-minded people in town to whom it does matter. Your learning will make sure you have a place here when I'm gone."

Sasha fidgeted. He hated it when his mother got serious. Whenever Mama talked about leaving him, Sasha always got a lump in his throat. "Are you still going to let me go to Kolya's tonight?"

Anastasia ran her fingers through his silky hair and glanced out the window. "I'm not sure. It's already starting to get dark. Hurry and pack, and we'll see."

With a speed his mother wouldn't have thought possible, Sasha dashed up the stairs and prepared his things for the "overnight trip." He had his own room now, small but private. There was a cot, a small window, and a chest for his clothes and toys. The ten-year-old rummaged through it now, looking for his sack. His aunt Ludmilla, a willowy, attractive young woman who had just turned twenty, stuck her head in and almost caught him with a handful of the rosy wooden disks. "Better hop along, little bunny," she teased him, grinning.

"Don't call me that!"

"It's getting late, little bunny," Ludmilla continued, ignoring him. "Wolves come out when it's late. Grrr!" He stuck his tongue out at her, and she continued down the hall to the room she shared with Anastasia, laughing.

When Sasha scurried back down, he found his mother standing by the open door, searching the sky anxiously.

It was a magnificent summer's twilight. Purple and orange struggled for domination in the cloudless sky, and the moon was already visible as a ghostly orb near the horizon. The birds twittered to one another as they prepared for their sleep.

In any other place, lovers would sit on grassy hills and watch the spectacle with awe and anticipation. The harried inhabitants of Barovia, however, could spare no time to appreciate the beauty of sunset. For them, it symbolized a handful of safe minutes before the arrival of the dreaded night and all that lurked within it. "Perhaps you'd better not go stay with Kolya's family tonight," Anastasia murmured.

"Mama, you promised!"

"I know, but the Kalinovs live all the way on the other side of the town, and it's almost dark now."

"I'll be fast!" Sasha assured his mother. "There's plenty of time if I leave right now!"

Anastasia hesitated, grimly aware that time was ticking away relentlessly. "Oh, very well. Take this." She removed a pendant that hung about her neck and slipped it over Sasha's dark head. The boy rolled his eyes at what he regarded as his mother's over-protectiveness.

He had never seen anything resembling a vampire or a werewolf in his entire life, not even the one that had rescued his parents. Sasha was rather hoping that tonight he and Kolya might meet this mysterious, golden elf-vampire. The boy did not even bother to examine the pendant. He knew what it was—a simple disk of silver with protective signs etched in it. "Hurry, now," Anastasia bade him, planting a quick kiss on his wide forehead and sending him off with a gentle smack on the bottom. Sasha took off running, delighted with his freedom.

Anastasia watched him go with a sad smile on her careworn face. "Oh, Petya, he's so much like you," she whispered to herself. The burgomaster's daughter said a quick prayer for her headstrong child as she closed the heavy wooden door and bolted it.

Kolya was waiting for him as he had promised, a doleful expression on his pudgy face. "I was afraid you wouldn't show," Sasha greeted him. Kolya merely glared, falling in step with the burgomaster's grandson as they trudged down the overgrown path that wound through the forest to the ring of stones on the hill. Kolya tripped on roots several times, and at one point Sasha stopped and lit a lantern so they could see better.

The circle was the same place where Sasha's parents had stolen a few moments together, which made it special for the boy. Also, it was rumored that it had once been a place where powerful, good magic had been worked, centuries ago.

Sasha laid one of the pink wooden disks at the foot of each stone, then placed everything else on the large, flat rock in the center. Kolya lit the lamps and candles, then the two boys curled up in the blankets they had brought.

Gathering his blanket up to his neck, Kolya glanced at the shadows that loomed just beyond the flickering of their smoky oil lamps. The strong smell of the chain of garlic cloves around his neck was starting to make him feel nauseous.

"I want to go home, Sasha," he moaned.

Sasha threw him a withering glance. "Look, we're perfectly safe. This place is enchanted, and we've got all kinds of things to protect ourselves with."

There came a sudden, sharp sound. Kolya shrieked and dove for the pile of charms, brandishing the mirror in the direction of the sound. "Idiot," Sasha said disgustedly, "You've just thwarted the attack of an undead rabbit. Congratulations." Indeed, Kolya could see the rabbit's white tail disappearing into the dark. He blushed hotly.

Sasha ignored Kolya's distress, instead picking up the book he had brought and flipping through it. "Here we are," he said triumphantly. He lay down on his right side, the book stretched out in front of him, and carefully positioned the lamp. An owl hooted ominously. Sasha listened and grinned. Then, making his voice as deep and ominous as a ten-year-old can make it, he began to read.

"Once upon a time, many moons ago, in the town of Vallaki, there lived a boy named Pavel Ivanovich. He was not just any boy. He was the heir of the Sun, and his purpose was to hold back the Darkness. His father had given him a piece of the sun, but it was stolen from Pavel's cradle. The Darkness hid it far, far away, but when Pavel grew to become a man, he realized that he had to recover the piece of the sun. To do that, he entered the lands of the Dark.

"So he walked, alone, to the black pasture where the Nightmares graze and the river of Forgetfulness flows, and he met the first Guardian of the Darkness. He was a tall, pale man, with sharp teeth and claws. 'Stop!' said Nosferatu, for so Pavel knew the guardian to be. 'Stop,

that I may drink your blood and live upon your death.'
But Pavel said to Nosferatu, 'You cannot stop me, for I
am the heir of the Sun, and I will show you the evil that
you are.' Pavel held up a mirror. When Nosferatu saw
how evil he truly was, he roared in pain and dissolved
like the mists in the morning sunlight . . .''

Kolya hugged his knees and tried not to listen to the
ghost story. He was certain he would not sleep a wink
tonight. It was his imagination, probably, but Kolya just
couldn't shake the idea that someone was watching
them.

Outside the circle of stones, Count Strahd Von
Zarovich laughed and drew back into the shadows. "It
would almost be worth it to attack, just to see their
faces," he told Jander. "Still, the little ones are so small
they would scarcely be an appetizer for us."

Jander thought the statement held just a touch of
bravado. Surely Strahd sensed the powerful magic of
the place. The huge gray stones protected the two foolish children as surely as any physical wall. Then again,
this realm belonged to the count. The elf glanced back
uneasily at the three slaves. They stood quietly behind
their master, three vampiresses who had clearly been
attractive in their lives and were now coldly obedient.

These three were typical of the kind of woman Strahd
found attractive. They were all taller than average, with
dark, red-brown hair and dark eyes. Their figures were
slim, unlike those of most Barovian women, who tended to be rather stocky. They resembled Anna closely
enough to cause Jander to think about his beloved every time one of the slaves appeared. It was torturous.

Strahd glanced at Jander. "You are pleased?"

Jander shrugged. "As you say, their blood could hardly feed us all. And," he added, "I'm sure you can sense the
amount of protection they have at their fingertips. I don't
think these puppies are worth the trouble."

Strahd's eyes searched Jander's, then the lord of
Barovia nodded once. "Come," he said, "I know a place
where a banquet awaits us." Casually he reached out a

sharp-nailed hand and stroked the cheek of the nearest slave. "Are you hungry, my love?"

The slave bared long fangs, her eyes blazing as she nodded. Jander, too, was ravenous. The cursed thirst burned inside him like a fever, demanding to be slaked. The very scent of these children was enough to cause him to salivate in anticipation. He wondered where Strahd was taking them. Was there an adventuring party or an army of sorts nearby?

"Let us feed, then. Into wolf form, my beauties, and we shall head into the village." Obediently the vampiresses shape-changed into sleek, brown wolves. Their master, flamboyant as always, twisted into his own wolf form, that of a monstrous black beast. Jander dropped to all fours, wolfen also. The pack followed the path that Strahd set and, tails up and ears back, trotted down into the unsuspecting village of Barovia.

As they slipped unnoticed past the Wolf's Den, Jander saw that a wreath of garlic cloves now hung on the door. He had not had much luck in obtaining victims anywhere here in the village, but the inn had been the best of a poor lot. He cursed mentally. He would have to visit Vallaki more often now; they were less careful than the villagers.

The elf followed Strahd and the she-wolves as they cut across the square, silent shadows in the darkness. He saw that they were heading down Burgomaster's Way, where the better families of the village dwelt. Jander felt a flicker of foreboding. Something was not right here. Strahd's gait was filled with a carefully reined enthusiasm that the elf instinctively did not like.

Jander was shocked when the end of their trail placed them at the burgomaster's mansion. Trepidation filled the elf at the sight; he had promised Anastasia long ago that she would come to no harm through him. The black wolf halted, arched, and shimmered into Strahd's human form. He gestured for the others to do the same. As soon as he could, Jander demanded in a whisper, "Just what kind of game are you playing?"

Deliberately ignoring Jander's disrespectful tone,
Strahd answered him smoothly, "Kartov has been
cheating me. He has been levying harsh taxes on the
peasants in my name, yet I have not received a single
copper."

Jander's heart sank at the icy timber of Strahd's voice.
"What is money to you, Your Excellency?" he said, trying
to avert what he feared was about to happen.

"It is not the money itself, but the fact that the arro-
gant mortal thinks to trick me." Surrounded by pressing darkness, Jander had no trouble seeing the red fire
in Strahd's eyes. "I plan to teach him a lesson." He started to move toward the door, then paused. "I thought,"
he said affably, "that you were hungry."

Jander's mind raced for any excuse. "They won't let
you in at this time of night."

Strahd smiled. "I have no need of their permission.
Don't you remember?"

Jander did remember his first glimpse of the depths
of Strahd's anger, the time he had shouted, *I am the
land! . . . Every home is my home.*

Surely Strahd will not kill the burgomaster's family in
their own home, the elf thought desperately. A vampire
cannot simply ravage a town for a lark. The continued
existence of Strahd and his minions depends on secrecy.
The count realizes that. He has to, Jander told himself.

Strahd began to chant in a musical, barely audible
voice. Jander winced, his dislike of magic not fading in
the face of his need for blood. The door started to glow,
emitting a soft radiance. "It's protected," Jander said.
Strahd glared at him with open contempt.

"What is a simple ward to the lord of the land?" he
replied, his deep voice containing a hint of laughter. He
again chanted, and the blue radiance vanished. The
count's body dissolved into a fine mist that seeped under the door. The elf heard a bolt slide back, then the
door swung open. "Come in," Strahd bade them, smiling at the irony. The three slaves rushed into the house.

Jander followed more slowly. "Now," Strahd told the

vampiresses, "do you remember my instructions?" Expressionless save for the hunger that danced in their blank eyes, they nodded. "Excellent. You may sup wherever you like."

Like hounds on the scent they are, Jander thought as he watched the beautiful undead women sniffing the air. He, too, however, was excited by the fragrance of so many humans in the house. Two of the vampiresses scurried into the servant's quarters on the first floor. The third vampiress ran soundlessly up the wide staircase. Jander and Strahd followed. At the top, the elf ducked into the first bedroom he came to and felt Strahd brush past him in the hall. There was a little cot and a few pieces of furniture in this first small bedroom, but nothing else.

The next bedroom was large and well-furnished, with two beds and a beautifully carved table between them. In one of the beds a young woman of about twenty summers slept contentedly.

For a moment Jander thought it might be Anastasia. He drew near and gazed down at her, marking her regular breathing and the long, black lashes that lay against sleep-flushed cheeks. No, this girl wasn't Anastasia, although the resemblance was strong. Jander guessed it was her sister. He sat beside her on the bed. Gently, like a lover, he laid a golden hand on her dark hair. With a bite that was as tender as any mortal kiss, he sliced a nick in her throat. A bead of blood welled up, and he licked it off, savoring the sustaining liquid. He placed his lips to the wound, gathered the girl in his arms, and fed. He took his time despite the hunger in his gut; she would not wake, and there was no hurry. When he had finished, several long minutes later, he laid her back on her pillow.

It wasn't until Jander was back in the corridor, closing the door quietly behind him, that he caught the hot stench of spilled blood.

 **TWELVE**

A cry of pain and fear rent the air. Swifter than a thought, Jander followed the stench to the master bedroom at the far end of the corridor, breaking open the door. "Strahd!"

One of the vampiresses was leaning over the prone body of an elderly man. It was Burgomaster Kartov. His throat had been sliced apart, as though the vampiress had ripped her fangs like daggers through the flesh. The wound gaped like a ghastly, misplaced grin, and what blood had not gone to feed the feral beauty spattered her face and soaked slowly into the rich blue-and-gold carpet. The burgomaster's wife, too, was dead, sprawled brokenly on the bed. Her limbs lay at grotesque angles, as though every joint had been torn apart.

Strahd held a young woman in an unbreakable grip. The count had obviously enjoyed slaking his thirst, for he had taken his time feeding. She was still alive, though ghostly pale and very weak. At the sound of the breaking door, her head lolled in Jander's direction. The elf's eyes went wide.

"Anastasia!" he cried.

"You promised," she whispered in a trembling voice.

Jander leaped toward Strahd, his ferocity surprising the other vampire. Jander tore the dying Anastasia from Strahd's arms, knocking the larger, more powerful man to the floor. Immediately, Strahd's three slaves tackled Jander, answering their master's sudden flare of surprise and rage. But the elf was ancient, his will as powerful and better trained than Strahd's, and his own rage and horror burned hot. He shook the three slaves off like a wolf scattering an attack of foxes, and lifted Anastasia in his arms, his gaze on Strahd, hot and full of hate.

The count rose slowly, with dignity. One white hand slicked back disheveled hair. His eyes were red. "How dare you come between me and my prey?"

"Prey is one thing. This is a massacre!"

"Only of humans. What do I care? You are soft, Jander, and that will be your undoing!" Anger turned to malevolent humor. "Of course, unless you wanted her for yourself." He smiled, his mouth smeared with red and his fangs long and sharp.

Jander kept his eyes locked with Strahd's. In his arms, Anastasia trembled and went limp with a horrible finality. Forcing himself to bridle his grief and horror, the elf turned to Strahd, his face showing a mirror of the count's own cold arrogance.

"You are the one who is courting death, Strahd," Jander said coldly. "You've got these people frightened, yes, but you don't want to make them angry. We are vulnerable—you even more so than I. I can control how deeply I sleep. You can't." The elf laughed, his normally musical voice made savage and ugly with his emotions, and laid Anastasia's pale corpse at Strahd's feet.

"One peasant farmer with a planting stick, Strahd, and you could be no more than this—less than this, for you would not even rise as a slave! Remember that this dawn, as sleep takes you."

Strahd's red eyes narrowed in anger, but he held his tongue. Jander knew he was listening. "Have you ever seen a lynch mob?" the elf continued bitterly. "I have, from both sides. It's a frightening thing. Individuals can be terrorized, but if you have a group of people who have been pushed far enough, they're going to find you and you won't be able to stop them from destroying you."

The vampiress next to Strahd snarled and raised a clawed hand. The count stayed her with a twitch of his finger. "Leave him alone."

Jander's eyes never left Strahd's. "I've seen it happen. A group of vampires had the whole town for the taking back in my homeland. They grew prideful and began a wholesale slaughter. The folk rallied and destroyed them. No vampire has ever been able to enter that village again. The people are eternally poisoned against strangers—much like Barovia. For the sake of your own neck, Count, try to exercise a little caution. Not everyone in this forsaken hellhole is a fool."

To Jander's amazement, the red in Strahd's eyes had faded and the count wore a thoughtful expression on his flushed face. "Jander Sunstar," he said slowly, "you are right . . . to a point. This is my land. I do whatever I wish here, and tonight, I wished to raise the black beast of panicked terror within the breasts of the Kartovs." He smiled icily. "I have done so. Now I shall listen to what you have to say regarding, how shall I put it, 'covering our tracks,' hmm?"

The elf didn't know what to say. Strahd had skewered his argument in a masterful fashion. The count had yielded to Jander without giving up a single thing. As if he could read the elf's thoughts, Strahd began to smile.

"Well, the first thing would be to destroy the bodies." Jander glanced at the nearest vampiress. "You have far too many slaves already." He thought the count would contest this point, but Strahd nodded thoughtfully.

"Take them all downstairs," he told the vampiresses. Wordlessly each of the beautiful undead picked up a corpse and silently bore it down the corridor. "Then what would you have me do?"

"We should burn the house down. Make it look like an accident. If we destroy all the evidence, there'll be no reason for anyone to suspect anything." Jander planned to wait until the last possible moment and then carry out the young woman upon whom he had fed.

The corpses were gathered in the main room downstairs. The powerful vampires broke the furniture easily and built a pyre in the middle of the room, piling the corpses upon it. Jander couldn't watch; it conjured up a centuries-old memory for him. Carefully, Strahd lit a torch from the still-burning fire in the hearth and placed it to the pyre. It smoked sullenly at first, then the wood caught and began to burn. Black, oily smoke curled up from the flames. Unnoticed, Jander moved to the stairs.

Suddenly the vampires heard a loud shout, followed by others. "Fire! Fire at the Burgomaster's!" came the cry. Strahd cursed, then dissolved into a mist that twined its way out one of the open windows.

Jander hesitated, throwing a concerned glance up the stairs, noting with disgust that he had stepped in a puddle of blood and left crimson footprints down the steps. The pounding on the door made up his mind for him. The would-be rescuers would find the girl upstairs. Unfortunately, they would also find the corpses.

The pounding increased. They'd break the door down soon. In a last effort to hide the tragedy, Jander grabbed a burning piece of wood and lit the draperies, which flared immediately. He tossed the brand back on the pyre, shimmered into bat form, and flew outside, dodging the burning draperies, just as the bolt on the door gave way.

The elf left behind the bloody scene and escaped into the welcoming dampness of the night, bitterly musing on what had just happened. Strahd hated weakness; Jander knew that this whole thing had been staged for his benefit.

He felt the bloody tears start, and he tried not to think of Merrydale and the horror that had happened there so many centuries ago. Of course, the memory returned.

*   *   *   *   *

The red dragon of the Dales was dead, thanks to the adventuring group that called themselves the Silver Six. Merrydale treated the heroes accordingly, opening

the Swan's Song Inn to them free of charge. Jander and
his companions—Gideon of Waterdeep, Trumper
Hillhollow, Lyria "The Lovely," Kellian Graycloud, and
Alinora Malina—were surprised and pleased with their
reception. When Jander had suggested they rest up in
the hospitable dale before moving on to new adven-
tures, no one had objected.

That had been three days ago. Trumper's thieving
habits had since gotten him in trouble with the law, although the halfling had managed to talk his way out of it.
Golden-haired Lyria had received two marriage proposals
and many propositions, and had found the attention so
annoying she'd threatened to turn her latest suitor into a
leucrotta. "Your breath is bad enough already," she told
the humiliated young man. Shy, dark-haired Alinora and
the even more reserved ranger Kellian were getting better
acquainted, and Jander and the cleric Gideon merely
roamed about the town together.

Tonight, the Silver Six were gathered at the Swan's
Song for a leisurely dinner. A trio of musicians performed by the fire that snapped and blazed warmly in
the large hearth. The happy chatter of a relieved town
filled the room with a comforting buzz. The serving
maid was prompt, polite, and comely. It was an idyllic
setting for a pleasant evening with good friends.

Trumper blithely packed away enough for any two
other people, and the rest of the Six were enjoying the
fine fare. All except Kellian, whose blue eyes were circled with purple rings and whose normally tanned face
appeared unusually pale.

"Does your throat still hurt?" Alinora asked, concern
in her hazel eyes. Shyly she laid her rough warrior's
hand over his. Kellian nodded listlessly, stirring the
broth Jander had ordered for him with his spoon. The
ranger had complained of a sore throat for days now,
and with each passing hour he grew more exhausted.

"Probably picked up something from those bug
bites," Trumper said with his mouth full, waving a chick-
en leg at the two tiny marks on Kellian's neck.

"Sorry, Jander, but I can't eat this," the ranger said in a hollow voice, pushing his bowl away. Lyria frowned, her emerald eyes narrowing, but she said nothing.

"Try," Jander urged. "How can your body fight off the infection without nourishment?"

Kellian glanced at the elf with haunted eyes. "I'm just not hungry, that's all," he murmured. "I'm going to bed. I'll be fine in the morning. All I need is a good night's sleep." Jander tried to push the bowl back in front of Kellian, concealing his shock when his hand touched his friend's wrist. Despite the fact that Jander had commandeered the table closest to the huge, well-tended hearth fire, Kellian's flesh was icy cold.

The ranger was dead in the morning, and the task of informing the rest of the companions fell upon Jander. Alinora was heartbroken. Lyria, too, was in tears, and even the halfling Trumper Hillhollow was subdued. The funeral was held that afternoon. Jander piped his friend to the eternal sleep, and the good folks of Merrydale, sympathetic to the strangers' grief, would not take a copper in return for laying the unfortunate Kellian to rest.

The next morning Alinora woke up with a sore throat. She, too, was looking pale and had the same curious insect bites on her throat as Kellian had. Jander was definitely worried. He made it a point to ask around the town and discovered that fully a quarter of the populace was coming down with this mysterious malady. "I don't like this," said Gideon when they stopped in at the Swan's Song for their noon meal. "This is no natural sickness."

Jander took a sip of his wine. The crowd at the tavern that afternoon was scarce, due to the large number of would-be patrons down with the illness that was rampaging through the town. Gideon, a bear of a man who had been a warrior until one of the gods had called him into service, stared at the amber ale before him. "Alinora didn't respond when I tried to cure her," he said, his voice low. The priest raised sad brown eyes.

Jander tried not to let his surprise show. Gideon was a cleric of great skill and tenderness, despite his gruff

demeanor. Jander had never seen anyone fail to rise after Gideon had pleaded with Ilmater on their behalf.
"Maybe she really isn't that sick," he suggested, knowing how feeble the excuse sounded. He couldn't meet
Gideon's eyes. Ilmater was the god of the martyr, patron
of all who suffered. It was inconceivable that he would
not wish to ease Alinora's pain.

When Alinora, too, died quietly in the night, Gideon
was devastated. This time, the folk of the dale accepted
money for disposal of the body; far too many corpses
were accumulating for them not to. Slim, pretty, tom-
boyish Alinora was buried in a shabby coffin that had
been built hastily, and Jander saw Gideon's eyes grow
shiny with tears when the elf piped a dirge for the second fallen comrade.

Back at the Swan's Song, Jander noticed that many
of the patrons who had before bought them rounds of
ale now stole covert, hostile glances. "I think we may
have overstayed our welcome," he said quietly to Lyria.

The mage flipped her long blond hair out of her perfect
face. "I agree with Jander. Who's for leaving tomorrow?"

"Me," said Trumper. "Soon as they stop paying for my
beer, I'm gone."

Jander turned to Gideon. The cleric was staring,
brooding, at the fire. His bushy brown beard hid the
frown that Jander knew was on his best friend's lips.
"Gideon?" the elf prompted.

"I heard you," Gideon snapped, his rough tone failing
to hide his pain. "Yes. Let's leave this place."

Jander's silver eyes met Lyria's green ones. This
whole tragedy, they both knew, had been hardest on the
cleric.

The next morning the entire town was under quaran-
tine, and the group wouldn't be able to leave for at least
another week. The populace was dying off at a staggering rate, too many to bury adequately. Some suggested
that the corpses be burned to cut down on the spread of
infection. The more superstitious in town concluded
that the recently buried corpses should be dug up and

burned alongside the freshly dead. A bonfire was lit that night, and the bodies—some fresh, some a few days old—were heaped upon it. Various clerics came and intoned a few words. The remaining inhabitants of the town glanced at the four strangers nervously, and Jander's sharp elven ears caught hostile muttering.

Shattering the silence of the mourners came a howl of pain and rage, the like of which Jander had never heard and which he prayed he would never hear again. He gasped, his silver eyes going wide with astonishment and terror.

The corpses on the pyre were moving.

Filled with a purposeful animation, they were hurrying as best they could to escape the flames. Some were partly burned already and bellowed their pain, shuffling monstrosities of rotting and charred flesh. Others were intact and began to leap upon the mourners. Jander dimly noticed Lyria beginning to chant a spell as he raced back to the inn to get his sword. When he came thundering down the stairs and out into the street, he skidded to a halt.

Alinora was there, waiting for him. Her innocence had ripened and rotted into lasciviousness, but there was nothing attractive about her well-toned figure anymore. Her short, dark hair was matted with blood and filth. The red mouth opened, and Jander saw long, sharp fangs as she sprang at him.

He swung at her with his sword, managing to cut deeply into her torso. She shrieked in agony, but the injury served only to enrage her. Alinora reached out her long, sword-strengthened arms and seized the elf in a powerful grip. Red eyes blazed with hate-filled light, but Jander's elven blood was protection against her hypnotic gaze. The gold elf continued to struggle, grateful that he would at least die fighting.

The vampiress's strength was staggering, and Jander knew he could not break free. Alinora bared her teeth, preparing to sink them into his neck. Jander heard a sharp cry behind him.

"Begone, demon!"

Alinora shrieked and cringed. Abruptly released from her unnatural grip, Jander tumbled to the earth. The vampiress hissed angrily, thwarted, and her form dissolved into mist. She was gone, for the moment.

The elf peered up at his savior. Through the flickering light of the torches that lined the street, he recognized the strong features of Gideon, who had been brandishing a medallion etched with the crossed hands of Ilmater. "Thank you, my old friend," the elf breathed, letting himself be helped up.

Gideon examined his neck and wrists with narrowed eyes. "Did she?" Jander shook his head. "Good. Jander, do you understand what's happening here and what we've got to do?"

Jander nodded, his face solemn. "Vampires have invaded Merrydale. We've got to send their souls to rest." It sounded like a brave and noble venture, and perhaps it was, but the elf discovered that he was totally unprepared for the sheer, wracking horror that was vampire-kind. Evil was easier to deal with when it was an ugly, inhuman creature than when it took the shape of a friend.

The elven warrior and the fighter-turned-priest clung to one another as they hesitantly made their way to the nearest holy house. Though Jander knew that a temple to Tymora, Lady Luck, was just around the corner, the brief trip took an agonizingly long time. Unearthly sounds filled the night air: shrieks and moans and, most hideous of all, malicious, nearly human laughter. Some of the undead tried to approach them, only to hiss in furious surprise when they encountered Gideon, wielding the power of his martyr god.

Some of the dalefolk had reached Tymora's house before the heroes and had locked the door securely against the night creatures. As Gideon and Jander banged with growing frustration and fear on the heavy oaken door, a familiar voice came from behind them.

"Move aside and guard my back!" Lyria commanded, her eyes slitted and her full mouth hard. She muttered something underneath her breath, then clapped her hands three times. The door swung open to reveal dozens of frightened dalefolk cowering within.

"Come on, what are you waiting for?" Lyria asked her companions, tossing her blond tresses. "It's only vampires who need invitations!" They hurried inside, hauling the door closed behind them. Lyria and another wizard began magically sealing the door, while Gideon sought out the skittish priestess of Tymora.

"Wondering when you folks would make it here," Trumper greeted Jander. His tone was light, but there was affection in his grip when he shook the elf's hand.

After a sleepless, terror-fraught night, Jander and his companions began stalking the vampires as soon as the sun touched the horizon. The dalefolk, somehow blaming the Silver Six for their sudden misfortune, were more of a hindrance than a help, although their own clerics and soldiers dispatched many of the undead.

Trumper, agile and sharp-eyed, ferreted out the creatures' coffins. Some hiding places were obvious; graveyards and crypts yielded several fresh-looking, bloody-mouthed corpses. The halfling also found vampires in more unlikely places, such as the wine cellar of the Swan's Song. "Fitting name," Trumper mused as Jander pounded a stake into a vampire child's heart. Jander swallowed his disgust, taking what relief he could in the expression of peace that settled upon the little girl's dead face as her soul was released.

With a sigh, the elf dragged his arm across his sweaty forehead, sitting down on the cold stone and leaning his aching back against a wine barrel. He was exhausted. The four of them had slain fifteen of the ghastly beings today. "I feel like I've been doing this for a year," he groaned. "What's the hour, anyway?"

Wine the color of blood drenched Jander as powerful white arms tore through the wine barrel at his back. The elf barely had time to react as the icy hands of the vampire locked on his throat. With all his strength, Jander flung himself forward, yanking the vampire off balance, pulling the creature down after him, down among the shattered barrel staves. The sharp pieces of broken wood pierced the belly of the monster, and it writhed and howled, its savage grip momentarily weakened.

A moment was all Gideon needed. The priest of Ilmater pulled his friend out of the way with one hand and impaled the vampire on a broken barrel stave with the other. The creature gasped and flailed as blood mixed with wine. It convulsed once, spat blood, and lay still.

Jander hugged Gideon tightly, both of them gasping to catch their breath. "Gentlemen . . ." came Lyria's voice, tighter and higher-pitched than usual.

"What is it, Lyria?" Gideon asked. The beautiful mage, her face pale, pointed at the vampire they had just destroyed. Jander closed his eyes in sympathy when he recognized the wine-stained body as that of Kellian.

That night there was no time to make it to the temple. Gideon drew a circle in which they were able to take turns catnapping in safety. The next day was similar to the first, save that they divided forces. Lyria and Gideon took one side of the town, Jander and Trumper the other. The elf didn't like the idea very much. "There's strength in numbers, Lyria," he protested, but everyone else agreed with the plan.

That night, Trumper and Jander made it to Tymora's Temple before sundown. It was nearly midnight when Lyria joined them, her lavender gown bloody and torn and a wild look in her eye. "They almost got us that time," she gasped as Jander eased her down on the rushes and Trumper expertly began to tend to her scratches. The elf inspected her throat and wrists; she didn't appear to be bitten. Lyria closed her eyes and lay back into Jander's lap. She was obviously near collapse.

"Where's Gideon?" the elf asked. Lyria's green eyes opened, and Jander saw fear in their emerald depths.

"He's not with you?"

Trumper, for once, didn't say anything, but kept his eyes on Lyria's cuts and scrapes. Jander began to tremble. "No, he's not here. . . ."

"There are other churches open to those seeking shelter," Lyria offered, her slim strong hand reaching for Jander's gold one. "I'm sure he's—"

"What if he's not?" Jander's words came out as a shout, and more than a few heads turned in his direction. The elf didn't care. He and Gideon had been friends for over ten years. Jander's mind went back to the days when the two had been HellRiders of Elturel and had fought Tiamat in her own lair. It was then that Ilmater had come to Gideon, and the mighty warrior had gladly put aside his sword. Since then, they had been inseparable, riding wherever they were needed, but always together.

Jander didn't notice that he had begun to silently weep, crystal tears meandering down his sharp-featured face. Neither did he notice when Lyria took him in her arms, laying his head on her breast and rocking him into a fitful slumber that was haunted by blood-red sunsets and corpses who wouldn't stay dead.

They had no chance to discover what had happened to Gideon, for the three strangers were driven out the next morning. Less than a week earlier, they had been heroes in a town that had for centuries been synonymous with hospitality. There had been no locks on any doors and no stranger had gone hungry. Now the folk of Merrydale ruthlessly expelled all but their own to face the dangers of the night. The remnants of the Silver Six, now a pathetic three, made it to the next village, where they went their separate ways.

Merrydale had been ravaged by a pack of malicious, clever vampires who had deliberately capitalized on the dale's reputation. The folk never recovered from it. They built a huge wall around the town, and Jander later learned that every inn was symbolically burned. Their habit of constantly wearing daggers was remarked upon and became a standing joke in other lands. Thus Merrydale, the most welcoming community in Faerun, had become the most aloof and hostile: it became known as Daggerdale.

 **THIRTEEN**

Despite his trepidation Kolya had fallen asleep and was snoring loudly. Sasha's eyelids, too, were growing heavy, but he was firmly determined to keep watch all night long. There'd be plenty of time to sleep after the sun rose. He hadn't seen *anything* even remotely exciting tonight, and he was darned if—the boy frowned. The ring of stones was set atop a small hill. It was enough of a vantage point that Sasha was able to see a light over in the village where there shouldn't be any.

Curiosity chased away the ghosts of sleep, and Sasha got to his feet for a better look. He still couldn't see clearly, so he clambered atop the nearest large stone. Trying to keep his balance, he eased himself up, arms extended, and peered at the village. Yes, there was definitely a light—and a lot of people were awake.

"Hey, Kolya, wake up!"

"Huh?" the other boy muttered.

Sasha didn't spare him a glance, but kept his eyes fastened on the commotion in town. "Something's going on. Let's find out."

"Oh, no." Wide awake and remembering where they were, Kolya wasn't about to budge. "I'm not leaving here till morning."

His friend glared at him. "Fine. I'm going. You can stay here all by yourself for the rest of the night, Cow-

ardly Kolya." Sasha jumped off the stone and began to
pile his belongings back into the sack. Muttering under
his breath, Kolya followed suit, and the two boys
tramped to the village. The night seemed somehow less
hostile than it had before, now that curiosity about what
had happened in town pushed to the forefront of
Sasha's mind.

When they got to Market Street, lights were on in the
houses, and people still clad in their nightclothes were
milling about. Several were carrying buckets. Sasha saw
the town seamstress, Cristina, throw open the shutters
and yell something to someone across the street. Cristina's brown hair, normally fastidiously pinned back,
tumbled wildly about her shoulders, and her sharp face
was filled with worry. Something was definitely wrong,
and the two boys followed the scurrying villagers.

"Burgomaster's Way!" Sasha cried and took off at a
dead run down the street that led to his home. Kolya
followed laboriously.

It was the longest distance that the half-gypsy boy
had ever traveled in his short life, those four hundred
yards from the square to the flaming house. The image
loomed ahead of him like a bad dream, the orange-red
flames licking the sides of the two-story mansion like a
dog slobbering over a bone. His legs were like rubber,
and his throat was raw from calling "Mama! Mama!" as
he ran, praying for speed when he knew there was no
way he could get there in time.

Rastolnikov grabbed him by the arm. "Easy, lad,
easy," he bellowed in what was meant to be a gentle
tone. Sasha was crying, from fear and from the acrid
black smoke that filled his eyes and lungs. He coughed,
feeling as though his lungs would be expelled with each
wracking heave. Rastolnikov placed a cloth about
Sasha's mouth. "That'll filter out some of the ash," he
told the boy.

Sasha rubbed his eyes furiously, trying to clear them
so he could see what had happened. The fire had now
been put out, but part of the house had been destroyed.

"Where's my family?" he demanded, trying to sound commanding and succeeding only in sounding very young and frightened. Rastolnikov didn't answer at once.

"We'll . . . tend to them in the morning, son. There's bad magic in there, too powerful for any of us to challenge tonight," the baker said cryptically.

"Is that the boy?" came a hard, angry voice. Rough hands grabbed Sasha, and pulled him away from the baker. "It's him!" Sasha found himself looking up at Andrei the butcher, who fixed him with a hateful gaze. "This is all your fault!"

The stunned boy couldn't even form a reply. "Vistani vengeance!" came another voice, shrill and female. "That gypsy that Anastasia was with. Kartov beat him, and now look! Remember, the gypsy cursed Kartov? Remember? And did you see what happened to them? Dear gods, their throats . . ." The woman who had spoken began to sob. The people around Sasha drew back, murmuring prayers and making signs against the Evil Eye.

Sasha looked again at the charred house. He stood up a little straighter. "I'm going inside," he said to anyone who would listen. He turned to Kolya, who had finally caught up with him. "Are you coming?"

Kolya looked up at Rastolnikov, who shook his head. The boy glanced back at his playmate, then averted his eyes. "No, Sasha. Guess I am a coward."

Sasha stared at his friend. "I guess you are, Kolya," he said slowly, not wanting to believe it. He tied the handkerchief about his face to screen out what smoke he could and leave his hands free.

Alone, Sasha walked toward what had once been his home. The angry, frightened crowd parted for him, muttering as they did so. The boy moved through the open wrought iron gates, across the now-wet cobblestone courtyard, and up to the door. The bucket brigade had broken it open in order to get inside, and the flames had blackened the thick wood. Gingerly the boy stepped through the jagged hole they had made, ducking his head to avoid the sharp edges. The wood was wet, but Sasha could still feel the heat.

He looked down as he entered, and it was then that he noticed the crimson footprints.

They appeared and disappeared through the still-thick, black smoke that swirled sluggishly throughout the room. Made by a pair of boots, the footprints descended the stairs and continued on out the door. Red blood now stained the carpeting that Grandmama so prized. Sasha's heart began to thump erratically, filling his chest so that he could hardly breathe.

Something terrible had happened here. More than anything at that moment, as Sasha stared at the bloody footprint, the child wanted his mother. He wanted to hug her, feel her hands smoothing his hair. Sasha took a deep breath, straightened up, and looked around.

A whimper began in his throat. His mother was there, all right, and so were his grandparents. They were half-charred bodies on a pile of lumber, still smoking and giving off a terrible burned-meat stench. Sasha's knees gave way. He barely had time to tear off the handkerchief before he threw up violently. He cried, and he gasped, then he managed some semblance of self-control.

The boy took a few more gulps of the comparatively cool air that circulated near the floor, then wiped his mouth with his sleeve and retied the handkerchief around his face. Something his mother had once said returned like a prayer to comfort him: *You are from a proud line. You are the grandson of the leader of your village on one side, and the child of a strong, free, magical people on the other. When the children tease you about the legitimacy of your birth, smile to yourself and remember what I have said.* Sasha got to his feet.

He didn't want to, but he took a few steps toward the smoking bodies. His family had been murdered, that much was clear, but how? And by whom? Sasha identified only three corpses—his grandparents and his mother. He felt bile rise in his throat again when he saw that their throats had been savaged, but he swallowed hard.

The manner of their deaths raised more questions. If they had been killed by wolves, as seemed apparent, who had tried to burn the corpses? Surely not the villagers. And where was the rest of the household?

Still feeling weak from nausea and the smoke, Sasha opened the side door which led into the servant's quarters. He moaned and leaned against the door for support. The torches flickering in their sconces provided ample if eerily distorted illumination. Here, too, were signs of slaughter. Ivan, the burgomaster's valet, lay sprawled on the stone floor. He somehow managed to still look dignified and imposing even though a chunk of flesh had been ripped from his throat. There was very little blood.

Sasha dragged his eyes from the floor and quickly noticed that the maids, cook, grooms and stable boys had also had their throats mangled. Part of Sasha's brain shrieked for him to panic, to mourn; he had known these people very well, after all. Another part of him, however, seemed frozen and calculating, and it was to this part that Sasha clung as he finished his grisly tour.

The half-gypsy boy left the servant's quarters shaken, but determined to continue with his investigation. Only one person remained unaccounted for: his aunt, Ludmilla. He walked past the piled bodies, keeping his head turned away from the sight, and stopped before the wide staircase. A torch burned steadily on the wall beside the steps. Sasha gently lifted it from its sconce and gripped it hard. He paused a moment, steadied himself, and began to ascend.

The firelight cast strange shadows that appeared and disappeared as he climbed. His heart beat even faster, and Sasha wiped suddenly damp palms on his breeches. The cold part of him was starting to melt, and the boy could sense the panic huddled at the back of his wounded soul waiting to burst forth.

He reached the top of the stairs and stopped, looking down the dark hall. The smoke was thicker up here than it had been on the floor below, and it moved in languid gray and black swirls, obscuring his vision and making his eyes water. Sasha could picture things hiding behind that protective shield of smoke. . . . Angrily he stilled his imagination and almost defiantly stepped into his room, thrusting the torch before him.

Nothing had been touched in the boy's room. His small bed was still neatly made, his toys and clothes remained out of sight in the large trunk. Yet everything had changed in the last few hours for the room's inhabitant. Sasha closed the door as he stepped back into the hallway.

The next room was where his Aunt Ludmilla and his mother slept. Sasha knew what had happened to Anastasia, and for an instant the panic got a foothold in his brain. Again, Sasha forced the fear down. He stood before the door for a long moment, trembling, wondering what was on the other side. Then he grasped the doorknob in his small hand, turned it as quietly as he could, and gently pushed the door open.

Moonlight streamed in through the opened window, silvering the room. There was a shape in Aunt Ludmilla's bed. As Sasha stood by the door, starting at the lump, it moved slightly.

Sasha almost lost control. What was in that bed?

A little whimper escaped him, and he bit his lip hard, tensing. The shape in his aunt's bed didn't move again. Shakily Sasha moved toward the form, his trembling hands making the torch dance crazily. He stood beside the bed. The shape had covered itself with the blanket. Before he could change his mind, the boy leaped forward, pulled the bedding down, then jumped out of range.

Aunt Ludmilla slept quietly. Sasha could see her rhythmic breathing. The boy let out the breath he had been holding.

"Aunt Milla!" he cried, reaching to shake her. It was then that he noticed how pale she was, whiter almost than the sheets upon which she lay. As he shook her, frantically trying to wake her, her head lolled to the side and her dark hair fell away from her throat.

Two holes, small and cleanly made, were visible in her neck.

He was a tall, pale man, with sharp teeth and claws. 'Stop!' said Nosferatu, for so Pavel knew it to be. 'Stop, that I may drink your blood and live upon your death.'

Nosferatu, Sasha thought, horror rushing through him. The First Guardian of Darkness. *Vampire.*

This time, the panic broke through. A cry welled in his throat, but somehow remained there. By some miracle, Sasha kept hold of the torch. He stumbled backward against the door, closing it. For a mindless instant Sasha pounded on the door before his reason reminded him that there was a knob. He turned it and sped out into the corridor. Luck alone saved him from a tumble down the blood-marked stairs. "Help!" he shrieked, finally getting a sound past the block in his throat as he dove for the damaged door and the sweet air outside.

Rastolnikov had been waiting for him and helped him outside. Sasha clung to the baker, jabbering incoherently. "Calm down, lad. Calm down and speak clearly," Rastolnikov boomed.

"Nosferatu!" Sasha gasped. "They were all killed by nosferatu! Come on, we've got to, got to . . ." He couldn't remember the legends, something about stakes in their hearts and cutting off their heads.

Sasha collapsed, and the baker, with a gentleness that belied his build, carefully picked him up.

"Not nosferatu," came a hostile voice from the crowd. "Vistani vengeance! Leave the boy to whatever horrors his people have brought here!"

"Vladimir," the baker's wife said, "you cannot take the boy in."

"He has no family!" Rastolnikov retorted.

"Then let him wander as the Lost Ones do, or else let the Vistani take him back," his wife replied, meaty hands on her sizable hips. "No one in the village will buy our bread if you shelter this bad luck boy in our home!"

The big baker ran a tongue around his lips. His wife was right. No good could come from a half-gypsy mon-

grel. Rastolnikov's wife had always been of the opinion
that Burgomaster Kartov ought to have disowned Anastasia, or at least made her turn her pup over to the Vistani. Rastolnikov was well aware that Sasha had caused
more mischief in the village than any three other boys
put together. Yet there was something quite pathetic
about the child lying unconscious in his arms. Without
the fire of his personality, the ten-year-old seemed almost birdlike in his delicacy, the bones underneath the
dark skin fragile and easily breakable.

With a sigh, Rastolnikov placed Sasha back on the
ground. The boy's eyelids fluttered and opened. Black
eyes fastened on the baker's face. "You're not going to
help me, are you?"

Rastolnikov's wife coughed. "No, lad, I can't," the
baker said, genuine regret in his voice.

The boy's lower lip quivered, and tears began to pour
down his face. Sasha could have sworn that he had exhausted his supply of tears, but somehow the droplets
kept coming. "P-please," he begged, his voice low and
trembling, "if you don't help me, they're going to come
get me, too!"

"Aye, and so they should, gypsy's bastard!" Someone
cried. A gobbet of spit landed on Sasha's face. With the
dignity of one much older, the boy wiped away the of-
fensive matter and stood unsteadily. "Go back to your
own kind!"

Other curses were shouted, but Sasha ignored them.
He walked stiffly to where he had dropped his sack and
rummaged through it. He took his time, and some of
the people watching him spitefully lost interest and returned to the safety of their homes. Still more left when
a stinging, needling summer rain began to fall. Finally,
Sasha was alone with his preparations.

A half-hour later, the boy stood in front of the broken
door to his home, looking like some childish caricature
of a vampire hunter. He was soaked to the skin, his silky
hair plastered to his skull. He had taken both his and
Kolya's garlic wreaths and draped them around his

neck. All the wooden disks adorned his neck, as well. Corked bottles of holy water were in his pants pocket, within easy reach. One of his small hands clutched a clumsily sharpened stake; the other held a hammer that was almost too heavy for him to carry.

"Are you sure you know what to do?"

Sasha looked around, surprised, and saw the tall, thin figure of Brother Martyn standing beside him. The cleric's pink and gold robes hung loosely about his slight frame, and his eyes were on fire with zeal. But his smile, as he looked down at the boy, was kind. Martyn, too, wore a variety of holy symbols and carried a bag that rattled woodenly when he moved. "Why don't you let me take that hammer," the priest offered. Sasha stared, unable to believe that anyone had taken his side in this nightmare.

Sasha's family hadn't been particularly religious. No one in Barovia was; with all the dreadful things that happened in the haunted land, few believed in the old gods anymore. When Brother Martyn had appeared from the Svalich Woods several years ago, babbling about the Morninglord, no one had believed him, but he had been permitted to live in the abandoned church as long as he didn't violate any of the town's laws. Sasha had always thought that Martyn was a little crazed. That didn't seem to matter now. Sasha burst into fresh tears of hope and hugged the cleric tightly. Martyn hesitated, then tentatively stroked Sasha's dark head. "Lathander is with us," he murmured to the child. "He will help us destroy our foes."

As he steeled himself to re-enter the charnel house that had been his home, Sasha Petrovich prayed fervently.

They stepped inside. Nothing had changed. The sinister scarlet footprints still descended the stairs. The oppressive, expectant silence still filled the air. Brusquely, unaffected by the sight, Martyn examined the bodies. "They have been drained of blood," he said coldly. "If they are buried, they will rise again as undead themselves. Hand me a stake and some garlic."

The cleric pulled the first body off of the blackened wood, tugging it free. Sasha turned away, his stomach roiling. The corpse was Anastasia. Her right arm had been charred and her clothes almost burned away. The right side of her face was also seared, and her hair had been scorched. Swiftly and efficiently Martyn laid her out on the carpeted floor. He glanced at Sasha, who had sat down with his knees pulled up to his chest.

"You do this one."

The boy's eyes widened with revulsion. "No!"

"Yes," Martyn insisted, going to the boy and kneeling beside him. "She's your mother. The hand of the one who loved her best should strike the blow that sets her free."

"But she's . . . No, Martyn, no. I can't!"

"You must. The rest will be sweeter to her for it. Trust me, Sasha." He fitted the stake into the boy's numb hand and folded the small brown fingers about it. "Trust me."

As one in a dream, Sasha rose and approached his mother's body. He tried to remember her as she had been in life—brave, sweet, loving, but always a bit sad. He knelt beside her, blinking away the tears, and positioned the pointed end of the stake between her breasts, directly over the heart. Sasha raised the hammer, then lowered his arm. "I can't do it, Martyn."

"You fail your mother, then," the priest replied, his face expressionless. Sasha shot him a hot, angry glance, but Martyn said, "You are denying her peace and condemning her to a horrible existence."

"You do it."

"I won't." Martyn sat down and stared at Sasha with uncanny pale blue eyes. "This is your task."

The boy realized that the slightly mad priest was serious. If he didn't plunge the stake into Anastasia's heart, Martyn would leave her to her fate. It made Sasha angry, and he took that anger and channeled it into strength. Gritting his teeth, he brought the hammer crashing down with all his ten-year-old might.

It was enough; the stake went deep into the chest cavity. Sasha half-expected Martyn to have miscalculated and the body to rise up against him, but the corpse only twitched with the force of the blow. Again Sasha struck. What blood was left in the sapped body oozed out of Anastasia's mouth. A third blow, and Sasha felt the tip of the wood hit the stone beneath the body.

His mother was not a vampire, but the soul had been trapped nonetheless. When Sasha looked again at Anastasia's features, they had changed subtly, and a faint trace of wonder brushed the boy's soul. The stories were true. The spirit did reclaim peace. Horrendous though the task had been, much good had come from it. He wiped the sweat out of his eyes with a hand that trembled, but his child's mouth was set in a firm line.

He rose, leaving the stake still in Anastasia's heart. "Well done, my child," said Martyn, gently placing soft, pale hands on Sasha's shoulders. "You have done great good here today."

The boy sagged, leaning against Martyn's body for support. "I understand, Martyn. Thank you. It was really hard, but . . . thank you."

"I shall attend to the rest of the ritual," Martyn offered. Sasha winced, knowing what the priest had to do to Anastasia's body before the gruesome ritual was completed. Martyn would cut off her head and stuff her mouth with garlic. Only then could she be safely buried. "Can you do the same to the rest of these poor people?"

Sasha stared at the bodies of his grandparents, then nodded slowly. "Yes, Martyn."

They worked together throughout the day. When Sasha's arms got tired, Martyn instructed him to put garlic in the mouths of all the bodies to which the priest had not yet attended, while he finished the bloody work by himself. When dusk settled on the land, the boy and the priest found that their arms ached, their clothing was drenched with blood that stuck to them as it dried, and their bodies shook with exhaustion.

Yet Martyn was filled with a sense of exultation. Surely he had been put here to do Lathander Morninglord's work. The bloody task he had just completed had not unnerved him in the slightest. Sasha, however, was wrung out. His nerves had been stretched to the breaking point. Martyn put a sympathetic arm around the boy's shoulders as they sat on the stairs.

"Let me tell you a story, my son, that might help you make sense of all this," Martyn indicated the beheaded corpses. "Once, there was a young child, just about your age, who lived a very happy life with his family. They were traveling to another town when suddenly mists surrounded them. They stopped for the night.

"When the mists cleared, they were in a completely unfamiliar forest. The people in the nearby town were cold and unfriendly and wouldn't give the group shelter. With nowhere else to go, they tried to spend the night in the forest." Martyn fell silent for a time, his fey eyes distant.

"Brother Martyn?" Sasha prompted.

Martyn stirred himself and continued. "The boy woke up to a hideous sight. One hundred wolves, all twice as big as normal wolves, surrounded the little camp. Beautiful women were kissing the boy's uncles, but when they raised their heads the boy saw that they were really just drinking their victims' blood. Naturally the boy began to scream at the sight. A tall man, as white as death and as black as night, gazed at him with flaming red eyes. The man moved toward the boy, slowly, and the boy knew that he was going to die.

"The boy's mother pleaded with the evil man, but he ordered his wolves to eat her. He was about to kill the boy when suddenly, Lathander Morninglord appeared." Martyn had completely forgotten Sasha in his ecstatic trance. His face was aglow with an inner light as he spoke. "The boy had seen pictures of the god, so he recognized him by his beautiful face and golden skin and hair. Lathander, too, had blood on his face, but he stopped the dark man from killing the child.

"'You shall not have the boy,' said the Morninglord in tones of music. 'Nor shall you suffer your evil women to feast upon him. Let him go, for he is under My protection and guidance.' And the evil dark man bowed before the power of the Morninglord, and the boy lived to see the dawn."

"That happened to you?" Sasha asked.

Martyn looked down at him and nodded. "As I live and breathe, I swear the tale is true."

"If the Morninglord is so good, why was his face bloody?"

"Often I have asked myself that. I believe that this land is so dark, that nothing completely good can dwell here. Lathander Morninglord himself is changed when he comes to Barovia. He is a little evil, because this land is evil, but he is mainly a god of goodness, of hope and renewal. He saved me. And, Sasha." Martyn looked at the boy intently. "I think, terrible though this has been for you, that it was for a purpose. I think you have been called. You have no family now. Would you like to come and live in the Morninglord's house? I would raise you, and teach you the true path."

Sasha gazed at Martyn, his black eyes searching the priest's blue ones. Was it true? Was there finally a place for him in this unfriendly village?

"Sasha," came a thin voice behind them. As one, Martyn and Sasha wheeled around.

Ludmilla stood at the head of the stairs, looking like a ghost. She was pale, and her sleeping chemise draped her like a shroud. Her brown eyes stood out darkly against the white of her skin.

Martyn was stunned. How could a vampire walk in the daylight? He felt for his vial of holy water. With a cry of "Die, demon!" the priest charged up the stairs. He grabbed Ludmilla's wrist with one hand and poured the vial of water over her torso with the other.

Ludmilla glanced down at the dampness on her chemise and covered herself. "Brother Martyn, what *are* you doing?"

Sasha began to laugh. Ludmilla wasn't dead! He ran to embrace her.

 **FOURTEEN**

The years following the attack on the burgomaster passed like so many minutes during Jander's stay at Castle Ravenloft, and time blurred the intensity of the elf's desire for revenge. After all, fifteen years meant little to a being who had expected to experience hundreds as a mortal, even less to an undead creature who sadly looked forward to eternal existence.

Not so for the human inhabitants of Barovia.

The fall sky was a cloudless, bright blue, and the red and rust hues of the leaves made for a pleasing contrast. The rain that had fallen the night before yielded a morning rich in the fragrance of damp earth. Leisl breathed deeply of the fresh scent, brushed a stray lock of mousy brown hair off her face, and took a huge bite out of the apple she'd just stolen from the fruit cart.

Market day in the autumn was a thief's paradise. There was so much going on and so many different items to steal that the cutpurse known as the Little Fox hardly knew where to begin. She figured the apple was a good start and took another bite as her quick hazel eyes flickered about.

In addition to the usual wares on display—Kolya's pastries, Andrei's fresh cuts of meat, Cristina's fabrics—the farmers from the outlying areas came into town in the fall. Shiny, newly harvested apples were everywhere to be seen. Carts brimmed with potatoes, cabbages, and turnips. Others were filled with pumpkins and squash. Just arriving was a fisherman with a string of salted trout on lines that stretched across his wagon. Leisl's mouth watered. She loved trout, fried in a pan with garlic, onions, and pepper . . .

The clop-clop of hooves behind her caused Leisl to turn, and a gaily colored gypsy wagon clattered into the square. Tethered to the back of the wagon and struggling to keep pace were two dozen bleating sheep. The Vistani driving the wagon was whistling merrily, but his shepherd passenger merely glowered. The Little Fox's sharp features softened as she grinned to herself. The shepherd was likely cursing at the ten gold pieces the Vistani had charged him to carry him through the choking fog.

Another few bites, and Leisl finished her apple. She dropped it into the makeshift pigpen one of the farmers had constructed to showcase his pink, oinking wares. A big sow lumbered over to the core and snuffled at it.

More horses were coming down the muddy path from the farm areas, and Leisl thought she saw a young foal with dark golden coat and a flaxen mane. Was it really a sorrel? Hardly anyone in Barovia bred sorrels. Leisl noticed the gypsy wagon driver sitting up and peering at the approaching steeds with an appraising gaze. Wanting a better look at the three-month-old foal herself, Leisl clambered atop the pig pen.

"Hey! Boy! Get off of there before you fall in!" Leisl knew it was the pig owner, and she turned to face him with an apologetic grin.

"Sorry, sir, I was just looking at—whoa!" Leisl's arms flailed as she tried to keep her balance. She cast a terrified glance at the filthy sty. Muttering, the farmer reached a thick arm to steady her and help her down. "Thanks a lot, sir," she apologized. "I'd have hated to fall in there."

"Aye, well, don't go standing on other people's property, and it won't happen," the farmer snapped, glaring at her and shaking his head. Leisl touched her cap politely and strode off, easily merging with the swarm of people and animals in the square.

The Little Fox put her hands in her pockets and fingered the coins she had just stolen from the pig farmer. By the size and shape, she guess it was two coppers and a silver. Not bad, but she could do better, and would by sunset today.

Slim and athletic, nineteen-year-old Leisl had often been mistaken for a boy. It suited her just fine, and she fostered the illusion by wearing men's clothing. Because of the unseasonably warm weather today, she wore a loose cotton shirt with the sleeves rolled up, brown breeches and brown, knee-high leather boots. On top of her head, disguising her short ponytail, was a small black cap. Everything about her appearance bespoke the ordinary. Average height, slender build, mouse-brown hair, muddy hazel eyes—that was Leisl. The very incarnation of nondescript, there was nothing memorable about her at all. That, her uncanny ability to be in the right place at the right time, and her light-fingeredness made the Little Fox a fine thief.

She had taken up "the profession," as her small circle of associates called it, through necessity. After twelve years at thieving, Leisl was a master of it. She'd learned to recognize who was gullible and who was too clever to get near, who carried a lot of money and who didn't, and . . . She narrowed her green-brown eyes. And, she thought to herself, who was a stranger in town.

A handsome young gypsy on a sleek black mare had galloped into the square with a grin on his dark face. Clinging to him was a pretty young woman, who looked around fearfully with large, deer-soft brown eyes. No sooner had the spirited mare come to a halt than the Vistani slipped off her back and extended his arms to help the young woman down. Leisl snorted as she observed the gypsy contriving to press the girl's ripe figure against him frequently.

The silly girl seemed too innocent to even have noticed. Leisl leaned up against the side of the Wolf's Den tavern and watched, amused. This was better than the Midsummer play. The girl apparently thanked the gypsy and fished in her pouch for payment. The Vistani looked deeply offended and gesticulated vigorously, declining the coin the girl offered. He bent over her hand for an unusually long period of time, then reluctantly took his leave.

As he remounted the black, bell-bedecked horse, someone called out something that Leisl couldn't quite catch. The gypsy obviously heard it, though, and jabbered something back, accompanying the verbal insult with a gesture that Leisl recognized as being hardly polite for mixed company. Affronted, the gypsy galloped down the path toward his encampment.

The girl looked around helplessly before heading for the Wolf's Den, carrying a large bundle. Unobtrusively the Little Fox meandered a distance away, apparently very interested in the cabbage farmer's wares. The girl put the bundle down, adjusted her long, curly dark hair, and knocked on the door.

"Go away," the innkeeper called from within. "We don't open until midday."

"Please, sir," the girl said in a sweet, trembling voice, "I'm hoping that you might need some help. I'd like to be a barmaid."

There was a pause, and Leisl heard the innkeeper's heavy footsteps. The door creaked open, and the innkeeper's wary face peered out. He looked the girl up and down critically. "Well, you're attractive enough. I guess you'll do. Who's your father?"

The girl licked her lips nervously. "Please, sir, I'm not from the village, I'm from Vallaki. My father was a fisherman, but he drowned this summer. Mama can't make enough money sewing to support us all, and—"

The innkeeper slammed the door in the girl's face. She jumped at the loud thump, and tears filled her eyes. Slowly she bent to pick up her pack.

"Let me help you with that," came a clear masculine

voice behind Leisl. She blinked, startled, and slipped back even farther behind the cabbage cart. The Little Fox recognized that voice. It was the young priest, Brother Sasha. Leisl's heart began to beat painfully. Being around the handsome priest always made her nervous.

"Thank you, sir," said the girl in her sweet voice, beaming at him. Sasha smiled in return, hoisting the girl's pack easily despite his slight build. His crimson and pink robe trimmed with gold was belted with a yellow sash, and the delicate pastel colors contrasted sharply with his dark hair and complexion.

"Where shall I take it, my lady?"

"Oh, call me Katya, please. Actually I don't have anywhere to take it. Maybe you can tell me of someone who might need my help?" Katya's look and tone were pleading. "I'll do anything—that is—" She blushed and looked down. "Anything that's . . . you know, respectable. I can cook and clean and mend clothes. Oh, please, sir, can you help me?"

Brother Sasha smiled. "I'm sorry you haven't been able to find any work. The town is rather suspicious of strangers. I'll tell you what. Brother Martyn and I are terribly bad about cleaning the church, and neither one of us can cook. Would you like to come work for us? I'm sure we can find you a place to live here in the village, of course," he added. "We have to observe the proprieties. It wouldn't do for a lovely young lady to live with two old bachelors like us, even if we are priests."

Sasha grinned, his brown eyes bright and warm. In her hiding place, Leisl felt a heat inside that went all the way to her toes. Katya's brown eyes brimmed, and her full, pink mouth quivered. She began to cry. "Oh, sir, you're so kind. I was so afraid—"

"Please don't cry, my dear, and definitely don't call me sir. My title is Brother Sasha." He shifted the pack to one shoulder and tilted her chin up with his free hand. His dark eyes searched her face critically. "When did you last eat?"

Katya shrugged. "I don't know. Two days ago, I guess."

"Two days! Come on. We'll get some food into you, and then we'll go meet Father Martyn. All right?" Together they walked to Kolya's store, and the rest of their conversation became inaudible to the eavesdropping Leisl.

"Are you going to buy anything or are you going to just stand here and keep away the other customers?" snarled an annoyed cabbage farmer.

"Sorry," Leisl muttered, shoving her hands deep in her pockets and walking away. Without really understanding why, she suddenly wished for the sky to cloud over and the rain to start again.

*   *   *   *   *

Jander's silver eyes opened. Again he had slept clear through the day without a single dream. It was a relief, but also a torment. He had ceased dreaming about Anna a few years ago, after he had exhausted every avenue of investigation.

Sadly, the elf had come to the conclusion that the beautiful, tormented girl had been what the Barovians called a "Lost One," men or women driven to despair by the horrors they had witnessed. They wandered forlornly from town to town, seeking what mercy they could find. Wherever Jander had asked about Anna, no one had ever heard of anyone with that name who matched her description. Besides, the villagers had often asked suspiciously, why did the elf want to know about a woman who must have died over a hundred years ago anyway?

Jander couldn't tell them. He could only thank them, and continue his inquiries.

Now he rose, stretching, and looked about his room. In this one place, at least, he'd been able to make some real difference; the bedchamber had been restored, if not to opulence, to comfort. The furnishings were clean, the bed hung with sky blue and indigo curtains. A comfortable reading chair graced a corner near the window, whose sealed shutters were hidden behind lines of graceful drapery. Jander looked longingly at the window. The moon ought to be full tonight, he recalled. It would be a splendid time to visit the garden.

The straggling, dying garden that Jander had discovered nearly a quarter of a century ago was a thing of the past. He had tended it diligently, pruning and planting and experimenting with a variety of different plants. Now it was a lush green oasis for the vampire, a thing of beauty restored solely by his efforts. He sat down on the wall and surveyed the growth happily, finding a small measure of peace.

It was autumn again, time to begin pruning in preparation for winter's sleep. Jander knelt beside the white rose bush that grew near the chapel door and examined it carefully. One last flower bloomed, made unearthly in the luster of the moon's glow. Gently the elf leaned forward to smell its clean, sweet fragrance and feel the soft petals, as soft as Anna's cheek, against his face. He closed his eyes and inhaled deeply, smiling sadly.

When he pulled away, he opened his eyes and gazed at the bloom. His smile fled. The flower, which seconds before had been in full, proud bloom, had withered and died. Its petals fluttered mournfully to the ground in a silent reproach.

Stunned and horrified, Jander backed away from the rosebush. A clump of night-blooming violets were clustered near his foot. Slowly, apprehensively, he extended a golden finger and touched the purple blossoms. They wilted as he watched, and the brown of death began to seep through the green leaves. This time, he felt the tiny death of the plant like a knife in the belly.

What had happened to him? Without warning, his nurturing touch had become fatal to these flowers. The vampire clenched his hands and brought them up to his chest, as if to ensure that no other innocent flora would fall prey to his evil. Jander leaned on the stone wall, grateful for the cool, rough sensation of unfeeling dead stone beneath his golden, killing hands.

Nearly weeping, he gazed over a low wall at the moon-whitened mist slowly moving around the cliff face. There were occasional gaps through which the vampire could glimpse the jagged edges of rocks. For a moment, Jander debated leaping into the mists. He dismissed the idea almost at once. Such an action would do nothing to mitigate his pain. He could not die.

The elf found himself keenly missing the colors of the daytime. Night's palette, while beautiful, was limited. Indigo and inky black of sky and earth, pearl-white of moonshine, dark green of forests and fields—these were the only hues he could see now. What happened to sky blue? To pink, and lavender, and all the delicate daytime pigments? Gone beyond his viewing.

The vampire closed his eyes tightly, willing himself to remember the tints of the day. "Anna," he said to himself, "Please come back. I miss you so much."

He didn't know what he hoped to happen, if his longing could bring back the painful, joyous dreams in which he and his beloved enjoyed glorious dawns and sun-saturated afternoons. Jander concentrated, formed an image of Anna in his mind. Tall, beautiful, with that mane of curly auburn tumbling down her back, brown eyes full of unspoken laughter . . . *Anna*. Jander opened his eyes and gasped.

Standing in front of him was just such a woman. For an instant his mind shrieked Anna's name, but then the thought fled as he looked more closely at the girl. Dark eyes and auburn curls she had indeed, but her slight frame was much too small to be Anna. The eyes were the right hue, but the expression in them was all wrong. Her full lips curved in a sardonic smile as she gazed at him.

"Ah, Jander," Strahd purred, stepping into the elf's field of vision, "allow me to present my new friend, Miss Katrina Yakovlena Pulchenka. Trina, this is Jander Sunstar, a visitor from a far distant realm."

For an instant Jander thought that the young woman on Strahd's arm was merely another newly created vampiress, but she was emitting a curious scent that was certainly alive. As Strahd put a proprietary hand on Trina's shoulder, he literally towered over her. She was dressed in the customary clothing of the village folk, but it was obviously not made for her. Her slight figure got rather lost in it.

Yet there was nothing vulnerable in either her expression or attitude. Her eyes were bright and took everything in swiftly. She seemed to have no fear at all; that trait, in Barovia, was remarkable.

"I am pleased to make your acquaintance, Jander," she said in a voice that was pleasant but too laden with self-satisfaction to be appealing. "Strahd has told me much about you." She patted the hand Strahd had placed on her shoulder. "Is it all right if I . . . ?"

Strahd nodded, and Jander caught a glimpse of a savage smile as Trina suddenly arched her back as if gripped by a deep inner pain. Astonishingly the contortions wrought no cry from her, and the elf watched with a horrified fascination as her face lengthened into a wolf's muzzle and her limbs stretched and flexed into long, lupine legs. Her fingers and toes contracted, going stubby as the nails sharpened into claws. Powerful muscles swelled, bursting through the confining clothes. Before a full minute had passed, a brindled gray and brown wolf stood where Trina had been, draped in now superfluous clothing. Its tongue lolled as its eyes narrowed and its ears relaxed.

"Trina lives in the village, where she is courted by a rather ardent young suitor. She has little time to herself and consequently prefers to be in wolf form when she visits the castle," Strahd explained. The wolf glanced from one to the other and wriggled out of the clothing. She padded to the elf and sniffed him curiously, her black nostrils flaring.

"She is the first mortal woman to voluntarily enter Castle Ravenloft in well over a hundred years," Strahd commented. "I cannot take her blood. The wolf taint spoils it for my palate."

"Then why bother?"

Strahd waggled a cautionary figure. "Be careful, Jander. She can understand every word you say!" To affirm this, Trina barked sharply. "I enjoy her company, more so than the slaves. She is almost as ruthless as I. That is hard to become in ten years!" He laughed without humor. "The ideas of good and evil intrigue her, but she is as the wolf of the forest—totally unburdened by scruples. She makes an excellent spy and a merry bedfellow." He turned his attention back to the wolf. "Come, my dear. I have been your guest before. Now, it is time for me to return the favor."

Jander watched them go—the tall, elegant vampire and the calculating, amoral werewolf—silhouetted against the torchlight as they returned to the castle. He shook his head at the sight. What will Strahd's slaves think of Trina, he wondered, and how will the werewolf react to them?

Hunger stirred inside him, but the vampire ignored it. He was so weary of this place. His trips to Vallaki and into the village provided little comfort, and the projects he had worked on over the last few years seemed paltry efforts. He sat down on the cool stone by the overlook and leaned his head against the wall.

"You have forgotten me," came the sweet, clear voice that Jander both hungered for and dreaded.

The elf was afraid to open his eyes, afraid that he was awake and his mind was playing tricks on him. "Dear gods, Anna, never. You know that," he whispered. He heard a rustle of clothing and caught the sweet perfume of her skin as she seated herself beside him. The vampire still kept his eyes closed.

"Look at me, beloved." Her voice was soft, gentle, the sound of wind in the trees on warm summer's afternoon.

"No. I can't."

"Are you afraid to see what your forgetfulness has

done to me?" Jander emitted a soft, pained cry at the blow. Turning toward her he slowly, reluctantly, opened his silver eyes.

And cried out again, this time in horror.

Anna looked worse than she had in the asylum. Her lustrous hair was dirty and tangled. Filth smeared her face, and her clothing stank of rot. Her eyes held an expression of lucid, sane agony, and that was the hardest thing of all for the vampire to bear. "Anna," he whispered, guilt racing through him, "have I done this to you?"

"I cannot rest until you have avenged me," she said softly, tears welling up in her pain-filled eyes. "You are my only hope. Why have you not sought my company these ten years past?"

"Because," he murmured, wanting to avert his gaze but powerless to do so, "it hurts too much."

Her hand caressed his cheek. "Did you think I was not in pain, my love? It hurt me, too, living as a madwoman. Jander, where did they go? I had a mind, thoughts, dreams—where did they go when I became insane? What happened to them?"

Jander pulled away. "I don't know how to help you!" he cried, as angry at his impotence as at her. He rose, paced, and turned his back on her. "No one seems to know you. No one can even give me any clues!"

"You must find the clues, and with them, find my destroyer," she said sweetly. "The knowledge you need is closer than you think." He swung around, questions on his lips, and discovered that she had vanished.

The elf blinked, caught off-balance by this sudden occurrence. The sky was turning gray with the approaching morning. For a moment Jander wanted nothing more than to stay where he was and gaze at the east while the sun rose in all its splendor and beauty and pain. That would end everything . . . but solve nothing.

The weight of resolution pressing down upon him, Jander closed his eyes briefly and turned to the castle.

 **FIFTEEN**

Trina was bored.

Jander could tell she was bored by the frequent sighs and fidgeting he heard behind him, but he continued to concentrate on his work.

Standing on a ladder, he used a finely honed chisel to scrape away the decades of dirt that had filled the carved letters below the fresco. Instead of being completely illegible, the inscription now read: THE GOBLYN KING FLEES BE ORE TH   OW R O   H   O YSM O   F RA EN   . With the patience that only the dead have, he began to work on the F of "BEFORE."

The fresco itself was in a sorry state, but Jander could still make out a strong figure standing atop a hill, arms outstretched, before a horde of cowering creatures. He assumed this fresco depicted Strahd vanquishing creatures that had once threatened Barovia.

"Gods, Jander, how can you *stand* this?" Trina, in her human form, peered up at him. Her pert little nose wrinkled with disgust.

"Little wolfling," he replied, a hint of a smile in his voice, "I would rather do this than track innocents for sport."

Strahd would have taken offense; Katrina simply noted, "That's what we're supposed to do. I'm a were creature."

"Not all were-creatures are evil," Jander pointed out absently, narrowing his silver eyes as the F began to take shape beneath his delicate touch. "At least, not where I come from."

She laughed, clapping her small hands in delight at his joke. "That's funny!"

"It's true."

"No! *Really?*"

"We have wereowls, and werebears, and even weredolphins on Toril. And some of those are righteous, loving creatures who abide the law and strive to uphold it. A weredolphin befriended me once. It saved my life."

"What's a weredolphin?"

Jander paused, surprised, then shrugged. Barovia appeared to be landlocked, so of course Trina had never seen the ocean. He pitied her for that, and a sudden longing welled up inside him for the beautiful shores of Evermeet. "A dolphin is an animal sort of like a large fish. They're warm-blooded, however, and their young are born live, not hatched from eggs. Weredolphins change from dolphin to human."

Trina was amazed. "What strange animals they sound like. Was this weredolphin in your debt?"

"No. He just saw I was in trouble and came to help."

Trina frowned. "How silly," she mused. "You might have been feigning, trying to trap him and sell him."

Jander stopped what he was doing long enough to glare down at her. "Not everyone's mind works like yours," he snapped.

"Good thing, too," she purred. Jander resumed his work, beginning on another letter. "Tell me how you traveled here."

"The mists brought me. Not unusual."

"That's what happens to everybody. Doesn't anybody ever come here through magic?"

Jander occasionally enjoyed the werewolf's prattle, but she had ventured onto his least favorite topic and his patience was wearing thin. "Trina, I don't know anything about magic. Why don't you ask Strahd?"

She didn't answer at once, and when she did reply her voice was sulky. "I'm not talking to him. He spent last night with Irina. *Again.*" Trina kicked the stone step angrily, then rattled off a string of curses that would do a sailor justice.

Oh, yes, Jander remembered Irina now. Strahd's newest "acquisition," still human at the present moment but not for long. "Then why are you here?" he asked Trina.

She shrugged her small shoulders. "I don't know." Her voice suddenly dropped, became husky. "Maybe I came to see you."

Jander looked at her. She had stepped up on the ladder, one small, bare foot still on the floor, and was smiling up at him. The werewolf's eyes were intense and her mouth red and inviting. Feeling very sorry for her, the elf maneuvered himself so that he could see her more completely.

"Trina, you're a very attractive girl, but I'm not interested. Besides, if you think I'm going to even *think* about getting involved with one of Strahd's ladies—"

"*One* of them!" She glowered at him. "I am not just one of Strahd's ladies!"

The elf didn't answer. Below him, Trina continued to fume. "I'm sick of being told that. Why can't he be satisfied with just me? Why does he want those stupid slaves who have absolutely no minds of their own? He says he likes that I am my own person!"

"I believe he does," Jander replied.

"Then why—"

"Trina, Strahd likes your independence. He also likes feeling in control of things. Let him have his slaves. They're nothing to him but . . . sport." He didn't say that he privately thought that Trina, too, was little more than sport to the lord of Barovia.

"I don't like it," she muttered, sitting down on the stone stairway and resting her chin in her hands. Her pretty face reflected her inner misery. For all her casual violence, Trina could look like a lonely child at times.

Jander climbed down the ladder, carefully put his tools away in the protective pouch he had designed, and sat next to her on the stairs. The werewolf didn't look at him, and when the elf gently turned her face to his she kept her eyes lowered. Huge tears glistened on her lashes. He put a sympathetic arm around her shoulders.

"I only put up with the way he treats me because of the magic," she said in a thick voice. "He's teaching me, you know. I've learned a lot already. I'm going to wait until I've learned enough to make him want only me."

"That's all magic is to people, isn't it?" Jander exclaimed, his pity transforming into anger. "Magic! 'I can be rich, I can make someone fall in love with me, I can rule the world.' Gods!"

"You hate magic?" Trina shook her head, puzzled. "Magic can do so much. That fresco you've been working on forever, for instance. All you need to do is ask Strahd to say one little spell and it'd be fixed in a second."

"I enjoy working on the fresco. Its beauty is coming back to life right under my hands. Magic takes away the pleasure of doing that. Besides," his voice grew hard, "Strahd doesn't have any use for something that doesn't immediately benefit him."

"That's not true!"

"Oh, yes it is. If you're looking for someone to love you, what's the matter with that young fellow you're allegedly having a romance with in the village?"

"Him? Don't be ridiculous! I only agreed to see him because Strahd thought it would be a good idea if I were involved with someone in town. People would be less suspicious of me."

"So you do whatever Strahd tells you to. You're no better than those slaves of his. In fact, you're worse, because you choose to obey him."

Trina opened her mouth to retort, then froze as the truth of Jander's words sank in. "No," she whispered, "I'm not his plaything. I'm not. He loves me."

She looked so young and miserable, so much like a simple human girl in the throes of her first adolescent romance that Jander was moved. He held her affectionately, feeling the incredible amount of tension in her small body. Her slim shoulders shook as she sobbed, her small hands clinging to his blue tunic. There was no way her affair with the lord of the land could end happily.

"Well, what a pretty scene we have here, to be sure," came Strahd's voice. Jander and Trina sprung apart like two children caught doing something wrong.

"Strahd—" Jander began. The look on the count's face quelled the words before he could speak them. Strahd's eyes were red points of light, and his aquiline face was livid with rage. He raised his hands menacingly, and his lips twisted into a sneer that could only be described as pure hatred.

For a moment the elf was convinced that he had pushed Strahd too far, that the other vampire had lost patience and was about to destroy him. The red glow faded, and Strahd's gaze again became cool and slightly distant. He lowered his hands, and Jander closed his eyes in relief.

"Jander Sunstar, my old friend," Strahd said in a voice that was soft but threatening, "you may not approve of magic. You must, however, remember to respect its power . . . and the power of those who use magic."

The count turned his attention to the werewolf. In her fear, Trina had begun to transform. She had flattened herself against the wall of the curving stairwell and was whimpering softly. Completely human eyes gazed fearfully out of a wolfish face, and long furry claws pressed on the stone.

Strahd smiled charmingly. His eyes kind, he held out a strong, sharp-nailed hand to the frightened creature. "Trina, my dear!" he coaxed. "Do not be afraid. It is already forgiven and forgotten. There, that's my Trina!" he approved as the woman, thoroughly wolf now, came to him and pranced happily about his feet. The vampire reached and petted her affectionately. "Perhaps I have been neglecting you, my dear."

The count and the werewolf began to ascend the stairs. Halfway up, Strahd paused and turned slowly to look at the elf. Jander met that dark gaze evenly.

"My old friend," the count said in an icy tone that belied the warmth of the words, "we have not sat and talked in far too long. I shall come for you tomorrow, after sunset, and we shall feed and converse as we used to, hmmm?" He turned, not pausing for a reply, and continued his ascent.

Jander stared after him, his mind a riot of emotions. He debated resuming work on the fresco, but dismissed the thought. He was far too shaken to be able to concentrate. He wished heartily that Trina had left the dark subject of magic alone. Much of the pain in Jander's long years of existence had been caused by magic. Even on magical Toril, the practitioners of the arcane arts could help him little with his curse of undeath.

Painful memories flooded Jander's mind, though he tried to hold them at bay.

* * * * *

The elven vampire leaned on the small wrought iron gate, trembling with exhaustion. He gazed down the flower-lined path that ended at the cottage. Now that he was finally here, Jander hesitated, wondering if he'd have the courage to go through with it.

It had taken him many weeks, traveling by night and resting by day, to make it to Waterdeep in his weakened condition. Since he had destroyed his master, Cassiar, he had refused to feed upon human blood, despite the fact that his undead body craved the fluid. Even drinking the blood of the forest creatures disturbed him, so he had forced himself to feed only when absolutely necessary.

Out of a stubborn pride, he had not even shapechanged to speed the journey. A wolf or bat would have reached Waterdeep more quickly, but Jander clung to his elven heritage. He made the journey on his own two feet.

He had thought Lyria "the Lovely" long dead, crumbled to dust a century or more ago. When he had learned that she lived by means of her magical skills in Waterdeep, of all places, he had been filled with a renewed hope. Now he mentally took a deep breath and opened the little gate, walking across that small but yet gigantic distance to his former comrade's door. He used the knocker to announced his presence.

At first the cottage was silent. Jander knocked again. A light flickered on in one of the upper rooms, and his superior hearing caught the creaking of stairs as someone descended.

"It's late, you know. I charge double after hours."

Jander half-smiled. "Let me in, you round-eared wench," he replied, trying to sound as light-hearted as he had been a century ago.

There was a pause, and Jander heard the grating of the bolt sliding back. The door creaked open. "Only one person in the world calls me round-ear, twig-finger," Lyria teased happily.

She had scarcely changed. Whatever potions she was imbibing, they certainly worked. Her hair was no longer the color of the sun, but a pale creamy white that somehow suited her. Wrinkles lined her fabulous green eyes, but her body, draped in the multicolored garment she called her "rainbow robe," was as lithe and slim as ever. With a whoop, she flung up her arms and hugged the elf energetically about the neck.

Taken aback, he hesitated before returning her embrace. They pulled away, regarding each other. "Lyria the Lovely," Jander said, his voice warm with affection. "You look as beautiful as ever."

"The elves always were the best flatterers," she quipped. "Well met, indeed, my old friend. Come in, come in! Your hands are like ice!"

Fussing like a mother hen with a solitary chick, she ushered Jander inside. The room suited her, at once welcoming and elegant. A fire blazed in a hearth of gray stone, driving away the damp from the high bookcase flanking it on either side. Two low divans, opulent with fat burgundy cushions, faced each other across a low table of inlaid woods.

In the center of the table a tray of etched silver held a decanter of dark wine and four graceful drinking vessels of blown glass, as delicately opalescent as bubbles on the face of a stream. Lyria gestured Jander towards one of the divans, then indicated the decanter. "A goblet of wine to take away the chill, perhaps?"

"No, thank you," said Jander too quickly. "I don't drink alcohol anymore."

"*What?*" Lyria began to laugh her musical laugh, and even Jander smiled. He, too, remembered his contests with Trumper Hillhollow. The halfling had usually won, but Jander had managed to drink Trumper under the table on at least two occasions. "A hundred years can change a person, I suppose." She smiled as she poured herself some of the ruby liquid. "Perhaps something else? You're positively arctic, Jander, and you've looked better. Is something troubling you?"

Jander felt the weight of his burden resettle on his slender shoulders as if it were something tangible. "Lyria . . . what *do* I look like?" For almost a hundred years Jander had been a vampire, unable to see his reflection.

Lyria frowned. "That's an odd question. Here, let me get you a mirror, and you can—"

"*No!*" Jander grabbed the mage's hand before he realized what he was doing, and he forced himself to let go. "No, just—just tell me what you see."

Lyria's emerald eyes grew speculative. They roamed over the elf critically, appraising what they saw. "Let me see. Your hair is the same color, that gorgeous wheat-gold that I so envied. Your eyes . . . They're not quite silver. More iron gray, I'd say. It's your skin that's really different. Kind of tan, not so bronze anymore. You're awfully thin, Jander, and cold."

The elf's gaze fell to the floor. How to put this into words? He was so intent on his own grief that he failed to notice when Lyria rose and began moving about. "Old friend," he began, lifting his eyes from the stone, "I—"

He shrieked in agony, toppling from the divan. A flailing arm caught two of the goblets on the table, sending them crashing to the floor. Lyria had found a reflective surface and had directed it at him. The mage looked, horrified, at the cringing elf on the floor. "It's only a—" She glanced in the mirror, and, suddenly, she understood.

Reflected clearly in the mirror was the divan and the burgundy cushions. The broken goblets were there, too, as was the floor and stone walls of the cottage. There was no reflection of Jander.

"Oh, my poor friend," Lyria breathed, filled with pity. "My poor, poor friend." Still trembling, Jander glanced up at the woman. His gaze was filled with agony, and a single bloody tear trickled down his cheek.

Lyria's hands were gentle as they helped him back into his seat. She drew up a chair opposite the elf. "How?" she asked.

Jander laughed, a dry sound empty of humor. "I wasn't even adventuring. I was returning here, to Waterdeep. I'd had enough of the wandering life and was planning to board the next ship to Evermeet. Two days away from home. I was—" He stopped in mid-sentence, wondering if he should tell her the blackest part of a dark story. He decided against it as he looked in her green, concern-filled eyes. There was no sense in inflicting more pain on her.

"Go on," she prodded. He licked his lips and continued.

"I was surprised by a vampire in my sleep. The master of the mob of undead, Cassiar, was fascinated by me. He'd never heard of an elven vampire, so he let me alone for a long time. I was a novelty for him. It took me almost a century to kill him.

"I resolved to find you. If anybody could lift this curse, it would be you. It took me a long time." Suddenly he seized the mage's hands. "I haven't really changed, Lyria. I stayed an elf. I'm so pale because I haven't had human blood for months, haven't even had animal blood for days. The gods don't care; they didn't save me. But you can, because you know magic. You can cure me, can't you?"

Now it was Lyria's turn to look away uncomfortably. She pressed Jander's icy hands, then rose and began to pace. The elf's gut twisted. He knew the mage well enough to realize that pacing was a bad sign. "Lyria . . ."

She waved an impatient hand, silencing him. "Jander Sunstar, I remember when I first meet you, before we formed the Silver Six. You told me all about your land of Evermeet and how you had always wanted to come here, to Faerun. Your face was on fire with enthusiasm. I remember trying to drum some magic into that sane, stable, non-magical head of yours. We've been through so much together: the dragon, Daggerdale—" Her voice caught, and her eyes grew bright. "You know that if there were any way, in this or any—*any*—world to help you, I would."

The pain in Jander's gut increased. "That sounds like a no."

The tears escaped the prison of her eyes and slid down her face. Lyria dashed them away with the back of her hand. "That's because, old friend, there is nothing I can do. There is no cure for vampirism, save one, and that's death. Death cures just about everything."

Jander's mind raced. "Could you kill me and then resurrect me?"

"Oh, certainly I could. I'd resurrect a vampire, though, because that's what you are now. There's no magic that can help you."

A red haze seemed to descend upon Jander. "No . . . no . . . I'm an elf! *I'm an elf!*" Nervously he began picking up the pieces of glass. "I can't be one of . . . I was at Daggerdale. I know what vampires do. I know what they are. I remember. Lyria, please, I beg you, tell me I'm not—"

He realized that he had clenched his fist about a sharp fragment of glass, but he felt no pain. Barely aware of what he was doing, he pulled out the piece of glass. The wound did not bleed.

"I don't know how you did it, but you've clung to who you were. That's something to be proud of, something to get strength from. There's no magical cure for you, but that doesn't mean you have to be one of those Daggerdale horrors. Maybe you can—" Lyria's voice faltered and died before the stricken look that Jander shot her.

"There's no hope," Jander whispered. He buried his face in his hands. Gently Lyria placed a hand on the elf's shoulder.

"No magic can save you. There is only one way to end your curse. Should you seek true death, my sweet, gentle Jander, come to me and I shall deal it mercifully. It is better to die at the hand of a friend."

With a roar, Jander sprang from the divan and charged at her. The mage was quicker, though, and leaped to the side. She scrabbled frantically in a box of odds and ends until her hand closed on something. She swung about and shoved the object into Jander's face.

The vampire stumbled backward, thrusting his arms up and hiding his face. "Lyria!" he cried in a broken voice, "you mock my pain!" Then he vanished, and Lyria was alone.

Catching her breath, the mage studied the object that had driven the undead elf away. It was a small, pink-hued wooden disk—the symbol of Lathander Morninglord. Lyria closed her eyes in sympathetic pain for her friend. Jander had once been a follower of the beautiful, golden-skinned god of the morning.

 **SIXTEEN**

The musical sound of the rain pattering against the window woke Sasha. He lay in his small, snug bed for a few moments longer, enjoying the languid sleepiness and was silently grateful for the rain. It meant that he and Martyn wouldn't have to perform their daily ritual of greeting the dawn in Market Square.

It was not that Sasha was an irreligious man. Since that awful night fourteen years ago, he had made Lathander Morninglord the center of his world. Even today, he and Brother Martyn would hold their own dawn ceremony here in the church, leaving the door open for anyone who cared to join them. Sasha just didn't like the fact that they had failed to convince more than a handful of the Barovians of Lathander's truth. It was discouraging to stand up on a podium in Market Square for an hour when no one cared what he had to say.

The distant roll of thunder made Sasha open his eyes. Reluctantly he yawned and stretched, then swung his feet onto the floorboards, tugging on a robe to ease his shivering. It was still dark in the small, cold room, so the young man lit a candle. He rolled out his prayer rug and sat down, composing himself for his own private moment with the Morninglord.

Below, Brother Martyn was already preparing the altar. He hummed as he worked, laying a clean white

cloth over the altar and reverently placing the candlesticks on it. In his mid-thirties, he had changed little on
the outside. On the inside, however, Martyn was being
eaten up by a dark growth. He had known about the disease for some time and had long ago recognized it as
the will of the Morninglord. Hence, he had never mentioned it to Sasha.

"Sorry I'm late, Brother Martyn, but the rain delayed
me a little," came Katya's sweet voice, echoing in the
empty nave. She stopped at the door and shook her
damp hair, sending droplets scattering. Shivering a little, she quickly removed her dark green wool cloak and
spread it atop one of the pews to dry.

"My dear, don't worry. Sasha is being a lazy slug-a-
bed, and I haven't even seen him yet this morning."

Katya laughed, her warm eyes dancing. "I found
something to tempt even you into eating, Brother," she
teased as she walked toward the altar with a covered,
rain-speckled basket on her arm. "Your favorite—a
plum pastry. I also have some bread, and some cheese,
and some dried sugared apples."

The priest was touched. "Katya, how did Sasha and I
ever get along without you? I'm afraid, though, that I'm
still not very hungry. You and Sasha can share the pastry. I will," he added, "eat a little bit of those sugared
apples."

Katya put her hands on her small hips and glared at
him. "And?" she prodded.

"And some cheese."

"And?"

Martyn laughed. "Mercy, I pray you!" he protested
mockingly. A sound at the church's back caused them
to look up. Cristina, the seamstress, hurried inside, her
black cloak pulled tightly around her as much for disguise as to shield her from the rain. Her sharp face was
flushed, and her dark eyes wary as she scurried down to
the altar.

"I don't know how much longer I can keep coming
here, Brother Martyn," she said in a low voice that trem-

bled. "If my husband finds out—"

"Sister," Martyn said kindly, taking her strong hands in his own smooth ones, "Lathander will take care of you. I only wish the Morninglord had touched Ivar as he has touched you."

"Greetings, Sister Cristina, Sister Katya," called Sasha as he entered, clad in his formal robe of embroidered pink satin. Cristina had made it for him last year, and he wore it with pleasure and pride. The harried seamstress smiled a little when she saw him in the garment.

"Greetings, Brother Sasha," Katya murmured, suddenly busying herself with lighting the candles in the nave.

Sasha looked at her, more hungry for that sight than for the food she had brought. It had been six months since the girl had arrived in the village, six months during which Sasha had seen her every day. It was becoming more and more difficult for him to hide his growing infatuation.

It was her looks that he had fallen in love with first. Who wouldn't? There was no denying Katya's beauty, with her dark curls, trim figure, and large, expressive eyes. Besides, Sasha was half Vistani, and it was a saying in Barovia that Vistani men always had an eye for the prettiest women.

There was more to this girl than looks, however. In the end, it was her gentle disposition that thoroughly won Sasha's heart. Now he watched her moving from candle to candle with a lit taper, reaching up to light the large, fat tallows. As the wick caught, it illumined her features with a soft, warm glow. Sasha reached a decision. He tapped Martyn on the shoulder. "Brother, a word with you?"

"Certainly, Sasha. What is it?"

The young man walked them a little bit away from Cristina, then spoke in a low voice. "I've been doing a lot of thinking these past few months," he told the priest. "I was wondering—we never talked about this, but . . . can priests of Lathander marry?"

There, it was out. Sasha felt relieved to have finally brought it up, no matter what Martyn might say. The priest smiled, looking from Sasha to Katya. "It's her, isn't it?" The young man nodded and smiled a little sheepishly. "As long as your bride is one of the faithful, there is no reason you cannot marry. Now, my boy," he said, his tone growing serious, "there is one obstacle standing in your way."

Sasha looked up at him, concerned. "What?"

"She has to say yes." Martyn's voice was still sober, but there was a twinkle in his pale blue eyes.

The young priest looked again at Katya. She had finished her task and was now sitting with Cristina in the first pew. The two women, one older and harried, one young and full of life, had their heads close together. As Sasha watched, Katya pressed Cristina's hands impulsively. Feeling his eyes on her, the girl met Sasha's gaze, smiling shyly. The priest smiled back, somewhat giddily. He would ask her this very day, right after the dawn ritual.

"It is almost time, and we are not prepared," Martyn chided him. Sasha grimaced in apology and hurried to help Martyn finish decorating the altar.

A few busy moments later, the sun rose, little more than a lightening of the grayness. Few in town noticed the difference, but the four huddled in the church bowed their heads in thanksgiving for the dawn. The Morninglord had vanquished the long Barovian night, chased away all the terrors that used the darkness as a cloak. That was no little thing. They passed around the Sun Cup, a gold-plated chalice filled with white wine, and each took a sip. Sasha led the Prayer of the Morning, and afterward they sang a song of praise for another safe night.

Sasha's pure tenor carried easily. The rain increased, drenching a small, boyish shape that huddled outside the church door. With the door open a crack, the Little Fox could hear the song, and her chilled lips moved as she mouthed the words. Leisl wiped away a bead of moisture from her face, unsure if it was a raindrop or a tear.

* * * * *

Jander had seen Strahd angry before, but it had never been like this.

The black-haired vampire bellowed his rage from the entryway, echoing the sinister boom of thunder outside. The count prided himself on his poise, but Jander had always known there was a quick, fathomless rage that lurked beneath the polished surface. Now, as Strahd stood drenched with rain and blood, carrying a dripping corpse in his arms, he was livid.

"Who dares!" the count cried to no one in particular. "Who dares?"

"What happened?" asked Jander. Trina, who had come scurrying into the room when she heard the commotion, smiled a little as she took in the scene.

Angrily Strahd tossed the corpse to the floor. It hit with a soggy thump, and now Jander saw that it was missing its head and there was a great hole in the breastbone. Strahd was shaking in his rage. "Someone has killed one of my slaves!"

Jander bit back a retort. He could have predicted this. In fact, he had tried to warn the count about having so many slaves; Strahd's rage stopped him from mentioning this now, though. "Curse him, I wasn't done with her yet!" Strahd turned his attention to the surprised elf. "Do you have any idea which of those wretched creatures down in the village might have had the gall to do such a thing?"

Jander shook his head. "They're all cowed by you, Your Excellency. Mothers warn their children of the 'devil Strahd.' Perhaps some newcomers?"

The count began to pace, his strong hands clenching and unclenching. "No, the Vistani have not told me of any wanderers in a long time."

"Someone could have come in through the mists and avoided the gypsies," Trina pointed out, descending the stairs and going to Strahd. The count paused in mid-stride and glared down at Trina, considering.

"True," he admitted. "I shall find out."

"What about the clerics?" Jander suggested.

At this, Trina laughed aloud. "What, Martyn the Mad and his skinny little apprentice? No, Jander, those two are no danger at all."

"There is somebody else, somebody in the village who has chosen to defy me." Strahd smiled cruelly, his fangs glinting in the torchlight. "He shall regret it bitterly. Jander, how would you deal with such an individual?"

"There is something you can do that will guarantee he'll trouble you no more," the elf replied. "I don't think you'll like it, though. Just wait him out."

"That is the coward's way!" Strahd exclaimed scornfully. "You suggest that I, the lord of Barovia, permit some upstart mortal to murder my creatures?"

"That's exactly what I'm suggesting. Right now there's nothing to connect you with the vampiresses. If you start punishing the Barovians for the attacks, you're playing right into the hunter's hands. Let it go, Strahd. Let him destroy your slaves if he wants to. He can't touch you, and in a few years he'll be dead and you won't have lost a thing."

Strahd's eyes narrowed with displeasure, and his nostrils flared. "You were right, Jander. I do not like this plan. However, I concede that it has merit, and I shall consider it." He glanced at the corpse and shook his head. "Poor, pretty Irina. Jander, get one of the zombies to dispose of this. You, my pet," he said to Katrina, extending a grave-pale hand, "come with me." He and the werewolf ran lightly up the stairs, Katrina's the only pair of feet to make sounds on the stone.

Jander studied the headless body that had once been a beautiful woman. He picked up the carcass easily and bore it out to the wild chapel garden. There, in the moonlight, with the rain beating down, he buried Irina himself.

The elf rose early the next evening and went to the chapel. He stood at one of the broken windows, staring out at the twilight. During the course of the day, last night's rain had turned to snow. The colors of the sunset had barely finished fading on the distant horizon, and, in the chapel garden, the thick, newly fallen snow softened the mounds of Irina's and Natasha's graves.

Strahd's arrival was sudden and completely unheralded, yet Jander turned smoothly to greet the younger vampire, neatly snatching from the air the gray wool cloak Strahd tossed to him. The count stretched his lips in a smile, seemingly in high good humor. Jander stiffened a little, careful to keep his face neutral. Strahd's idea of fun had little in common with the elf's.

"Come, my friend," Strahd said, when Jander did not immediately don the cloak, "we have business to take care of tonight!"

"Aren't we hunting as wolves?" Jander asked carefully. Usually when he and the master of Castle Ravenloft hunted together, which happened less and less as the years went by, they did so in lupine form. Fur was much more discreet than cloaks.

"It is a surprise. We have a call to pay on someone in the village," said Strahd, and that was all he would reveal. Turning, the count lead the way through the castle and down into the courtyard, where a pair of black horses waited, harnessed to Strahd's magnificent coach. Jander felt his shoulders loosen a bit at the sight. Surely Strahd would not take the coach and horses if he were planning another "discipline" of slaughter like the one he had visited on the burgomaster and his family.

The midnight steeds began the long trek down the steep road toward the village. Spring was in the air, but snow still blanketed the earth. The moon was waxing, a few days short of full, and its light on the snow brightened the scene considerably.

The two vampires sat in silence for a time. Jander wondered what the count had in mind tonight. Apparently he was going to be subjected to another one of Strahd's little "tests." The irony of the situation did not escape the elf. Here they were, possibly the two most powerful individuals of their kind, thrust together in this dark land that seemed to nurture them. They could have been an unbeatable team, yet they were far too different to ever become comfortable allies.

There was much in the count that the elf admired. The count was unquestionably good company, with his easy conversation and extensive knowledge of a variety of subjects. But something about Strahd was too hungry for Jander's liking. They were not friends, despite the count's constant use of that term. Comrades in arms, perhaps, bound by their undead natures and strong sense of individuality, but not friends.

Jander caught Strahd watching him, and the elf smiled a little. "I wish you'd tell me what you're up to."

"And ruin my surprise? Never! When centuries stretch before one, surprise keeps the senses honed. Staying off-balance is the only way to keep the intellect sharp, do you not agree?"

They passed through the ring of fog, clattered over the bridge, and continued on. Soon they reached the outskirts of the village. Jander saw white faces at the windows, staring out fearfully. The horses trotted on, making a sharp turn to the right and passing through the village square before taking the first left.

At last they halted before a small shop. The sign, too worn to be legible, creaked in the wind. All the other shops were dark—either closed or abandoned. A light burned in the window of this one, however.

Strahd jumped out of the carriage and strode to the entrance. As always, he was determined to make a fine appearance, and he looked debonair and commanding as he approached the door. He knocked forcefully.

For a moment, silence reigned. "Who is it?" came a thin voice at last.

"Your liege lord," Strahd boomed. "You were told to expect me."

There was another silence, and Jander could smell fear behind the wooden door. He heard the bolt slide back, and the door eased open a crack. A sharp female face peered out, then the door opened fully.

The woman dropped into a curtsey, perhaps to hide her fear. "Good evening, Count," she said in a voice that quivered. "My name is Cristina. All is ready for your visit."

"Excellent, my dear!" said Strahd in a pleased voice. He extended a thin hand to bring her to her feet, and she rose and stepped back, ushering Strahd and Jander into a tiny, rather bare sitting room. The elf glanced briefly around the room, taking in the stiff, thread-bare chairs and old but well-polished tables that stood between them. Framed color sketches of men and women in evening clothes crowded the walls, the only things that seemed personal in the little room at all.

Strahd took Jander's arm and guided him into the center of the room. Cristina trailed after them. "This is my companion, Jander Sunstar," the count told her. "He is the one you must see."

The woman turned frightened brown eyes to Jander, but moved closer, obedient. She reached up to the elf, as though to touch him, and, startled, he stepped hastily away from her. He darted a questioning glance at Strahd, who was smiling. Cristina stepped up to Jander again and slowly but firmly ran her hands over his shoulders and arms, examining his tunic. "It should be no problem at all, Your Excellency," she said. The elf was, by now, completely confused, and his puzzlement showed on his sharp-featured face.

The count burst out laughing. "Cristina, we are confusing our friend! Jander, Cristina is a seamstress. I asked the burgomaster to tell the finest tailor in his village that we had need of her services. Your clothes are hardly fit for the spring celebration."

"The what?" Jander asked, still confused.

Strahd ignored him and returned his attention to Cristina, who seemed to have relaxed slightly. "My dear, have you prepared a selection of fabrics and colors, as I requested?"

"Indeed, sir, I did," she replied and led them through a door into a much larger room. Here were the tools of her trade, shears and manikins and fat cushions of pins and needles, racks of thread and bright yarn for embroidery. One table had been covered with multiple bolts of fabric. "I only hope that something I have pleases you."

Once she began to concentrate on the business at hand, Cristina lost some of her apprehension. She was a woman in her late thirties, whose face was careworn but whose eyes sparkled when she talked of her craft. She had done admirably in gathering a fine assortment of cloth. Jander, who tended to favor strong colors like blue and red, selected gold silk and an indigo velvet. He also picked out a bolt of crimson broadcloth and trim of gold and silver.

"Do you not like my style of clothing, Jander? I think it would suit you admirably," Strahd suggested, indicating the highly tailored, layered clothing that he himself wore.

"No, Your Excellency, it seems there are altogether too many buttons for my taste. New clothes based on what I wear now would be fine. And gloves," the elf added suddenly, sorrow brushing his features. "Several pairs of gloves." Perhaps a layer of cloth between his killing flesh and the delicate flowers would enable him to work in the garden once again.

"I do wish I was going," Cristina said. "I'd love to see all the people in their pretty clothes! Here, half a moment. I'll fetch the mirror, and you can see how the colors look against your skin."

"Ah, no thank you," said Strahd. "We are running late for an appointment as it is. When can you have the outfits ready?"

Cristina thought for a moment. "I can send them within the week."

Strahd frowned. "Three days."

The seamstress grew pale, but nodded. "Whatever

Your Excellency wishes."

"Here's for your effort," and the count casually scattered a handful of gold coins on the table. When a shocked Cristina had finished gathering them up, she discovered that her customers had disappeared.

She sat down on a stool, trembling. Many were the whispers about Count Strahd Von Zarovich, all of them fantastic and most of them sinister. The strange, golden-hued being that accompanied him, kind though he seemed, also was mysterious. Cristina clutched the coins to her breast. It was more money than she'd ever seen in one place before. Count Strahd had done all right by her, and she'd not be saying anything against him or his friend.

Not on her life.

"You're looking for someone at this spring celebration, aren't you?" asked Jander when Strahd brought the elf his new clothes three nights later.

Strahd turned his head sharply to look at Jander, piercing the elf with a needle-sharp gaze. "What makes you say that?" he asked, his voice soft, his tone dangerous.

The elf wasn't sure what trap he'd sprung in Strahd's dark mind, but he ventured ahead carefully. "You're going to see if you can learn anything about the vampire killer."

The count relaxed, and the sharpness of his gaze faded somewhat. "Ah. Yes, actually. Your advice was good, but I must continue my own investigations. Besides, I have not made a public appearance in Barovia for far too long. I don't want the people forgetting about me."

"I hardly think that's likely," said Jander. "But why am I going with you? I really would rather not."

The count raised one raven brow. "Ah, Jander, after all the years you have huddled here in Castle Ravenloft, it's time the people knew you as my guest, so they may treat you accordingly. Have I made so many demands on you these years past that you should refuse me the pleasure of your company?"

"No, but—"

"Do you not like the new clothing I have had made for you? Is that what has upset you? Shall I return it to Cristina and demand my money back?"

Jander cursed inwardly. Strahd would do it, too, and the thought of poor Cristina being denied her hard-earned money filled the elf with anger. "The clothes are beautiful, Strahd," he said wearily, "and I'll wear them to the celebration."

"I shall have you looking like a nobleman yet," the count approved, choosing to ignore Jander's resentment.

A half-hour later, as Jander admired the feel of the fine fabric against his skin, he had to admit that the count had been right. He wished he could see himself in a mirror, for he knew that the clothes were well-made and striking. The cotton shirt he wore beneath the short-sleeved indigo tunic of velvet fit him perfectly. The tunic itself had patterns of gold thread embroidered on it. The gold silk breeches also fit well, tapering into a pair of supple, white leather boots. Dutifully Cristina had provided several pairs of gloves, also made of the same milk-white leather.

When Strahd entered, he paused, his eyes raking the elf from top to bottom. "Turn around," Strahd commanded absently. Reluctantly Jander complied. When he turned around again, the elf could see approval in the count's dark eyes, mixed with a tinge of self-satisfaction.

"Now you are every inch a worthy companion of the lord of Barovia," Strahd complimented him with a little bow.

That night they entered the carriage once again and went down to the village, swooping like a hawk on its prey.

SEVENTEEN

The event was held in the burgomaster's mansion.
Jander felt very uncomfortable, recalling the last time
he had entered that building. Repairs to the damaged
areas had been made over the years, however, and the
new burgomaster seemed determined to make every effort to erase the incident in the public mind.

Coaches milled about the place; poor things in com-
parison with Strahd's beautiful carriage, but the best
the less-than-wealthy Barovians could afford. Their
clothing, too, was far less sumptuous than that worn by
Jander and Strahd, and suddenly the elf wished that he
had not been clad in a manner that so flagrantly boasted of the count's wealth. He smiled ruefully to himself.
Not, he mused, that he could ever hope to blend in with
the crowd. The Barovians were an insular lot, and even
a strange human met with distrust in this unhappy
realm. Jander was clearly alien, and therefore suspect.
Clothing would do nothing to mitigate their misgivings.
Besides, he was obviously with "the devil Strahd."

The carriage clattered through the open iron gates.
At the main entrance, the two black horses halted and a
servant stepped forward to open the carriage door. His
face was carefully neutral but noticeably pale. Strahd
stepped out of the carriage with a flourish.

He was met with silence. After a long moment, a few

of the bolder guests who were also just arriving murmured, "Good evening, Count."

"It is a beautiful evening indeed, my good people," Strahd replied blandly. He turned and motioned to Jander, who stepped down with considerably less flamboyance than the other vampire. A few people transferred their stares from their liege lord to his companion.

"Come," said Strahd under his breath as he gripped Jander by the elbow and guided him purposefully through the crowd. The elf could feel the eyes boring into his back, and he was acutely uncomfortable. They ascended the steps where the burgomaster and his wife were waiting, preparing to greet their guests.

The burgomaster was in his early forties, tall and straight with dark hair and a neatly trimmed beard. If he was distressed at having Count Strahd Von Zarovich and his mysterious friend attend the function unannounced, he did not show it. "Your Excellency, you do my home great honor by your visit," he said in a strong voice, bowing low. "Allow me to present my wife, Ludmilla."

Ludmilla, in her mid-thirties, was a handsome, full-figured woman who curtsied deeply, her eyes on the ground. She looked familiar to Jander. "I echo my husband's welcome, Your Excellency," she said.

"Ludmilla Kartova, is it not?" Strahd asked as he bent to press cold lips to her hand.

"Why yes, Your Excellency. Until I married."

"My sympathies on the demise of your family, madame. I complement you on your house's restoration."

"Th-thank you, Your Excellency."

Jander cringed inwardly. Now he knew where he recognized Ludmilla. Strahd's audacity stunned him. "Burgomaster Radavich," the count continued, "allow me to introduce my friend, Jander Sunstar. He is a visitor from a distant land, as is no doubt readily apparent."

"My lord, my lady," said Jander, "It is a privilege to meet you. I also extend my sympathies for your loss."

"Yes," cut in Radavich quickly, with a surreptitious squeeze of his wife's hand. "Please come in and make yourselves most welcome."

Jander and Strahd allowed themselves to drift past the burgomaster and his wife. The count collected the obeisances of his people as he and Jander slowly moved out of the small, elegant reception hall and into what Jander could only call a great hall.

There was little similarity between the charnel house Jander had fled and this elegant, well appointed chamber. It was evident to him that several of the charred walls of the earlier residence had simply been removed, so that what had once been three or four rather dark rooms was now a single large room, full of light and air. Pillars of carved wood fruit helped to support the expanse of ceiling, set with molded white plaster panels that bore a pattern of apple blossoms.

A small fortune in candles burned in four multi-tiered chandeliers. The simple ironwork holders had been painted white to match the ceiling, making the flames on the candles they held appear to float freely in air and shadow. Candelabras and graceful oil lamps added further light, gleaming amid garlands of apple blossoms and spring wild flowers on the mantlepiece of the large hearth. Their perfume complemented the soft music of a single flute and the murmur of conversation of the assembled villagers. In recognition of the balmy spring night, a fire had been laid ready but remained unlit, and the wide double doors were thrown open to the garden. Lanterns had been hung in the trees, casting soft yellow light over sprays of blossoms. Were there still lovers in Barovia bold enough to seek privacy under the night sky? Jander wondered.

"Morninglord!"

The man who had shouted the title forced his way through the crowd. He was tall and thin, probably in his mid-thirties, with pale blue eyes that held the glow of a zealot. The formal pink and gold robes that marked him as some sort of cleric fluttered as he dropped to his knees in front of Jander, bowing his head in abject servitude. "Morninglord, you have come to us at last!"

The elf felt sick.

It was not the first time in his long existence that his resemblance to the god of the dawn, Lathander "Morninglord," had been noticed. Yet did the priest known of the human god from Faerun? Perhaps he, too, was a victim of the land's strange, evil mists.

"Good sir," Jander said firmly, "please rise. I am not Lathander Morninglord. Look upon my face."

"No, no. Thou art the Morninglord, who has come to put an end to the nights of terror in this cursed realm!" the cleric babbled.

"Leave the elf alone, fool!" Strahd spat. The cleric only continued gibbering, clinging to Jander's leg, his face on the elf's white leather boots. Jander didn't know what to do, and he could sense Strahd's patience evaporating like mist under a hot sun.

"Come, good Brother," came a clear voice. Gentle hands reached down to the priest and eased him up. A young man compassionately put his arm around the Morninglord's cleric. His garb was similar to that of the priest's, but was much less ornate. "The Morninglord has not come. Not yet."

The youth, a slender young man in his early twenties, bowed gracefully to Strahd and Jander. "I apologize for Father Martyn's behavior. His wits are addled. However, my noble elf lord does indeed resemble the image of the god. Your Excellency, do we have your forgiveness for this outburst?"

The young priest's voice was resonant and strong, and he kept his eyes politely averted. Strahd was pleased and graciously waved his hand. "We celebrate spring tonight, not winter's harshness. I can be generous to the courteous. Take him away."

"My most noble liege is too kind." The young man led the priest away. Conversation began again, and Jander was relieved to find that some of the attention was beginning to drift away from him.

Strahd was watching the elf, amusement brimming in the depths of his dark eyes. "You upstage me!"

Jander shrugged. "Cults come and go. Lathander will die with his cleric. You, Count Strahd, are certain to outlast any daylight deity." Strahd laughed aloud at that.

For the rest of the evening, Jander held back, watching everything and participating in nothing. Strahd, however, cut a swath through the throng. He selected the most beautiful women as his partners and performed the steps of the elaborate Barovian dances with catlike grace. As he watched, leaning up against a door that opened into a small garden, Jander noticed the expressions of the women going from frightened to shy to enamored as they danced with the count.

The elven vampire shook his head mournfully. Strahd was undoubtedly planting suggestions in those minds. One by one, the women would wander up to Castle Ravenloft over the course of the next week or two. Their families would never see the girls again.

At least, they would pray not to.

"I have in my hand a pendant that, should I brandish it, will cause you great pain. Not only that, it will reveal your true nature to every person here. I don't think you want that."

Jander did not move for a moment. Then, slowly, he turned to the person who had dared address him so boldly.

It was the young man who had aided the priest earlier. The boy watched him, but avoided direct eye contact. "What do you mean, my 'true nature?'" the vampire inquired mildly. "You are threatening a guest of both the burgomaster of your town and Count Strahd Von Zarovich."

The young priest continued to keep his gaze averted and smiled a little. "I don't think you want to risk it, nosferatu. Turn around slowly and step out into the garden."

So, Jander mused, the priest knew what he was doing. He was right—any disturbance now and he would advertise the elf's vampirism to the population of the village. The townsfolk's reaction would be predictable and violent. Jander did as the priest requested, thinking to lure the youth into the shadows.

"Stay in the light of the doorway."

"As you will." There was something uncannily familiar about the young man. The priest was of slight build,
but the way he set his shoulders—not to mention the
deft way he had managed to confront Jander—
indicated a stubborn will and inner strength. His face
was handsome and delicately made, almost pretty, but
a square jaw and sharp black eyes curbed any hint of
weakness. There radiated from him a sense of great sorrow and loss, but a great determination as well.

"Very well. You have me," Jander said quietly. "You're
not as stupid as you'd like the villagers to think, are
you? What do you wish to do?"

The black eyes roamed his figure almost hungrily. "I
know more about you than you think, nosferatu. You
are Jander Sunstar. You are an elf from another world.
Nearly twenty-five years ago, you arrived here in Barovia. You saved a gypsy boy from a lynch mob. A girl, the
boy's lover, swore the friendship of her family to you."

Jander waited, expectant.

"I have been looking for you for a long time. My name
is Alexei Petrovich. They call me Sasha in the village. I
am Anastasia's child. It was my father's life you saved."

The voice was steady, with only a hint of the deep-set
anger and pain. Jander marveled at the youth's self-
control. "You are a very lucky young man, Sasha
Petrovich, on many counts. How did you escape the fate
of your family?"

"I was not home that evening. A friend and I spent the
night outside. I came home the next morning to
find . . ." His words trailed off.

"You were reading the book," Jander remembered
aloud, "in the circle of stones. You were wise to camp
there. That really is a holy place. The undead will rarely
have the strength to violate the sacred ground."

Sasha tensed, and Jander realized he had made a
mistake. "How did you know?"

Jander did not answer. Sasha's mouth set in a hard

line, and his hand closed about the medallion again. He lifted it, prepared to present it against Jander. The elf averted his face. "*How did you know?*" Sasha demanded hotly.

"We were there," Jander admitted. "You and your friend escaped death by a hair's breadth. If . . . my fellows had been hungry enough, we could have braved the sanctity of the circle for your blood."

Anguish filled Sasha's face. "Did you . . . ?"

Jander knew what the boy was thinking. "No. I did not murder your family. You resemble Petya very much, Sasha. I didn't know your parents very well, but they seemed like good people." He kept his voice calm. "I mourned your mother's death, and she did not die by my hand. That, I swear to you."

The youth's eyes finally searched Jander's. After a moment, Sasha relaxed slightly. "You could have saved my father and done . . . that . . . to my mother anyway. I want to believe you, but you are . . ."

"A vampire? Yes, and I have been for several centuries. That doesn't mean that I cannot be saddened by slaughter. Sasha, you trusted me a moment ago when you looked into my eyes. You knew that to be dangerous. I choose not to harm you, just as you are choosing not to betray me."

Sasha swallowed. "My mother told me about you. I swore never to harm you, if I ever met you. It is not a choice, vampire. I'd expose you to the crowd if I could, but I am crippled by my honor."

"Many years have passed since I last drew breath. I have forgotten more than most mortals shall ever know, but I have not forgotten honor," Jander said slowly. "I shall not harm you or yours, child of Petya. More, I cannot do."

A breeze stirred the night air, causing Sasha to shiver. He did not speak for a time, and Jander respected his silence. Moments passed. Finally, Sasha said in a low voice, "I was born in this house. This village is my home. Its people are my people, whether they want to claim me or not. There are things worse than dying, Jander Sunstar, and what you and your kind do is one of those things. How is it that you look so like the Morninglord and yet are his worst enemy?"

Sasha's dark brows were knotted in puzzlement and pain. "How is it that you saved the life of a boy you didn't know and yet live by drinking blood? I can't begin to understand such things. Maybe humans aren't meant to. I shall keep the bargain my parents bound me to. More, *I* cannot do."

He disappeared as quietly as he had come, blending almost as easily with the night shadows as the vampire did. Jander marveled at the skill; it was probably a trait he had gained from his gypsy ancestors. With a sigh, the elf returned inside and directed his attention back to the crowd.

As the evening wore on, Jander noticed a young woman stealing not-so-covert glances at him from the shelter of her fan. She was fairly attractive: blond, with warm brown eyes. When she caught his gaze, she smiled teasingly.

Jander held that gaze. He crooked a finger, inviting her to approach. Hiding her giggles from behind her fan, she exchanged knowing looks with her friends, who pushed her toward Jander with coy smiles of their own. The elf's mouth began to ache, and he realized how hungry he was. It was time to feed.

*   *   *   *   *

Sasha had sought refuge from his emotions by walking in the courtyard. He breathed deeply of the cool night air, fragrant with apple blossoms and other flowery scents, and tried to calm himself down. Sasha couldn't believe what he had just done. He had exchanged words with a vampire.

The priest looked up as a horse clattered into the courtyard. Katya, her cloak flying, rode up to him. "Sasha," she said in a worried voice, "it's Martyn. I think you'd better hurry."

Sasha's heart sank within him. He had asked Katya to take Martyn back to the church, but apparently something had gone wrong. Without even bothering to get his own horse, Sasha clambered up in front of the girl and grabbed the reins, turning the beast toward the church.

It wasn't far from the burgomaster's mansion to the church, but to an anxious Sasha it seemed to take forever. "What's the matter with him?" he asked Katya as they hurried along.

"He seems to have lost all reason, and he's in very great pain. I don't know what's wrong with him."

Sasha slid off the horse as they reached the church, turning to help Katya down. Together they opened the doors into all but complete darkness. "Martyn?" Sasha called, blinking.

A single candle at the altar provided the only illumination. Sasha made out a huddled shape near the wooden table. "*Martyn!*" He ran down the aisle to the priest. Katya hurried about, lighting more candles so that Sasha could see.

Martyn was moaning softly and clutching his side. His pale face was twisted with terrible agony, yet when Sasha touched him his eyes opened and he smiled. "Sasha, you've been like a son to me," he gasped. "I shall miss you when I go, but I have seen the Morninglord, and He has called me!"

"Martyn," Sasha said gently, "that was not the Morninglord. That was an elf. He's not divine. Let me heal you, please!"

Martyn shook his head, arching with pain and gripping his side harder. "Nay, my boy. Don't waste a prayer on me. He has called me, and I must go. I tell you, that *was* the Morninglord. I remember him. I remember that kind face covered with blood . . ."

Sasha felt a chill shiver through him. Martyn's family, like Sasha's, had been destroyed by vampires. Yet a being Martyn thought of as the Morninglord had spared him. It had to have been Jander. The young priest began to tremble. Then . . . was it all a lie? Was there in truth no Morninglord other than Jander? It couldn't be, it just couldn't.

"Martyn, please, don't die, I can heal—"

"No!" Martyn protested in a surprisingly vigorous tone. His pale blue eyes were distant, unfocused. "Aye, Morninglord, I hear . . . I come . . . ah!" He gasped with mingled pain and pleasure, and he reached out a slender, trembling arm to something Sasha couldn't see. The arm fell just as the priest shuddered and sighed one final time, then lay still.

Stunned, Sasha could only stare for a few moments. At last he folded the cold hands across the corpse's sunken chest and closed the pale blue eyes. Tears started in his own. For nearly fifteen years, Martyn had been his family. Ludmilla and her husband Nikolai had been kind to both Sasha and Martyn, but the half-gypsy youth knew where his heart lay—with Martyn and the Morninglord. Now, he had begun to have doubts.

Gently, Katya knelt beside him and slipped a comforting arm about him. Just as gently, Sasha disengaged himself.

"I'll be all right," he told her, touching her soft cheek lovingly. "I shall tend to Martyn shortly. Can you leave me for a little while? Right now, I must be alone with my god. I have many questions for him."

*   *   *   *   *

Jander was down in the cells again because he did not trust the mindless skeletons and zombies or the evil vampiresses to deliver the proper food to the newest prisoner. He unlocked the door with the iron key that hung outside, and it creaked open.

The little girl gazed up at him with huge eyes. "Here," said Jander, setting the plate of food down. "Eat."

She looked at the food, wrinkled her nose, then looked back at him. He turned to go. Tentatively the child reached toward him, tugging on his pants. Her face was solemn as he squatted down at her level. The elf could see the angry red puncture wounds on her neck. Jander had learned to feed delicately and with little trace if he so desired, and he had taught this technique to Strahd. The other vampires that Strahd created, however, were all bloodlust and savagery. Strahd found them eminently disposable, and even Jander found it easy to care little about their true deaths whenever Strahd wearied of them. The slaves were vicious; this child would not survive a second feeding.

Without knowing why, and more than a little annoyed at himself for his weakness, he said, "Do you want to go home, little miss?"

"Yes, please, sir," she said, her sweet voice trembling. What Jander was about to do bordered on reckless, but he had sat idly by for too many years now. What was one little child to Strahd? Without another word, Jander picked her up in his powerful arms. She locked her own arms about his golden neck and rested her head, as naturally as if he were her nurse, against his shoulder. A few minutes later, she was asleep.

Jander made his way carefully up to the entrance hall, wary for any sound that would indicate another vampire. He encountered a few skeletons, but apparently all the slaves were away hunting. Strahd, too, was out for the evening. The count had started disappearing almost nightly, never inviting Jander or Trina along and never saying what he was up to.

Anyway, Jander said to himself, if one of the slaves remarked about the child, Jander could always claim he was taking her elsewhere to feed. The cool night greeted him as he went out into the courtyard. The elf closed his eyes in relief.

A sharp bark startled him, and he looked around. One of the wolves that made Castle Ravenloft its home was sitting next to the elf's feet, tail thumping on the cobblestones. Jander was wary, as the wolves were now by and large Strahd's creatures. Yet when he tentatively prodded this one's mind, he sensed nothing more hostile than the wolf's quest for companionship. *All right, my girl,* Jander told the wolf, *let's go for a run.*

Jander ran swiftly despite the slumbering burden he carried. The wolf who had accompanied him was panting heavily. Even so, it was only an hour till dawn by the time they reached the village. He paused at the bridge. Swollen with the recent thunderstorms, the brown, turgid lvlis was running swiftly. It would not do to fall in. He glanced at the bridge. Twenty-five years ago, he had not been able to cross it under his own power; Petya had had to carry him. Since then, he and Strahd had either flown or run in bat or wolf form directly to the village, or else they had crossed the river in the carriage.

Jander's powers had changed since he'd entered Barovia. The land had cruelly taken away his contact with nature by giving him a touch that was lethal to plant life. Yet he noticed that he needed less sleep here than in Faerun and that his grip was stronger than before. He wondered what would happen should he try to cross the bridge.

Before the thought was fully formed he was halfway across, the child still resting peacefully in his arms. Elation began to bubble inside him as he neared the other side, and when his feet touched soil once more he was hard put not to leap for joy. What else might he do that had been forbidden to him? Wear holy symbols? Look in a mirror?

See the sunlight?

His musing was interrupted by a low growl from his wolf companion. The animal stiffened, her ears swiveling forward and her black nostrils flaring. With a whuff, she bounded off into the shadows, heading back toward the castle. Jander gazed in the direction the wolf had been looking. The elf's infravision showed him a large red shape up ahead. Shifting his slumbering burden slightly, he moved with absolute silence.

Further inspection revealed the figure to be the young priest Sasha, and Jander thought he knew what the youth was up to. The young man was not clad in his usual garb of gold and pink robes, but completely in black. A hood bobbed about his throat, and his face was pale and drawn. He carried a sack stained with blood over his shoulder.

"Well again, Sasha Petrovich," Jander called in a traditional Faerun greeting. His voice held a hint of amusement. "So you are the one killing off the undead. I suspected as much."

Sasha started violently, whipping around and half drawing a medallion. When he recognized who had hailed him, some of the tension dissipated. When he saw what the vampire was carrying, however, he was horrified.

"Drop her this instant!" he commanded.

Jander smiled humorlessly. "She'll have a nasty bruise if I do that. It's not what you think. I'm bringing her back from . . . where I found her." Sasha's expression registered suspicion. "By the tresses of Sune, boy, do you think I'd call out to you the way I did if I was supping on the girl?"

Sasha ignored the comment, dropping his sack and walking toward the elf with his arms outstretched. "Give her to me."

Jander didn't move at first. "You still do not trust me."

"You're a *vampire!* How can I trust you?"

"Would you trust me if I bargained for her, then?"

Sasha's face grew dark with anger. "What do you want, nosferatu?"

"You live in the church, the only place in the town that has books and records. I'm looking for someone named Anna, who was born about the year 333 of the Barovian calendar. Let me know if there's anything there about her."

"Why do you want to know?"

Jander was becoming exasperated. "Not for any malevolent reason, I assure you. There's little in you that knows trust, Sasha, or laughter. I miss the boy who used to tell ghost stories."

Sasha's lips thinned with a growing impatience. "That boy died that night, along with his family. I have little left to laugh about."

Something broke in Jander with an abruptness that took them both by surprise. His blond brows flew together in a terrible frown. "Nothing? You're alive. You're young. You don't have to feast on innocents to survive!" He thrust the little girl out in front of him with a vehemence that woke her. "You can feel the sun, know the love of a woman, of your fellow humans . . . Gods! If I were you, son of Petya, I would give thanks on my knees every day, and I would laugh every minute!"

The girl began to cry. Sasha snatched her and cradled her close. As soon as the young man had taken the girl, Jander changed into a wolf and bounded off, ears flat and tail bushy.

Sasha was surprised at the elf's outburst. Jander had been right. There was a lot that he was taking for granted, and it shamed him that it had taken an undead creature to point it out.

"Where'd the gold man go?" the girl asked.

"You're safe now, little one. I'm taking you home."

"I want the gold man! And I want to get down."

"We'll put you down as soon as we get to the village, hmm?"

Sasha's mind wasn't on the girl's prattle, but on the peculiar elven vampire. He was halfway home when he heard the sound, a low moan and a deep, throaty laugh. For an instant he blushed with embarrassment, thinking he had stumbled upon a pair of young lovers. He realized almost at once that the moan had no pleasure in it and the laugh was full of cruelty.

Quickly he put the little girl down. "What you doing?" she asked. He slipped his own medallion of Lathander over her head and took out a length of rope. "I'm coming right back, little one. I'm tying you here so you don't wander off in the mists and get lost, all right?"

"No!" she protested, her pink mouth puckered in a frown.

Sasha winced at the noise. "We're going to play a game, all right?" he whispered. "It's call the Quie

ame. And the little girl who can be the quietest gets
ome dried sugar apples."

The girl brightened considerably as he finished tying
er to the tree. She put a finger on her lips, and he did
kewise. His eyes narrowed, he hunted for the source of
he sounds.

A beautiful woman was crouched over the body of a
ounger woman. Her lips were fastened to her victim's
eck, and she sucked deeply, a thin trickle of crimson
scaping her hungry mouth and dribbling down to dis-
ppear in her victim's collar. Lounging beside the vam-
ire was a gray-brown wolf, eyes half-shut, tongue
lling. Thankfully Sasha was downwind, and neither
ight creature noticed his approach.

The familiar anger welled up inside Sasha. Gods, how
e hated these monsters. The fear, the eternal fear, also
lled him, but as always he fought it down. Taking ex-
ert aim, he hurled a vial of holy water toward the vam-
iress's head. The vial shattered and spilled its
ontents, burning her flesh and blinding her. She let out
unearthly wail.

The wolf leaped to its feet, hackles raised, and
rowled menacingly. "Demon of darkness!" Sasha bel-
wed, shattering the night. "In the name of Lathander
orninglord, I command you to leave this place!" He
rust a pink wooden disk before him forcefully, the de-
rmination on his young features making him look
uch older than his twenty-four summers.

The vampiress hissed. All trace of beauty had van-
hed from her twisted features. Her face was a mask of
ood and charred flesh. She cringed, howling, and
en disappeared. The wolf who had accompanied her
apped its sharp teeth, then bounded into the envelop-
g night. Sasha said a silent prayer of thanksgiving to
athander as he scurried forward to the fallen villager.

The young woman's breathing was shallow, but she
as still alive. With speed born of practice, Sasha
eaned the wound with holy water, applied gentle pres-
re to stop the bleeding, and bound it. When he got the

her back to safety, he would pray to Lathander to heal
her. At the moment, however, Sasha was afraid to waste
time. He covered the unfortunate woman with the
cloak, then left to fetch the little girl.

"I'm being very quiet," she whispered loudly as he un-
tied her from the tree.

"I know, little one," Sasha whispered back, "and I'm
very proud of you."

When they returned, the young woman was trying to
sit up. At Sasha's approach, she attempted to draw a
dagger from her boot. She failed, her fingers fumbling
uselessly.

"Easy, easy," Sasha murmured. "You're going to be a
bit weak for a time."

Her eyes focused, and she looked up at Sasha. The
priest started at a horrible realization: he hadn't put his
hood on. Did she know that Sasha was a vampire
hunter? Had she seen him attack the undead creatures?
His carefully crafted image of a shy priest would be destroyed unless he could convince her to keep his secret.

"Wh-what happened?" the young woman murmured.

"You were attacked by a vampire."

"You're the priest."

"Yes, that's right."

"So you drove it away?"

Sasha hesitated. "Well—"

"I can help you." The young woman was weak, but
she was obviously serious in her offer. She blinked dazedly; still in shock, Sasha assumed. "My name is Leisl,"
she said, her voice growing faint, "and I can help you.
I'm not afraid of those . . . things, and I hate that the
night isn't safe for honest thieves." Her eyes became unfocused. "You can't keep doing this all by yourself, you
know. What if you got . . . hurt . . . ?"

Weakened by the effort and the loss of blood, Leisl
fainted. Sasha barely moved quickly enough to catch
her.

 EIGHTEEN

Light streamed warmly over Leisl's face. She blinked
sleepily, squinting against the brightness. When her
eyes had adjusted, she looked around.

The golden sunlight—probably late afternoon, the
Little Fox guessed—poured in from a single small window that was open to let in the early summer warmth.
She was resting in a small but comfortable bed, covered with a single wool blanket. As she looked around
the room she noticed that it was small and the walls
were at odd angles. An attic of some sort, she decided.
A stool and a table supporting a basin and candlestick
were the only furniture apart from the bed that she
noticed.

As she craned her neck to look around, she winced.
One hand went up to touch the bandage on her throat.
Memory flooded back, and Leisl wondered where she
was.

A young, attractive woman entered through the suddenly open door. Her face lit up with a smile when she
saw Leisl was awake. "Where's Sasha?" Leisl demanded.

The girl seemed taken aback, but continued smiling.
"You're awake. That's good. My name is—"

"Katya, I know. Where's Sasha?"

Katya raised her eyebrows in surprise. "He's away at
the moment. He told me to look after you. You're in his

room here at the church. Do you feel up to eating anything?"

The thought of food made Leisl nauseous, but to get rid of Katya for few moments she replied, "Yes, I'd love something to eat."

"Good. I'll be right back. You just lie here and rest." Katya patted Leisl's hand in a sisterly fashion, then left, closing the door behind her.

This is just wonderful, Leisl thought to herself sarcastically. In the bed of the man I love and being taken care of by his fiancee. Just wonderful. Carefully Leisl eased herself up and noticed that someone had changed her clothing. She was now wearing a man's cotton shirt that was too large for her and nothing else. Leisl blushed hotly.

There was a knock on the door. The Little Fox drew the covers up to her chest protectively. "Come on in. That was fast cooking, Kat—oh."

It was Sasha, a thin line of worry between his eyes. He was clad, once again, in his priestly garb. "Good morning. Leisl, isn't it? Are you feeling better?"

She nodded. "Yes, thanks."

"Look," he began, pulling up the stool and sitting next to her, "we've got to talk."

Leisl leaned back on the pillow and folded her thin arms across her chest. "Go ahead."

"You said last night that you were a thief."

She went cold inside. Had she really said that? "You insult me. Calling me a thief when you don't even know—"

"You said it, Leisl," Sasha repeated in a weary tone. "You were weak and not thinking clearly, but I know it's the truth."

Leisl looked away. "You going to turn me in?" She'd be flogged in the public square, at least. If the burgomaster was in a particularly bad mood, he might even order her hands cut off.

Sasha shook his head. "I'll bargain with you. No one knows that I . . . I do what I do at night. I have to keep it secret."

"That's understandable. We'll keep things discreet."

"You can't come with me."

"Why not?"

"It's too dangerous."

Leisl snorted. "Sasha, listen, you don't know dangerous from your—"

"Well, I see you two are having a fine conversation,"
said Katya as she entered, carrying a tray. Despite her
earlier queasiness, Leisl sniffed appreciatively at the
food. Katya had brought her some hot porridge, bread
and butter, fried eggs, and a large jug of fresh milk.

"I think," said Leisl as Katya adjusted the tray on her
lap, "that I am going to eat all of this very quickly."

"Good," Katya approved. "It'll put some meat on your
bones." Leisl glared at her, but the other woman appeared oblivious. "Shall I leave you two to chat?"

"Please," the priest replied. Katya bent and kissed his
cheek.

"Call me if you need anything," she told the Little Fox
as she left.

An uncomfortable silence fell. Leisl tackled the eggs
hungrily. "These are real good. Want some?" she offered, her mouth full.

Sasha grimaced. "No, thanks."

Leisl pointed at the door with her fork. "She know
about your, uh, hobby?"

"No, and I'd like to keep it that way. I told her I found
you on the doorstep this morning, very early." He
paused. "I appreciate your offer of help, but it's dangerous enough for one. Two, especially a girl—"

Leisl threw him a murderous glance. "I've stolen for a
living since I was seven years old, Sasha Petrovich," she
snapped, "and I've wriggled out of situations that would
turn that black hair of yours snowy white. Maybe that
sweet-faced little maiden couldn't handle it, but that
doesn't mean I can't. So just shut up about me being a
girl, all right?"

"You have a very poor way of thanking somebody
who has just saved your life," Sasha said, very quietly.

Leisl's eyes fell to her plate. "Sorry. You're right. That's just a sore spot with me." She continued eating. "Katya cooks very well," she confessed.

"So, can I trust you to not betray my secret?"

Leisl began to butter the bread. "Yes. I'll keep my mouth shut, provided you do the same."

"Thank you, Leisl. You're free to stay here until you feel well." He rose and left without another word. Leisl looked after him, a softness on her face that would have stunned Sasha had he seen it. Then she returned her attention to Katya's excellent cooking. The Little Fox was not about to leave until she'd finished her meal.

* * * * *

The vampiress sniffed, and a slow smile spread across her face.

Human blood.

The wolf at her heels also caught the scent, growling faintly with eagerness. Together the two predators moved toward the kill.

The human, dressed in black, would be easy prey. Small and slender, he stood in front of the fast-running Ivlis, aimlessly tossing pebbles into the black water.

Soundlessly she was upon him, but it was she who was surprised. The minute her hands closed on his shoulders, he hurled himself into the pool, reaching to return her embrace.

The vampiress wailed, but the inky waters of the river rushed down her open throat, filled her nostrils. They sank like stones, the vampiress totally unable to swim. She felt the boy attempt to pull free of her grasp and tightened her arms about his slender body. Damn him, if she was going to die, she would take him with her . . .

From her hiding place in a tall, gnarled tree near the river, the Little Fox watched anxiously. She'd seen everything; Sasha was, without a doubt, the stupidest young man she'd ever seen. And she'd seen a lot of stupid young men. She had to admit, though, he seemed to know exactly what he was doing. After all, he had saved her from a vampire.

Leisl became a little anxious when a flurry of bubbles burst on the surface with a series of pops. She became even more worried when no further bubbles came up. When several long seconds had passed, she cursed heartily and dove in herself.

By the gods, but the water was cold, even in summer. The shock to Leisl's system almost caused her to gasp and lose her lungsful of precious air, but she bit down hard against the impulse and swam deeper. Her hands touched yielding flesh.

The vampiress was dead, but her weight and her death grip prevented Sasha from freeing himself and heading for the surface. It was too dark for the Little Fox to see anything, but she figured that the struggling one was Sasha, and pried the dead hands from around his neck. Chunks of flesh, ripped from the undead's bones by the merciless currents, brushed passed Leisl. For a few precious seconds, Sasha fought her, but then he shot to the surface. She followed.

They both coughed like consumptives for a moment, wheezing and gasping, then Sasha struck out for the shore. After they both clambered onto the bank, shivering violently, Sasha found his cloak and held it open for her. She accepted the woollen warmth gratefully, wishing she could make her teeth stop chattering.

"You shouldn't have followed me," Sasha said. "You could have been hurt, even killed. What I do is dangerous work."

The Little Fox snorted. "Obviously. You'd have d-drowned without me." She opened her cloak. "C-come on in. You'll die yet if you don't get w-warm."

Sasha hesitated, an image of Katya flashing into his mind. He dismissed it. Leisl hardly counted as a woman and was certainly no threat to Katya's place in his heart. They moved close as Sasha tugged the cloak closed for warmth.

For a while they walked toward the village in silence. Leisl was nearly as tall as the priest was and matched his stride efficiently. "So," she said, "when do we go out next?"

Sasha stopped and glared down at her from a distance of four inches. "What makes you think I'd take you with me?"

"Oh, you will." She smiled wickedly. "Or else I'll tell your precious Katya what you do after dark."

Sasha flushed deeply with anger. He was not in the least ashamed of his vampire stalking, but he had no wish involve his innocent bride-to-be in this dangerous activity. Should his identity be discovered, she would be in more than mortal danger. Besides, Katya had had enough pain in her brief life. He would not add to it by making her worry about him.

The Little Fox arched an eyebrow. "Well? What do you choose? Do you have a partner or a frantic fiancee?"

There was no choice, and she knew it. He did not even bother to reply, but pulled his cloak off her and strode on ahead. "Hey!" she called and scurried after him.

"You're going to have to swear allegiance to Lathander Morninglord," Sasha stated, not looking at her. "It's the only way I can be seen with you."

"That's fine. I kind of like the idea of him, anyway."

"You're going to have to take orders from me without questioning them."

"That's fine, too."

"And no more thieving. I will not work with someone who steals for a living."

Leisl opened her mouth to protest, then shut it. "Agreed. So, am I in?"

Now he did look down at her, exasperation warring with amusement. "You're a real pest. You know that, don't you?"

The Little Fox grinned.

* * * * *

"Your move," said Strahd silkily.

Jander frowned to himself as he scrutinized the board. They were playing a game Strahd himself had invented, called Hawks and Hares. Naturally the lord of Barovia always insisted on being the Hawk. As the elf learned the nuances of the game, however, he was starting to give Strahd a bit of competition. There was a long pause, in which the crackling fire provided the only sound. At length Jander moved his Hare two squares to the right. "I can reach my warren in five moves," he announced.

Strahd frowned, his dark eyes searching the board, totally engrossed in the game. "Not if I bring my Goshawk into play," he purred, his piece "swooping" down on Jander's Hare. He picked up the gray stone and moved it to the pile of others he had taken from the elf during the course of the game. "Jander, you always forget to guard your back."

"And you," Jander said, pleased with himself, "always forget about details." He moved the piece that was the Rabbit Doe forward two hops. "The Doe has reached the warren. According to the rules that gives me—" he counted the remaining pieces on the board "—five more Kittens to introduce into play." His silver eyes bright with amusement, he reached over to the pile of gray stones and selected five.

"You play on the defensive," Strahd noted.

"I'm the Hare. That's what I'm supposed to do."

"I'm bored," moaned Trina, who'd been moping around all evening. Strahd was seldom home at nights anymore, and Trina definitely didn't like it that the count had chosen to play a game with Jander rather than pay attention to her. Now she sprawled by the fire, one arm draped over the big gray wolf who drowsed there.

"Silence," growled the count. There was a knock on the study door. "Come."

It was one of Strahd's slaves. "Excellency, there is a Vistani here to see you. He says it's important."

Strahd gave the slave his full attention, the game forgotten. "I shall come down. Jander, Trina—I won't be gone long." He rose, paused, made a move, and smiled icily at Jander. "Your Doe is dead." With a flourish and a rustle of red and black silk, he was gone.

Trina slipped into the chair he had vacated. "Teach me how to play this game, Jander." She peered at the round, polished stones.

"Not tonight." After a pause he asked, "Do you know where Strahd has been going these months past?"

She frowned. "No. He used to take me with him. He doesn't, not anymore. He says he's looking for someone. Why are these stones gray and those all different colors?"

Jander wasn't paying attention to the werewolf. He was thinking about the count and wondering if Strahd himself had noticed how much he had changed. So, he was "looking for someone." That didn't surprise the elf. What did surprise him was that Strahd hadn't instigated a methodical massacre of the population in pursuit of his unknown nemesis. Instead, the count had taken to disappearing for a week or so at a time, conducting his own quiet investigations as well as enhancing his network of spies.

Strahd's restraint, however, did not indicate that the count was calmly accepting his lot. Jander knew that, eventually, the net would close in on Sasha. He mentally wished the boy luck.

"The Vistani have found another one of mine," Strahd announced, startling Jander out of his reverie. The count stood in the doorway to the study, trembling with contained fury.

"What happened this time?" Jander asked.

"He drowned her. It was Marya. Damn him, *damn* him!" Jander remembered Marya, the newest addition to Strahd's bevy of lovelies. The count had been quite taken with the voluptuous woman with the large, hypnotic eyes. No wonder he seemed particularly upset.

"This enemy of mine is uncanny! Time and again I

have told my slaves not to travel alone. They are warned. And yet, he keeps surprising and killing them. He blinded Shura so she could not identify him to me. It makes me wonder if this mysterious foe is something more than mortal." Strahd smiled craftily. "It is well that I have new spells with which to fight him."

Absentmindedly playing with the pieces on the board, Trina muttered something under her breath. Strahd frowned. "What was that, my pretty?"

Trina pouted. "Nothing," she said sullenly.

The count's carefully reined temper broke. He strode over to the girl and yanked her head back. "Remember who your master is, little wolf-girl," he snarled, his lips close to her throat. "I can't take sustenance from you, but I can take your life. *What did you say?*"

"Strahd," Jander began.

"Silence!" shrieked the other vampire and followed the command with a jumble of unintelligible words. Jander tried again to speak and found himself mute. His hands flew to his throat as if he could pry the words out. "Speak!" Strahd ordered the werewolf.

Trina was crying now, from anger as much as pain. "I said, 'if you wouldn't make so many of your stupid slaves, you wouldn't lose them!'"

With a sneer of disdain, Strahd released his grip. Trina fell from the chair, writhing into her wolf form. Strahd looked at the board, and his expression grew even darker. "Trina, you have been playing with my pieces. I told you never to touch my game!" Before Strahd could punish Trina further, she had completed her transformation. The werewolf sped out the door, bushy tail between her legs.

"Jealous little bitch," Strahd said, his anger turning to self-satisfied humor. "She hates it when my attention wanders from her. She'll come cringing back in a bit. I have her for as long as I want her. She craves my magical knowledge—and me." He glanced at Jander and released him from the silence spell.

"I've told you of my abhorrence of magic, Strahd!"

Jander spat angrily. "Why can't you respect that? The lives lost, the atrocities committed—and for what? A violation of the laws of nature! Magic can't bring *you* peace of mind, can it?"

Strahd's eyes went red. "Careful what you say, friend Jander," he said, his voice dangerously soft. "Remember whose guest you are. And remember also, you yourself are a violation of the laws of nature."

The elf froze as if struck. Strahd ignored him, rearranging the pieces on the board. "Shall we play again?"

Seeking the solace of the forest, Jander stormed from the study. A breeze blew at his back all the way from the castle, rich with the fragrances of summer. Once in the shelter of the forest, the elf took out his flute and began to play a frenetic melody, his fingers dancing as he channeled some of his anger into his music.

A violation of the laws of nature. I am that, Jander noted bitterly, but I am also other things, things Strahd will never comprehend. For a moment he considered trumpeting the count's crimes to the village, but the thought of committing treachery did not rest easy with the elf. Back on Toril, treachery had cost him everything, his life, his happiness, perhaps even his undying soul. Memories of the traitor's evil deed pushed all anger from Jander's mind, and a deep sadness washed over him as he became lost in remembering.

* * * * *

The fire spat as Jander put a fresh armload of dead branches on its red-orange heart. The elf stepped back as the flames crackled, sending a shower of tiny sparks spiraling upward. The fire subsided after a moment to a cheerful glow.

The elf was not cheerful. He was very tired and still had several days of traveling before him. A few yards away, his horse cropped contentedly, occasionally cocking an ear in her master's direction. Jander spread out his bedding and rummaged in his pack for something to soothe his growling stomach. He grimaced at what his search yielded. All that remained of his supplies were a hunk of salted, practically inedible pork and some stale traveler's bread. He gnawed with little enthusiasm on the hard bread, knowing that he ought to bestir himself and set a snare for a rabbit.

His heart did quicken slightly at the thought of finally going home. Two hundred years of wandering Faerun, fighting evil, making friends, sleeping on cold, hard earth—surely that was enough to wear anyone down. He had held up the reputation of the Sunstar family at all times. Evermeet sang to his soul now, calling him home after his wanderings. *Evermeet, Evermeet, home of the People . . .*

Alone with the night, Jander reached for his flute. He had carved it himself back on Evermeet, and it had traveled with him, his one unchanging companion over the last two centuries. The elf carefully unwrapped the instrument from its layer of protective coverings and raised it to his lips.

Sweet as a bird's call and haunting as the waves' eternal sigh, the uncanny, nearly magical music filled the air. Jander's mare paused in her feeding to harken to the sound for a few moments. Gideon used to claim that the very beasts of the forest stopped whatever mischief they were about to listen when Jander played. Whether this was true or not the elf couldn't say, but he knew that it always soothed his own troubled soul.

The pure sound lingered in his heart, even after he put the flute down.

"There's no one else in Toril who can play like you do, old friend," came the voice.

Jander's sword was drawn and in his hand in a heartbeat. "Who's there?" he challenged, unsettled by the fact that he hadn't heard the intruder approach.

As an answer, the figure moved closer to the firelight. His bulk was better suited to a warrior than a cleric, but the big, bearded man wore the garb of a priest. Jander's breath caught in his throat and for an instant emotion blocked all words. "Gideon," he breathed softly. "I'd given you up for lost at Daggerdale!"

"So I would have been, were it not for Ilmater's Miracle. I am blessed. He came and took my pain from me."

Jander had heard of Ilmater's Miracle. Occasionally, when a devout priest was in great pain, the god of the martyrs would manifest and take the priest's place. It was far from a common occurrence, but the elf could think of no one more worthy of such a gift than Gideon.

Sheathing his sword and tossing it onto his bedding, Jander strode toward his friend, arms outstretched in welcome. A huge smile on his face, Gideon met him halfway, nearly crushing him in a bear hug. "Oh, thank the gods, thank—"

Jander's prayer turned into a choking cry as two small points of white heat stabbed into his neck, piercing his soul as well as his flesh. The scalding pain traveled down to his gut, and it felt as though his soul were being pulled out through the two small holes in his jugular. Dimly the elf felt droplets of his own blood trickling down his throat and staining his blue tunic.

The elf tried to push Gideon away from him, but he was too weak, and his hands pushed feebly against the cleric's massive chest. The feeding continued mercilessly, and Jander felt his consciousness coalesce into a tiny point of light behind his eyelids, then fade altogether.

Awareness returned some time later. Something cool and moist and filled with the rich loam fragrance of earth covered the elf, pressing damply against his face. He shifted and tried to wipe the dirt away, but found that soil covered the rest of his body, as well. Panic gripped him, and he flailed frantically, scraping at the dirt on his face and clawing his way out of what he now realized was a shallow grave.

Fear lending him energy, Jander scrambled a few feet away from the lightly dug pit. He sagged, too weak to stand and get his bearings. He could only stare at the trench, an ugly gash in the forest's fertile soil, and say a prayer for his narrow escape.

"Good evening, Jander," came a strident voice. "Hope you slept well." Nervous laughter followed.

Jander sat up, turning weakly in the direction of the voice. A slender young man emerged from the shadow of a nearby tree. The youth was pale, his hair a mass of coppery curls with one stray lock trailing across a milky brow. His eyes were large, with a rather doelike quality, and he gnawed his lip nervously as he twisted a pair of fine calfskin gloves in his white hands. The rest of his clothing, from leather boots to linen shirt, was equally fine.

"Who—" began Jander, but the sound emerged as a croak. He licked dry lips and started again. "Who are you? Where's Gideon?"

Again the youth laughed, a short, harsh bark. "Your friend wants you, cleric."

The former priest stepped into Jander's limited range of vision. His eyes glowed an eerie red, and he smiled, showing white, sharp teeth in a beard matted with blood. With a cold pang of loathing, Jander realized that the blood on Gideon's face had come from his own throat.

"You're one of us now, Jander," Gideon said in a voice that was nothing like the strong, sad tone that the elf remembered. The voice of the cleric-turned-vampire had a hard, sneering edge to it.

You're one of us now. Jander's hand groped for his throat. It was smooth, unmarked. The elf closed his eyes in relief. They hadn't gotten him yet, so if he—

"No, Jander Sunstar," the red-haired young man was saying. "You are indeed a vampire. Feel for a pulse. You've been dead for a full day now."

Slowly, keeping his eyes on Gideon and the stranger, Jander stretched one thin hand to the other and felt at his wrist. He frowned to himself and readjusted his grip.

There was no pulse.

Still lying on the earth, the elf craned his neck to look up at the strange young man, who was staring down at him appraisingly. "I do like this one, Gideon, very much. You've done well. Bring him something to eat. Jander, my name is Cassiar, and I am your master now."

"No," Jander whispered. "Gideon . . . we were friends!"

"Gideon the mortal was your friend," the evil creature snarled at him. He approached Jander, and the elf saw that Gideon was carrying a towheaded child in his arms. "I am Gideon the vampire, and I have little use for things from my past. Cassiar is my master now, and I obey."

"You're very hungry, Jander, aren't you?" Cassiar purred. Suddenly the elven vampire was hungry, and he realized that his newly undead body craved fresh blood from the little boy's throat. He could smell the blood, and the elf felt a curious sensation in the roof of his mouth. Fangs were growing in response to the blood-scent, and fresh horror overwhelmed him.

"No!" he cried, covering his face with his arms. "You can't make me do that to a child!"

Cassiar frowned, his boyish mouth puckering in annoyance. "You have no say in the matter. You *will* obey me, and I say drink!"

Jander was too young, too weak a vampire then to resist the command his master had given. With loathing, he bit into the boy's white throat clumsily, gracelessly. Blood splattered softly on his golden face. Even as his mind was overwhelmed by revulsion at what he was doing, his body drank greedily, messily.

Afterward he looked up at Cassiar, and his silver eyes were filled with hatred. Though it would take him nearly a century, he eventually slew his evil master. That act of rebellion allowed him to forge his own future, but it did little to free his soul from the curse his traitorous friend had inflicted upon him.

 **NINETEEN**

Sasha was horrified to find himself shaking as he stood over the corpse of his latest victim. He steadied himself for a moment, kneeling in the forest litter. Even after this pause it took him two tries to pull the heavy wooden spear from the vampiress's breast, and sweat beaded his brow as he stuffed the beautiful mouth with garlic. He stubbornly ignored the Little Fox, who stood quietly, observing his distress.

Picking up the small hatchet, he prepared to cut off the head. His hands, however, were trembling so badly that he couldn't manage it. "I'll get this one," Leisl said, stepping in so smoothly that it seemed completely natural. Gratefully he handed her the hatchet and watched in admiration as she coolly proceeded to behead the corpse. She was such a professional about this—no trembling, no tears. Not for the first time, Sasha wondered if she had any heart at all.

The vampiress had only been undead for a few weeks. The scent of blood and decay assailed his nostrils, and Sasha turned a sickly shade. Stumbling to his feet, he made it to the nearest tree and vomited. Leisl politely ignored him, concentrating on her work.

The priest fought to control his shivering as he slumped against the tree, wiping his mouth with the back of his hand. Of course he was afraid. He was always afraid. Only a fool would not have a healthy respect for these powerful, clever beings. A fool—or the impulsive, innocent child he had been on that long ago night, when rashly he had braved the darkness outside only to lose his family in the sanctuary of their own home.

The fear did not bother him. This sudden weakness did.

At the edge of his vision, something white fluttered. Sasha was instantly alert, adrenaline suddenly pumping through him. Another vampire? He caught the image again and recognized it. "*Katya!*" he cried, his voice a sharp violation of the thick, enveloping silence of the late summer forest. Without thinking, he sprinted off after her.

"Sasha, wait!" Leisl called. Cursing, she gathered up their tools in her blood-drenched hands and took off after him.

She caught him easily, for Katya, or whatever it was, had disappeared. The priest was breathing raggedly and real fear haunted his face. He looked down at Leisl in agony. "*Katya!*" he said, as if the one word would explain everything.

Leisl's heart sank. She knew where they were going.

In his apprehension, Sasha set a hard pace, and by the time they had reached the village they were both panting heavily. Sasha pounded frantically on the door of Katya's tiny cottage. "Katya? Darling, it's me. Please open the door!"

There was a long silence. Sasha's face reflected his anguish as he nervously dug with a thumbnail at a splinter in the wooden door jamb. At last, the door eased open a crack and Katya peered out fearfully. Her small white hand clutched her holy symbol about her neck. "Sasha? Oh, Sasha!"

With a sob, she flung herself at him. He held her closely. "Darling, what's wrong? What happened? I thought I saw you—" He stopped himself just in time. "Outside."

"Oh, Sasha, you may have. That's what's so horrible!" She gazed at him, her brown eyes enormous and full of tears. "I . . . sleepwalk," she confessed, the last word a whisper.

Sasha went cold inside. Sleepwalking in Barovia was an invitation to disaster. The priest knew, better than anyone, just how dangerous it could be. Suddenly frightened, he moved her thick brown hair off her neck, fearing to discover the telltale tiny puncture wounds. He sighed with vast relief when he saw that her throat was unmarked.

"I have such terrible dreams," she continued. "Dreams about blood and somebody stalking me in the shadows. Then I wake up, and I don't know where I am!" The tears began again, and she buried her face against Sasha's chest. "And I wish . . . I know it isn't right, but . . . I wish you were here with me when I sleep, just so I'd know I wasn't alone."

"Hey, you two, it's getting cold out here, and I'd like to get a little bit of sleep myself," came Leisl's sharp voice.

Sasha started. He had forgotten about the Little Fox, so upset was he at Katya's distress.

"Of course," sniffled Katya, drawing back from the priest shamefacedly. "I'm so sorry, Leisl. I'm all right now." Katya didn't fool either of her visitors, however. Her eyes were still huge, and her lower lip quivered.

"Here," said Sasha, slipping his medallion of Lathander off his neck and placing it around Leisl's. "Go back to the church. I'll see you there in the morning. I don't feel comfortable leaving Katya alone right now."

A little, grateful cry escaped Katya's lips, and she clutched his hand hard.

"Fine," snapped Leisl. "See you there." She looked at Katya, started to say something, but thought better of it. A quick exit was better than a retort this time; had she lingered any longer, they might have seen the tears that filled her eyes. She couldn't hate Katya. The girl was too sweet. Yet Leisl was fiercely jealous, and she gulped hard as the tears rolled down her face.

Sasha, troubled, watched her go. The Little Fox gave him no end of confusion. What was bothering her now?

He returned his attention to Katya. "No more bad dreams tonight, love. I promise," he teased, kissing her cheek. Her cottage was small but functional, a two-room, one story house with simple furnishings. Sasha carefully checked the locks on the door and the two windows. "Tomorrow at dawn, when Lathander's power is greatest, I'll place some wards on the doors. Right now, let's get you to bed." Obediently Katya climbed back into bed and pulled the covers up to her chin. She watched him with large, sleepy eyes as he pulled up a chair next to her.

"Thank you for staying," she murmured, yawning.

"My pleasure. Now get some sleep."

Sasha fully intended to keep watch until daybreak. He must have been more tired than he thought, for he bolted awake some time later. Katya was writhing on the bed, clawing at her throat. "No, no," she cried, her eyes tightly shut.

Instantly Sasha was at her side, pinning her arms to the bed in a desperate attempt to stop her thrashing. She awoke, her eyes wide and fearful. "Sasha!"

"You had a bad dream. That's all." He gently took her in his arms, holding her tenderly as her trembling subsided.

"Sasha," she said again, but there was a new note in her voice. He craned his head to look at her. Her eyes were dark, and her lips seemed very red. "Sasha."

Suddenly he was kissing her, all his good intentions completely forsaken as her beauty and unexpected passion drove the thoughts of darkness from his mind.

* * * * *

Pleased with the work so far, Jander straightened, stretched, and reread the inscription beneath the fresco. THE GOBLYN KING FLEES BEFORE THE POWER

OF THE O YS M O   FRA EN   . He was almost finished. He had to admit, he was curious as to what the rest of the inscription might be.

He heard a door slam and the patter of eager feet. "Jander? Jander, where are you?"

"By the fresco, Trina," he called. She hurried up to him. Her eyes were wide with childlike glee, and she clutched an enormous book.

"Look what Strahd said I could study while he was gone!" She waved it up at him. It was some sort of spellbook. The elf tried to hide his disgust.

"That's wonderful, Trina."

"It's got all kinds of spells in here. Listen: A Spell for Curing Serious Injuries. A Spell for Seeing Things Made Magically Invisible. A Spell for Opening Magically Sealed Doors . . ."

Jander wasn't listening. A Spell for Ignoring Prattling Werewolves, he thought to himself with a slight smile. A Spell for—

"What was that last one?" he asked, trying to keep his voice calm.

"Um . . . here it is. A Spell for Opening Magically Sealed Doors."

"That's a very difficult one, I hear. You'd better not try that one yet."

As he had hoped, Trina frowned up at him. She was sitting on the stairs, the book spread out in her lap. "If it's in here, I can do it. You don't appreciate magic. You don't realize just how much Strahd has taught me over the last few months."

"I still don't know if you're up to that one," Jander countered.

"You show me a door that's magically locked, and I'll open it for you," she boasted.

Jander pretended to think. "I can't think of any right—wait a minute. There is one door that's been magically locked."

He and Trina hurried up to the study. Jander was filled with nervousness and elation. He had been wanting to get into Strahd's mysterious room for a long time now. Every other place he had looked for information on Anna had turned up nothing. He knew for a fact there were books in that room, perhaps something that would tell him more about the woman he loved.

They climbed the winding stairs, and Jander pointed to the door across from them. "I believe that one's been locked. Give it a try."

Placing the book on the waxed table in the center of the study, Trina perused the spell for several minutes. Jander feigned nonchalance, pretending to scan some of the book titles.

"Jander, watch this," Trina crowed. She stood in front of the door and closed her eyes. Raising her hands and spreading her fingers, she muttered a long string of words under her breath. The outline of the door began to glow with faint bluish light. Abruptly the light disappeared. There was a barely audible click, and the door swung forward an inch or so.

"Oh, Trina, you are clever," Jander approved. She smiled hugely, obviously very pleased with herself. "What else can you do?"

More than anything he could recall wanting in recent memory, he wanted to enter that room, with its teasing, open door. Before he could do that, however, he knew he had to allay any suspicions the werewolf might harbor as to his motive. Feigning interest in her newfound skills, he followed her around for the next hour or so while she moved objects without touching them, caused the fire in the hearth to blaze brightly and then fall to embers, and demonstrated other easily mastered feats. "A Spell to Fall like a Feather," she read, her eyes growing huge. "Is that like flying?"

"I don't know, but you'd better make sure you study that one well before you go leaping off the ramparts."

Trina laughed. "I will."

"Is there anything else you can show me?" the elf queried, hoping desperately that they had reached the bottom of Trina's bag of tricks. Quickly the werewolf scanned the spells and shook her head.

"Nothing that I can do right now."

"Well, in that case, would you mind practicing else-where? I have some work I have to do."

She fixed him with a wary gaze. "Like what?"

For a horrible instant, his mind went blank, then: "I'm going to oil these bookcases. They're so lovely, but Strahd hasn't really taken the time to bring out the lus-ter of this wood—"

"Sure, Jander. I'll leave you to it" the werewolf said hastily, fleeing in the face of boredom. "I'm going to try the Falling like a Feather one in a bit. See you later." She left, closing the book but keeping a finger in it to mark the page.

At last, the elf was alone. After Trina had gone, he closed the study door, locking it for good measure. He turned to the door of the secret room, his mouth going dry with excitement and nervousness. He hadn't been this reckless in years, but Strahd had just recently left and would not be back for at least a few days. What was it that Strahd was so insistent Jander not see? He couldn't even imagine what it might be.

A twinge of remorse touched the elf. He had given the count his word that he would not enter the room. For a brief moment, honor warred with curiosity and the fierce hope that, here, at last, he might find some trace of Anna. Jander stepped up to the door.

With a bit of trepidation, the vampire reached out and hesitantly pushed open the wooden door. It swung inward with a creak to reveal a large, dark room. There was a stench within, of decay, and his nose wrinkled. His eyes quickly adjusted to the darkness, but he took a torch that was fastened on the wall to his left and lit it from the fire in the study. Thus armed, he entered.

A long table stretched before him. Once, like so many of the objects in Castle Ravenloft, it must have been a thing of great beauty. Now it was covered with a layer of dust. That did not surprise him; it was what was on the table, underneath that thick dust, that caused

Jander to raise an eyebrow in surprise.

The table was laid in anticipation of a meal that had never arrived. There was a disgusting pile of rotting matter in the center of the table. Jander drew forward, raising the torch for a better look. It had once been a cake—judging by its many tiers and the tiny figure of a white-clad woman on its top, a wedding cake.

Jander tasted a faint flavor of fear. Something was very, very wrong here. He took a stepped away from the table onto an object that crunched under his foot. He glanced down to see what it was, and his apprehension increased. It was the other half of the cake decoration— the tiny figure of a groom. The head was missing from the tiny man.

Jander turned his attention to the rest of the room. The table and what remained of the cake indicated that this had once been a dining hall. It was also a picture gallery. Jander was surrounded by the faces of the Von Zarovich family. Some of the names seemed familiar, others were completely new. He paused when he came across a portrait of a handsome young couple.

According to the plaque at the bottom of the picture, the pair were Barov and Ravenovia Von Zarovich. This painting was done when they were but recently married, and they were a stunningly attractive pair. By the date on the picture and the striking similarity to Strahd, Jander assumed them to be the count's parents. Barov's features were clearly echoed in his son's; the dark eyes, the finely-chiseled nose and cheekbones were almost exactly like the present count's. Ravenovia had been a beauty, and the skilled artist had managed to capture the fire and intelligence of her large dark eyes.

The next picture was of three men. Strahd was one of them. He was seated in a plush, red velvet chair. He had changed little since the portrait had been painted, and Jander guessed that it had been completed shortly before his transformation. On the count's left hand, standing slightly behind the chair, was a man in his late thirties. He was rather squat, but had a kindly, benevolent expression and was clearly close kin to Strahd. On the right, kneeling beside the count with his hand on the arm of the chair, was one of the most handsome young men Jander had ever seen. His features, too, were Strahd's, but they were different—clearer, bearing a stamp of youthful vigor and a curious combination of power, self-respect, and innocence. This man was only in his twenties. Oddly, he seemed strangely familiar to Jander. Both this man and Strahd wore military uniforms, though of different ranks and orders. The young man wore a beautiful, sun-shaped pendant. Strahd's breast was encrusted with medals.

Jander read the names: Strahd, Sturm, and Sergei Von Zarovich. An attractive trio of brothers, had the artist been less perceptive and not painted to perfection Strahd's troubled countenance. His dark eyes were grim, the eyes of a man who saw neither joy nor beauty anywhere he looked, the mouth a thin, humorless line. Even in life, when blood and breath had tied him to the sunlight world of the living, Strahd had obviously been an unhappy man, despite the honors that crowded his chest.

There were many more paintings. The costumes changed through the years, although some suits of armor and pieces of jewelry recurred as if they were family heirlooms or formal regalia. Aimlessly Jander wandered about the room, glancing at a few of the portraits.

At the far end of the room, there was a small table set up. Unlike most of furnishings in Castle Ravenloft, this table was meticulously kept. A clean, white cloth was draped over it, and pieces of jewelry were carefully laid out: a necklace, earrings, a bracelet. There were two candles in well-polished holders and two leather-bound books. One was obviously very old and well-thumbed. The other was much newer.

Jander picked up the newer book and rifled through it aimlessly. It was written in Strahd's curious shorthand, but over the last few decades Jander had had ample time to decipher it. He replaced the book on the table, not bothering to look at the other tome.

Above the table there was another portrait. It was covered with a white cloth similar to the one that draped the table. Jander frowned. Why hide this one? With a swift movement, he tugged off the cover.

He stared, horrified, at the two figures depicted there. A man and a woman posed happily in their wedding finery. Yet someone had taken a knife and slashed through the man's face repeatedly. That, however, was not what struck Jander to his heart. It was face of the woman on the man's arm.

It was Anna's face. It could be no other's.

She was smiling radiantly up at the now-faceless young man. Her expression was one of absolute joy, and love shone in her eyes. She was wearing a beautiful white dress and carrying a bouquet of flowers. A veil trailed over her auburn curls. It had been her wedding that had been celebrated in this room.

Jander stared at the portrait for several minutes, trying to make sense of the senseless. At length his gaze straggled down to the names of the couple: "Sergei Von Zarovich and Tatyana Federovna, on the Occasion of their Wedding, 351."

The elf staggered back, shaking, his mind reeling as he tried to comprehend what had happened. So this wasn't Anna, but someone named Tatyana. A sister? A twin, perhaps?

His gaze dropped to the books. Perhaps they had some information regarding Tatyana. He picked up the newer one and opened it. It was entitled "The Tome of Strahd." Despite his agitated state, Jander snorted derisively. Trust Strahd to pen something so ostentatious. He sat down by the shrine to Tatyana, cradled the *Tome of Strahd* in his lap, both eager and afraid, and began to read.

I am The Ancient, I am The Land. My beginnings are lost in the darkness of the past. I was the warrior, I was good and just. I thundered across the land like the wrath of a just god, but the war years and the killing years wore down my soul as the wind wears stone into sand . . .

Jander frowned to himself. This was no chronicle of the past. This was Strahd's propaganda, his writing of history as he wanted to see it—just like the tale, riddled with falsehoods, that he had told Jander years before about how Barovia had entered the mists. Some wild, distorted story about a rival and a woman and—

Staring wide-eyed, Jander looked up at the painting again. Was this bright young man Strahd's rival, who "enchanted" Tatyana and "stole" her from the count? False, all false, and he knew it to be, though he did not know how he knew. It was impossible to conceive of two people more in love than the couple depicted in the painting, impossible to ever cast them as schemer and slave.

Disgusted, the elf put the book down, reaching instead for the other one. Carefully, aware of how fragile it was, Jander eased it open. The pages were yellow and threatened to crumble at his touch. The writing was barely legible, and the shorthand made it difficult for Jander to read as quickly as he wanted. He could make out enough to see that it was a diary, dating back to 349 on the Barovian calendar—nearly two hundred and fifty years in the past.

Before Strahd became a vampire.

Jander began to tremble. Clutching the book close, he made for the study. He had several hours until sunset and would not be disturbed. He replaced the torch in its sconce, settled down in one of the overstuffed chairs, and began to read.

 **TWENTY**

Twelfth Moon, 347. At long last, the war is over. The enemy has been decimated, destroyed, or driven out. I have found a valley that lies before the ruins of the warlord's castle. I have taken both . . .

Sixth Moon, 348. Peace gnaws at my soul. I do not like it. The inhabitants of Barovia do not like me, either. I care not . . .

Third Moon, 349. Work proceeds on the castle. In honor of my mother, I shall name it Ravenloft. It is becoming a suitable home for the Von Zaroviches . . .

Eleventh Moon, 349. All is in readiness. I shall call for my family, to make this cold place a home . . .

Fourth Moon, 350. They have arrived, and Sergei, my youngest brother whom I have never before met, is with them. How young he is, both in body and spirit! If he had not nearly bested me in sparring this morning, I would call him a summer soldier, but in all honesty, his skill is staggering.

We have become fast friends as well as blood-bonded soldiers. He is suited to the new age of peace in a way that I, with the chill of death in my bones and the taste of war still on my tongue, could never be. What would I give to be him now, young and carefree, with those dark good looks that captivate women? What an irony that, as he is the youngest son, he is pledged to become a priest!

I must be growing old—the cold night in its futile quest for the beginning of day. Never before have I wanted a family. Now that Sergei has come, I find myself imagining a woman by my side and a child on my knee . . .

Sixth Moon, 350: The Most High Priest Kir has died suddenly, and Sergei has insisted I declare it a day of national mourning. Sergei must now take up the position of Most High Priest, an honor that has the lad quite humbled. He is not permitted to wear the formal garb of a priest, as he has not yet been ordained, but the clergy has given him leave to wear the Priest's Pendant, a pretty enough bauble to which Sergei attaches a great deal of—perhaps even too much—emotional value.

* * * * *

It was the year 350 by the Barovian calendar, and as Count Strahd Von Zarovich gazed out over the River Ivlis, watching it twine its way through the mountains and the Svalich Woods, he knew he was the absolute and unquestioned master of everything he surveyed.

The thought gave him no pleasure. Little did, these days.

There had been a movement, a few years past, concocted by some frightened burgomaster in one of the little villages, to turn the count's birthday into a national holiday. The burgomaster had sought to turn Strahd's displeasure for the paltry tax money that had come from that particular village. He had picked the wrong tactic. Strahd never celebrated his birthday. He had once joked, calling it the "death day." Now it was never discussed at all. Strahd's youth had fled, squandered in fighting and killing.

The unfortunate burgomaster had turned up dead, his head neatly separated from his body by one sure sword stroke. The issue of the count's birthday had never again been raised.

This day Strahd returned to his study, picking up the

journal he had begun when he had first conquered this
land.

*I hate the Barovians! They do not know when to leave
well enough alone.* He paused, then scratched in, *Has
Sergei picked up this trait as well?*

*He has developed a disconcerting habit of venturing in-
to the village, trying to, as he says, "do some good for
these people." There, he is treated like some sort of young
god. The folk throw flowers in the path of his horse and
practically deafen the boy with cheering. No good can
come of this. Sergei's place is above the people, here in
Castle Ravenloft, a proper Von Zarovich. He should not
be wallowing in peasants' dust.*

There came a burst of knocking on the study door.
"Come," called Strahd absently.

It was Sergei. His handsome features were alight, his
curly dark hair in disarray. "Oh, Strahd, I must tell you
what happened today!"

"Must you?" his brother replied as he reluctantly set
down the book. "What can you possibly have found in
that dismal village to interest a Von Zarovich?"

Strahd frowned to himself as Sergei drew up a chair.
He had never thought Sergei's enthusiasm and forth-
rightness becoming to the ruling family of the land. Today Sergei was a veritable frolicking puppy. Something
of portent indeed must have happened. "I met a girl."

Strahd waited, but that apparently was the extent of
Sergei's announcement. With a trace of annoyance, the
older man picked up the diary. "Good heavens, Sergei,
if you come bounding in here every time you want to
'save' one of the local whores—"

"If you were anyone other than my brother, I'd kill
you for that!" Sergei was on his feet, anger in his face. "I
met her doing my work in the village. She helps people,
she . . . You've never met her. I'll bring her here shortly,
and you can see for yourself."

"You shall not sully this house with harlots!"

"*You* shall not speak of Tatyana in that fashion!"

"Oho, the tart has a name!"

With a visible effort, Sergei mastered his rage. He deliberately reseated himself, and when he spoke it was in soft tones. "Brother, you know the love I bear for you. I would ask that you not refer to Tatyana as a whore, or tart, or with anything other than complete courtesy. She is of low birth, that's true, but she is perfection itself. Never have I seen a brighter soul. And, Strahd, she will be mine. I plan to marry her."

"Out of the question. First of all, she's not of proper rank. And secondly," he reached to touch the priest's amulet that Sergei wore, "you're pledged elsewhere. Remember?"

"You know that Mother and Father had no particular desire for me to continue with my vocation. The custom that the youngest son enters the priesthood is merely that—custom. Not a law!"

"You seemed suited to it."

Sergei had to nod. "I was. Am, still. Had I been meant to continue down that path, surely the gods would not have made me love Tatyana so. When you meet her, you will love her, too. Besides, what does it matter if I wed? You are the heir, and after you comes Sturm. You see—" he flashed the familiar all's-right-with-the-world grin "—there are advantages to being the youngest son."

"Sergei," said Strahd, his patience wearing thin, "wed whom you will. I care not. If you've found some potato-shaped ragamuffin from the village and can clean her up enough so that the servants don't object, you can marry her tomorrow for all I care. Leave me, now. I'm quite busy."

Sergei frowned. His clear blue eyes searched Strahd's face. "I know many years separate us, and I know you think me impossibly young and immature. I've always admired you, Brother, but I've never understood what made you so bitter when you had won so much and had so much in your favor."

"Sergei—"

"Damn it, Strahd, nobody knows better than I do the things you've done for us all. You've put an end to a war that had been going on for generations! You bought us this peace. Your part is done, and you did it beautifully. I don't have that kind of pride in something I've done. I can't win a war. I can only live and do what I think is right, here in these quiet times." The young man rose. "I'm sorry you had to spend your youth on a battlefield, but it's not my fault."

Strahd watched him go, shaking his head. There were times that he completely despaired of Sergei—and other times when he admired his brother beyond all men.

Sergei had been the last and most radiant flower on the Von Zarovich vine. He had brought love and comfort to his parents while Strahd was away fighting battle after battle and Sturm's interests led him away from the immediate family. Sergei had grown to manhood not knowing his eldest brother, and when Strahd had settled in Barovia and called for his family, the eldest and the youngest brothers had met for the first time.

It was brotherly love at first sight. Sergei clearly worshiped Strahd, the gallant war hero, and Strahd could not help but respond. And why not? There was so very much to like about Sergei: he was intelligent, full of good humor, a fine sparring partner on the field.

As much as the aging warrior could, Strahd loved Sergei.

It was no paradise in Castle Ravenloft. Strahd wanted his youth back. He not only loved Sergei, he wanted to *be* Sergei—twenty-seven, with his whole life spread in front of him like a banquet, to be enjoyed and savored until one was sated. Strahd's youth had been poured on the soil to appease the gods of war, and now, at age forty-five, he had very little that was precious to look back upon. He had no family, no intimate friends. All the good he had once thought of doing had somehow bowed to expedience; he had made no law that had changed the world, had annexed no territory that had brought him new life. It would serve Sergei well to be saddled with some cabbage grower's daughter, Strahd thought bitterly.

He picked up the quill and wrote in strong, bold letters: *For all the love that is between us, Sergei angers me from time to time.*

Five days later, when Sergei's betrothed stepped out of the carriage and looked about shyly, Strahd knew a sharp despair.

The girl was beautiful—perfection indeed, as Sergei had assured him. She was tall, with long, rich auburn hair that curled down her back in waves. Her simple clothes clung to her full breasts and narrow waist, and her skin was tanned from the sun. Sergei held tightly to her hand, beaming with pride and love. And when Tatyana glanced up at her future husband, her warm eyes glowed with devotion. Somehow Strahd got through the introductions, even the lengthy formal dinner that night. However, his heart had been lost to this lovely jewel from the valley.

Her genuine sweetness made things even harder to bear. She often slipped her arm through Strahd's when they were walking, called him "brother" and "elder," with a great deal of respect. How could she know that he envied his brother with all his heart?

Sometimes the count fancied that she loved him, too; but always, that fragile deception shattered when she laid eyes on Sergei. Then she came wonderfully, fully alive with love. All who saw the young couple together took joy in their joy, so genuine and obvious was their mutual devotion.

All save Count Strahd Von Zarovich.

His dreams that she would fall in love with him continued, growing ever darker as the months passed and the wedding drew near. He began consulting various spellbooks, but could find nothing that would suit his needs. Strahd became ever more irascible, often staying up until the dawn, searching for something, anything, that might help.

One afternoon, he sought distraction by playing the organ. The diversion worked for a while, wrapping him up in its reverberating music that sang to the soul. His fingers flew over the keys, coaxing chords that echoed his torment yet brought release from it.

Sounds from the entry hall broke his concentration and he ceased playing, his fragile peace shattered. Going to investigate, he frowned with displeasure. It was not to be a quiet afternoon, it would seem. Laughter and amiable chatter filled the hitherto silent halls as the hunt, hounds and all, spilled into the dining room. The dogs' nails made little clicking sounds on the stone floor as they ambled about happily, tails wagging.

"Strahd!" Sergei waved at his brother. "You missed a fine hunt!"

"Indeed, Old One, even you would have laughed for joy, if we could only have dragged you away from your books," Tatyana added, smiling warmly at the count.

Strahd returned the smile, although his was forced. "Books are good company. Fox hunting is a waste of time."

"Ah, you'd have enjoyed this one. And you'll never guess what happened at the Wolf's Den afterward!" Sergei caught his brother's arm and propelled him toward the table, where unobtrusive servants were uncorking dusty bottles and filling crystal goblets. Smoothly Sergei maneuvered a glass of the ruby liquid into Strahd's strong hand.

"Sergei!" Tatyana's face turned the color of the wine and, laughing a little, she ducked her head against Strahd's chest in a totally unselfconscious fashion. "Please make him stop, Old One, I don't want that tale told!"

Strahd closed his dark eyes, willing himself not to betray his inner torment. Oh, to have Tatyana's head on his breast thus and not have her love! Unable to help himself, he raised his arm to fold her against him.

Abruptly the beloved warmth against his chest was gone. Teasingly Sergei had tugged his betrothed free and was busy kissing her, despite her shy protests. "She taught me quite a lesson, Strahd."

"Gods know, you have much to learn," the count

growled, jealousy welling up inside him like a poisoned tide.

"We were drinking a pint of ale with the locals down at the tavern. All of a sudden, this big, hairy brute grabbed poor Tatyana. Just grabbed her. And before we could do anything, he was trying to—"

"*What?*"

The word exploded from Strahd's throat. Fury raced through him. The other members of the hunt stepped back. The count was hardly known for his gentleness of manner, but this crimson rage that contorted his face went beyond what even the most unfortunate of them had ever witnessed. Even Tatyana was frightened and drew closer to her future husband. Only Sergei, whose love for his brother was absolute, was unaffected. He continued his tale.

"Trying to beat her head on the floor," Sergei finished. "Well, naturally, I and a few of these good fellows pulled him off her the instant we regained our wits. We were going to take him outside and give him a drumming he wouldn't soon forget, but Tatyana wouldn't let us."

Startled, Strahd glanced at the girl. Her color was high, but her eyes met his evenly. Gods, those eyes.

"She told us that she knew this man, that they had grown up together. She said that he was angry because she'd been lucky enough to marry a Von Zarovich, while his family starved. Then do you know what my dove did?" Sergei smiled proudly down at Tatyana, his arm tightening about her shoulders. "She took off every piece of jewelry she had on and gave them all to this man. 'Buy food for your children,' she told him, 'and as long as I live, your family shall never go hungry.' And that monster, that big, hulking bear—why, Strahd, he began to cry, just like a baby, and kissed Tatyana's hands. Isn't she a wonder?"

A cheer rose from the hunters, and a toast was drunk to Sergei's bride-to-be. She beamed happily.

"Tatyana, you are a fool," Strahd said bluntly. Her eyes filled with pain. He ignored her, turning to Sergei.

"And you, Brother, are worse. You have just dragged the family name through the dirt of that filthy town. You ought to have slain the dog for his insolence. If a servant of mine had behaved as you did today, I'd have him flogged raw. Unfortunately, you are my blood kin, so that option isn't open to me. Believe me, I regret that. You will excuse me."

He stalked out of the dining room, hurling his goblet to the floor. Stunned silence marked his departure. Everyone was embarrassed, but no one knew what to say. Tatyana spoke first. "Poor Strahd. I think he may need our pity and care more than Yakov in the village."

"My dear," said Sergei softly, kissing the top of her head, "I believe you may be right."

Scrawling furiously, Strahd vented his anger in his journal: *I must find something, some spell, some potion, that will make this angel mine. I must! There is nothing I would not give to win that woman!*

Strahd was awake well into the early hours of the morning. He sighed deeply, rubbing eyes that were heavy and full of grit. Every part of his weary body screamed at him to abandon the quest, at least for this evening, and rest.

By a great effort of will, the count shook off his lethargy. Should he not discover some magical means of making Tatyana his own, he told himself sternly, there would be plenty of nights alone in his bed for sleep. With hands that trembled from exhaustion, Strahd grimly selected another book of spells, seated himself heavily, and began to peruse it.

He was turning a page when he noticed that two pages were stuck together. He frowned. Why had he never observed this before? What secrets lay between those two pages that he had yet to explore? Sudden eagerness surged through him, bringing him fully awake. Carefully, wary of damaging the old parchment, he separated the two pages. He began to smile, hardly daring to believe the evidence of his own eyes. In a flowing script on the yellowed pages, some long-forgotten wizard had penned the following:

A Spell For Obtaining The Heart's Desire.

He skimmed through the spell quickly. There was nothing too unusual about it; it boasted no out-of-the-ordinary magical ingredients. *Bat's wool* . . . Gods, that was certainly easy enough to obtain in this forsaken place. *Ground unicorn horn* . . . If he remembered correctly, he had some of the precious powder around somewhere. Then something curious happened. Strahd's vision blurred for an instant. Impatiently he again rubbed at his overworked eyes.

When he looked back down at the spell, the list of ingredients had changed.

"What?" he muttered to himself. As he watched, the letters twisted and turned, reforming into new words. Suddenly alarmed, Strahd dropped the book on the table. It landed with a loud *clap*.

That's a very old book. You should handle it more carefully, came a voice that raised the hairs on the back of Strahd's neck.

His head whipped up, and he looked quickly about the room. There was no one save himself in the study. "Who's there?" he called.

You ought to know, came the voice again. It was full of silky, suppressed mirth, and seemed to come from every corner of the room. It rasped on Strahd's ears like dead leaves scudding over a tomb. *You called me. I heard your hate. I am here to give you your Heart's Desire.*

"Show yourself," Strahd demanded.

The voice laughed, low and drily. *You could not tolerate the sight.*

Suddenly Strahd believed that whispery, cold voice, and a part of him cried for him to leave the study, leave the dead voice that crept through him like a poison, leave Tatyana to Sergei.

"No," Strahd whispered. "She will be mine."

Shall we begin?

"I—I have not even performed the rite," the count

stammered, trying to collect his scattered thoughts.

You do not need to. The spell was only there to . . . pique your interest. As you undoubtedly noticed, it is constantly changing. Just like a mortal's mind.

"What are you?"

At the question, the volume of the voice grew like wind on a stormy night. It laughed, swelling until it pressed upon the count like some physical being.

I am every nightmare every creature has ever had. I am the dark thoughts of murder and treachery, of fear and lust and obscenity and violation. I am the cutting word that kills the soul and the bloody knife that kills the body. I am the poison at the bottom of the cup, the noose around the thief's neck, the cry of the wronged, and the shriek of the tortured. I am the lie. I am the black pit of madness. I am Death and all things worse. You know me, Count Strahd Von Zarovich. We are old, old friends, you and I.

Strahd began to tremble, but his voice was steady. "Have you come . . . for me?"

I have come on your behalf, the graveyard voice sighed, its sound again as faint as a dying man's last breath. *You have fed me well. You are due your reward. You hunger for your brother's betrothed, for your lost youth. I shall remove the rival from your path, and you shall age not one day more . . . if you do as I tell you.*

For a moment the count hesitated. What this creature offered was temptation beyond belief. *Tatyana.* Strahd nodded. "What must I do?"

TWENTY-ONE

Gods! Gods! What horrors and miracles have been wrought here today! My hand trembles as I write, but from grief or joy I cannot say. I shall endeavor to put down events as clearly as I can, so that I may read them later, when my mind is calmer, and try to make sense of it all . . .

* * * * *

An hour before the ceremony, shortly after dusk, Strahd knocked softly at Sergei's door. "Come," the younger man called.

Strahd entered, smiling. Sergei looked quite splendid. His bright blue uniform, decorated with epaulets and medals, had been cleaned and pressed for the occasion. His boots were black and shiny, and the platinum priest's medallion around his neck flashed as he moved. Sergei had just finished buckling on his sword and was now plucking nervously at his uniform. He glanced up at his mirror to see who had entered. When his eyes met Strahd's, a huge smile spread across his face.

"I wasn't sure you'd be here!" Sergei exclaimed, turning and holding his arms out to Strahd. The count hesitated, then embraced him. "I didn't know if you were still angry about that incident with Tatyana and the villager."

"Nay, little brother, I was overhasty and cruel. I have come to ask forgiveness of you."

Sergei's eyes, the bright blue of his uniform, filled with quick tears. "There are those in this land who say there is no good in you," he said thickly, "but I always knew that there was the soul of an angel in the 'devil Strahd.'"

"Step back and let me look at you," the count said enthusiastically, uncomfortable with the emotional turn the conversation had taken. Sergei obliged, smiling bashfully. Strahd whistled mockingly, and his brother landed a good-natured, gentle punch.

"You're going to break more than a few hearts today," the count said. "There will be a rash of suicides in the village, I'll wager. Every matron in the land shall mourn the death of Barovia's most eligible bachelor."

"Ah, but I trust that they shall raise a glass to the most happily married man in the world shortly thereafter!"

A cold, sluggish anger began to creep through Strahd's veins. He had almost decided against sealing the bargain he'd struck with the mysterious dark entity. Sergei's obvious love for him and delight at his presence had strengthened that resolve. Now, though, as Sergei beamed with joy for his upcoming marriage, the dark monster of jealousy began to stir inside the count.

He reached a slender finger to touch Sergei's medallion. The piece glittered, the crystal in its center flashing as it swung gently. "You'll have to give that up, you know."

Sergei's hand reached up to clasp the medallion. "Yes, I know. Can't be married and be a priest, can I? Although I never did think that was quite fair. You can do your duty to your gods and your family. Love for one doesn't eclipse the other."

"Sacrilege!" Strahd exclaimed in mock horror. "You'll have to start your own religion, Sergei."

The young man laughed at that, releasing his hold on he platinum pendant. "Maybe I will, if I can still keep his. It's been a source of comfort on some long, dark ights, I can tell you."

The red tint of anger mixed with the green of jealousy n the palette of the older man's soul. What could this child possible know of long, dark nights? What kind of ell had the spoiled youth clawed *his* way through? Serei had never had to fight for anything in his brief life! Raised in the lap of luxury, he fought for pleasure and exercise, not for life, not for lands. Women flocked round him, and he, the idiot, always turned them down vith some polite excuse. He was an excellent and couraeous young fighter, but damn him, he ought to have een a priest. What had he done to deserve Tatyana? And what had he, Strahd, done to be denied her?

"You could have had any woman in the world," Strahd aid suddenly. "Why her?"

Sergei's eyes widened in surprise, then grew soft with ity. "Oh, Strahd," he whispered, his voice trembling vith emotion, "don't you know?"

In his heart of hearts, Strahd did know, and he knew vhat Sergei meant by the question. It was merely the hetorical question of a lover so in love that he thought he whole world must see his betrothed as he did.

Strahd's jealousy and bitterness chose to warp the weet words. *Don't you know?* The simple question beame a taunt in the count's poisoned mind. Curse him! Sergei knew Strahd loved Tatyana, and he was marrying he girl himself to spite his older brother!

Somehow Strahd reined in his anger and realized hat Sergei was speaking.

"My joy is complete save for one thing. I wish you had omeone like Tatyana."

"For the groom, I have a present," Strahd said, ignorng the comment and handing Sergei a carefully rapped bundle of embroidered fabric. "It's magical nd quite old. Well suited to the day."

Smiling, Sergei unwrapped the present. It was a small

dagger, its hilt decorated with red, black, and gold. The sheath was an odd kind of leather, of a peculiar color. Sergei glanced up at Strahd, confused.

"I see you recognize it," Strahd said, "the time-honored weapon of the Ba'al Verzi assassin. The sheath is made of human skin, usually from the weapon's first victim. The carvings on the hilt are runes of power."

Sergei's face registered shock. Calmly the count took the weapon and pretended to examine it. He drew it gingerly; the blade was bright and flashed candlelight. "Legend has it that it is bad luck to draw the dagger unless you can give it blood. I'm generally not superstitious, but I think this time it's better to not tempt fate. Don't you agree?"

Before Sergei could react, Strahd plunged the blade into his brother's heart. Crimson fountained onto the murderer's hand. He met Sergei's final, questioning gaze with a savage joy. Confused to the last, the young man died without a sound. He collapsed limply into Strahd's arms.

Working quickly, the count laid the body out on the floor. Just as the entity had demanded, Strahd withdrew the knife. He gazed at the shiny crimson on the long blade and took a deep breath. Bringing the bloody knife to his mouth, he licked it clean, fighting the nausea that welled up inside him. He grimaced, then tore open his brother's uniform and white cotton shirt, exposing the small wound that still pumped bright blood.

Drink of the blood, first from the instrument and then the chalice, the entity had told him. Strahd knelt beside the still-warm corpse of his favorite brother, placed his lips on the wound and drank.

He choked, coughing and gagging, and lost some of the precious fluid. Anger at his weakness flooded him. Exerting the discipline that had made him a veteran warrior, he ordered his body to continue. Strahd sucked at the lips of the wound, pulling more coppery-tasting blood down his throat, until, imperceptibly, the action became easier. After a moment, he began to relish the taste.

Energy filled him. Suddenly he became aware of the texture of Sergei's fine clothing beneath newly sensitive fingers. He could smell the blood and sweat on his brother's body. He heard the voices of the other guests, even though they were many rooms away. On a whim, Strahd picked up Sergei's body with one hand, simply because he could. This was glorious! He laughed aloud and dropped the corpse carelessly. It sprawled, and abruptly Strahd realized what had happened.

The count began to tremble, and he knelt by his brother's body, touching the pale, still face gently. He gathered the corpse in his arms, and when he cried out loudly, his grief was unfeigned.

"Damn you, Sergei, damn you. This is your own fault! You weren't supposed to marry! You were the youngest son, you were supposed to have been a priest . . . Why didn't you just do what you'd been born to do?"

Strahd's powerful hands were knotted in Sergei's thick, curly hair, his flushed cheek pressed against his brother's pale one. Quick footsteps were heard in the corridor, and Anton, Sergei's personal servant, threw open the door. He stared, horrified, at the bloody scene. He dragged his shocked gaze from Sergei to Strahd, imploring the count to do something.

Strahd held out the Ba'al Verzi knife. Anton recognized it, and his eyes, already wide, grew even larger. "Sergei is dead," the count said brokenly. "It must have happened just a moment ago. Tell the guards to seal off the castle at once. We must find my brother's murderer!"

The servant nodded, still in shock, staring at Sergei's limp, blood-soaked form. Anton's eyes filled; like all in Castle Ravenloft, he had loved the young master. Then he was gone.

Strahd was astounded. It had been so easy. He had never lied before; as the unquestioned master of first his troops and then his land, he had never had to. He had doubted that he could brazen his way out of the murder of his own brother, yet he had, and with so small a lie. He wondered if this easy way with falsehood was yet another part of his dark gift.

Suddenly he went cold. He had drunk Sergei's blood. Had his mouth been stained with the fluid when Anton was present? Quickly Strahd got to his feet and went to inspect his face in the mirror. When he peered into the glass, he received a profound shock.

His reflection was starting to become transparent.

Strahd clutched at his chest, relieved to find it solid to the touch. It took an effort to conquer the sudden rush of fear that welled up inside him, but then, Strahd had never been weak-willed. Stubbornly he forced the fear back and bathed his face and hands. The water in the basin turned red.

From the chapel he heard a high-pitched wail of despair, followed by shouts and weeping and other sounds of lamentation. The door to Sergei's room again burst open, and four of the castle guards entered. Their swords were drawn. "Your Excellency," said their captain, "we have sealed off all exits to the castle, as you requested. We have no idea who might have done the deed, but no one shall leave until you are satisfied as to the identity of the killer."

Strahd, calm again, nodded. "Excellent. Confine everyone to either the chapel or the dining room, whichever one they happen to be nearest."

"Aye, Your Excellency." The guards turned to leave.

"A moment." Strahd had paid the bloody price. It was time to collect his promised reward. "Where is Tatyana?"

"Out behind the chapel, in the garden. She refuses to let anyone near her."

"She'll let me near her," Strahd said. He smiled thinly. "She has to."

He made his way to the chapel, ignoring the tears and questions of the devastated guests. Dozens of candles provided illumination in the chapel, enough to cause the stained glass windows to cast colored shadows on the statue-still figure of the angelic young girl who huddled, shattered, in the dewy grass of the garden.

The bride's face was white with shock, her dark eyes enormous. Tatyana seemed to have no care of the dirt and grass on her beautiful, painstakingly sewed wedding gown. She did not look up as Strahd approached. Gently he eased down beside her.

"Come, my dear," he said tenderly, folding her in his embrace. She remained immobile for a moment, then he felt her relax, come back to life, and begin to weep. Her slim body shook violently with each sob, and she clung to him as if she were drowning. Strahd tightened his grip, his newly heightened senses drinking in the feel of the smooth white silk, the scent of her skin and hair, the warmth of her young body. He murmured soft words, soothing, comforting.

At last her sobs quieted, and she began to speak brokenly. "Wh-why? I don't unders-stand. Who would— who *could* do something like this? Oh, Strahd!" Her sobs began afresh, and her hands clung to him desperately.

"Shh. I know it is hard for you now, my darling, but soon all will be well. Out of great pain comes greater joy, and, in time, you will deem yourself the most fortunate of all women."

She froze, then suddenly wrenched herself away from him, slapping his face. Her eyes were wild, filled with agony. "Old one," she whispered, "he's *dead!* How can you say such things to me?"

"Because you are free. You are free to marry me now. He stood in the way of our happiness, but no more, my dear, no more! Tatyana, beloved, I can give you—"

"No!" Her agony turning to revulsion, Tatyana struggled to escape the murderer of her fiance. Strahd's grip was unbreakable.

He was filled with a sudden anger at her ingratitude. If she would just stop struggling, just let him explain what wonders had been wrought, and all for her, *all for her*. He clamped his hands on either side of her face and kissed her. Her mouth was sweet, but there was a new hunger growing inside him, and he wanted more from her than just a kiss.

He bellowed in pain, and his grip slackened. One hand went to his mouth and came away red. Pain throbbed in his lower lip where she had bitten him.

From a few inches away, Tatyana stared at Strahd for an instant. Her eyes widened with a new horror, then she was up, hiking the long, trailing skirt of the dress up to her knees and running as though her very soul depended upon it.

And perhaps she was not so wrong.

Strahd cried his anger, and the sound echoed through the castle. Then he, too, was on his feet and in pursuit of the terrified girl, running with unnatural speed and silence.

Tatyana fled, her heart pounding, sweat pouring down her face, stinging her eyes and blurring her vision as she raced through the garden. Rose thorns tore at her dress, and she wondered with a new burst of panic if even the plants were under Strahd's command.

There was nowhere for her to run, really. In her mad flight she didn't realize that, neither would she have cared. The only direction was away from Strahd, away from the lonely old warrior who had somehow become a monster and murdered Sergei.

Tatyana could hear him behind her, crying her name, demanding that she wait. She had seen what a hideous, bloody-fanged creature he had become, and she would never let him touch her again. When the low, stony walls loomed in front of her, Tatyana did not even slow down. Strahd seized the hem of her dress, but with a strength that startled him, the girl tugged it loose from his iron grip.

The mists roiled below as Tatyana threw herself over the garden wall, embracing the sky as if she were reaching for Sergei. Her cry as she hurtled downward hundreds of feet toward the jagged rocks was not so much a wail of anguish as of sharp, pure joy at having escaped Strahd's grasp.

The count's flailing hands clutched at empty air, and

he almost lost his balance. He could see her white form falling like a dying swan until the mists and the darkness far below engulfed her, mercifully sparing him the sight of her body being shattered on the rocks.

Pounding impotently on the wall, the vampire arched his back in agony and screamed. His cry echoed back to him mockingly from the mist-shrouded depths that yawned open a few feet ahead.

An arrow whizzed past his right ear. Strahd whipped around, staring with fury at the castle. By now, the identity of Sergei's murderer was clear, and the guards knew their duty. The archers had assumed their posts and directed their arrows through the slits in the wall.

The air was suddenly filled with angry, singing sounds as dozens of arrows found their mark in the body of the castle's lord.

Yet Strahd did not die.

He looked down at the arrows protruding from his chest and abdomen. A slow smile spread across his features, and, enjoying the terror he knew the sight would cause, he slowly and deliberately plucked out the feathered shafts one by one. He held the huge bundle they made in one hand and with the other snapped them easily. Then, with a terrible purpose, he walked back to the castle.

Strahd Von Zarovich had been denied the only thing he had ever really wanted in his life, and he would exact payment for that loss from everyone within the walls of Castle Ravenloft, perhaps even everyone who dwelt within the borders of Barovia.

 **TWENTY-TWO**

Jander found he was trembling. There were no words for the pity and horror that churned inside of him. What a fall from grace. What a slaughter of innocents. He forced himself to read on.

Tenth Moon, 400: She has come back, come back to me! I have been granted another chance! My beloved Tatyana has been given new life in the body of a villager named Marina. This Marina looks exactly as my dear Tatyana did, but there is something subtly different about her. I cannot say what. In truth, does it matter? I have begun to court her. Surely, this time, I shall make her mine . . .

Twelfth Moon, 400: There is none so cursed as I. Tatyana, my love, is dead once more, this time by her father's hand. The fool said he would rather see her dead than my bride. I slew him at once, of course. I slew the whole family, then returned to these prison walls to nurse my grief. Darling Tatyana, will I never hold you in my arms and see you look at me with love?

Fourth Moon, 475: Again, Tatyana has returned. I believe this terrible land is testing me, trying to make me prove my love. This time she goes by the name of Olya, but I know the truth. She bears my beloved's face, although she acts not at all as Tatyana did. It is as though a part of Tatyana is missing from this otherwise perfect pic-

*ture, as though Olya is a not-quite-finished work of art.
As before, I care not, and I will bend her love to me . . .*

*Fourth Moon, 475: I cannot bear this torment! To have
almost had her and see her slip away from me yet again!
A fever claimed Olya, they said. Nothing to be done, they
said. But no one came to me, to see if there was anything
I could do!*

Something penetrated Jander's dazed horror. The
fourth moon of 475. He had arrived in Barovia around
that time! The name Olya was somehow familiar. The
elf concentrated, and it came back to him: Olya was the
girl who had died of a fever, the very night that he had
entered Barovia, the very night Anna, also burning with
fever, had died by Jander's hand.

Could they have been somehow linked? Were they
the same woman? Anna had been traumatized, unable
to utter more than fragments of words. Anna: *Tatyana*.
"Sir," her name for Jander: *Sergei*. Somehow, Tatyana
had yearned so desperately to be free of Strahd's enveloping evil that part of her had escaped the night she
leaped into the mist, escaped into Waterdeep. She was
but a shattered, partial soul, with fragments of memories, deemed a madwoman by all who saw her.

Hungry for more information, Jander read on and
was brought up sharply when he recognized his own
name.

*A stranger has entered my dark realm of unhappiness.
Undead, as I am; yearning for life, as I do; but unlike me,
he will not pursue his dreams and goals. He is as soft as a
newborn, with feelings that bruise and a conscience that
will not even let him drain his victims dry. How has such a
one survived so long as an undead? And further, why
does such a one appear so wise? For this Jander Sunstar,
elf from another land, harbors much worth knowing inside that golden head.*

*I crave his knowledge. Why can I not draw his secrets
from him?*

*He thinks he is a guest here. He thinks I am his friend.
So easily tricked, yet so difficult to plumb. He is the wisest*

fool I have ever known. I shall keep him here, and learn what I may . . .

Third Moon, 500: Another generation has littered, and the children have grown to adulthood. It is time to begin once again looking for Tatyana. I may not find her this year or the next, but I cannot risk losing her. I must search.

So, that was where Strahd had disappeared for weeks at a time. He wasn't looking for the killer of his slaves, as Jander had assumed. The master of Barovia was looking for his love, Tatyana, *Anna,* so that he could continue their eternal dance of mutual torment.

It had to be stopped. Jander had been brought to Barovia to quench his thirst for revenge, and he was going to do just that. More, he would relish it. The elf began to shake, and he felt the red haze of berserk anger descend over his consciousness like a crimson curtain.

*   *   *   *   *

Sasha was ten years old again, and entering the slaughterhouse.

Red liquid poured down the staircase, saturating the rug that covered the stone floor. The child climbed, as if drawn against his will, up the stairs that loomed darkly ahead. The boards creaked under even his slight weight.

At the top of the stairs, his mother stood waiting for him. Her long brown hair was loose and tumbled down her back. Her eyes were full of concern.

"Where have you been?" the voice boomed, echoing crazily. "I've been *so worried.*" Long arms reached for him, pulling him to her breast, then white teeth flashed and yellow eyes rolled back into her head. *Mother! Mother!*

Sasha bolted upright, nearly falling out of his pallet in the process. He was absolutely soaked in perspiration, and he labored to catch his breath as his senses readjusted from the nightmare. The moonlight spilled in coolly from the window.

His heartbeat slowing, Sasha fell back on the pillow. Many nights had he awakened thus, tormented by nightmares that kept returning like the long Barovian nights themselves. The frequency of these horrifying dreams did not mitigate the terror they inspired. Sweet Lathander, how many more vampires must he kill before the dreams stopped and he knew peace again?

He took a deep breath and rose from the bed, bare feet padding softly as he went to the small table and poured water into the basin. The priest bathed his flushed face with the cool liquid, forcing himself to calm down.

There came faint tapping on the window. Sasha was instantly alert, his ears straining for the sound. He heard it again—a soft, cautious noise, but definitely real and not part of his dreams. A shape moved outside the window. Sasha's gaze flickered from the figure outside to the moonlit floor. There was no shadow there. Sasha knew what that signified. A vampire lurked outside, apparently waiting for him.

The cleric smiled grimly to himself. This particular undead had picked the wrong victim. When he sent this one's soul to rest, he would have twenty vampire deaths to his credit. Quietly and swiftly, Sasha gathered his tools: a garlic wreath, which he slipped over his head; a vial of holy water, honestly gotten from the altar this time; and Lathander's medallion. He said a quick prayer, took a deep breath, and prepared to do battle.

The tapping came again. It was louder this time, as if the horrid creature was growing impatient. The undead did not, however, lose interest and fly away. Slowly Sasha crept toward the window, staying away from the puddle of moonlight on the floor. Then, with a cry of "Lathander!" he sprang, ripping away the curtain and opening the locked window in one fluid movement.

His free hand was closed tightly about the pink wooden holy symbol, but when he recognized the vampire, Sasha let his arm fall. Jander threw up one hand in a gesture of self defense, but still clung to the side of the church wall, his gloved hands and booted feet finding holds that no mortal could have used.

"Jander!" Sasha hissed furiously. "What are you doing here?"

The glance the vampire threw Sasha pierced the youth, who suddenly realized that the elf was covered with crimson. Biting back a cry, the young man took a step backward, filled with revulsion. "I have to talk to you, Sasha. I . . . need your help."

The priest shook his head. "What makes you think I'll help you?" He could not tear his eyes away from the ghastly vision the vampire presented. The blood on Jander's clothing gleamed blackly in the moonlight, and his handsome face was sticky with the fluid.

Realizing how he must look, Jander said quickly, "It's not human blood. Meet me in the cemetery in ten minutes. We'll be less likely to be seen there. Bring a basin of water with you." Jander's shape shimmered, faded into a mist, and then coalesced into the form of a small brown bat. The winged rodent fluttered off into the night.

Sasha was shaking, and part of him wanted only to return to bed and pull the covers over his head. What did he owe this monster, to go traipsing around a cemetery at night?

His father's life.

Sasha sighed and reached for the water jug. Quietly, so as not to disturb Leisl asleep in the next room, he descended the stairs. One of the steps creaked loudly, and he froze, listening. There was no sound from the little thief's room, so Sasha continued.

Jander was waiting for the priest by the Kartov family grave site when he appeared a few minutes later. Leaves swirled about the vampire's feet in the autumn wind. The moon cleared a cloud, and its light fell full upon his slender shape. Again Sasha was filled with a mixture of horror and appreciation. The vampire was a beautiful creature, his golden skin taking on a magical sheen in the moonlight, his form straight and tall. What a shame he was such an evil being.

Sasha handed the basin and the water pitcher to him. Wordlessly Jander placed them on the ground and knelt. Removing his white leather gloves, he poured some water into the basin and splashed his bloody face with the cool liquid. Sasha had brought a towel and handed this, too, to the vampire. With hands that trembled, Jander buried his face in the towel.

Sasha remained standing, his arms folded. "Say what you came to say," he stated flatly. "I swore I'd not kill you, but that's all. I shouldn't even be here." He almost regretted his words when Jander lifted his head from the towel and threw him a stricken look. "What happened?"

"First, please remove that garlic wreath, Sasha," Jander said. "It's a nauseating smell. I promised I'd not hurt you."

Sasha made no movement. More swiftly than Sasha could have dreamed, Jander sprang from his kneeling position and ripped the wreath from his neck, tossing it away. The priest's hands flew toward his unprotected throat, but Jander made no further movement toward him.

"You aren't supposed to be able to do that!" Sasha quavered.

Jander smiled humorlessly. "There are a lot of things I can do here that I shouldn't be able to do. Mark that, Sasha. This place changes the rules." His smile faded and was replaced with the sorrowful look the priest had seen there when last they'd met. The vampire sat down on a clump of grass and rested his head in his hands for a moment. When next he spoke, his voice was shot through with a thread of pain.

"I asked you to look for records on a woman named Anna. Do you remember?"

"Yes. I'm sorry, Jander, I looked, but there was—"

"No, there wouldn't be. I loved this Anna, if you can believe that. She was insane, but I loved her. She fell ill, and I knew she was dying. I couldn't bear the thought of existing without her, so I tried to make her a vampire like myself." He waited for Sasha's response, his silver eyes glittering.

As Jander had expected, the priest was appalled. "That's not love, that's the most selfish . . . By the Morninglord's glory, you *are* a fiend!"

The elf continued, ignoring Sasha's outburst. "She had no relatives, no one to take care of her. She needed me. Do you know how wonderful that feels, to be needed? I loved her. I would have taken care of her for all eternity. That's why I wanted to give her a chance for a kind of immortality. I thought that, with time and love, she might recover."

Sighing, Jander shook his head sadly. "She refused to take my blood and died because of that choice." He looked at Sasha calmly, his voice taking on a cold tone. "When I came to Barovia, when the mists brought me, my thoughts were crowded with revenge. I wanted to find the man who had destroyed Anna's mind. Tonight, I learned who it was." He paused. "I have a great anger sometimes, and tonight, I was enraged. The blood you see was from a flock of sheep. I slew them all. It is well your people keep to their homes after dark, Sasha, else I surely would have slaughtered any unlucky enough to have crossed my path."

Jander reached slender fingers into his pouch and emerged with a handful of items that glittered in the moonlight. He handed them to Sasha. "Give these to the owner of the flock. Tell him it's reparation from the gods or some other nonsense. He'll find that easier to believe than the truth." He smiled sadly.

Sasha did not know what to say. Abruptly Jander changed the subject.

"Have you ever heard of anything called a crimson death?" Sasha shook his head. "Perhaps it is called something else here. It is a gaseous creature, but shaped like a human. It feeds like a vampire, on blood. It is terrifying to behold. As it feeds, it flushes from its natural color of pale white to red, and takes on a solid form. Only then can it be killed and only by magical weapons."

Sasha's face registered disgust. Jander continued. "It is rumored that crimson deaths are the spirits of vampires, that when one of us is destroyed, we become a crimson death." Now he gazed intently at Sasha. "You have slain many of us. Have you ever seen a creature such as I have just described?"

"Never."

"You must be absolutely certain."

"I am. Jander, I may know more about the evil beings of Barovia than they know about themselves."

"Do not brag so, young one." Jander smiled thinly. "Though we may put that boast to a test. As I said, I am here tonight because I need your help."

Sasha looked at him skeptically. "I find that difficult to believe."

Jander did not reply immediately. "I have a score to settle with Strahd."

Sasha stiffened. "I bear no love to the lord of the land, but I will not raise my hand against him merely because you say I should."

"Sasha, think! When did you first see me? As the honored guest of the count at the spring celebration. You know what I am. What do you think *he* is? *He's a vampire!*"

Sasha's face went pale. "No," he whispered.

Jander nodded. "All the other vampires in the land answer to him, all save me. I am the only other free-willed vampire in Barovia, the only one strong enough to defeat Strahd."

"Then do it. What do you need me for?"

"He has magic at his fingertips. I have none, save those skills that came with my transformation. Besides—" his musical voice grew harsh "—I am an undead creature. A mortal, especially a priest, can do things I cannot."

Sasha licked his lips nervously, his black eyes darting back and forth like a trapped animal's. He remembered his nausea the last time he had put a vampire to rest. "Jander, I have responsibilities in the village. Now that Martyn's gone, I'm the only trained priest left. Katya and I are to be wed next summer. I can't just—"

Jander's silver eyes flashed with anger. "I don't want to hear about your responsibilities. I don't care about your fiancee. Do you not think that someday Strahd will slake his thirst with her blood? With the blood of your children and their children after them? What are your responsibilities to a monster like that? Gods, who do you think slew your family fourteen years ago?"

Sasha's mouth opened in a soundless cry, and he buried his head in his hands. Jander rose and began to pace, trying to control his anger but driven by his need.

"You must understand," the vampire continued. "He became what he is through a pact with some dark entity, a pact sealed in the blood of his own brother. He drove a beautiful, innocent girl to suicide with his reckless lust for her. So he believes, but I don't think she died. Not all of her." Unable to subdue his rage, he gripped Sasha's shirt and hauled the young man to his feet, impaling the boy with the stab of his glance.

"I believe part of her escaped, fell through some kind of portal into my world. By the time I found her, by the time I loved her, she was only a part of a soul. Strahd had broken her mind. We both lost her, that poor child who never did a thing to hurt anyone."

He tossed Sasha to the ground and clenched his fists tightly. He could feel the rage welling up inside him again, the urge to drop to all fours and kill. Jander forced it down. When he spoke again, his voice was calmer.

"That is what the lord of the land has done. That's not the end of it, though. Apparently this girl, Anna, Tatyana, whatever her true name is—she is reincarnated every few generations. He keeps inflicting his torment on her and on your fellow citizens, creating vampire after vampire." The elf paused again and took a breath. "I will make a vow to you, Sasha Petrovich. I have never created a vampire by my actions, and I swear now that I never shall. Destroy Strahd, and you destroy all the vampires in Barovia. Can you deny me aid when I am in pursuit of such a goal?"

"Only tell me one thing." Sasha hesitated, his serious brown eyes searching Jander's. "What . . . was it like?"

Jander gazed at Sasha with searching silver eyes for a long moment. "Why," he said finally in a weary voice, "would you want to know? You are of the light. Be thankful that you know so little of the mysteries of the dark!"

"I have to know. What was it like to die and yet not die? How does it feel to—"

"To live on others' lives?" Jander's voice, like his beautiful face, became hard. Varying emotions warred for prominence within his breast, and so many words— words of fear, of anger, of longing, of caution—crowded his throat that he choked on them and said nothing for a long time. At last, he spoke.

"The blood need is a thirst like no other, a hunger that has no parallel. The man stranded in the desert, his tongue thick within his papery throat, yearning for the tiniest drop of moisture to ease the parched, cottony feel of his mouth—that is nothing to my thirst. A prisoner trapped in a cell, denied food for days; he feels his stomach hollow within him, he looks at the rats who share his cell, the filthy straw upon which he sleeps, his very own flesh as sustenance—he knows nothing of my hunger. And every night, we awaken thus."

He gestured at the tombstones about him. "We creep out of our coffins, our crypts, our caves, our places of hiding among the dead, for we are dead and yet we live. We spring from the shadows or lull an unwary traveler, and then steal from her something more precious than any material item. We hold her, a stranger, and perform an act more intimate than that shared by lovers. We take her blood and live upon it, Sasha. Can you even partially grasp the horror of the thing? And, all the gods forgive me, it feels wonderful!"

Sasha was frozen with pity and horror as Jander, for the first time, finally told another being of his inner torment. He was no longer looking at Sasha. His eyes were distant, turned inward, gazing at something the priest could never see.

"The bridegroom going to his beloved for the first time has only a shadow of our ecstasy. The painter finishing his masterpiece barely glimpses our joy. The blood *is* the life, and there is nothing so beautiful as taking it, feeling it pour into you as if you were an empty vase that is filled at last. It is a false rapture, and we know it—we *know* it—and yet we continue on.

"Then the moment is over, and when it is over, I look at the limp form in my arms and I curse myself. Oh, she lives on. I assuage my conscience with the fact that I take a life only when I must or when my reason is pushed beyond endurance. But I have violated that woman, and I am ashamed.

"And for her, the fangs are heat and cold, piercing and commanding, and she feels the blood leap from her veins as though her very heart was being ripped out. She is helpless, utterly, completely helpless, more so than the babe fresh out of the womb. But there is a hellish balance. We, too, are helpless. We need mortals. We can smell them, the bloodscent, just like that newborn babe smells the warm, milky scent of its mother. We are called to it like the waves to the shore and are as incapable of resistance. There are none so cursed as we."

The elf fell silent, and Sasha thought he had finished. When he spoke again, his voice was soft, gentle, and full not of anger but of sorrowful regret. "When I breathed, I was not a wicked being. I was a warrior for just and noble causes. The beasts of the forests were not unduly afraid when they caught my scent. All men were either brothers or worthy foes; women were to be honored and respected. I do not boast if I say the world was better where I touched it.

"Now I suffer what you cannot even imagine. Horses will not carry me without command. The forest animals flee in terror at my approach. I am shut off from the company of others, save those wretches like Strahd who care nothing for me and for whom I care even less. The sun, for whom my family was named, is fatal to me. There is nothing beautiful in my world anymore. I live in darkness and destruction, and I spread it like a pestilence. The very earth loathes me. See what my touch now does!"

Furious once more, the elf slammed his bare hands onto the grass by the grave. Sasha heard a faint crackling sound. When Jander lifted his hands a few seconds later, the priest saw dead, yellow grass where the elf had touched the earth.

"And Anna . . . oh, Anna!" Jander sobbed aloud. "Strahd destroyed Tatyana and will keep on doing so. But it was I who took Anna's life. If I pay for that with my agony to the end of the world, it would not be enough. Many are my sins, Sasha. I have never claimed otherwise. How many, also, are my inner wounds. Son of the gypsy boy, will you help me? Will you help me avenge her and save the lives and souls of all you love?"

Jander's plea would have softened even the hardest heart, and Sasha's was all too vulnerable. He had been fighting evil for more than half his life, prowling in the shadows of a nightscape that was home to the lords of the undead, hammering stakes into their hearts, cutting off their heads so that they could not rise again. Having Leisl help eased the burden, but not enough.

Now Jander wanted him to attack the most powerful vampire in the land. Sasha was tired. Hadn't he done enough? Would there ever come a respite? Would he never be able to hold his beloved Katya safely through the night, untroubled by memories and nightmares?

Things darker than memories and nightmares troubled nights in Ravenloft. He could not know this and still do nothing. Sasha closed his eyes. "All right," he said. "What must we do first?"

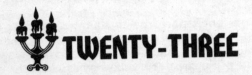

TWENTY-THREE

Leisl was waiting for Sasha in his room when he came back, sitting on his bed with her feet tucked underneath her. She had prepared a hot mug of wine to take off the chill of the graveyard and handed it to him wordlessly. He accepted it and drank in equal silence.

"I assume you saw the, uh, elf," Sasha finally commented wearily, leaning back on the pillows and rubbing his eyes with his free hand.

"So that's what they look like. I saw him. I also saw that he didn't cast a shadow in the moonlight and that he had blood all over his face." She tried to keep her voice calm but didn't quite succeed. "What crazy scheme have you gotten yourself involved with, Sasha Petrovich? I thought we were supposed to be killing the things, not chatting with them in graveyards!"

Sasha debated not telling her, but the Little Fox already knew too much. What might be worse was if she decided to "help" without his approval. Things could get very, very bad very, very quickly.

He took a deep breath. "The vampire is named Jander Sunstar. He saved my father's life many years ago. He's sort of a friend of the family." He smiled with no humor. "He stays with Count Strahd up at the castle."

"Oh, isn't that great." Leisl wrinkled her nose. "A vampire and a crazy mage tyrant. You have nice friends, Sasha."

"Leisl!" The priest tried to be indignant, but, as always, her candor made him laugh through his shock, and he began to relax. The wine's exactly what I need, he thought as he took another sip. Leisl was uncanny, the way she always seemed to know what he wanted even before he did. "It's not quite how it looks," he continued. "Jander's plotting against Strahd. It appears as though the lord of Barovia is also a vampire." He watched her face, anxious to see her reaction.

She cocked an eyebrow. "If they're both vampires, why does Jander hate him?"

"Doesn't it frighten you?"

"Why should it? You and I go out tracking the godsforsaken things nearly every night. Vampires I can deal with. Humans—" her voice went hard "—are less predictable. They're the real monsters, if you ask me."

"Leisl," he began slowly. She tensed, her hazel eyes going wary. "Why did you become a thief?"

"I don't want to talk about it," she said shortly. She crossed her arms, and her lips drew into a hard line. Normally Sasha would not probe, but he had to know if she could be trusted on this most dangerous mission.

"Look, I respect your privacy, but I am not about to take you into Castle Ravenloft with me if I don't know what's going on inside that head of yours!" he snapped.

The Little Fox studied him for a moment, her eyes searching his. "All right," she said, a trace of hostility in her voice, "I'll tell you. I was born to a farming family. We lived on the edge of the village. When I was seven, a pack of wolves decided to turn my whole family into their dinner. I was the youngest of four children, and I had my own small room in the attic. I was safely out of reach. I stayed there, scared to death, for four full days before I got so hungry that I climbed down.

"Nobody in town would take me in. I ate off the refuse piles for weeks. Then this old man said he'd take me into his family. Family, my foot. The man was named Fox, and his family consisted of orphans like me that he was teaching to steal for him. I was good," Leisl said softly, a tinge of hate and pride creeping into her voice. "I was so good that Fox began calling me the Little Fox, so good that he kicked me out of the group. He said I was ready to go it on my own.

"I was thirteen, Sasha. Just thirteen, and scared to death. I made it because I always watched my back and I never trusted anybody. I still don't." Her eyes went soft. "Except you. So now, you know you can trust me, too."

Sasha forgot how much this skinny young woman annoyed him at times. He forgot how troublesome she could be. He reached out and folded her into a gentle hug. She was stiff in his embrace at first, then relaxed, thin arms creeping up to clasp him in return. They held each other for a long time.

Jander had said he would come back to see what they had found within a week. Sasha and Leisl began searching for information that could even the odds in their quest to defeat the lord of Barovia. Sasha performed the duties of his position efficiently, but his mind was elsewhere. He spent several hours in prayer, sitting on his rug alone in his room: "Lathander, we need your help now. Please guide us . . ."

The Morninglord did not manifest, neither did he inspire Sasha with any divine insight. So the priest and his cohort turned to the moderately stocked church library. It was a small, cramped room, with poor circulation of air and no windows. The room smelled of dust and mold, and the books had gone for far too long without feeling the touch of a human hand. Now all the books, a couple dozen of them, had been pulled down from the shelves where they had been moldering and lay open on the rough wooden table.

Leisl sneezed and continued munching on the lunch Katya had prepared for them, washing the food down with a sip of wine. Resting his cheek on his hand, Sasha turned another page. The rustling was the only sound in the still room. Leisl fidgeted, wishing for the first time in her life that she could read. At least then she might be able to aid the priest.

"Anything yet?" she asked hopefully.

Sasha sighed, flipped hurriedly through the rest of the book, then closed it gently. "No. Not a thing. These books are mainly records—crop reports, births, deaths, marriages—that sort of thing. Nothing of any consequence."

Sasha leaned back, stretching and tilting the chair so that its front two legs were off the ground. He laced his fingers behind his head and closed his eyes, letting his mind wander where it would. Vampires were evil creatures, but few people really believed in them now. They were things of legend. How did one fight a legend?

Leisl stared moodily at the pile of books on the table. She started when Sasha abruptly lowered the chair, and the two legs thumped to the floor. His eyes were bright.

"Pavel Ivanovich," he said, his voice tense with excitement.

"Who?"

"The old story. You know, Pavel Ivanovich of Vallaki, the heir of the Sun. Don't you remember that story?"

"I didn't have a mother telling me bedtime stories. Remember?"

"Oh, Leisl, I didn't mean—" He looked so crestfallen that Leisl waved his apology aside.

"Tell me about this Pavel."

"Well, he was the heir of the Sun, born to keep the Darkness at bay with a piece of the sun his father had given him," Sasha explained. "The piece of the sun was stolen by the Darkness and hidden in the darkest part of the land. Where in Barovia do you think that would be?"

Leisl began to grin. "I don't think you want me to answer that."

Sasha frowned. "This is no time for jokes, Leisl. The darkest part of Barovia is Castle Ravenloft, right?"

"I suppose so."

"On his quest, Pavel confronts many guardians of the Darkness. The first, and the most evil, was Nosferatu—a vampire." Sasha was growing more and more excited.

"Don't you see? This all makes perfect sense. The legend goes on to say that when Pavel recovered the piece of the sun, the curse upon the land was lifted. And Strahd certainly is Barovia's curse."

"Sasha, this is just some stupid folktale," Leisl snorted, thoroughly unimpressed.

"Of course. Folktales often have a grain of truth in them, though. It could be that there really is something in Castle Ravenloft."

"Yeah. A couple of vampires."

Sasha's patience was wearing thin. He glared at Leisl, making no attempt to hide his anger. "Nobody asked you to get involved with this. Nobody asked you to come kill vampires. In fact, nobody asked you to do a damn thing here. If you're that sure it's a fool's cause, why don't you get out and leave me alone?"

Her face didn't change, but the priest sensed an inner turmoil beneath her calm visage. "I'm with you. You know you can count on me."

Which was, Sasha knew, very true. "Sorry," he muttered.

"All right." Leisl moved some books out of the way so she could sit on the table. "Suppose this legend is true and there's a piece of the sun in Castle Ravenloft, a piece that will help us destroy Strahd. What exactly *is* the piece of the sun?"

Sasha dropped his gaze. "I don't know."

"Well, that's handy."

"Leisl, I'm doing the best that I can."

"So am I."

He didn't reply, only bent his head over the thick tome in his lap.

He sighed to himself. He hoped Jander's search was more fruitful or else they'd have to tackle the master vampire without the aid of magic. That, Sasha mused bitterly, was a frightening thought.

The priest had no village elder he could turn to, either. Martyn's death had made Sasha the most prominent scholar in Barovia. He thought about sending Leisl

Vallaki, to see if anyone there would be willing to give
them some information. That might be the best thing,
although he hated to do anything that would take time
or attract attention.

If only there was someone here in the village who
knew magic or—

He began to smile. Or perhaps someone *outside* the
village . . .

"The gypsies," he said.

The next day was Market Day, when the Vistani occasionally wandered into town to do some trading. It took
some convincing, but for fifteen gold coins and a promise of "aid should I ever request it," a shifty-eyed man
named Giacomo sold Sasha and Leisl bottles of the
magical potion that would let them pass safely through
the poisonous fog that encircled the town. He also let
them ride on his wagon through that deadly ring of
mist.

Autumn was now well and truly settled on the coun-
tryside, and the trees were naked silhouettes against a
gray sky pregnant with snow. Leisl and Sasha bundled
close together for warmth. Soon the dread wall of fog
came into view, swirling like some living thing.

"Drink now," Giacomo told them, lifting a flask to his
own lips and swallowing. The two passengers did as
they were told, though they gagged a bit at the bitter
taste.

A few seconds later they were in the thick heart of the
fog. It smelled stale, but thanks to the potion they
would survive. So thick it was nearly solid, the fog was
oppressive to say the least. Leisl and Sasha could barely
see one another's faces, and the Vistani driver they
could not see at all. Giacomo and his ponies continued
on, and then suddenly the mist thinned and disappeared altogether. Both young travelers breathed sighs
of relief.

They continued along the trail toward the Vistani encampment. Leisl noticed a profusion of small gray and
white birds in the skeletal trees. She pointed them out

to Sasha. "*Vista chiri,*" he replied. "They follow the gyp
sies. My mother said it is because the birds are the soul
of dead Vistani."

Despite his heritage, Sasha had never attempted t
visit the gypsy encampment or tried to find his father
There was a very real possibility that he would run int
Petya here today; it was a risk that had to be taken. H
was reconciled to it, but his heart thudded painfully i
his chest with every clop-clop of the ponies' hooves.

The piercing wind shifted, carrying with it the smel
of a campfire. They were almost there.

*   *   *   *   *

Maruschka stared into the crystal ball, her eyes see
ing what was hidden to others, her lips moving soundelessly. At last she emitted a quavering sigh and drew th
purple velvet covering over the shining orb. Sh
blinked hard, trying to clear the tears that had blurre
the last scene the ball had displayed. Rising, she wen
into the autumn morning.

The passing of twenty-four summers had left its mar
on the Vistani Seer. She had come into the full Sight o
her twenty-second birthday, two years after the golde
elven vampire had rescued her brother. As she mad
her way to the campfire, her icy hands reaching eagerl
for the warmth, her nephew Mikhail plowed into he
knocking her into the leaf-spotted brown grass.

"Sorry, Aunt 'Ruschka," he apologized, helping her t
her feet. Maruschka glared at the boy, Petya's younges
and was reminded of all the years that had gone b
Mikhail had known only seven summers, but it wa
abundantly clear he had inherited his father's knack fo
trouble.

Petya himself and his wife, Ilyana, lingered insid
their *vardo.* Maruschka could hardly blame them. Wh
would want to leave the warmth of a spouse on a col
morning? The Seer had never married. As she had bee
born to be, Petya's sister became the leader of the trib

When Eva had died four years ago, Maruschka was well prepared to take her grandmother's place.

She rubbed her hands at the fire. The rattle of a wagon caused her to look up. Inwardly she winced, though her dark face remained composed. Seated in the wagon was a young man who was the image of her brother. He was also the figure she had seen in her vision earlier that morning.

The young man was not cloaked in the priestly raiment of pink and gold that he had worn in the vision. Instead he had clearly made an effort to dress as casually as possible, no doubt trying to be "typical" of his people with their standard garb of cotton shirt, sheepskin vest, and dark wool breeches. He and his companion, a skinny youth, clambered out of Giacomo's wagon. The Seer already knew what they had come for, and when Giacomo pointed in her direction, she fixed Petya's son with a mysterious smile.

"You bear our blood," she said without preamble when Sasha got within earshot. He blinked, caught off-guard.

"That is true enough. I am a wanderer from a far distant land—"

"You are Sasha Petrovich, son of the Vistani Petya and the burgomaster's daughter. You are currently the priest of a god who is not known for his dealings with our folk. Why do you seek my aid?"

He was thoroughly taken aback. He had told Leisl this disguise wouldn't work. It was fine for *her*, she was used to playacting and disguises . . .

"And perhaps the young lady would like a cup of tea?" Maruschka suggested. After a pause, she said, "Come into my *vardo*, then." She turned to lead the way. "I am presuming you can pay?" she said as they walked, but it was more a statement than a question.

For answer, Sasha dug into his pouch and presented a handful of gold that glittered in the wintry light. Leisl winced, knowing heads would be turning. "Put that away," she hissed, "or else we're not going to make it back with our throats intact!" Suddenly she realized how that must sound to the gypsy Seer and lifted mortified eyes.

Maruschka only smiled a little. "Little one, you know more of the ways of the world than your friend here. Priest, you would do well to listen to her. Come, both of you."

Over the years, Maruschka's *vardo* had grown more elaborate as her influence within and beyond the tribe expanded. Fresh paint and ever more gilt adorned the ornate carvings of the exterior, and her ponies' trappings sported an assortment of bells and tassels that made every move of camp seem like a festival procession.

Inside, shadow and mystery vied with splashes of wild color. The necessities of comfortable living—carved trunks for her bright clothes, colorful weavings for her bed, and countless embroidered cushions glinting with gold thread—contrasted with the more mysterious objects that nourished and supported her Sight. Books sat on tables and nestled in odd corners. Carefully tied bundles of herbs hung from the ceiling and lent the caravan their strange fragrances. Her cards, wrapped in a piece of white silk so old it was nearly transparent, rested in a special box amid a brass burner for incense, a black clay bowl for scrying, and a huge chunk of rock crystal whose facets drew the eye down into the heart of stone. A fat white candle on a squat stand presided over the whole, its flame glittering like a single pale eye. A black bird in a large cage drowsed, ignoring all interruptions.

As Maruschka lit the lamps that hung from the *vardo*'s central roof beam, Sasha looked about, thinking to himself, all the trappings are here. But the power was here, as well, and the priest had enough of his father's blood in him to realize that that power was in no way dependent upon the scent of herbs or the influence of firelight dancing on mysterious objects. He hoped he was doing the right thing.

Maruschka rummaged through the clutter, her skirts swishing gently and the many bracelets on her dark arms clanking with musical tones. She waved a ring-encrusted hand absently, and Leisl and Sasha seated themselves on the pillows on the floor. A tap on the door caused them to jump, but it was only Mikhail with their tea. Maruschka held her breath. To her, the resemblance between the half-brothers was obvious, but neither boy showed any sign of noting the similarities. She let out her breath.

"Now," she said after she had handed each a cup of hot, fragrant tea, "tell me what you wish to know."

Sasha gazed at her with dark, solemn eyes. The steam from the cup rose softly around his face, wreathing it with mist. "I want to know my fortune. Doesn't everybody?"

Maruschka went cold and closed her eyes. *So, already the vision comes true. So soon, so soon . . .* "Drink the tea," she said shortly, "and then hand me the cups."

Obediently they did so. She placed the cups on a clear space on the floor in front of her, closed her eyes, and breathed deeply. Then, slowly, she picked up Leisl's cup and gazed into it.

"You have fear in you," she murmured. Leisl snorted, but Maruschka ignored her. "For many things, there is no fear at all. But you fear two things: the night's Gray Singers and the loss of something you care for. Your path is leading you into the Dark, and you will have to face both of these fears in the near future."

Leisl hid her expression, keeping her face carefully neutral even though her heart sank. The night's Gray Singers—wolves—whom she did indeed hate and fear. She only cared for one thing: Sasha. Now this gypsy was telling her that Leisl would lose him. The thief blinked hard, hoping the young priest didn't see. She needn't have worried, for Sasha's gaze was fastened on Maruschka's face.

"And you, gypsy-blooded," the Seer continued, keeping her voice soft, "you are over-burdened with a task you have set yourself. A great loss is coming your way. It is not clear what form this will take—the loss of love, of belief, or something as concrete as an object or person. You seek the light in the paths of the dark. The stones—" Her voice dropped even lower. "The one who has loved best has the heart of stone. Stone will tell you what you need to know."

"Will . . ." Leisl swallowed and began again. "Will we die?"

The gypsy looked up, a slow, wide smile spreading across her face. "Why of course, little one. All things die. That is—" the smile faded at the corners, "—*almost* all things die."

There was an uncomfortable silence, during which the two young people sat wrapped in thought. At last, Sasha stirred. "How much do we owe you?"

Maruschka was about to state the usual fee, then abruptly changed her mind. "There is no charge. I know your father well, and for his blood, this time, it is my gift."

Sasha was about to protest, then thought better of it. "Our thanks, Madame Maruschka."

The Seer rose and opened the door, leaning out and jabbering something in the Vistani tongue. "It is time for you to leave, children. No one should trouble you. The trip safely through the fog also is my gift."

Sasha and Leisl rose. "Goodbye, Madame," Sasha bade the gypsy Seer, bowing low. Leisl bobbed quickly, then followed the priest. Maruschka watched them leave, then closed the door and sat down heavily among the cushions. Pika squawked, and she smiled wearily up at the black bird.

She was proud that she was at least able to give them a true seeing, even if . . . For a brief instant she wished with all her heart that she had never been granted the Sight. Then she would not have to make the kind of choice that had now been foisted upon her.

Maruschka had responsibilities to her tribe that went far beyond familial duties. Her ties bound her to all Vistani, to everything they were. Their protection must always take precedence over the happiness, even th safety, of strangers. She must do nothing to jeopardize their existence. Eva had complicated matters by involving the Vistani with Strahd and his machinations, but Maruschka knew that it would be foolish to defy the lord of Barovia. She could not, would not do so, even for the life of her brother or for that of his son . . . her nephew; not even for the only being who had ever made her think of romance, however briefly—an alien creature, golden of skin and fair of form. He had been of another race, and worse, had known a totally different kind of existence. Angrily she recalled the fortune she had revealed for him. She had promised success, success with the sun and with a child.

The irony of it welled up in her like bile. How could a vampire succeed with the aid of the sun? How could an undead creature produce a child?

Maruschka shook her gray-streaked head sadly. "Aiee, Jander," she said softly, "if you remember me at all, when the disaster strikes, forgive my hand in it."

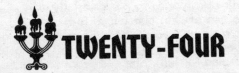 **TWENTY-FOUR**

Jander had no idea when Strahd would be back. It could be five months or five minutes. He had to make every instant count, for he knew he would be unable to control his anger when Strahd returned.

Yet he also had to maintain an unruffled exterior. Strahd's slaves were vicious creatures, by no means as clever as either Jander or their dreadful maker. Still, they had eyes, and they could observe. Whenever he was around the other undead, the elf made sure that he didn't reveal his inner turmoil by word, look, or deed. He had no need for such pretense around the skeletons or zombies; they were completely mindless.

Sharp little Trina, however, was another matter entirely. He could tell she sensed something amiss when she visited him two nights after the meeting with Sasha. In order to drive her away, he feigned painstaking interest in his frescos. "I'm hoping to recapture the original sparkle of that beautiful sunburst pendant," he had told her. "Yes, that one there. Lovely, isn't it? I think a mixture of silver, with just a hint of white . . ."

It worked. Trina heaved a sigh of supreme annoyance and flounced down the stairs. He heard her footsteps change into the patter of paws halfway down. When he ran to the nearest window, he saw her scampering across the cobblestone courtyard.

In a flurry of speed, Jander abandoned his brushes and paints and returned to the study. He did not even know what he was looking for—a clue, a spell, anything that might help destroy the plague of Barovia, Count Strahd Von Zarovich.

Two things culled from of all his perusing stuck in the elf's mind. One was the chapter from the history of Barovia's ancient army. He found the segment now and reread it: *The Most High Priest of Barovia, a young man named Kir, led the people in prayer. He was granted the use of the mysterious Holy Symbol of Ravenkind to wield against the goblyn king. While Count Strahd fought and led his men to victory, the Holy Symbol was used in secret, as well. Afterward, Most High Priest Kir carefully hid the Holy Symbol in a secret place.*

No one knows what the Holy Symbol looks like, or where it is hidden. To this day, no other priest has been able to find or use it. Unquestionably, however, its powerful magic aided our noble Count Strahd to his well-earned victory.

"The Holy Symbol of Ravenkind," Jander repeated aloud. "Something of great power for good, and nobody knows what the damned thing is." He laughed humorlessly at the irony.

The other item that stayed with him was an old folk tale about an intrepid young hero called Pavel Ivanovich and his quest for a piece of the sun. Jander recalled hearing fragments of the story from Sasha on the night Strahd slaughtered the priest's family. The elf forced down the remorse that rose in him even at this late date, and concentrated on the story. This Pavel was able to defeat Nosferatu. Maybe there was some truth to his legend.

A week passed, and Jander spent his time in frantic searches through the books that were hoarded in Strahd's collection. On one particular night, he paced about the castle, impatient for the nightfall. Shortly after twilight, he left the keep in his wolf form. The first snow of the season, a light dusting of flakes, had fallen during the sunlight hours, and the forest was draped with crystals and ghostly white drifts. The night was clear, and the moon was almost full.

Jander ran easily and swiftly toward the village. His nose caught the hot scent of a fresh kill, and the scent reminded him that he, too, needed to feed before the night was over. Mingled with musky wolf and coppery deer blood was Trina's unique scent, and Jander made a quick detour toward her.

He found her in a small clearing, far enough from the edge of the forest that she was unlikely to be spotted by any of the villagers. Jander considered that wise, for she was in half-wolf form, using her clawed hands to tear off chunks of meat, spattering the snow with blood. The kill steamed in the chill air. Several other wolves fed noisily nearby.

Jander changed into his elven shape so that he could speak with Trina. "Do you know when Strahd will be returning?" he asked, hiding his aversion as he watched her feast on the deer she and the other wolves had pulled down.

Trina gazed at him with human eyes in a wolfish face. She shook her head and ran her long, pink tongue about her jowls. "Not for a while, I don't think. He takes me with him on short trips." Her voice, while understandable, was several octaves deeper than usual and came out as a throaty growl. She bit hungrily into a bloody haunch, twisting her lupine jaws for a better grip on the meat. Jander heard bone crunch as he turned away.

Returning to his own wolf form, Jander headed toward the village. Once out of the cover of the woods he went cautiously, his lupine shape moving like a shadow across the snow. At the edge of the churchyard he crept into the tiny copse of trees that bordered the village' graveyard. Sure that he was safe at last from unfriendly eyes, he shimmered into his elven form and crossed the graveyard to the church.

Sasha was waiting for him. Someone else was wit

the priest, too. The two shapes were huddled together on a crude wooden bench nestled against the side of the building. They stood as the elf approached.

"I thought it was to be the two of us," Jander commented, a bit suspicious.

"It was, but she can be trusted. Jander Sunstar, this is Leisl, my . . . partner in nocturnal stalking." He paused, then added, "She knows about you."

Leisl was openly staring. "I didn't know elves could become vampires. Of course, I don't know all that many elves. Or vampires."

"Now you know both," he said in a slightly sarcastic tone, bowing mockingly. "Tell me, Leisl. Why are you here tonight? I know what drives Sasha. But what of you?"

"I can't let Sasha tackle Strahd all by himself, can I?"

A smile played about Jander's lips. The Little Fox's answer seemed to satisfy him, and the elf turned to the priest. "I have been unable to discover much useful in Castle Ravenloft, although I sense that somewhere in the count's library are the answers we seek. There are two things I think we should investigate further. First, do you know anything about the Holy Symbol of Ravenkind?"

Sasha shook his head blankly. "I haven't uncovered very much about Barovia's early religions. There's nothing in the church on them."

"That is very peculiar."

"I thought the same thing. It makes me wonder if documents have been deliberately destroyed."

"Or taken elsewhere. Well, so much for that."

"What was the Holy Symbol of Ravenkind?" asked Leisl, feeling a bit left out. The elf turned his silver gaze upon the Little Fox.

"Apparently it's a very powerful holy object. It was wielded against the goblins at the same time that Strahd's army fought to liberate Barovia. Unfortunately," Jander said ruefully, "it was kept secret and no one but the initiated knew exactly what it was. The information was passed from priest to priest, I think, and somewhere along the line the chain got broken. I was hoping Sasha might tell me more, but . . ." His melodious voice trailed off sadly.

"What was the other piece of information?" Sasha prodded.

"You're going to think I'm grasping at straws, but there is an old legend, some nonsense about a piece of the sun and a young hero. But—" he smiled "—there is sometimes truth to be mined from legends. The question is, how to uncover it."

To his surprise, Sasha and Leisl exchanged grins. "Leisl and I reached the same conclusion. That legend is the only clue we were able to find, too. Oh—and maybe you'll understand this—we've heard a few cryptic musings that might lead somewhere. Does 'the one who has loved best has the heart of stone' mean anything to you?"

Jander frowned. "No, not really. Usually the one with a heart of stone can't love at all. Any other riddles for me? I used to be quite good at them, once."

"All right, then how about: 'Stone will tell you what you need to know?'"

"I told Sasha I think it refers to carvings," Leisl suggested. "A statue, or perhaps some writing on a wall somewhere. That sort of thing. I mean, how else could stones tell you anything?"

Jander nodded slowly, but a frown furrowed his forehead and he began to pace. Leisl's was a logical assumption, but something in the elf knew it to be an incorrect conclusion. The answers, or at least some of them, were there, *right there*, on the outskirts of his cognizance. If he could just concentrate . . . Suddenly he knew.

"There is a spell that enables stone to speak," he said. "Do you know it?"

Sasha shook his head. "Do you really think it's that important?"

"Well, let's see. Are there any stones—or walls, or

buildings—in Barovia that might have been witness to events that might give us some help?"

"Castle Ravenloft," offered Leisl.

"Obviously," replied Sasha, "but that's too dangerous." He looked about him at the cold gray shapes, dusted with whiteness, that marked the places where the dead lay. "Tombstones?"

Jander shook his bright head. "No. I don't think much happens in a cemetery that could benefit us. We know where the vampire is."

"The market square?" Leisl suggested. "I'll bet a lot of people have crossed over those cobblestones."

"Too busy, even at night," Sasha murmured. "We can't risk being seen. The church is of wood, unfortunately."

Jander, who had been pacing and listening with only one ear, turned to them. "The circle of stones!" he exclaimed. "That is definitely sacred ground. How long has that circle been there, Sasha?"

"I don't know. Centuries, I think." He began to smile. "Jander, that's it. That's got to be it!"

"Shall we meet here again tomorrow, after you have had time to prepare?" asked the elf.

"Do we have the time to spare?"

Jander shrugged. "I have absolutely no idea. Strahd could be gone for another month, or he could be back at the castle now."

"Then we don't have the time." Sasha's mouth drew into a firm line. "This is a good cause. Surely Lathander will bless it and give me the magic we need. I'll go to the altar and pray. You two can come inside and—oh." Jander's face was filled with sorrow. Sasha cursed himself for his insensitivity. Of course, the vampire couldn't enter a holy house.

"Leisl, why don't you go in and keep warm?" Jander said smoothly. "We undead do not feel the cold as mortals do."

Leisl's hazel eyes narrowed as she regarded the vampire speculatively. "No, that's all right. We'll be fine,

Sasha. I promise I'll come inside if I get cold."

"All right. I don't know how long this'll take." Sasha glanced from the elven vampire to the thief, and for a moment amusement brushed his soul, despite the seriousness of the situation. "Strange bedfellows," he muttered to himself, then headed back into the church.

For a while neither the elf nor the human spoke. The wind picked up, stirring Leisl's brown hair. Grimacing against the chill wind, she pulled her cloak tighter. "Must be convenient, not feeling cold," she commented to fill the silence that gaped between them.

"I suppose so," Jander replied. "Although if I could be mortal again, I'd be happy to wander naked in a blizzard."

She turned toward him, her face a white oval in the moonlight. "You don't like being a vampire?"

Surprised horror spread over his features. "No!" he snapped, pained. "What gave you that idea?"

"I don't know, I just . . . Sorry." Again the uncomfortable silence fell. "Why do you want to destroy Strahd?"

Jander didn't reply at once. Then slowly, he said, "He hurt someone I loved."

"Did he kill her?"

"No. Strahd broke her heart and her mind. He murdered her fiance and drove her insane."

"Oh, Jander, I'm sorry," Leisl said sincerely. "No wonder you want revenge."

"Revenge and an end to my love's misery." He fixed Leisl with his sad silver eyes. "You see, she returns to life every few generations. Every time she's born anew, the count hunts her down and tries to make her love him." The silver eyes went hard with hatred. "It's going to stop."

"I understand. Love makes you do things that you might not normally do."

The vampire smiled, his teeth glinting a little in the dim light. Oddly, the sight didn't frighten Leisl now. "I believe you do understand. Does Sasha know how you feel?" The Little Fox began to stammer a protest, but he waved her silent. "It's all over your face whenever you look at him."

Blushing, she looked away. "No, I don't think he knows. He's too wrapped up in Katya to notice me. Don't tell him, please?"

"Your secret is safe with me."

A third time the two fell silent, but this time the stillness was companionable. "Here comes Sasha," Jander said after a moment. He and the thief rose.

With a swift, sure stride, the priest approached. When he got near enough so that they could make out his features, they saw he was smiling gently, his eyes alight. "Unto the favored of Lathander," he said in a voice that trembled, "even the very stones shall speak. I have the tools. Shall we go?"

The stones stood silent sentinel on the hilltop. Nothing about the scene had changed since Jander and Sasha had last been there, fifteen years ago, and the quiet steadfastness of the rocks indicated that nothing ever would. The stones were covered with small white caps from the recent snow. No marks, of animal or other creature, had yet disturbed the virgin drifts. Sasha and Leisl trudged into the center of the circle and spread out a blanket. Jander did not follow them. So sacred a place would admit the vampire only if he concentrated on violating its protective barrier. Rather than weaken himself so, he preferred to linger outside.

Sasha stood for a moment, drinking in the power of the place, feeling it soak into him. He gazed at the sky for direction and began to set up a small altar in front of the largest stone. Jander watched attentively from his position outside the circle, and Leisl fidgeted, shifting her weight from one foot to the other.

After seating himself, Sasha indicated for Leisl to do likewise. Along with the various holy symbols, Lathander's cleric laid out a bottle of a silver liquid and a small lump of clay. Carefully Sasha worked the clay, shaping it so it looked like the large stone in front of him. He began to hum, his voice soothing and sweet, and then to chant slowly.

The hair on the back of Jander's neck stood up as the spell began to work. He recognized some of the words Sasha was using. How many long years had it been, he wondered sadly, since he had watched a cleric chant holy spells?

Sasha poured the silvery liquid into the snow in front of the clay replica of the stone; Jander recognized it as mercury by its peculiar movements. The young man's voice rose, then halted abruptly. A brief, tense silence followed, then the trio waited expectantly, unsure as to what would happen. Their answer came quickly.

The large stone in front of Sasha began to glow. Jander's sharp ears caught a low hum. The sound was joined by others, swelling, growing into a chant, a variety of voices that were not human. As the sound swelled, Jander saw the awe and fear on the faces of his companions as they, too, heard the song:

Hark to the song of the stones, not sung for far too long.

In the Early Age, stone only were we. Deep below, we guarded the treasures of the earth. Men came and harvested here, using these earth-gifts to good ends. Stone and metal, bones of the soil; they were freed and became objects of beauty and sacredness.

In the Mid Age, forgotten it was that we were the guardians of riches. We were moved and shaped into holy things and became the guardians of men's souls. Joinings were here, and beginnings, and endings.

In the Later Age, forgotten it is that we were holy. Few come to worship here in the Dark Times. Fear rules this land. Yet what was sacred once cannot be completely defiled. In the Later Age, we are the refuge of the lost, who have no shelter; the lonely, who have no love. We protect them from harm and discovery. And so shall we continue to do, until Time has crumbled us and the wind has scattered the dust.

Ask of us what you will, and we shall answer.

Sasha licked dry lips, and when he spoke his voice

quivered. "Great stones, we are looking for two items: the Holy Symbol of Ravenkind and something known in legends as a 'piece of the sun.' Can you tell us about these?"

What you seek, we have seen.

Before the dawn of the Later Age, in the midst of the Nine Nights of Fear, the Great Weapon was blessed here. Made by a holy man, yet not made. With his last breath he brought it here, and we blessed it.

Lost, lost now is the Piece of the Sun, which was also the great Holy Symbol of protection for the Raven's Kind. It rests near those it was meant to protect. More, we cannot tell you.

This is the song of the stones, not sung for far too long. We shall not sing again.

The chanting became unintelligible and faded quietly on the clear, still air. The stone's glow died, as well. Jander felt an odd feeling of peace, and the even the silence of the night sounded harsh after the haunting song. Sasha's face was filled with rapture. "Thank you, blessed Lathander," he whispered. Even skeptical Leisl's face was filled with incredulity and a puzzled wonder.

They were respectfully silent for a moment. "So they're the same thing!" Leisl said at last, then she added morosely, "But we still don't know where the artifact is hidden."

"Yes we do," Jander corrected. "The Holy Symbol was made for the Raven's Kind—Strahd's family. Their crest is a raven, their castle is Ravenloft. So that means that it is hidden there, near the ones it was meant to protect." He turned his gaze on Sasha. "Perhaps," he said with a chuckle, "we should rename you Pavel. Are you ready to enter the land of the Darkness?"

Sasha smiled back at him, his face still alight with the magic of the place. "Ready when you are, Nosferatu."

 **TWENTY-FIVE**

Sasha gazed out Katya's window at the deceptively bright morning. A fresh layer of white snow blanketed the streets, hiding the rough spots and refuse. Only a few prints, of horses and humans, showed that a few souls were up and awake. The priest sighed to himself and closed the shutters.

He turned to find Katya blinking sleepily. She smiled and stretched, yawning, the flush of sleep still on her face. Sasha's heart filled with a love for her that was almost painful, and he went to her and kissed her forehead.

"Why did you not leave for the dawn ritual?" she mumbled. "And your clothes . . . Where's your robe?"

Sasha's eyes roamed her face eagerly. Katya was so beautiful, so fragile and gentle. "I have something very important to do today. I may not be back for a while. If— if I don't return in the next couple of days, I want you to read this." He placed a sealed note on her bedside table. "I love you, Katya. I will do everything I can to come back to you. I promise."

His anxiety brought her awake fully. She frowned. "Sasha . . ."

Before his will could fail him, he turned and left, pulling the door shut behind him.

"*Sasha!*" He ignored the pleading cry. For all their sakes, he had to.

Leisl was waiting for him impatiently when he returned to the church. As usual, she was clad in functional men's clothing. Her mousy brown hair was braided
tightly so as not to be a distraction. Their two horses
were saddled, ready to go. She had gathered their tools
together and strapped them securely on the horses'
backs.

"About time you got here," she grumbled, frowning.
"Sun's been up for an hour. We're wasting time."

"We're wasting time quarreling, too," Sasha shot
back as he vaulted easily onto his gray mare. "Come
on." He squeezed his thighs together, and the horse
sprang into a canter. Cursing, Leisl mounted her own
steed and followed.

They rode down Church Street and through the market square, where there were more signs of life than
near the church or Katya's cottage. Sasha, his mind
crowded with unpleasant thoughts, didn't notice at
once that Leisl had dropped behind. After a few moments, as he began to reach the outskirts of the village,
the silence behind him penetrated his brooding, and he
pulled his horse up. Ten minutes later, he saw Leisl clattering down the street toward him.

"What were you up to?" he demanded. "I thought you
were impatient to get going."

She smirked at him. "Just picking up some food for
when we get hungry."

"I hope we won't be there that long."

"If we are, you'll thank me."

"You think more about eating than anyone I know!"

Leisl's hazel eyes narrowed. "That's because I've been
hungry enough at times that I can't help but think about
it," she snapped. Sasha was properly rebuked and lowered his eyes. He tugged his mare's head back toward
the road. They continued on in silence, their horses settling into a comfortable pace.

Sasha mentally reviewed his spells. Lathander had
been generous and had filled his priest's head with a
number of useful incantations in reward for several

hours of deep prayer. As for more mundane preparations, between them Sasha and Leisl had an array of
weapons—holy symbols, stakes, hammers, holy water,
and garlic. They also had a few non-sacred items of pure
silver, for Jander had warned them that encountering a
werewolf within Ravenloft's walls was entirely possible.

They clattered across the bridge that spanned the
Ivlis, and Sasha saw the ring of rolling fog a short distance ahead. He halted his mare and fished about for
the magical potion. Leisl did likewise, and they shuddered at the bitter taste. Gritting themselves for the
always-unpleasant journey through the malevolent
mist, they squeezed their horses into a slow trot.

Cold dampness engulfed them, completely obscuring vision and sound. Sasha hoped the Little Fox was
right behind him, but there was no way to be certain. A
few hundred feet later, the mist thinned and cleared.
Leisl was waiting for him, grinning. "Slowpoke," she
teased, but there was real kindness in her voice. He feebly returned her smile.

The journey to Castle Ravenloft took longer than
they expected as the road twined up through the mountains. They debated leaving the beaten path to follow a
trail that branched to their right, but the risk of getting
lost was too great. Better to follow the road and take a
little longer than to lose their way in the forest.

As they headed into the mountains, the horses
slowed slightly with the extra effort. Sasha patted his
mare's gray neck, and she whickered and swiveled her
ears back in her master's direction.

"What's that?" Leisl asked, pointing toward their left.
A road stretched into the distance. Even though it was
approaching midmorning, the huge gate that barred
the distant road seemed menacing to the young woman. The fact that the gigantic statues standing sentinel
had had their heads removed added to her discomfort.

"The gates of Barovia," Sasha answered, his voice
solemn. "They say that Strahd can open or close them
just by thinking about it."

Leisl looked at the gate again and couldn't suppress a shudder. Sasha, too, was growing a bit nervous as they neared their goal, and he kicked his mare with more vigor than was necessary. The horse leaped into a gallop.

After a few more tense moments, they saw Castle Ravenloft looming into their vision. Tall and black against the clear, wintry sky, it represented everything Sasha knew was evil about Barovia. Here was the seat of the villagers' fears. Here dwelt the monster responsible for the slaughter of the priest's family. Here was the nightmarish master of the land. And he, Sasha Petrovich, walked into it willingly. It didn't make much sense on the surface, but the priest knew his course to be the right one.

As they rode closer, Sasha saw two guard towers ahead and then noticed a rickety drawbridge spanning the deep chasm. He doubted their horses would be able to cross. "Whoa," he muttered, drew his horse up, and sat, thinking. Many beams on the bridge had rotted away, and the iron looked very old and rusty.

"What do we do now?" Leisl asked, halting her own mount. She glanced up at the two stone guardhouses. They were vacant, save for the stone gargoyles that grinned wickedly down at the travelers.

Sasha sighed and swung off his mare. He began to unpack her. "It's too unsafe to bring the horses across," he explained. "We've got to let them go here."

"Let them go?"

Sasha turned and looked at her. "If we tether them, they're easy prey for anything that comes along. If we set them free, chances are they'll wander back to the village and safety. Besides," he added grimly as he hauled another bundle off his horse, "if we make it out with the job done, we'll be able to walk back in utter safety. If we don't, well, we won't need horses."

Leisl didn't reply, only began to unpack her horse. Sasha gathered their tools into a single sack, reluctantly deciding to leave some items behind. They would do him little good if their weight caused him to fall to his death. He straightened and eyed the drawbridge, but it didn't look any sturdier than it had before. Sasha shook his head and slung his pack over his shoulder. "Let's go," he said with a confidence he didn't feel."

"I should go first," offered Leisl. "I'm lighter, and I'm pretty nimble. Maybe I can help you across."

Sasha hesitated. He didn't like the idea, but Leisl had a point. "All right. You first."

Carefully the Little Fox ventured onto the first board. It groaned, but held. She gripped the iron chain tightly, easing herself onto the next board and then the next, feeling her way and shifting her weight when necessary. She kept to the sides as much as she could, as they were better supported. Her eyes carefully examined each board before she put her weight on it.

"Step where I step," she called.

By the Morninglord's glory, it looks unsafe, Sasha thought. He clutched his sack tightly with one hand and used his other to grip onto the rusty iron chain. Tentatively Sasha stepped onto the board. First step safely planted, he said a quick prayer of thanks, one he repeated with each safe step.

When the priest looked up again, Leisl was already three-quarters of the way across, but that glance cost Sasha his concentration. He frowned as he looked at the next board. Was it there Leisl had put her weight, or on the other side?

He stepped gingerly, but the board snapped beneath his weight anyway. Sasha's right leg went through up to the hip. Flailing frantically, he clutched at the swaying chains. His pack tumbled down to the sharp rocks a thousand feet below. He hadn't realized he had cried out, but his throat suddenly hurt, and Leisl was there holding onto him. He fixed her with a frightened stare and dug his fingers into her freckled forearms.

"You're going to be all right. Just relax," the thief murmured, her voice calm and reassuring. "Grab onto that beam there. It's sturdy," she said in a sharper tone. The priest pried his fingers loose from Leisl's arms and obeyed. Calmly the thief talked him back onto his feet. It was then he realized he'd dropped his pack.

"Better to lose the pack than to lose the priest," Leisl said. "Your powers are more important than any holy symbol. Come on."

Sasha's next steps were tentative, but he made it across. "Leisl, thank—"

"Forget it," she said, though the appreciation in his eyes made her glad.

They continued, walking through a covered tunnel and emerging in a cobblestone courtyard. The entrance to Castle Ravenloft loomed ahead, its entry doors covered with beautiful carvings.

"Look at those doors," Leisl murmured. "I've never seen anything so gorgeous in my life."

"Yes, they are lovely," Sasha admitted, his dark eyes roving over the ornate carving, "but remember what this place houses." He stepped forward and reached for the latch.

Jander had told him that he would be unable to meet them at the door because of the sunlight, but that he would leave it open. As promised, the door swung outward easily, and the two hurried inside. Sasha pulled the door closed behind them. After the bright morning sunshine, it seemed very dark inside.

"I'm glad you made it here safely," came Jander's musical voice. The elf stepped into the entryway. Sasha's eyes adjusted enough so that he saw they were in a small room, dimly lit by flickering torches. "Was there a problem? You're late," Jander continued.

Sasha threw him a dark, unhappy look. "Did you think we weren't going to come?" The elf said nothing, only raised a golden eyebrow. Sasha's shoulders sagged. "I had to say goodbye to Katya."

"I was only worried," Jander offered. "Strahd's spies are everywhere."

Leisl, who had been quietly looking around, gasped suddenly. Her curious gaze had wandered up to the four dragon statues that perched above the entryway. They stared down at her balefully, their eyes gleaming.

"They are only stone," reassured Jander, although he, too, was always unnerved by the glittering jeweled eyes. "How are you armed?" he asked them.

"We brought many holy items," Sasha answered, "but I lost my pack on the bridge, so we'll have to make do with what Leisl has."

Jander smiled. "I spent the morning carving some stakes," he informed them, pleased. "What about weapons?"

Sasha shook his head. "Only a hammer or an axe, if I have to fight. I hope I don't. Leisl?"

Grinning, the thief patted her boot. Jander saw that a small dagger was neatly tucked into it. "All I need for a fight is in here."

"Then I have a present for you," Jander said. He handed her a small, evil-looking dagger. Its blade shone even in the torchlight, and its sheath looked very odd to Leisl. She took it curiously.

"Jander, that's a Ba'al Verzi dagger!" Sasha exclaimed, repulsed. "Why do you want to give her that awful thing?"

The elf turned his silver gaze to the priest. "Because," he answered coolly, "the blade is pure silver. I, too, am armed . . . just in case," he said, indicating the short sword that hung at his side.

"Is it magical?" Leisl asked.

"No," the elf replied shortly, "merely functional. I leave the magic to you, Sasha. I have one request for you now. Do you think you would be able to find Strahd if he were in the castle?"

Leisl's eyes widened, and her mouth opened. The elf dammed the flood of questions by adding, "I said if. I don't think he's here, but it would be a good idea to check."

Sasha shook his head. "I'm not sure," he said slowly, "but I can try." He seated himself on the floor, shifted a bit to get comfortable, then closed his eyes. The priest began to murmur a soft chant, then fell silent. His eyes moved rapidly beneath their closed lids. At length, he opened his eyes and met Jander's questioning glance.

"I turned up nothing. I can't be sure, though."

"Thank you for trying. That will have to do." Jander strode to the torches that lined the gray stone walls and liberated two from their sconces while Sasha busied himself lighting a shuttered oil lamp Leisl had carried.

"Our first destination should be the catacombs," the vampire told them as he handed Leisl a torch. "We've got to kill the slaves before nightfall. Come." He led the way out of the hall. Leisl and Sasha followed.

Jander set a swift pace, and the two mortals had to hurry to keep up with him. Leisl was silently grateful that she didn't have time to examine things too closely. What little she glimpsed as they half-walked, half-ran down the silent stone corridors unnerved her sufficiently. She kept telling herself that the gargoyles that lurked above were only stone carvings, that the beautiful yet cold statues they passed couldn't *really* be following her with their eyes.

The Little Fox was by no stretch of the imagination a coward, but she had never before been in this kind of situation. Stealing food, knifing an enemy in a street fight, even slaying the vampires out in the open was one thing. Being inside this dark, brooding edifice of stone, shadows, and distorting torchlight was something else entirely, and the thief couldn't shake a curious, pricking sensation of foreboding. Leisl kept her eyes fastened on Sasha and the elven vampire, although her ears were alert for the slightest sound.

Sasha, too, was unsettled by the oppressive darkness of the castle's interior. He was used to the small streets and alleys of his village. The church, dilapidated though it had been, never had this stifling sense of night-at-daytime that Strahd's dwelling place radiated, and the burgomaster's home had been a cozy cottage compared to the sprawling if decaying grandeur of Castle Ravenloft.

What struck the cleric most, though, as the three of

them moved purposefully through the dark halls, was
how out of place Jander appeared. The vampire was all
color—gold skin, blue tunic, red breeches—in sharp
contrast to the monotony of gray stone that pressed
about them. The elf had seemed more at home when
Sasha had encountered him in the woods and even by
the church than he did here. Suddenly the cleric recalled Jander's impassioned words about the misery of
the vampire's nature. Now he realized just how bitter a
fate it was to the elf. Jander had been meant for green
forests and golden sunlight, not this dark, shadowy existence of living death.

They came to a halt in front of a pair of double doors
as finely carved as the front doors had been. "This is the
chapel," Jander explained. "I should warn you, Strahd
has many minions here. Most of them are mindless en-
tities, and they have been instructed not to harm me or
anyone with me. I doubt we'll run into anything more
dangerous than a skeleton or a zombie. At least," he
amended, "not during the daytime." He pulled open the
double doors.

When he touched the doors, he heard the expected
soft rattling sound behind him. As it had done perhaps
a thousand times before, the skeleton who guarded the
chapel contested their entrance. It shuffled toward the
vampire and the mortals, worn leather boots slowing its
progress. Jander had almost come to regard this guardian as a friend; at any rate, its mere appearance no longer distressed him. There was no real threat in the
skeleton's attempt to bar them from the chapel.

Then, as if to prove Jander's earlier point, the skeletal
guardian stepped aside, the bright medallion that hung
about its neck swinging gently with the movement. Jander swept past him, and Leisl and Sasha followed,
though not without a backward glance or two. Sasha quietly mourned the destruction of the place as he gazed at
the broken pieces of wood that had been pews.

"Here we are," Jander said as they passed through an
alcove. An entryway to a spiral staircase opened befor

them. Chill breezes wafted out. The air smelled stale, as if it had been trapped there for centuries. "We follow this to the catacombs. Leisl, put out your torches. We should save them if we can. I don't know how long this is going to take."

The three were silent at first as they wound their way deeper into the cobweb-draped heart of the castle. The cold increased the farther they went, and the mortals began to shiver. Leisl listed to the echoing sounds their feet made on the flagstone as they descended.

"Hey," she whispered suddenly. Her voice seemed incredibly loud.

"What?" Sasha hissed back from a few steps in front of her.

"Jander, have you ever gone down this stairway before?"

The elf paused, glancing back up at her. His sharp features looked distorted in the wavering orange light of the torch he held. "No, but I know where it leads."

"How do you know there's not some kind of trap here?"

There was an absolute silence. Jander had no idea if Strahd had rigged this convenient stairway with anything dangerous. It would be just like the count. He grinned wryly to himself. "I don't know, Leisl. You've raised an excellent point. Would you like to go first and spring any traps you might see?"

"You bet I—hey!" Leisl scowled as she caught Jander's dark-humored joke. To his own surprise, Sasha snorted with sudden laughter, and even the Little Fox began to chuckle, though she shook her head in mock exasperation. The elf smiled up at her, the torchlight almost glinting off his golden skin, his silver eyes warm with humor. Suddenly Leisl realized that, strange though it was, she was starting to like the vampire. "Seriously," she noted, "if you would like me to check as we go—"

"No," Jander said. "I'll stay in the lead. Any traps here would be far more dangerous to you." He turned and continued on, adding darkly, "That is only one of the benefits of being dead."

It was impossible to calculate how much time passed before they finally reached the bottom of the stairs, but Jander's torch was almost burned out. Before they entered the catacombs, the elf took Leisl's torch and lit it from his own dying one.

"Behold the hall of the dead," Jander said grimly. He placed a hand on Sasha's shoulder. "It is not a place for the faint of heart."

Sasha gazed up at him steadily, the light from his lamp throwing shadows on his face. The long descent had given him time to steady his nerves and reinforce his sense of purpose. He blazed with an inner fire that glowed in his features. Jander recognized the expression; he had burned like that, once, long, long ago. "I'm not afraid," the priest replied in a calm voice. "Where do the vampires sleep?"

Jander almost laughed. "Everywhere," he said flatly. "Every coffin in here might house one of Strahd's slaves."

Sasha couldn't help it. He shut his eyes, wincing. "There are three of us, and it is daylight outside," Jander reminded him. They stepped up to the first crypt.

"Look at them," Leisl said in a tone of faint disgust, her hazel eyes fastened on the dark ceiling. Sasha followed her gaze, and even he had to swallow. The ceiling of this dank place was covered with hundreds, perhaps thousands of bats. Even though the priest knew they were harmless, he felt a rising tide of panic as they shifted and fluttered.

"We should begin," Jander said.

As Sasha and Leisl retrieved their tools, the vampire strode to the first crypt. With only a little effort, he lifted the huge stone lid and peered inside. A skeleton, draped with ruined bits of finery, slept its eternal sleep untroubled by undeath. Tension building in his muscles, pulling them taut, he moved on to the next crypt.

* * * * *

A few hundred years ago, the innocent young elf that Jander had been would never have imagined that so grim a thing as death would become routine. Things change, he mused morbidly as he held the writhing body of the vampiress so Sasha could pound a stake into her heart. Twenty such "murders" they had completed so far, twenty beautiful, deadly, evil creatures, with lips the color of the blood that bubbled up from their hearts. Jander remembered Daggerdale as they worked. For an instant, he was mortal again, tasting bile in his throat as he and Gideon sought out and dispatched the unholy things, much as he and Sasha were doing now.

Death ought not to become so routine, even the death of a vampire.

They had worked out a system, the elven vampire, the wiry little thief, and the half-gypsy priest. Jander, with his superior strength, removed the stone slabs. He held the vampires down while Sasha pierced their hearts with sharpened wood. Leisl was left with the unpleasant but less dangerous task of cutting off the heads and stuffing the mouths with garlic as Jander and Sasha moved on to the next crypt.

"My hands are going to stink for the next ten years," Leisl muttered under her breath as she crammed one more garlic bulb into the gaping mouth of the vampiress she had just decapitated. Concentrating on her work, ghoulish as it was, alleviated some of her trepidation, but not all. She still felt as though they were, somehow, under surveillance, and now and then she glanced around sharply. "You're getting jumpy, girl," she said to herself, "and that's bad for your profession. Just calm down."

She finished the task and caught up with her comrades. They had reached the last coffin, and, as Leisl approached, the infernal creature shuddered and died. Her face became pale and composed as her soul drifted toward peace. Sasha and Jander drew back, and Leisl severed the head from the neck with a few quick hacks and completed the grisly ritual.

Jander looked at Sasha. The priest's shirt was soaked with sweat and his breath was labored. A drop of red meandered down his cheek like a bloody tear. Without thinking, Jander reached over to wipe it away.

Sasha jerked back, then looked flustered. "I'm sorry. You startled me."

The elf nodded as if he believed it, but he realized the truth with a weary sense of resignation. Sasha did not yet trust him fully. He could hardly blame the boy, but it was a sad thing nonetheless. He looked about. The ghostly shapes of the stone coffins loomed like slumbering monsters. Distorted by the wavering torchlight, they appeared to move. Those less brave than Sasha and Leisl might have been driven mad by the eerie place long before now.

"We have done good work here," Jander said. "We have eliminated most of our enemies. Now we must find Strahd's coffin and sanctify it, so that he has no place of refuge here."

Sasha nodded slowly, tired from his exertions. He flexed his hands, cramped from clutching hammer and stake. If it had been possible, Jander would have suggested that the priest take a rest. Time, however, even more than the master of Ravenloft, was their enemy.

Jander was not certain where Strahd's coffin was, but he could make a fair guess. He, Leisl, and Sasha had investigated every one of the dozen crypts in the main area of the catacombs. There were a few alcoves off to the sides; no doubt specially prepared for the members of the count's immediate family.

The first such chamber they came to was that of Strahd's parents, the handsome Barov and Ravenovia, Castle Ravenloft's namesake. Steps led down into the small, peaceful room. The two sarcophaguses appeared well-sealed and untroubled. Jander continued on, letting the nobles sleep undisturbed. They had died before

Strahd had made his evil pact with the dark entity, so it was likely that Barov and Ravenovia enjoyed true death.

A second chamber was labeled for the use of Sturm and Gisella Von Zarovich. Sturm had been Strahd's second brother, Jander recalled. Yet this room was completely empty, even of coffins. The fortunate Sturm appeared to have lived out his prosaic life away from Castle Ravenloft and its diabolical inhabitant.

A third room for the dead was also empty, although some preparations had been made. One open, empty sarcophagus clearly bore the name "Sergei Von Zarovich." Jander shook his head sadly. After brutally murdering his youngest brother, Strahd had not even bothered to inter the corpse. No doubt the unfortunate young man had been left to rot where he lay while Strahd pursued his malevolent desires. The sight of the second sarcophagus caused the elf to close his eyes in pain. If time had passed naturally, the coffin in the crypt would have borne the words, "Tatyana Federovna Von Zarovich."

Anna would never rest in such a place. Her body was ashes, burned in a madhouse and now scattered to the winds. And Tatyana was doomed to return to Barovia over and over . . . A gentle touch on his arm brought the elf back to the present. Sasha was looking up at him, concerned. "There is nothing for us here," Jander said, his voice thick.

The final chamber had to be Strahd's. As with Barov's and Ravenovia's tomb, steps led down into the fifty-foot-long room. From here, the trio could see the count's coffin. There appeared to be no obstacles to their entry. "We should proceed with caution," the elf said in a soft voice to Sasha. "It looks too easy."

Slowly, carefully, Jander began to descend into the crypt of Strahd Von Zarovich.

 **TWENTY-SIX**

A sharp stinging sound filled the air as arrows flew from bows concealed in the wall and embedded themselves in Jander's body. Within a heartbeat, Leisl, daggers in hand, had flattened herself against the wall while Sasha had seized his holy symbol. "Jander!" the priest cried.

A dozen shafts protruded from the elf's body like pins from a cushion. Unperturbed, Jander plucked them out one by one. He did not bleed, did not even appear injured. "I'm all right," he reassured the cleric. "As I said, there are advantages to being dead."

Leisl shook her head, smiling a little. When he had removed all the arrows, Jander continued his descent alone. Nothing further happened. When he reached the bottom, he looked around. His infravision picked out several warm red shapes in various corners of the room. Before he could tell Sasha or Leisl not to follow him, the wolves emerged into the dim light of the trespassers torches.

There were easily a dozen of the great beasts, who approached with frightening slowness. The fur on their necks was raised, and their ears were plastered to their skulls. A low growl rose from every corner, and Sasha and Leisl could now see the flash of sharp white teeth and the red gleam of hate-filled eyes. The rank smell usky fur filled the room.

"Oh, gods," whispered Leisl, coldness filling her gut. ne night's Gray Singers. Without thought, she stepped oser to Sasha.

Jander cursed to himself. The beasts now were rahd's creatures, but he had to try to turn them before e started hacking at them with his sword. He sent a ental command. *Easy, my old friends. We mean no arm. You don't want to hurt us. . . .*

The wolves, stiff-legged, closed in for the kill. Jan-er's gloved hand went to his sword. *No. Leave us alone. ur master's orders were not meant for us!*

One of the wolves paused. Her ears twitched, and she acked her head a little. The elf stayed tense, hoping jainst hope that his will was stronger than Strahd's ower over the wolves. A second wolf seemed confused id sat down, whimpering. *Leave. You have guarded ell. Now it is time to go. . . .*

A third, then a fourth, relaxed. One by one, the huge imals ceased to threaten the three interlopers. The st female suddenly ran up the stairs, and the rest fol-wed until they had all abandoned their sentry posts.

The vampire closed his silver eyes in relief. Sasha and :isl stared, dumfounded. "That is how, once, I saved ur father's life," the elf told the young man, and Sasha niled as he remembered his mother telling him the ory.

"This is very encouraging," Jander continued. "I had ought the wolves to be completely under Strahd's ntrol. That I was able to turn them means the count 1't as all-powerful as he'd like me to think." Leisl took deep, shuddering breath and deliberately forced her nse shoulders to loosen.

When they reached the closed coffin, Jander fully ex-:cted another sort of attack, but nothing happened. asha began to lay out the items necessary for the task hand: his holy symbol, a vial of holy water, some spe-al herbs that had been blessed.

"Do you think he's here?" Leisl whispered. Jander

shook his head.

"No." Carefully he opened the coffin, then stared. was wrong.

Strahd lay on the satin lining, his dark eyes close his gaunt features pale and waxy. His hands were fold across his chest, and he appeared perfectly compose The master of Ravenloft looked, as he was, quite dea

"Thank the Morninglord it's still daytime," the pri murmured. Jander nodded, moving Strahd's hands his sides so that Sasha could place the sharpened sta over the count's heart. The priest positioned the wea on, said a quick prayer, and raised the hammer.

We've got you now, you bastard, Jander thought w a sudden self-satisfied burst of hatred.

White hands shot up to clasp Sasha's neck, as t count, with a bestial roar, sat up. The priest dropped tools, his hands clawing at the fingers clamped arou his throat. He jerked back, but the motion only su ceeded in tumbling both himself and the count to t floor. Jander leaped at the count with a cry of his ov striking Strahd with a violent blow. The count's g slackened, allowing the priest to squirm free. He roll away, coughing and gasping.

Jander threw himself on Strahd with all his streng pinning the count beneath him. Strahd's eyes blaz red, and his sharp teeth snapped an inch away fr Jander's face. The elf didn't have to say anything to t Little Fox. She was already there, hammering a sta into Strahd's black heart with all the power she co muster. It penetrated, and Strahd screamed in ago Again Leisl hammered, and the stake went deep Blood drenched the fine white linen of Strahd's sh The count shuddered once, violently, then went limp

Jander permitted himself to collapse limply over body of his enemy. It was over so quickly. Somehow had expected the cunning master of Ravenloft to ha put up a better struggle. To his surprise, Jander felt riously unsatisfied.

Someone touched his shoulder gently. "Jand

came Leisl's soft voice, "I think you'd better take a look at this."

Wearily the elf lifted his head. Leisl, shaking with her earlier efforts, pointed at the count's body. Lifting himself, Jander studied the body beneath him. A shapely female vampire lay on the stone floor, a stake through her heart.

"Damn you, Strahd," the vampire whispered, closing his eyes as he rolled off the corpse. "I should have realized."

"An illusion?" Sasha coughed, rubbing his bruised throat. Jander nodded miserably.

Sasha respected his comrade's silence and went about sanctifying the coffin. Leisl turned her attention to decapitating the corpse.

Anointing the coffin's satin interior with holy oil, the priest murmured a prayer. He then doused the coffin liberally with holy water. He sighed and looked over at Jander. "It's done," he said. "Now what?"

The elven vampire shook himself from his lethargy. "We start searching for the piece of the sun."

* * * * *

The next few hours were among the most frustrating, tense, and essentially miserable ones any of them had ever spent. Jander's first thought was that Sasha might be able to magically locate the Holy Symbol, but this proved to be a fruitless effort.

Their only other recourse, Jander reluctantly informed his companions, was to search the castle.

"The whole damn place?" Leisl moaned incredulously. Jander nodded, and, almost overwhelmed by the task ahead of them, they began their search.

They left the sinister catacombs by way of the even more frightening dungeons. "Some of the former prisoners left treasure in the cells," Jander told them. "We might as well check here."

The elf remembered his first visit here, how the pitiful

wails and cries had disturbed him. Now the place was more or less quiet. Strahd's slaves were hungry, impatient feeders, and the larder was low. The elf unlocked the cells with the skeleton key that hung on a peg outside the center cell, and he and Leisl made a careful but swift inspection of each one. Sasha watched with horror.

"None of this moves you at all, does it?" the priest asked, a note of disgust creeping into his voice.

"It all moves me," Jander answered, refusing to get angry as he rifled through a rotting chest of gold pieces. "Especially what's in the farthest cell."

Curious, Sasha went and looked into the cell. A small boy was curled up, fast asleep, on a pile of rotting straw. "Don't disturb him," Jander whispered at Sasha's ear. "Gods know, he needs the rest from this horrible place."

"Why haven't you let him go?" Sasha whispered back angrily.

"Because I don't rule here. Strahd does. I do what I can, when I can. It's never enough. I've let prisoners go in the past, but he always takes more." The vampire snarled. "Only when we have slain the master, may we free his prisoners. Not before. Come."

"But—"

"Sasha," said Leisl sharply, "let him alone. Let's do what we came here to do and then we can save the world, all right?"

Sasha turned on the thief with a hot retort on his lips, but it died as he looked first at her, than at Jander. She was right. The elf, too, was pained by what surrounded him, but he had a plan that could accomplish everything they wanted to do. There was no sense jeopardizing that plan.

With a last, wounded look at the slumbering child, Sasha followed the vampire. Leisl brought up the rear, her sense of trepidation still with her. The stench of rot that assaulted Sasha's nostrils when they entered the torture chamber almost caused him to vomit, but his undead guide moved surely through the instruments of agony toward the balcony. Sasha stared. He couldn't

ear his eyes from the grisly tableau of slow-moving
ombies reenacting their deaths and grinning skeletons
ondling implements of pain.

The priest felt a gentle prodding at his back, and turn-
d to meet Leisl's level gaze. "Don't look," she said gen-
ly. "Just keep moving." In a state of stunned shock,
Sasha obeyed.

Jander halted and looked up at an observation balcony about ten feet above them. "Link your arms
around my neck, both of you." Puzzled, they obeyed,
clinging tightly. "Hang on," the elf instructed. He bal-
anced himself, squatted low, then leaped up onto the
balcony.

The three companions eventually headed toward the
chapel, though they stopped to examine the various
rooms and alcoves as they came across them. Their
search turned up nothing. When they reached the
chapel, gently rebuffing the guardian skeleton, each of
them set upon the room with renewed energy, aware by
the fading light outside that twilight was near. "Surely,"
Sasha said aloud, his voice full of hope, "a holy object
ought to be in a holy place."

Again, they turned up empty-handed. By this time
Sasha and Leisl were very tired; even the vampire was
starting to feel the strain. The young priest refilled his
oil lamp, lit it again, then lay back in one of the pews,
rubbing his eyes with his fists. Leisl had dipped into her
pack and was currently chewing on a hunk of bread. Her
bright hazel eyes kept flickering about, as though she
didn't feel quite comfortable in the place. "So, what do
we do now?" she inquired with her mouth full.

Jander didn't answer as he looked at them, his mood
black with failure. He mulled over the situation in his
mind. The helpless prisoners, most of them children,
still languished in the dungeons below. Anna had not
been avenged. Strahd would return eventually. Jander's
daring foray against the aristocratic vampire had accomplished nothing save the destruction of a few slaves
and coffins.

Jander swore softly. Leisl's query still rang in his ear so what do we do now?

He had no answer.

The elf heard the familiar, soft clatter that heralde the approach of the bony chapel guardian. Was it tim to close the church? he wondered facetiously. Wear discouraged, he turned to look at the guardian.

And saw something that caused him to bolt uprigh his whole body tense.

The vampire had looked upon this melancholy skel ton a thousand times. He could probably recite ever last detail about the walking pile of bones. But Jande had never before truly *seen* what had been resting wit in his grasp for decades. Shards of what had once bee formal clothing draped the guardian's shoulders; an belt had long since dropped off. However, the skeleto still wore ruined leather boots that tended to slow i movement. About its stalk of a neck, a pendant da gled, as it had for hundreds of years.

It was wrought of platinum and shaped like the su with a quartz crystal embedded in its center. The meda lion swung as the skeleton moved, tapping against th ribs with a hollow sound and catching the flicker of th torchlight.

Suddenly Jander remembered the covers of books the study, inlaid with that same sunburst. The elf's min raced to the fresco and the inscription he had dec phered: THE GOBLYN KING FLEES BEFORE TH POWER OF THE HOLY SYMBOL OF RAVENKIND. was all beginning to fall into place—Strahd's scathin comment in his journal about Sergei's becoming priest: . . . *the clergy has given him leave to wear th Priest's Pendant, a pretty enough bauble to which Serg attaches a great deal of—perhaps too much—emotion value*; the headless statue in the Hall of Heroes, with th same pendant carved around its stone neck; the po trait of three brothers, the youngest of whom wore th same pendant; Strahd's cry, as he bent over the body the brother he had killed: *You were supposed to hai been a priest.*

"The one who has loved best has the heart of stone," Jander said softly. The truth shone on him like the brightest sunlight; the quartz in the pendant was the piece of the sun, and the skeleton standing before Jander was all that remained of noble, loving Sergei.

"Jander?" came Sasha's voice, uncertain.

The elf exploded into action. With a cry, he swung at the skeleton with his bare hands, seizing the dry bones and scattering them like a madman. Ribs clattered to the floor. Arm bones skidded into corners. The skull bounced and shattered on the stone floor.

With his violent attack on the skeleton, Jander had freed the trapped soul. They were kin, in a sense, he and Sergei: the vampire couldn't help but love anyone who had loved Tatyana, Anna, so deeply. Abruptly the frenzy passed, and the elf gazed at the bones that now lay strewn about the chapel floor. He knew that the next time anyone approached the statue of the youngest Von Zarovich in the Hall of Heroes, it would be a stone statue and nothing more.

Sergei was at peace at last, and he had left behind that which Jander had sought—a way in which they could both have their revenge upon Strahd, the creature who had destroyed the woman they loved.

"There," rasped Jander, pointing a trembling gold finger at the medallion as it lay winking upon the floor. "That's it. That's the piece of the sun."

Wonderingly Sasha reached out a trembling hand and closed it about the medallion. It rested comfortably in his hand, the cold metal warming from his touch. Leisl peered over his shoulder as the priest traced the runes carved into the platinum. He recognized some of them: Truth. Compassion. Forgiveness. Justice. Light. . . . The Holy Symbol of Ravenkind did indeed appear to house a piece of the sun. It was altogether the loveliest thing Sasha had seen in his life.

"Boy, that'd fetch a pretty penny somewhere," Leisl commented, although her voice, too, was subdued with a sense of awe. Sasha smiled a little, then turned to the vampire with eyes that were shiny with tears. He knew how the elf loved beauty, and he suddenly longed to share the glory that was the Holy Symbol with the tortured soul. "Oh, Jander, touch this. You must touch it."

Jander, too, was enraptured with the beautiful object. As if drawn, he reached out a tapered, gloved hand to caress the artifact, but he snatched it back at once, blackened and smoking, and clutched it to his breast. A groan escaped his lips.

"Oh, Jander, I'm sorry, I'm so sorry! I only wanted to share it with you." Sasha's face was full of contrition.

"It's all right," Jander managed. "Obviously it was never intended for such as me." He smiled, his pain turning it into a grimace. "You see why I wanted you to come along, Sasha. If it did that to me with just a touch, think what it will do when you present it against Strahd."

"The heart of stone," Sasha breathed, his gaze drawn back to the object again. "Just like Maruschka said."

Jander's head came up. "Maruschka?"

Sasha nodded, too enraptured by the beauty of the pendant to notice the strained sound of Jander's normally mellifluous voice. Leisl, however, fixed the vampire with narrowed eyes. "When Leisl and I went to see the Vistani to have our fortunes told," Sasha explained. "She was the one who gave us all the clues."

"When did you go?"

Now Sasha met Jander's silver eyes, worried at the fear he saw there. "A few weeks after you asked me to help you defeat Strahd. What's wrong with that? I know gypsies are cheats most of the time, but this one—"

Jander was on his feet, glancing about the room. "Come on," he urged them. "We've got to get out of here." Leisl needed no further encouragement, but was on her feet and ready to leave. She'd been right all along. Something was wrong here.

"What's the matter?"

"Sasha, you're a fool!" Jander cried. "The gypsies are

Strahd's spies! If you went to see Maruschka and she told you about all this, then she knows we're here. And that means—"

"Strahd knows we're here," Leisl finished, growing horror on her sharp features.

Even in the flickering orange of the torchlight, Jander could see the blood drain from Sasha's face.

The torch and the oil lamp suddenly went dark. A blast of cold air came out of nowhere and whipped through the chapel, nearly knocking the companions down with its force. Though Jander could see nothing with his infravision other than Sasha and Leisl, the elf sensed a maleficent presence in this once-holy place. A low, satisfied laugh began to sound, rising to a shriek of evil mirth that was a tenor harmony to the wind's deep rush. Punctuating the other sounds was the hair-raising call of wolves on the hunt.

"Too late," came Strahd's velvet voice.

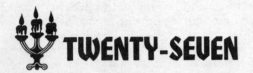

TWENTY-SEVEN

The wolves came as they had a generation before in the village, with a musical and deadly sense of purpose, bounding into Castle Ravenloft's chapel from the hallway, the alcoves, and from the door to the garden. Some even came crashing in through the stained glass windows, sending shattered rainbows flying. Jander formed a mental command to turn the half-dozen beasts.

His order went completely ignored. The elf was unable to even sense the wolves' minds.

"You humiliated me with that trick before," came Strahd's voice, tinged with satisfaction. "Not this time."

It was Sasha who recovered first. He began chanting an incantation in a voice that was clear and careful though high with fright, making a circle about himself and Leisl with holy water. The approaching wolves continued to charge them, only to halt abruptly outside the sacred circle the priest had created. They growled their frustration.

Jander had located Strahd. He was seated in one of the thrones on the balcony fifty feet above them, a dark figure of shadow with a pale white blur for a face. As Jander watched, the count rose and advanced toward the edge of the balcony.

More than anything in that moment, the elf wanted to

leap up and tackle his foe with his bare hands and teeth. He knew, though, if he made a move, the count would summarily destroy him. That was what happened to teachers who had outlived their usefulness. Instead, Jander summoned the patience of five hundred years of undeath and stayed motionless. He waited until he was certain he had Strahd's attention. When the elf caught the other vampire's gaze, he smiled, slowly, and dissolved into a fine mist that immediately dispersed to near invisibility.

Although he no longer had physical organs, Jander was capable of "hearing" and "seeing" what transpired next. The count, baffled and angered, rushed to the edge of the balcony.

"Jander! You shall not escape me so easily!" Strahd roared, his eyes glowing red. Suddenly his attitude changed, became languid. He turned his attention to Sasha and Leisl, who stayed well within the protection of the priest's ring. Just outside of the circle of holy water, the thwarted wolves shifted and growled, confused.

"Sasha Petrovich, cleric of Lathander," the count said smoothly, in an almost conversational tone. "You are a brave priest indeed, to walk into the lair of a vampire. Even braver to have befriended one. But your efforts were for naught! You and your thieving friend shall die useless deaths. Jander has deserted you. At the first sign of trouble, you see how he reacts."

Sasha didn't want to believe it, but it certainly appeared that way. The priest gripped the Holy Symbol of Ravenkind in one hand and pulled Leisl, who was trembling at the sight of the Gray Singers, protectively close to him with the other. "Be that true or no," he said, his voice youthful and clear with purpose, "you are still my enemy, Count Strahd. I take my revenge for the murder of my family!" He made as if to lift the medallion, but the vampire had vanished.

Confused, Sasha hesitated. An instant later, Strahd materialized abruptly, right at the limit of Sasha's ring of protection. He wore a smile of triumph, and in his cold, sharp-nailed hands, he clutched a terrified young woman.

Sasha made a terrible choking sound. The woman's doelike eyes were now huge and filled with fear.

"Katya!" the priest whispered, horror-struck.

The mist that hovered a few yards near the scene registered the information with an equal horror. *Katya? Sasha's fiancee was really Trina, the count's lycanthropic spy!* Jander wanted to materialize, warn Sasha against what he knew the young priest was about to do. The vampire fought down the impulse. Patience would win the game and nothing else. Dear gods, though, it was so hard just to stand by and watch Strahd play with the elf's friends as if he were sitting at a game of Hawks and Hares. . . .

Sasha stared, transfixed, an expression of unspeakable pain on his features. He had been standing straight, secure in his convictions of righteousness and the all-powerful might of his god. Now he slumped, defeated before the battle.

"Don't hurt her," he murmured. "Please, whatever you do to me, don't hurt her."

"It is in your hands, Sasha Petrovich. Throw down the amulet," Strahd purred, "and she lives. Make one move toward me, and she dies instantly." Sensuously, the vampire lord pulled Katrina's dark hair away from her white neck. He bared his fangs and brought them toward the beating vein . . . closer . . . closer . . .

"Sasha, don't, he'll kill us all," began Leisl. Strahd paused, fixing her with a powerful red gaze.

"Do be still, thief," the vampire commanded. Leisl held her tongue, suddenly no longer mistrustful. His eyes held her, and slowly Leisl felt her own will slip away under that crimson stare.

"All right," said Sasha in a broken voice. "For pity's sake, leave her alone. She's never hurt a soul."

The bitter, malicious irony of it ripped through Jander. Patience, he reminded himself.

The Holy Symbol of Ravenkind fell to the stone floor

from Sasha's nerveless fingers.

"Excellent. Sasha, I am so very pleased that you are reasonable. Now, please, kick it out of the circle for me," Strahd instructed. When the priest, too numbed with grief, didn't move, the vampire jerked hard on Katrina's arm. Playing her role to the hilt—or perhaps Strahd had really hurt her—she gasped in pain. Now Sasha did move, hastily kicking the beautiful object out of the ring. It slid along the stone floor with a scraping noise.

"Thank you so very much. For everything, really. You see, I let you find the trinket because I needed to locate it myself. If I have it, I can keep it safe, can't I?"

Jander's "vision" was beginning to fade. He had never lingered in mist form so long before. Usually he used it only for a brief instant—to evade capture or slip under a door. The elf didn't know how much longer he could wait. He let himself drift down, slowly, toward the scene.

"I knew about the famous Holy Symbol of Ravenkind," Strahd continued, "but I didn't know exactly what the cursed thing *was*. Most High Priest Kir died before he could tell Sergei the secret. I must confess, I had no idea that my dear brother's pendant was the awesome, sacred Holy Symbol. I overestimated the priests. I thought they would guard it more carefully than that.

"But, thanks to you, my dear friends—" he bowed mockingly to Leisl and Sasha "—I have the bauble in my grasp now. Pick it up, my dear," the count told Katrina.

As if she were tossing aside a costume, Katrina divested herself of her look of wide-eyed vulnerability. Her sprightly laugh echoed through the hall as she flung her arms around Strahd's neck and kissed his pallid cheek. "Oh, you are so *clever!*" Like a child gathering flowers, she scurried to the discarded holy symbol and picked it up eagerly. Sasha stared at her, his mind thawing only enough to make room for a fresh horror.

"Katya, no!"

Her smile widened, turned feral. "Now you're catching on, sweetheart. Oh, how easy, *easy* you were to fool!"

Sasha had recovered from the shock of the betrayal, and now his Vistani blood boiled within him at the deception. His black brows drew together, and a storm that would have done a pure gypsy justice began to gather in his eyes. With a snarl, he reached for the pink wooden disk that was Lathander's own holy symbol.

"Foolish priest!" Strahd roared. "You dare to threaten me in my own home! From nothing, you seek to destroy the land?"

Suddenly there was a hissing sound by Sasha's and Leisl's feet. Small columns of steam were rising as the holy water Sasha had poured evaporated. The disk Sasha clutched exploded into flames, and the priest cried out in pain. The seven wolves pranced agitatedly. "No, sit and guard," Strahd told them for Sasha's benefit. "See that the priest watches what happens to his friend. At least, for a while."

The vampire turned to Katrina. "You take him, when you are ready," he instructed her. Still holding the symbol, Katrina looked at Sasha. A slow grin spread across her pretty, savage face.

"Come, Sasha my love. Kiss me. Don't you want to kiss me?" Katrina threw back her head and howled, the inhuman sound exploding from her throat. Her skin rippled as thick hairs emerged and receded.

"Katya!" Sasha could barely believe the nightmarish reality that was being revealed to him. Katrina's eyes had not changed, but her nose and mouth were elongated in a grotesque parody of a wolf's muzzle. Gray hairs exploded out of her face.

Leisl did nothing. She stared, transfixed, at the vampire. "Come, my dear," Strahd invited in his velvet voice. "Come to me."

The Little Fox began to move slowly toward Strahd. "Since you were responsible for the deaths of my slaves, it is only fitting that you be my first new one, hmm?"

"No!" cried Sasha, his attention briefly diverted from the terrifying spectacle of Katrina licking her jowls a few feet away from him. "Let her go!" At his cry, Katrina paused. She swung her wolfish face toward Strahd.

"What?" she demanded in a low growl. "You will make *her* a vampire?"

"Yes, I think so," Strahd answered absently, running a thin finger along Leisl's jawline. "I do not think Jander Sunstar has really left. He is too noble to flee, the fool. It will hurt him to know what I have done to this child. It will hurt the priest also, to watch. Besides, I think she will make an interesting companion."

"You will not!" snarled the werewolf. She whirled, turning on Strahd. Her hands were still human enough for her to clutch the Holy Symbol of Ravenkind like a weapon.

Strahd's eyes registered surprise at the outburst, but he made no move. Not yet.

Katrina kept a tight grip on the Holy Symbol. "It was all your fault, you know," she growled. "You kept finding more and more women to take you away from me. You wondered how so many of them could be killed. I got them alone, I led them to Sasha in wolf form, and he got rid of them for me. And now I hear you tell him that you're going to make *her* a vampire and start the whole thing over again? No! I won't hear of it!"

"Katrina, my dear," Strahd exclaimed, turning away from Leisl, "surely you don't think this pitiful creature could ever take your place in my affections! She is a diverting amusement and a means of revenge, that is all. If it troubles you so much, then I shall just kill her."

"Do it," the werewolf demanded, tears of bitter jealousy filling her human eyes and trickling down her furry cheeks. She let her arm droop a little bit, relaxed her grip on the Holy Symbol ever so slightly.

"No!" Sasha cried.

Now, Jander thought.

Without warning, a sleek, golden-brown wolf leaped from the pack and seized the medallion between its teeth. Faster than he had ever changed before, the vampire transformed from wolf to mist to elven form, clutching the Holy Symbol of Ravenkind. It burned, as it had before, with angry, mocking pain. The stench of charred flesh wafted up from the seared hand. Jander ignored it.

Many things happened at once.

Katrina, flooded with anger, surrendered to the change and shivered into her lupine form. A massive gray and brown wolf now, she leaped straight for Leisl. She hit the thief hard, knocking her off her feet. The Little Fox, however, managed to reach the dagger that Jander had given her. Her left hand up to protect her throat, she stabbed at the wolf with the silver Ba'al Verzi blade. It bit deeply into Katrina's shoulder.

The werewolf howled her pain and twisted, snapping. Her teeth sank into Leisl's arm. The thief's dagger clattered to the floor as she cried out once, harshly. The Little Fox had never before felt such pain. The wolf-woman she wrestled with seemed to be everywhere at once. Claws raked her face. Fur stifled her breathing. Sharp teeth again found sensitive flesh, bit, severed.

The Little Fox was going to die, and she knew it.

She refused to give in, pitting every ounce of her rapidly dwindling strength against the fearsome creature. It was not for her own life that she fought, using her teeth and nails like an animal's, it was for Sasha's.

Hind claws ripped brutally across her belly, and Leisl wailed as she felt the blood gush forth. Hot breath, foul with carrion, came near her throat. Her sight dimmed.

Sasha dealt with the other wolves swiftly and efficiently. He leaped for the oil lamp and with a prayer dashed it at the animals. The puddle of oil exploded with a *whumph* as the smoldering wick sparked to life. Light flared about him, sending the darkness scuttling for the corners like guilty rats. Two of the wolves were caught in the flames and howled as they fled. Two more were singed and also turned tail. The two remaining

aped at Sasha. The priest defended himself with the
ammer he had used to slay the vampires. He killed one
f the beasts with a lucky blow to the head that
runched its skull. The final wolf decided it had had
nough, and Sasha was left unguarded.

Like an avenging angel the young priest sprang to
eisl's rescue, righteous anger contorting his hand-
ome, delicate features. With her vision fading, Leisl
eard him shout something and saw him bring some
littering object down on Katya's haunches.

The werewolf howled, a long, shrill sound that
eemed to take forever to die. When it had at last faded,
he creature had fled, her left haunch smoking, branded
y the pure silver of one of Sasha's holy symbols. Leisl
ayed conscious long enough to see the priest's dear
ace filled with concern, then her head fell back across
is arm.

Jander, meanwhile, had at long last confronted his
nemy. Despite the pain, he was filled with a hot, brutal
leasure. The elf lifted the Holy Symbol of Ravenkind,
eady to shove it into Strahd's face.

"You fool! You can't use that against me!"

"Can't I? I followed Lathander, Strahd! *Lathander
lorninglord!* And *this*—" he gestured with the medal-
on "—is a piece of the sun."

Something like fear flickered across Strahd's sharp
eatures. The scowl of fury softened, became placating.
What are you trying to do, my friend?" the vampire ca-
led, his voice sweet as honey. "Such an action would
estroy you as well, surely. Look at your hand!"

The voice lulled and soothed, but Jander did not
eld. He was buoyed by the white-hot hatred that filled
is breast. "You don't know the whole story," he spat.
Before we die, let me tell you about Anna."

"Yes, yes, I remember—that poor, insane girl whose
ormenter you came here to—" Strahd broke off. "Do
ou believe that I was the one who hurt her?"

"I know it was you. Her name wasn't Anna. After you
estroyed her mind, that was all she was capable of

uttering. Only a fragment of her true name, just as sh
was only a fragment of her true self—*Tatyana*."

Emotion flooded the count's pale face. "No," he whi
pered in pain. "You lie, elf. She fell through th
mists . . ."

"Oh, she fell through the mists all right," Jander co
tinued as he slowly began to advance on the other var
pire. The pain in his hand increased, became harder
ignore. "At least, part of her did. But not all. Some pa
of her wanted so much to be free that she made it ha
pen. Part of her somehow ended up in my world, h
mind gone from the horrors she'd witnessed. The ho
rors *you* had inflicted upon her!"

"No! I loved her! I only wanted to—"

"You destroyed her, you bastard. By the time I fou
her, she was just a shell. Even so, enough of her so
shone through that I loved her." Treacherous tears b
gan to fill his eyes, threatening to blur his vision. A
grily he blinked them away. "I wouldn't have cared if sh
had loved Sergei. He made her happy, he made h
whole. You had her complete, and you destroyed h
Damn you for that!" His voice rose, filled the room as
gave vent to his hatred.

"Jander . . . you would *die* for this?" Strahd was the
oughly shocked.

The elf let his actions be his answer. The elf forme
silent prayer to Lathander, god of the morning, foe
vampires. Just this one thing, he thought. Send me
whatever pit awaits me, but allow me this one last, go
act.

By now, Jander's hand was nothing but blacken
bones, yet he managed to retain his grip on the H
Symbol of Ravenkind as he lifted it and directed it
ward Strahd.

The elven vampire felt the power rise, using him a
vessel. It shuddered up his body, nearly bursting h
heart, and shot through his arms to coalesce in the pl
inum medallion. A burst of light streamed from t
crystal, the pain of the explosion wringing a cry fro

Jander's gut. The beam of brilliant golden light hit Strahd full in the chest.

The vampire screamed in utter agony. He arched backward, his face contorted with horrible pain, his body taut. Jander watched him, filled with hot, savage joy. Never before had he taken pleasure in another's suffering, but at this moment, brutal satisfaction made the agony in his hand insignificant.

Strahd's elegant clothes began to smoke and then burst into flames where the sacred sunlight struck. The glow burned its way deeper, began to blister and blacken the white flesh. The count staggered with the pain, moaning. He lost his balance and toppled behind one of the pews.

The movement broke the stream of light for just an instant. Jander moved quickly, refocusing the holy symbol's brilliance. The instant, however, was all the other vampire needed. Before the light fell on him a second time, the count finished uttering a spell, and to Jander's horror he affixed the elven vampire with a vicious grin of triumph laced with pain.

Strahd disappeared.

"No!" Jander wailed. So close. He had been so close. His legs refused to support him, and he collapsed to the floor.

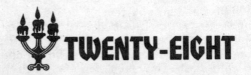 **TWENTY-EIGHT**

Jander opened his eyes weakly. He was still lying in the chapel, completely drained of energy. The vampire tried to move and succeeded only in twitching his hand slightly. He grunted softly with the effort.

Instantly someone was beside him. "Welcome back," Sasha said softly. "I thought we'd lost you there for a while."

The elf did not reply. He had offered everything to Lathander in order to be permitted to wield the Holy Symbol, and Lathander had accepted. Jander knew he was dying.

It was a bitter, unfulfilled death. He was angry; he had been cheated. *If you are to get your justice, it will be through the sun.* False Seer! he cursed. He had gambled everything, and Strahd was still out there, injured, but not completely destroyed.

He lay face down on the stone floor of the chapel. The room was not quite dark. Dawn was on its way, but not yet here. Jander felt his strength dripping into the dark heart of Ravenloft's stones. "What . . ." He did not have the strength to complete the sentence, but Sasha could see in his eyes what he wished to know.

"Strahd is gone. I think he was able to cast a spell at the last minute. Leisl, well, she was hurt badly, but I've been able to heal most of her serious injuries. You've been unconscious nearly all night. I drew a protective circle around the three of us, and I've been keeping watch." He smiled a little. "Thank goodness for Leisl's food. I've been eating all night and I feel much better."

"Here all night?"

"Yes. I don't know what's out there, and I was afraid to try to leave until Leisl was able to walk a bit. We'd be too vulnerable."

Jander tried to collect his scattered thoughts. A bit of strength was coming back to him, enough so that he could talk. "I think you're safe enough during the day. Strahd's been hurt, even if he's not dead." The elf tried to keep the bitterness out of his voice and failed. "Leisl . . She's been bitten. When you're ready to leave, go to Strahd's study. Take whatever interests you, but there is one book in particular which you must consult. It will tell you how Leisl can be cured."

"Cured? Jander, she's going to be fine."

"No, she's not. She's been bitten by a werewolf, and she'll turn at the next full moon."

Sasha went cold. The dreaded disease was highly contagious, and by now, the Little Fox was infected. Suddenly Sasha found it difficult to breathe. What would he have done if Leisl, dear, brave, stubborn Leisl, had died? His feelings for the girl surprised him—and warmed him. "I'm going for the book right now," he said, getting quickly to his feet.

Jander gasped softly, and his good hand groped for the priest. "Sasha, don't go. Not yet. I may not last that long."

Kneeling beside his fallen comrade again, the priest said, "No, Jander, you're going to be fine, too. If you made it through last night, I think that's a good sign. We'll . . . uh . . . get you some nourishment." He broke off, uncomfortable but desperately wanting to help. He looked around and noticed that Jander was lying directly beneath a hole in one of the stained glass windows. It had been broken last night when one of the wolves leaped through. The day was well on its way, and the sky was pale gray.

The priest hooked his hands beneath Jander's arm
and made as if to drag the elf to safety. The vampire
cried out once, sharply. "Jander, I'm sorry, I didn't mea
to hurt you, I was just trying to get you out of the path o
sunlight."

Jander shook his head. His thoughts were churning
and some kind of peace was coming from them. "Wait

Had he really failed Anna? Weak, freed from the dri
ing need for revenge, the elf carefully pondered h
"dreams." They had been both hurtful and joyous, b
suddenly he sensed a wrongness about them.

He considered everything he knew about Tatyana
nature. She had given her jewels to a poor man. She ha
fallen in love, not with a dashing war hero, but a gent
priest. Even in Waterdeep, less than a fraction of a pe
son, she had given her food to the other inmates an
denied herself nourishment. Would that sort of lum
nous soul urge Jander on to revenge? Punish him whe
he hesitated with nightmares?

No. The elf realized with a sudden clarity that ha
Anna's soul truly visited him in his dreams, she wou
have urged him to forgive Strahd for his sins. After a
she had already forgiven Jander for taking her li
Anna would be the first to offer gentleness for ill usag
That lay at the heart of her soul's beauty.

Then where had the dreams come from? They ha
been too real to have sprung from his own imaginatio
The elf felt his grip on consciousness fading, willed
back. He smiled to himself.

He had, finally, grasped the horrible, evil, carefull
crafted beauty of it all, the beauty of the spider's we
The land itself, or the dark powers responsible for i
heinous creation, was trying to trap him. It had been tr
ing to trap him ever since that terrible, oft-regrette
killing spree back in the asylum in Waterdeep. Barov
had been giving him strength, adding fuel to his fire f
revenge whenever it seemed at its lowest ebb. It had r
newed the pain and longing for the light in his soul.

had fed him foul sustenance, and his hatred had thrived.

The land would never let Jander destroy Strahd. It had brought him here as a playmate for its favorite child of darkness, nothing more. Strahd had learned a great deal from Jander over the years, and the land had fed happily on the elven vampire's despair. It was the perfect solution. He had been manipulated all along, allowed a tiny victory here, a false contentment there.

The dark powers did not want Jander destroyed. Rather they would keep him alive, lusting for revenge, eternally wallowing in the pain of his loss. They would drag Sasha down, too, either by destroying him or perverting him with too great a love for hunting the undead. As for poor, tortured Tatyana, nothing Jander could ever do would win her soul rest. She would return, century after century, for the land's amusement.

No, the dark powers wanted both master vampires alive. Even now, the elf felt the new strength seeping through his body and a deep part of him yearned for sanctuary from the merciless rays of the sun. Sasha's concern played right into the demonic hands of the place. Jander understood now, though, and he would snatch some semblance of victory from the desolation that loomed about him. *Through the sun and through children,* Maruschka had prophesied. She had not been a false Seer after all. "No," he said with a firm gentleness to the child conceived the night he had entered Barovia. "Let me see the light."

"You can't! You'll die—"

"Sasha, listen to your words!" Jander laughed tenderly as he looked up into Sasha's anxious face. "I'm already dead. I will never be able to destroy Strahd. We would be cursed to be enemies throughout the centuries, and I would become twisted and bitter, always striving for a victory that cannot be mine."

"You're just going to give up?"

Jander shook his head. "No. I choose this death of my own free will." He glanced toward the dawn. "Quickly. Listen to me. When I am gone, carry on our quest. For the sake of your soul and all those you love, do it for the right reasons. Destroy Strahd if you can. You will be giving him peace and you will be saving countless others from his terrible fate. Don't destroy him because of a vendetta."

"But—"

"Beware of the land itself. It will seek to corrupt you through your very virtues. Be sure of yourself, my friend. Now," he said, "when this is done and the day has come, go down to the dungeons and free those poor souls. Then you and Leisl must go into hiding."

Sasha shook his head. "There are people in the village who depend on the Morninglord."

"He will still be there, as much as he ever has been. They will find their own paths to his light. You and Leisl represent a threat to Strahd. He'll try to destroy you both as soon as he is well. I don't know when that will be, but he will be healed eventually, and he will come after you. That much is a certainty." He closed his eyes.

For a moment they stayed there together, Jander's head pillowed in Sasha's lap. Without wanting to, the priest found himself gently stroking the golden hair. It wasn't fair, he thought to himself. Jander hadn't asked for this. In his heart, the elf was as much a creature of the light, perhaps even more so, than Sasha or Leisl. He didn't deserve to die this way, burned to a cinder by the rays of the sun.

"No!" The refusal exploded from Sasha's lips with a vehemence that was unexpected even to him. "You are *not* going to die! Jander, don't do this." He wondered why it was so hard to see and why there was a warm wetness sliding down his face. Wonderingly, Jander reached up and touched the salty tears, rubbing them between his thumb and index finger.

"Do you know how long it has been since anyone wept for me?" he said softly, filled with emotion himself. Cruel and violent though this place was, it had given Jander much. This was the way to die. Not with a stake through the heart, or by drowning in the darkness, or by the fire that mockingly echoed the hell to come. To sit in the sun once again, to feel its rays, warm and loving, in the instant before the pain began—this was a good death. He recalled Lyria's words: "It is better to die at the hand of a friend." Now he understood. There could be no better friends than this brave, impulsive half-gypsy boy and the glorious sun itself.

"Don't mourn my passing. It is something for which I have hungered for centuries. But stay here, with me, while I . . . Will you stay, Sasha?"

The priest's voice was thick. "I'm not going to leave you."

Jander smiled and relaxed. "Help me sit up," he asked. Sasha did so. With weak fingers, the elf fumbled at his belt, removing the flute. With a great effort, he raised it to his lips, inhaled, and began to pipe in the morning.

He no longer cared what the sunlight might or might not do to him. He only knew that whatever it brought had to be better than this miserable existence he had endured for over five centuries. There would at last be an end to the darkness, to the undeath that fed upon life. Whatever he might be, be it ashes, or charred flesh, or something altogether unexpected and perhaps quite wonderful, he would no longer be a thing of the dark.

His music flowed like water as the sky lightened. The elf had seen through the land's dark deceptions. He, a thing supposedly of evil, had wielded the Holy Symbol against a fellow vampire. Perhaps the Morninglord had found a way to spread his beauty into this nightmare land. Perhaps the dawn would give Jander new, true life instead of peacefully ending his undeath.

His song as bright as the morning itself, Jander gazed at the lightening horizon with eager eyes and waited for the wonder. The sun cleared the horizon and fell upon him like a benediction. He closed his eyes and drank it in.

# EPILOGUE

Miles from Castle Ravenloft, deep in the mountains, a sleek gray and brown she-wolf entered a hidden cave. The beast limped through labyrinthine turns until she reached the coffin, secreted there by a cunning vampire for a special purpose. The she-wolf's shoulder was stiff from a dagger's bite, and her haunch would forever bear the mark of the silver brand.

She sniffed at the box. Her tail wagged slightly, then drooped with disappointment. The master would not awaken today. She leaped to the top of the dark mahogany box, yawned, turned around two or three times, and curled up to sleep. Surely, when he awoke, he would forgive her. And when he revived with the hunger clawing at the back of his throat, Katrina would see to it that he had a fresh victim waiting to assuage his thirst. Within minutes, the werewolf was asleep, breathing slowly.

The wounded vampire dreamed.

Strahd had been hurt—dangerously hurt. The sunlight had almost slain him. He was in searing, agonizing pain, and would need to rest for many weeks, perhaps months, perhaps even years. Yet, what was time to a vampire?

Jander had nearly destroyed him, but Strahd was the richer for the knowledge the older vampire had given him. He had new skills, new wisdom; and he now knew his most dangerous enemy.

He would see Sasha Petrovich again, and when he did, the boy would not be victorious.

And his Tatyana? Her soul had been allowed a brief respite, but the girl was as bound to Ravenloft, in her own sweet and sorrowing fashion, as Strahd. As he was doomed to love her for eternity, so was she doomed to reappear, with a different name but the same beautiful face and shattered soul, to be loved by him.

He would see her again. And, one day, she would love him. Strahd Von Zarovich was determined that this would happen, and he had the time to be patient and the power to make almost anything come true in Barovia. After all, the land was his to command.

The vampire rested and dreamed, and day dawned in Ravenloft.

Ravenloft™ novels

One step into the mists, and a world of horror engulfs you. Welcome to Ravenloft, a dark domain of fantasy-horror populated by bloodthirsty vampires and other unspeakable creatures of the undead.

Knight of the Black Rose

James Lowder

The fate of the villainous Lord Soth was left untold at the conclusion of the popular DRAGONLANCE® Legends Trilogy. Now it can be revealed that the cruel death knight found his way into the dark domain and discovered that it is far easier to get into Ravenloft than to get out—even with the aid of the powerful vampire lord, Strahd Von Zarovich. On sale in December, 1991.

novels

◇ The Cloakmaster Cycle ◇

Follow one unlucky farmer as he enters fantasy space
for the first time and gets caught up in a race for his
life, from the DRAGONLANCE® Saga setting to the
FORGOTTEN REALMS® world and beyond.

Book One
Beyond the Moons
David Cook

Little did Teldin Moore know there was life
beyond Krynn's moons until a spelljamming
ship crashed into his home and changed his
life. Teldin suddenly discovers himself the
target of killers and cutthroats. Armed with a
dying alien's magical cloak and cryptic
words, he races off to Astinus of Palanthas
and the gnomes of Mt. Nevermind to try to
discover why . . . before the monstrous neogi
can find him. On sale in July, 1991.

Book Two
Into the Void
Nigel Findley

Plunged into a sea of alien faces, Teldin
Moore isn't sure whom to trust. His gnomish
sidewheeler ship is attacked by space
pirates, and Teldin is saved by a hideous
mind flayer who offers to help the human
use his magical cloak—but for whose gain?
Teldin learns the basics of spelljamming on
his way to Toril, where he seeks an ancient
arcane, one who might tell him more. But
even information has a high price. On sale in
October, 1991.

Prism Pentad
BOOK ONE

The Verdant Passage

Troy Denning

KALAK: AN IMMORTAL SORCERER-KING WHOSE EVIL MAGIC
HAS REDUCED THE MAJESTIC CITY OF TYR TO A DESOLATE
PLACE OF BLOOD AND FEAR. HIS THOUSAND-YEAR REIGN OF
DEATH IS ABOUT TO END.

BANDING TOGETHER TO SPARK A REVOLUTION ARE A MAV-
ERICK STATESMAN, A WINSOME HALF-ELF SLAVE GIRL, AND A
MAN-DWARF GLADIATOR BRED FOR THE ARENAS. BUT IF THE
PEOPLE ARE TO BE FREE, THE MISMATCHED TRIO OF STEADFAST
REBELS MUST LOOK INTO THE FACE OF TERROR, AND CHOOSE
BETWEEN LOVE AND LIFE.